PRAISE FOR VANITY IN DUST

"Low immerses you in sensory details, bitter conflict, and characters you both love and hate. A deliciously decadent debut that will make you reconsider the world within which we live."

—Sara Dobie Bauer,
author of *Bite Somebody*

"[T]he story is really just beginning. I'll be watching for the next book in this series...Ms. Low has me hooked on her tale."

—The Book Faerie

"*Vanity in Dust* is…beautifully written, skillfully drawn, convincing and gripping, but leaving one feeling more sickened by the brutality of the world than entertained by escapism or sense of wonder. Perhaps not the read I was expecting, but a powerful and worthwhile one nevertheless."

—The Future Fire

"Low's debut is a valiant attempt to create a new magical world."
—Publisher's Weekly

VANITY
IN DUST

CROWNS & ASH: BOOK ONE

CHERYL LOW

WORLD WEAVER PRESS

Published by World Weaver Press, LLC.
Albuquerque, New Mexico
www.WorldWeaverPress.com

Edited by Laura Harvey
Cover designed by Linn Arvidsson.

First edition: August 2017
ISBN-10: 0-998702218
ISBN-13: 978-0998702216

Also available as an ebook.

VANITY IN DUST

To my first reader, my favorite writer, and my greatest love—Phong Chau.

CHAPTER ONE

Ferrin climbed the stairs one heavy leg at a time, a cigarette in one hand and a teacup in the other. The rooftop throbbed beneath his shoes with the beat of music pulsing from the warehouse below. He dropped his head back, silver hair falling away from his cheeks. Rosy lips parted to suck in a deep breath. It was soothing, for a second, before he replaced air with smoke. Long fingers brought a cigarette to his lips and he drew the dust-laden smoke deep into his lungs, making his skin shiver with delight.

It took some effort, but he lifted his head upright again and blinked at the midnight city. From the Low there was nowhere to look but up, toward the heart of the realm. The Queen's Tower was there, high above it all, far from where he stood now but not so far from his family's home. His cheek twitched with the start of a snarl in the face of that tower. Before he could think better of it, before he could think at all, he let loose a furious cry and hurled his cup into the dark toward that tower. It would never reach. Just as he would never quite reach.

Ferrin staggered back a step. Even the sound of the porcelain vessel breaking somewhere in the shadows didn't satisfy. His newly freed hand stroked back the unruly strands of his hair as he shuddered and tried to find composure. It wasn't like him to lose it in

1

the first place. He was always angry but it never felt this hot on his skin. Uncomfortable, he took another drag of his cigarette, and in the spread of that dust through his body, he forgot to worry.

It would shame him if his peers in the High knew how he crept down into the Low to party with the rats. Ferrin exhaled black smoke, glaring past it at the buildings obscured by distance. There were lights there, far away, ever glowing in those better parts of the city. Ferrin was always invited to the parties but it was mostly a joke. No matter how fine his suit or how close his house to the Tower, he could never escape the scandal of his father being from the Low of the Realm. The man was long dead and no one remembered his name, but that didn't matter. Up there, Ferrin was just a rat in a nice suit. But down here… down here, he was a king.

The scratching, fluttering sound of wings smacking against brick drew his gaze to the corner of the rooftop. One of the lamps had gone out, something that never happened above the Low, and the shadow there swelled with pixies.

Ferrin shuffled two steps closer and peered into the moving darkness. The nasty insects shifted about wildly, bumping into the wall and each other, grappling for space closer to him at the edge of the shadow. They stared back with nearly human eyes to match their nearly human, though miniature, bodies. In his dusted state, Ferrin was tempted to reach out to them, but then one smiled. Thin lips parted to expose rows of needle teeth and he twisted back. Sobering even just a fraction was enough to have him returning to the party inside, closing the door sharply behind him and drowning in the volume of the warehouse once more.

It wasn't often that the Low had parties like this, but he had the means to make it happen and a connection that sold him cheap dust. Ferrin had decided not to pry into how or why that particular lord had so much dust on hand to sell for so little. The price of dust never went down unless the quality did, and Ferrin had never known it to be so cheap. But answers were more dangerous than questions, and not knowing could be the difference between life and death. The Queen would not look kindly on one of her nobles cutting into her profit, and while Ferrin might scorn her daily in his thoughts, not even he was fool enough to put himself in her sights.

These parties in the Low brought a crowd from the Main. A crowd too poor to even dream of partying in their own district with the High born that came to slum it near their homes, but who earned just enough pouring tea and driving cars to buy entrance into one of Ferrin's parties. He turned a decent profit selling weak dust to nobodies. Once upon a time he'd dreamed of building himself an empire of wealth to scorn his peers, but now, with whispers of revolution in the back alleys of the Realm, his dream had changed. Some of those whispers spoke of a place outside the Realm. Of a world beyond the Ash.

Having no stomach for treason and no place to climb on the social ladder, Ferrin now dreamed of gathering enough wealth to flee before getting caught up in whatever terror the revolutionaries could spark in the Realm. The Queen was many things, but forgiving was not one of them.

Ferrin was halfway down the skeletal staircase bolted to the wall of the warehouse when a scream pierced the room, surpassing even the persistent beat of the drums. He caught the sway of his body on the railing and looked over it. The people that filled the room rolled like a wave, pulling away from one corner. His eyes narrowed to watch a woman launch herself at a man, grabbing at his face with fingers curled like claws and tackling him to the floor.

Ferrin reeled back from the violence, pressing up against the wall. His lip curled in disgust. This was the Low. People were unpredictable and brutish here. It wasn't uncommon for brawls to break out now and then, but he never appreciated the reminder of how far he'd fallen.

The music cut out. Shouting spiraled through the crowd. The woman screamed madly, as did the man losing his eyes to her fingers.

Another scream came from the middle of the room, away from the first scene, and within a matter of seconds the room exploded into violence. Men and women alike screamed in fury, lashing out at those closest, tackling and climbing on friends turned prey. When fists and nails wouldn't satisfy, they bit at their victims, tearing free chunks of flesh and spitting them out to bite again. Those not gone wild before his eyes struggled to escape, many slipping in the blood to fall short of the doors.

A floor packed with violence stretched between himself and the exit. The rigging of the staircase creaked loudly and swayed. Ferrin looked down the winding stairs to see it filling with people. Some rushed up in hopes of an exit while others gave chase, drawn by movement and the promise of a struggle.

Ferrin shuddered, dropping his cigarette from trembling fingers. His heart beat against his ribs, making his vision blur. His first impulse was to run, and run he did. He scrambled up the stairs, away from the violent fiends at his back and the madness blooming in the garden of broken bones below. He was almost to the top, almost to the promise of cold night air and escape, when rage twisted in his heart with the swirls of dust in his blood.

His shoulders hunched forward, teeth grinding and body staggering at the surge of blood in his veins. Twisting around to look down the stairs, Ferrin let out a cry of rage. His skin was unbearably hot and his teeth ached against his gums, throat dry and body hungry for the kind of satisfaction that only broken knuckles could give.

He came down the stairs two at a time, so hurried that he was falling more than running, hands pulling at the railing to bring him closer faster. He hated them. He hated all of them. For turning on him. For making his party a disaster. For being the same class as his father. For being at all. Most of all, he hated them because he could see them. Because they were almost within reach and the closer they came, the closer he got, the more he wanted to break bones and tear flesh.

The staircase shook and bolts tore clean from the wall. He grabbed onto the railing just as it lurched forward, the end higher up holding fast while somewhere in the middle it came free of the wall. The shock of it momentarily sobered him. People tumbled to the floor below, scrambling weakly only to be crushed as the lower end of the staircase gave way and crashed down.

Ferrin crumbled to his knees in his metal cage turned sideways. His fingers hooked into the railing beneath him. He had nowhere to look but down at the gruesome brawl. Suddenly, he missed his view of the Queen's Tower, and it was enough to have him laughing through his tears.

Seconds felt like hours and he couldn't will himself to move, afraid of falling and dying. When he felt eyes on him, Ferrin lifted his head to scan the farthest edge of the crowd. It wasn't difficult to find the one watching him. It was a testament to the bad dust that no one else had taken notice of the Queen's Wrath. He stood as a solitary soldier, with narrow body and silver eyes, occupying the doorway of the warehouse, staring through the mess of it all at Ferrin.

He felt the weight of that gaze and knew, with gut twisting certainty, that the Queen finally saw him.

He waited, desperate with hope that the Wrath would end the madness and save him. But that hope was madness all its own. The Wrath raised one arm, fingers dressed in the black armor that coated his entire body. He never broke eye contact with Ferrin, and Ferrin could not will himself to look away. The lights grew brighter. Brighter and brighter. Ferrin let out a strangled sob just before the bulbs burst, one after another, throughout the entire warehouse. Darkness swallowed them up.

The Queen's Wrath vanished from the doorway and in rushed the violent flutter of little wings, soon bringing the sounds of the room to a horrible pitch. The pixies would not care if the dust was good or bad. They would not care if it was left on the table, burning in a cigarette, swirling in the tea, or hot in their blood. It was rich with magic, and that was all their tiny stomachs cared to know.

Vaun woke with a mild start that began and ended in the flash of lids and the shrinking of pupils. The fingers of strangers curled in his dark hair and the comfort of foreign limbs folded around him, a thigh across his abdomen, an arm laced with his. Parted lips puffed steady, sleepy breaths against his ribs and sheets twisted somewhere between them all. The smell of sweat, sex, and mixed perfumes hung thick in the air, warmed by their collective body heat.

He moved and his muscles ached with delight, his skin peeling from those of sticky warmth. Some whimpered at the loss of him, still caught in their reverent sleep, while others simply shifted, too accustomed to these mornings to be bothered with waking.

He located the bathroom easily, though this wasn't his home. In fact, Vaun was relatively certain that he had never been here before. Nonetheless, he showered. He didn't bother with the frail lock below the polished doorknob. After a little more than a century prowling the Realm he could more easily count the bodies he hadn't slept with than the ones he had, and everyone knew that Vaun Dray Fen, second son of the Queen, never shared a bathroom. Not the shower, the sink, or even the mirror. And if anyone thought the entitled bastards of the Realm's households had tempers, they had never tried sneaking into a prince's mirror space before.

Vaun kept little privacy for himself. The city's gossip exploited his sexuality. The morning paper quoted his snide comments. Artists painted, sketched, and photographed his nudity in every position and action imaginable. There simply wasn't much he hadn't shown, given, or taken. Bedrooms might be a public forum, but bathrooms were a private luxury. He made sure of that.

He took his time in the shower, looking over his host's shampoos and soaps with a shrewd eye. From the scant selection of sterile and decisive bottles and the lack of floral or fruit fragrances, he was willing to venture a guess that his host was a man. In fact, the order of things reminded him of his own bathroom.

By the time he dried off with a fine, plush towel and perused the drawers of well-organized scent spells and eye, hair, and skin color charms—all the highest grade—Vaun was prepared to say that he liked this man.

When he re-entered the bedroom, the bed of lazy bodies had begun stirring with small moans and feminine giggles. He located his slacks and pulled them on, ignoring the invitations from his bedmates to return to the sheets and their arms. Though a few were familiar and enjoyable faces, they were hardly glamorous in their dull morning state.

Picking up his shirt from a chair, he made his way out of the room and down a hall that led to a broad, open parlor and dining room. His steps slowed to a near halt. At the head of a long table laden with a beautiful display of pastries, flowers, and neon wedges of fruit, a man poured dark wine for a woman to his right.

"Good morning, Vaun," Addom Vym said, putting down the bottle and taking a seat. "Breakfast?"

Vaun eyed the woman, but refused to let her put him off a perfectly good meal. "No coffee?" He wasn't complaining, just surprised.

"I've been up quite a while now. I can have more made," offered the son of one of the Realm's most powerful families, gesturing toward the chair at his left.

"Wine will do fine," Vaun said quickly and took a seat. "New apartment?"

Addom leaned back into the sturdy frame of his chair. His unrelentingly black hair framed startling pale gray eyes. Usually his eyes were red, making Vaun wonder if gray was his natural color. "The old one needed... airing out." He smiled to take away any subtlety and gestured to the sterile room around them. "Do you like it?"

Vaun sat down, making a careful effort not to look at the woman across the table while he plucked a few select foods for his plate. "It will do." He could feel her icy gaze boring into him but still he forced a casual bite of lemon sponge cake.

Addom lifted the bottle of wine with a raised brow. Vaun wasn't entirely sure what the other man's game was, but whether or not it was a trap, liquor wouldn't hurt.

"Please." The prince reached for an empty glass.

She moved fast, smacking the delicate vessel from his hand while seeming never to have risen from her seat to do so. Vaun had forgotten how good she was at that. And at breaking things. Just as quickly, she slapped the newspaper down in front of him, ignoring the personal space of his cake entirely.

He glanced at the front page and a rather large photo of what was obviously the start of a promiscuous evening. There he was, smack in the middle of those scandalous limbs and bodies in varying stages of undress. He tipped his head to the side to get a better look at it; his fingers were lost in the hair of a brunet in his lap. He looked happy enough. A shame he didn't recall knowing any currently brunet individuals.

Vaun leaned a little closer, eyes slanting in Addom's direction. "Was this taken in your bedroom?"

The man in question sipped from his glass and shrugged.

The prince frowned but needn't ask more. The Vym family had a long standing, unspoken agreement with the press. They let the cameras and reporters in, and they were never the subject of public scandal. Sure, they kept themselves in the public eye, but only on the terms they desired. Though the other households reveled in gossip, the Vyms clung to a twisted vision of honor that made their descendants vicious in the most cunning of ways.

Vaun often thought that his sister had been meant for them: deceitful, judging, sniping, and dangerous.

"What were you thinking?" she snapped, her lace-gloved hands in

8

her lap again, as though they hadn't produced the paper in the first place. "Do I even have to ask? Do you have any idea how this makes us look?" She practically hissed through her perfect teeth.

Some said that he and his sister looked alike, but Vaun couldn't see it past the dramatic shape of their eyes and the angle of their jaws. The black that lined her eyes and those endless lashes made the pale color of her irises that much more intimidating today. She dressed like a widow who loved to grieve. Full-length skirts, satin corset with ribbon trim, and fringes of lace at every edge of clothing that met with skin. She wore a hat today, with a veil that stretched to claw at her delicate cheekbones, though it never quite overcame the mound of dark curls atop her head.

"Well?" Fay demanded.

"How's your husband?" Vaun pushed the paper to the side and picked up his fork. She might have ignored his cake, but he would not.

The cringe never went beyond her eyes, but he saw it, and she knew it. Fay had never quite recovered from the scorn of being forced into a marriage with the oldest Vym son.

"Tell me you didn't rat me out to my own sister." The prince looked at Addom, taking a bite but only pretending to enjoy it. Eventually, even cakes became dull.

"She recognized the apartment," their host said with conversational intrigue. "I was rather flattered." Addom smiled slyly at his sister-in-law. "Usually she pretends she doesn't even notice me."

"But did you have to let her in?" Vaun swung his gaze back to her. Fay hated when he talked about her rather than to her, and he knew it. Just as he knew everything else she hated and even the few things that she liked. They might not have grown up in the same house, but that didn't make them any less related. He knew that she wasn't surprised by any scandal he made and, though she did enjoy fussing about it, it wasn't like her to go this far out of her way to chide him.

"I like her." Addom sipped his wine.

"She hates you."

Addom laughed and nodded as though they had reached a fair agreement.

"I saw your valet outside," Fay said.

Vaun almost stopped chewing. *Almost.* She never mentioned his valet. Not in the past seventy years since he first acquired one. When they were in the same room, Fay didn't even acknowledge her, her standard treatment toward all "lesser citizens," which seemed to include nearly the entire Realm. She hadn't even squawked when the paper began reporting on his personal assistant and plastering her photo right alongside his own. No. Fay never, before today, admitted she even saw the woman.

Vaun eyed her curiously, wondering if he was taking part in a cryptic conversation. Addom was hardly the sort of person to be sneaky in front of. He was a Vym, after all. Deception was their business.

Fay sighed and turned her head before Vaun could ask any more questions with his eyes. She offered her profile instead, a daunting portrait of annoyance, before rising. Both men stood immediately, a natural impulse when a person like Fay left her seat. Vaun liked to think it was because no one trusted her enough to stay seated and allow her the advantage of height. She straightened her skirts and ignored Addom when he pulled her chair farther back to make way for her exit.

One of her hands flicked toward the paper she had thrown at her brother. Her long, black lacquered nails gleamed in the morning light. "Take a good look, Vaun. Changes must be made before things worsen."

Addom followed her to the door, bowing slightly and offering a soft farewell in her wake. She could easily be called rude if she wasn't the daughter of the Queen. When Addom Vym returned to the table, Vaun was already sitting again and stabbing at a piece of colorful fruit with his fork.

"I am most thankful not to be my family's eldest son, even if it might have seen me married to your sister." Addom grinned at the thought.

Vaun laughed. "Indeed. Your brother has the great misfortune of being noticed regularly by my sister. It's one of the downfalls of being the eldest; businesses, responsibilities, all that." He shuddered for the drama of it and lifted his glass. "To good blood and being the useless youth."

Addom grinned widely and picked up his glass. "And to all of the misfortune that we bring to our families."

Vaun drained his glass and rose, tucking the newspaper under his arm.

The residence exited into a large stairwell of broad, marble steps and a vaulted ceiling painted with golden clouds. The steps swept around a lamp hugged by marble cherubs and flooded down to a pair of thick front doors, heavily carved wood panels inset with glass that looked out onto the street. It was almost exactly the same as Vaun's own townhouse in the Vym province of the Realm, with the exception of a few details. Vaun wasn't sure whether to be flattered or insulted, but when he saw the doorman at the bottom of the steps holding his jacket from the night before, all possible offenses were forgiven. He grinned and took the previously forgotten garment back, examining it while the man opened the doors and let in the cool morning air.

The prince pulled on the dark blue jacket while he stood on the sidewalk. He couldn't remember when or where he had lost it the night before but was relatively certain that someone had cleaned and pressed it since. Anyone out on the sidewalk at this hour stopped to take notice of him. His appearance didn't warrant their attention, at the moment, but his blood did.

Vaun ignored all of them without prejudice and walked out into the ever-gray where the dark clouds hung heavily in the sky above.

Tall lamps ran evenly down the sides of the cobblestone streets, glowing bright as ever in the dim of day. Thick, sculpted metal arches curved over the streets to dangle the heavy, glowing orbs. The lamps alone would have told him what part of the Vym province he was in, if he ever suspected that Addom Vym would take up living anywhere below the High.

The Realm was broken into three provinces under the three households, each stretching from the walls of the Queen's Tower at the center of the city down to the Ash at the end of the Low. Each province had a High district at its top, closest to the Queen and the heart of the Realm. No streets were cleaner and no buildings more beautiful than in the High of the Realm. Though the High district of each province differed in style, it was always home to the best the city could offer. The most pretentious of the High born made a point of never leaving that first circle around the Tower, his sister among their number. A shame, Vaun thought, since some of the best teahouses and seediest clubs were to be found in the Main.

The Vym family ruled over a third of the Realm, every stone from the top of the High to the bottom of the Low in their province fell under the dominion of Quentan Vym. His rule was absolute in his territory, save for the Queen's law and the will of royals.

A black car, parked just down the street, pulled up in front of him. Vaun pretended not to notice it until the driver got out and came around to open his door. He slid into the backseat, settling onto the soft leather before the door closed soundly. Within moments they were driving toward the Maggrin province, where he currently resided. He rotated between the three provinces, occupying one house for roughly six months at a time. This would be one of his last nights living in Maggrin for the next year. With a flick of his fingers he unbuttoned his jacket and took out the newspaper tucked inside.

Sitting across from him, a woman raised a skeptical eyebrow. "Since when do you read the paper?" Grayc Illan Sanaro asked. There was only one newspaper in the Realm and it claimed the title "the paper" long before Vaun could remember otherwise. A woman once told him that there had been many papers, each with different opinions. He could not imagine how differently opinionated a paper could be when reporting gossip and scandal.

Over the edge of headlines, Vaun looked at his valet and smiled. She wore a pin-striped pencil skirt, one so tight at the knee that she could not cross her legs and bob her stilettoed foot in irritation. It had a short matching jacket with white lace tufts at the shoulders and no hat or gloves. Grayc Illan had a habit of being horribly unfashionable in a splendidly odd way. Her hair, for instance, was stubbornly short while everyone else imitated Fay's length, intricate styles, and use of accessories. Grayc had worn her hair more or less the same for all the decades that he had known her, always between chin and shoulder and always a mess of black ringlets. No accessories. No braids. No change of color. At first he thought this was a sign of poverty, Grayc Illan having come from the Low district of Belholn, once upon a time. It was terribly functional. The more she messed it up the better it looked. But after a handful of years, he started to feel that a change would unsettle him and couldn't imagine her hair any other way.

"Did my sister speak with you?" Vaun half accused over the lip of his paper.

Her round face portrayed her confusion and annoyance beautifully. Grayc Illan was one of those individuals that showed off their negative emotions with clean ease, as though masking or containing them was unthinkable, but when it came to anything kindred to happiness or pleasure, she was a veritable statue. "Why?"

He shrugged and settled back into his seat as though it was particularly comfortable. "Let's make a stop at Gram's." Vaun flipped the large page and wrinkled his nose at yet another unflattering photo of himself.

His valet frowned. "Isn't it a bit early for a teahouse?" Her disapproval faltered at the corners of her painted mouth when she thought of something that bordered on devious. "Wouldn't you like to go home and rest before this evening's event? Maybe change your clothes?"

It was Vaun's turn to raise an eyebrow, flipping another crisp page. "Are you trying to seduce me?"

Her glare returned in full force. Her teeth clicked and her knuckles rapped quickly against the black glass panel between the cab and the driver. Soon the car turned toward the neighborhood at the bottom of the High district in Vym. When she didn't reply, or even bother to look at him again, Vaun returned his attention to the news.

He was about to flip the page and then possibly crumple up the entire mess of gossip, when he saw a strange set of bold letters. "Ferrin Gray dies in Low Riot'" cut across the middle of the page. He read through the callous series of sharp truths and glaring facts. The name made his back tight and his skin cold. Ferrin had been a socialite of the Belholn province, far from being a nobody, but also not a name that many would miss. Vaun held the paper a little more gingerly when he took in the brief story that summarized the man's death.

The article speculated why the High born citizen had been at a party in the Low, suggesting that perhaps he had relatives there in a most damning way. The riot-turned-slaughter at the party was attributed to the brutish nature of the Low born. Few survived the brawl and pixies made short work of those that did.

Was this what Fay had hoped he would read? The prince folded up the paper and dropped it onto the seat beside him. Fay had no connection to the dead man that he knew of. He sighed and scrubbed a palm over his face to wake himself from such dreariness.

Grayc Illan didn't bother to get out with him when the car stopped and the door opened. She sat silently in the car and willed discomfort on him until the door finally closed between them.

Vaun straightened his jacket on the sidewalk and allowed himself a smirk when his back was turned to her tinted window. He was beginning to see similarities between the women in his life. Aside from being rigid intellectuals with tongues like knives, they also possessed the notion that he cared when they ignored him. It worked in his favor on most days. Up until the point at which he irritated them into explosive outrage, they tried to punish him with glares and silence. The prince pushed the swinging door of Gram's Teahouse open and mentally patted himself on the back for his selection of female company.

The dimly lit establishment possessed the distinct, and sought after, feel of a shabby lounge. Mismatched, well-worn couches and chairs clustered around old and often wobbly tables. Inside, people played the part of tired bodies weighed down by the previous night's events. They slouched in seats and sipped tea, wallowing in the high it gave and staring off at the nothing that now held so much interest.

Vaun breathed in the smell of flavored smoke and tea, making his way into the belly of the room to one of its most familiar figures.

Ollan sat in the corner of a threadbare, emerald sofa. Her long, thin legs crossed at the knee and her body leaned onto the arm of the couch that held her elbow up high. Her suit was of the best quality but rumpled by too many nights of wear. Her jacket draped over the back of the couch and her vest was unbuttoned. A black cigarette burned down nearly to her fingers. Wisps of yellow smoke curled off its ashen lips to lick the air, holding the woman in rapture as her bloodshot, violet eyes stared intently at those ever-changing shapes. For almost too long to be comfortable, the prince simply stood beside the mock living room and waited for his friend to realize he was there. Staring wasn't impolite, but startling a person enraptured by smoke certainly was.

Ollan finally drew a shuddering breath and brought the cigarette stub back to her lips for one last drag before rendering its life useless. Her thin lips curled into a broad smile around the withering corpse when she saw Vaun. The woman exhaled a greeting with a puff of bright yellow smoke and stubbed her cigarette out on the face of the table. She stood to shake hands, her legs more wobbly than either of them expected. One arm waved the tea clerk over with another cup and a fresh pot.

"Have you heard about Ferrin?" was Ollan's first question, safely in her seat again.

Vaun sighed but found a smile as he settled himself onto the couch beside his friend. He nodded, watching the clerk set out the mismatched porcelain. The cold, empty pot was exchanged for a heavy, steaming vessel. The clerk took off the lid long enough to drop a few cubes of dust inside and then, after returning the lid, filled both of their cups.

"Terribly sad. Lovely boy. Bitter, but lovely," Ollan continued as she picked up her tea and breathed in the steam. Her eyes lingered in their closed state long enough for Vaun to wonder if the woman had already had too many cups—not that he could recall ever seeing Ollan sober.

Dusters like Ollan were not a rare breed in the Realm, but of them all, Vaun favored her the most. A few years back she had led a group for the better treatment of pixies—a truly hysterical movement, considering the men and women who gathered to talk of the poor, mistreated insects were the same ones sucking down their weight in dust every day. The whole movement had come apart when someone actually suggested they boycott the Dust Factories until change was had.

The Dust Factories were ugly buildings right on the edge of the Low districts, just before the dirty pavement turned to the dark ruin of the Ash. They belonged to the Queen, as did the drums of raw magic she sent down to them. The magic lured the pixies into the factories where the vile bugs filled whole rooms and fed on the magic until their bellies were so fat that their frail wings could no longer lift them.

After that, the pixies were strung up and roasted so quickly that their magic-rich bodies remained as small statues of their once living selves until being crushed into the fine dust that eventually found its way into their cigarettes, cakes, wines, and not least of all, tea.

"I was out last night," Vaun said. "I didn't see you."

Ollan shrugged and leaned back. "I don't get out much these days."

"Don't be odd," he scolded mildly and picked up his cup by its rim. "Only bores and poor people stay in."

With a laugh, Ollan nodded. "My apologies, prince." She reached up with the hand not occupied by porcelain and scratched the back of her neck idly. Her uncuffed sleeve sagged down the length of her gaunt arm, bearing an odd stretch of black ink.

Vaun frowned, squinting at what looked to be words scrawled across the woman's skin. "What is that?"

Ollan appeared confused before realizing what the prince was looking at. She shrugged and looked at the markings herself. "Don't rightly know." Her smile grew as she raised her cup to meet with her eternally parched lips. "Probably one of Charlie's pranks. Bunch of gibberish." She took a sip and then swallowed quickly as a thought struck her. "He and Jounas will be coming by in the morning."

Vaun smiled. "It is morning."

The woman laughed as though the prince had delivered the punch line to a good joke and proceeded to precariously refill her not-yet-empty cup. "Have you heard about that Ferrin boy? Terrible shame. Lovely boy. Bitter, but lovely."

The prince shook his head with a laugh and drained his cup in one tip. His eyes fluttered shut as the tea slid down his throat. It took seconds for him to feel the dust fan out inside of him, spreading like a quiet fire that had his heart beating just a little bit faster and his skin humming softly. He leaned back into the embrace of the sofa and let Ollan refill his cup. "Did you know him?"

"Who?" Ollan asked.

Vaun smiled at the ceiling. "The dead man."

Ollan shook her head and fished another cigarette from her slacks.

17

"No, no. But he had a pretty face in the paper. A shame."

The prince laughed too loudly. "If only someone ugly had died, instead." He started on his second cup, the faint hum under his skin becoming a solid and lovely strumming of veins. In the wake of his own sarcasm he struggled to think of a single ugly person. Staring up at the ceiling, he wondered why they never replaced it with something more attractive than old, rough wood, considering how many of Gram's patrons spent their hours staring at it.

Vaun wasn't sure how long he had been sitting there until a persistent and excitable voice finally forced him from his upward stare.

His neck ached and he reached up to rub it only to find his hand occupied by a cup. He stared at it for a moment. It was a different cup than before and it held a last sip of coffee at its core. Coffee? Were they already to coffee? He looked at the table in front of him, now occupied by a scattering of drained porcelain, cigarette remains, and a coffee press. Charlie sat across from him with Jounas, telling a lengthy and winding tale of gossip.

Somehow it had become early afternoon. Vaun set his cup down on the table and leaned over to Ollan, who was still sipping at tea. "How many pots did we have?"

"We?" Ollan sang with a shake of her head. "You had two and told me all about your night, though I most certainly did not ask."

"Vaun, are you listening?" Charlie interrupted with a whine of excitement. "You're not going to believe what I saw last night!"

"Was it me?" the prince asked casually as he gave the two men his foggy attention.

"No."

"Then I do not care."

Charlie's smile grew wide. "Oh, you'll care. It is possibly the best gossip the Realm has had in months!"

It had not been an exaggeration. It was the sort of scandal that would have men and women squirming in their seats with mental imagery. True or not, gossip like that would not be bound by whispers for long.

With short words, and somewhat wobbly knees, the prince bid farewell to his teahouse companions and made his way out into the gray of the afternoon. He stretched and smiled. The air tasted bitter with the dust still saturating his palate. His driver opened the car door and once again Vaun found himself sitting across from a sour woman. She was looking down at her little notebook with her pen poised near its page. How much time did she spend sitting in his car? Surely she didn't look so rigid and angry when he wasn't there, though some part of him dearly hoped that she did.

Grayc Illan drew a breath and let it out in an elegant sigh of boredom. Her eyes never left the half scribbled upon page. "To The Library?"

"You make it sound so dull," Vaun whined as the car pulled out and began its path up the street.

"After a couple of decades, shouldn't it be?"

The prince flicked a hand in her direction. "It has only been open a year. You are too dramatic."

Grayc Illan huffed to hint at the first breath of a laugh that never followed. "I'm the dramatic one?" She shook her head and closed the notebook before sliding it into her inner jacket pocket. "You should go home and get ready. Your tailors have been waiting five hours now just to present you with your evening outfit."

He ignored her and looked out the window at the passing streets.

Moving back up the High district of the Vym province, toward the Tower, he felt a wash of boredom sweep over him. His smile faded. Perhaps he understood what she meant. The Library was just a new building to house an old game.

The car stopped smoothly and he got out with all the elegance his still somewhat wobbly legs could manage. He paused with the door open, turning back and leaning down just enough to eye the woman still seated inside. "Not planning to join me?" he asked sweetly but waited to grin until he saw the way her lips twisted into a tighter frown. The Vyms made it clear when they opened The Library that it was not an establishment for anyone of Low birth.

With a laugh that bordered on indignant, he closed the car door and sauntered up the stairs to the entrance. A man and woman in matching suits of near outrageous color opened the tall double doors, bowing dramatically when he passed. The hall between the front door and the main room itself was just long enough to marinate the senses in the slowly nearing clatter of porcelain and low hum of voices. It would all be polite banter and modest laughs at a Vym establishment, no matter what terrors filled the pages of the paper that morning. Vyms were beautiful liars.

He lifted his chin a little higher when he walked into the open café, sweeping across the large floor of tables and guests. He stopped off at the largest table to pay his respects to the Vym family and his own sister. Fay replied to his warmly over-worded greeting with an imperial flick of her wrist before returning her conversational attention to her in-laws and guests.

Addom coughed, a bold sound in a vast room of hushed voices, and stood from the table. He promptly said something to his relatives about not letting a prince read alone and offered to join Vaun on his path toward the extravagant spiral of stairs leading up to the second floor, overlooking the first. Shelves of books lined the high walls all around them, stretching toward the ceiling only to vanish against the blinding lights of the chandelier.

The Vym son slipped an arm around Vaun's shoulders. "It's a good thing you came. I was so bored that I was contemplating drowning myself in a cup of tea."

Vaun plucked a modestly sized novel from the wall as they reached the second floor, never stopping to look at the title, and tucked it under his arm. "Nonsense. You adore your ridiculous relatives, and I know it." The prince selected a table near the railing with a picturesque view of the main floor. "Rigid as they may be."

Addom grinned and collapsed elegantly onto a small couch that made up half of the sitting area. "But what's the point of having relatives if I can't complain about them?"

Vaun rested an arm on the marble banister and looked down at the Vym table again. Even among all of the other aristocratic families of their province, the Vyms still stood apart, just like the royalty they loved to imitate. Perhaps that was one of the reasons their household had been so eager to make a union with The Queen's bloodline. Now they really did have a princess, though it came at the cost of tolerating her.

It had been a scandal when Fay took Quentan's last name rather than giving him hers. She had denied her husband the title of a prince and even, on occasion, called herself the Lady of Vym just to remind him of it.

Vaun watched the way they sipped their tea, most holding their books and pretending to read. His sister was likely the only one actually reading hers, not that she would ever admit to it. It was fashionable to pretend and Fay was a fashionable woman. They spoke of mundane things and left room to interject insults that wore the smiles of compliments. That, too, had become fashionable in the Vym Province and Fay excelled at it.

Vaun let his attention turn to the one woman at the table not feigning interest in bound paper. Evelet Vym was drinking her tea and looking utterly bored, that is, until she caught the eye of a handsome waiter. It was alarming how similar Evelet and Addom were, even for twins.

The prince's smile grew when he thought about the Vym siblings and the very reason he came to The Library in the first place. "Where is little Larc today?" Vaun asked as though the absence of the youngest Vym was noteworthy. Larc was a shut-in and all the Realm knew it.

Addom opened one eye, rolling his head to the side on the plush arm of the sofa. "Larc?"

Vaun waited.

"She's never been here." Addom sat up. "You know she never leaves the family house."

"Are you so sure?" Vaun grinned. "I heard otherwise."

Addom forced a smile but it was too careful to be cheerful. "Gossip?"

"Is it still gossip if there's a photo to go with it?" The prince opened his book to pretend to read, and almost laughed when he found the pages blank.

"A photo of my Larc, out in the wild?"

"Your Larc." Vaun thumbed a blank page.

"You saw this photo?"

Vaun hummed a confirming sound, then lowered his book enough to peer over it. "And she was not alone."

"Is that so?" The lord's voice darkened. "And who showed you this photo?"

The prince shrugged, reclining into the comfort of his seat. "It seems she was seen in the Low, of all places." He returned his attention to his book. "I am hoping to see the rest of the photos in tomorrow's paper. I was told they were quite passionate. No word yet on who her lover might be…"

Addom raised one brow and casually picked up his teacup, tossing back the poison of its porcelain belly. "You heard this first hand?"

The prince turned another page and nodded. "The telling was…explicit." From his friend's cheerless response, Vaun began to wonder if the story was more scandalous than a secret tryst in a seedy location. It wouldn't even be news worthy if Larc wasn't known to be frightened of her own cigarette smoke. "Is she under house arrest, your youngest sister?"

Addom looked up, surprised before smiling thinly. "What?"

"Larc. I've never seen her leave the house. Is she not allowed to?"

He laid his book on his chest thoughtfully. All these decades he, like the Realm, assumed she stayed home because the city outside was simply too frightful for her. "Is Larc a captive?"

The smile fell away and took with it all of those invitingly wicked bits about Addom's features that drew others to him. For once he looked completely serious and there was absolutely nothing inviting about him. "Careful with your words, friend."

Vaun felt the last bits of his morning high evaporate as a chill scaled his spine. He had not realized until that moment that they were, in fact, friends, and such could end right now. "I see."

Addom blinked, and the glimpse of his true self vanished. "So." He picked up his empty teacup and smirked. "Who started such an awful rumor?"

Vaun wasn't sure whether he opened his mouth to divulge such fragile knowledge or change the subject, but in the end it didn't matter because a burdened silence suddenly swept over the room. All eyes turned toward the door, even the prince's, and all lips parted to inhale surprise though none dared exhale sound.

Evan Kadem stood in the mouth of the entrance. Physically, he was very similar to Vaun, if Vaun had never smiled, laughed, or lounged in his life. Evan Kadem was coated in a plated armor reminiscent of large scales melded to his flesh, covering him completely save for his face, giving way to human skin near the birth of his jaw. He carried no weapons, for he never needed any. He was the first son, and the Queen's Wrath, a title given to him so long ago that no one could know for certain if it had been the lady in the Tower that named him so or the citizens of the Realm that whispered it first.

Fay stood from the table of Vyms and Vaun realized that he, too, had risen to his feet. It had been years since he had seen his brother in person. There were few reasons for him to leave the Queen's side in the Tower. The only sounds in the large room were those of Fay's skirts as she left her seat and walked to meet their sibling. He spoke low and, though all ears strained, none could hear what was not meant for them.

Vaun watched his sister tense. It was a subtle change, but he would have seen it miles away. She turned her head slightly and he felt as though she was resisting the urge to look back at him. When his gaze left her profile he found himself staring back at Evan Kadem. Silver eyes pierced the stretch of room, pupils too sharp in those large beds of color to be normal.

Fay's palm cracked against the Wrath's cheek.

Addom stood, as did Evelet and one of the other Vym lords at the table below, but it was too late for apologies, too late to offer themselves in her place. Evan Kadem's arm rose in reply, palm wide and gloved in that black armor. It descended and sent the residents of the High into a moment of complete terror.

It was only a matter of seconds, but Fay did not flinch. If possible, her chin lifted, her eyes daring the eldest prince of the Realm with the sort of anger only a sibling could harbor.

The arm of the most feared man in the Realm stopped short, the gust of air disorienting the normally obedient strands of her hair. Vaun shivered out an exhale, suddenly standing beside the two of them on the main floor. His fingers flexed against their hold on Evan Kadem's wrist. The material beneath his hand felt almost like rubber, but softer, making him wonder, not for the first time, if that armor wasn't truly the man's flesh. Cold eyes looked at him again.

"I think this has already gotten out of hand." Vaun's guts twisted under that awful stare. There was so little that was human about those eyes and nothing that he could read in them. "I don't know why you came, brother, but surely it was not for this."

Fay continued to stare up at the Wrath, willing him to leave, or maybe to die, with those eyes of hers.

"Merriam Fullan Vym," Evan Kadem said.

The woman in question let out a wailing sob and stood so quickly that her chair fell back onto the floor. Others rose, too, sobbing and shaking their heads.

To have your name spoken by the Queen's Wrath was to have your name spoken by the Queen.

"She is no one!" Fay shouted when Evan Kadem walked away from them and toward Merriam. All of the Vyms stood from their seats but none moved to stand in the Wrath's way.

Vaun stared after him, his hand sinking back to his side as it finally recognized the absence of a wrist between his fingers.

Merriam screamed. She shook her head, hands clenching and unclenching against the front of her dress. She begged for help, looking around wildly through her tears.

Fay started to follow Evan Kadem but Vaun grabbed her arm. She tore herself free of him. "She is no one!" Fay repeated.

The Queen's Wrath grabbed Merriam by the hair and pushed her ahead of him, toward the door. "Treasonous acts and the use of magic to hide herself from the Queen," he replied, voice stiff. "Is a traitor no one?"

"I'm not!" Merriam screamed, reaching out for Fay.

Fay didn't reach back, her hands balled into fists in her skirt. "Evan Kadem!" The princess shouted a name most didn't dare to whisper and, near the door, the Queen's Wrath stopped.

Silence fell over The Library and Merriam's sobs echoed in every corner. They looked on her as though she were a ghost, already dead. No one ever came back when the Queen sent her Wrath down with their name on his lips.

Evan Kadem's cold gaze found Fay again. "If you disobey your Queen, you will pay the price."

His gaze slipped past her to find Vaun, and for one horrible second, the youngest prince thought he saw a smile on those wide lips. "Happy Birthday."

The door closed behind him but the guests of The Library remained reverently silent.

They waited, as Vaun did, for Fay to decide what they should feel.

He watched her shoulders quake, her nails pressing into her palms to cut crescents of flesh before she finally shook them out. She rubbed the blood she'd spilled discreetly into the black of her dress, the skin healing over before she was done. When she turned away from the doorway and back to the room, her expression was perfectly poised. She returned to her table. Evelet picked up Merriam's fallen chair and a waiter appeared to take away her teacup. The Library returned to sipping and pretending to read.

"You made quick work of those stairs," Fay said from her seat without looking at him. She picked up her tea and took a drink. "You should take care how you use your magic, brother. Wouldn't want the Wrath to come with your name on his lips."

The exhaustion of her tone took the air from his lungs.

"You're welcome," Vaun spat, bitter that he ever thought things could change.

CHAPTER TWO

Grayc Illan Sanaro watched the entrance to the Queen's Wall from her seat in the car. Guests poured in, wearing their finest in hopes of attracting the prince's attention. Every year it was the same. They wore masks for his birthday. No one remembered who started that tradition, except for Grayc Illan. She remembered the day he decided to make them all wear masks more than fifty years ago.

She had never crossed the street to the Tower grounds before. This was as close as she had ever been.

The passenger door opened and a man slid onto the seat beside her. She didn't have to turn her head and look to know who it was. "I told you to stay away from me." Grayc Illan watched another car pull up across the street and Quentan Vym step out. He rounded the vehicle and waited at the other door for his wife to join him on the sidewalk. Grayc straightened. Fay never attended Vaun's birthday parties. To Grayc's knowledge, the princess hadn't set foot on Tower grounds since her wedding day. Others noticed, masked faces swiveling toward the Lord and Lady Vym as they entered the courtyard beyond.

"Maybe I'm here for his birthday." Udaro smiled around the words because they both knew it wasn't true. Udaro was a Belholn, but only by technicality, as one of the previous Lord's bastards. The High would always see him as a rat of the Low. He enjoyed many liberties, but no one with blood below the High was invited onto the Queen's grounds.

"It isn't safe to talk to me." They'd gone over this before. "All she has to do is ask and I will tell her everything."

"You wouldn't," Udaro insisted.

"I would have no choice."

"Come with me tonight," he suggested. "He's gone where you cannot follow."

Grayc Illan watched another set of cars arrive. Addom and Evelet Vym poured out with four guests between them. "I can't leave him," she confessed.

"Because she said so?"

"Because I won't." Her cheek turned and her eyes took him in. The shadows in the car made the tattoos creeping up from his white collar look sinister.

"He is everything that is wrong with the Realm," Udaro whispered harshly.

"He is important." She turned her gaze to the gates again. "We cannot burn down the house without a spark."

Udaro shifted uncomfortably beside her, sucking a breath through his teeth. "He is more than a spark, Illi. He is an inferno waiting to devour us all. You cannot wield him." He stayed a moment longer before shaking his head and swallowing whatever he meant to say next.

She let him leave because she had no reply that would sooth him.

Vaun Dray Fen was a sleeping dragon and she had no intention of wielding him, but one way or another, she was going to see the Realm burn.

Vaun walked into the courtyard nestled at the base of the Queen's

Tower, past the wall that divided it from the rest of the Realm. Floating lamps drifted overhead like perfectly rounded paper clouds, setting the cobblestone paths, fountains, steps and iron railings aglow. Hundreds of intimately small tables were set out with dainty dishes of brightly colored, miniature Bundt cakes and squares of cheesecake topped in shining, dust-coated flowers, each a masterpiece that would meet a gruesome end tonight, either swallowed by painted lips, dropped onto those cobblestones as the party developed over the night, or thrown out in the morning.

Away from the courtyard and down the steps, gardens of flash flowers bloomed almost violently. Giant, tight buds opened right before the eye, rainbow petals spreading wider and wider to birth more layers, the old dying and falling like confetti to the ground while the centers still bloomed. Eventually it would end, fade, and begin again. The fallen petals faded as soon as they touched the ground, leaving the faint glittery residue of magic behind. It was a display of excess that only the Queen could afford. There were junkies in the Main and Low districts that would have gladly licked that leftover magic from the ground. Even the families that attended this event by exclusive invitation wouldn't waste magic, not if they could sell it, horde it, or use it themselves.

Vaun let his attention slide past the gardens to the high walls of the labyrinth that surrounded her Tower. Some thought of it as the Queen's version of a moat, her last defense to keep out unwanted guests, but Vaun knew better than to think that his mother would run out of defenses. It was just another display; just another game. He had played in it as a child when his governesses would bring him to visit her. He had always hoped to get lost inside, trapped so that he could not come when she finally called him out for their formal chat.

He hated this place, but tradition dictated that his birthday celebration be held on Tower grounds so that all three households could pay their respects without the chance of deception. Entering into an enemy province came at great risk to the ruling families of

Vym, Belholn, and Maggrin. Their reign extended only to the edges of their own borders. No family would dare feud in the Queen's home, though she stopped making appearances at these events decades ago. He supposed that was something to be grateful for.

The dust-laden wine, pastries, and tea turned the dance floor into an aggressive swirl of colorful hair, skirts, and coats that left most onlookers wobbling. Laughter swelled up around Vaun until he was sure that he was drowning on his feet. There was an arm around his waist, he realized, and a dainty hand against his chest, while another fed him bites of cake.

The night felt interminably long, even if it was his own party.

Every year his birthday played out more or less the same. It was possibly his least favorite event of the year, despite its subject. It was one of the few nights when all of the Realm's lords and ladies occupied the same floor. Belholns took up most of the dance floor, while those that had downed enough tea and inhaled enough dust to have their legs falling out from under them lounged comfortably off to the side.

Xavian Ren Belholn, the eldest son and head of the Belholn household, sat at the table beyond those languid bodies with his wife. They smiled and laughed and would appear to be the calmest of the families in attendance that evening, should anyone be fool enough to underestimate them so gravely. Belholns were always more alert than they appeared and armed to the teeth. Fighting was a sport in their province, even in their High.

The Vyms sat in joyful clusters around their tables, pretending with great accomplishment not to notice the Belholns at all. And the few Maggrins in attendance stayed near the exit, always skeptical of their enemies. They took great pleasure in whispering behind fingers and teacups, eyeing the other families as they did.

Vaun's group of interlinked limbs stumbled their way down the steps and into the garden, spilling wine and cackling at the mess as they went. It was a miracle they did not fall on the stairs, if miracles spent themselves on such petty creatures. They reached the walkway between the ever blooming flowers only to tumble into a heap on the cold stones. Giggles exploded from two decidedly female throats while someone started to work open his belt.

Vaun sighed pleasantly, sprawling on the ground much like he had as a boy, staring up at the ever present clouds that filled the sky as they twisted around the spire of the Tower like old coffee down a drain. He reached up to take the thin mask from his face and held up the frail metal accessory. The gold had been cut to look like lace, catching sparkles of light from the lamps before he dropped it carelessly onto the ground.

Suddenly, he found himself chilled and alone. The prince sat up on his elbows in time to watch his cluster of would-be playmates slink back up the stairs to rejoin the party, looking more than a little dissatisfied. His lips parted to call them back when he saw the figure standing at the railing that overlooked the garden. For a second he thought it was the Queen herself, only to realize that it was an even more unlikely guest: Fay. His sister stared down at him, her expression lost in shadows. Vaun stood immediately. It was not like her to attend events at the Tower courtyard. Suspicion and perhaps an ounce of fear pulled him toward her, but before he could take a second step he heard a shoe scuffing cobblestones.

Vaun turned away from his sister and the party to stare at the woman there against the backdrop of the gardens. She wrung her hands, face drawn and eyes wide. He wondered if she had been trapped when he and his cowardly companions blocked the path to the stairs.

Vaun smiled widely at the woman in front of him. He slunk closer, straightening his clothes, though a part of him was already devising plans to make them askew again. The prince chanced a glance back to see if his sibling was still on the terrace. Fay had vanished as quickly as she had appeared, leaving him to his new game. His attention fell on the woman in the garden completely, finally taking in the oddity of her appearance. She did not look entirely out of place among the rose bushes and falling petals, but he could not imagine her blending into the party in the courtyard. Her dress was simple; elegant, but modest.

Her hair was mostly down, dark but not black, midnight blue, or maroon. He squinted as he neared. Was that brown? She wasn't jeweled, painted, or tattooed, save for the white feathered mask she wore and the gold ring on her left hand. His smile practically split his cheeks. This was an interesting costume, if only because it was the only plain one he had seen in decades. Modesty was not in fashion.

"You like to watch?" Vaun stopped less than an arm's reach from her. Had her cheeks actually *colored*? He took another step and breathed deeply, wanting to inhale a hint of whatever magic she was using. It had to be an exquisite spell if it could make her blush so naturally. His senses fluttered, but it was not from the high he expected. She had a scent, but it was not any magic that he knew; he found it indescribable. It reminded him of fabric, of lemons, of silken hair, but none of those truly came close. It made him want to lean in closer and breathe deeper but he did not want to give her all of the power in this game, at least not yet.

He took her hand in his and held it up to look at the simple band around her finger. It looked cheap and wore a little at his smile. Why would she falter on such a small detail?

"Happy Birthday," she said.

Vaun looked up and for a moment caught the gleam of her blue eyes before she looked away again, this time at the buttons of his jacket. He knew her. He had to. There was no man or woman in the High of the Realm he did not know. "Did you bring me a gift?" He searched her face for some hint at her identity.

Her blush returned and his heart raced. He needed to know what that spell was. He was not sure he had ever seen a woman blush before. No. He had. It was there, somewhere, in the back of his memories. He had seen this. He had seen her.

"My apologies, my prince. I merely wanted to wish you well."

Still holding her hand, he took her arm in his and turned them, walking toward the labyrinth. "Then you will be my gift. I could use the company." There was hesitation to her steps but he did not allow her to pause. "Which family are you from?" he asked as they slipped into the stone walled path, shadows playing from every corner.

She looked up at him, holding onto his arm cautiously. "You don't remember me?"

There was some hurt in her voice but mostly relief. A curious response, since most women and men cried when they realized the prince had forgotten them. "I suppose that makes it my turn to apologize." His fingers rubbed that cheap little ring of hers. "Do I know your husband?"

"Everyone does." She spoke more easily now, bolstered by her anonymity. Her gaze wandered the turns and he realized that she was trying to remember them.

His mind searched through names, trying to connect any of them to this woman. He let go of her hand when they came to a small, circular, dead end. Leaving her to stand in the middle, Vaun walked around her, looking her over thoughtfully and tapping his lips. "I do not know how I have forgotten you," he admitted, offering her more credit than he was sure she deserved. "Won't you give me your name? Let us start again."

Something in her eyes sparkled then; a hope perhaps, small and desperate. "Could we start again without a name?" the lady asked, turning to look at him fully. There was a plea in her eyes that made him want to recoil in the same breath that he swept closer.

"And if I say no?" the prince whispered and it was suddenly less than sweet. "If I demand your name?" He leaned in until their noses almost met and the feathers that curled off her mask tickled his cheek. She trembled when his hand curled around the broad curve of her hip, sliding up to her waist and feeling just how thin those layers were between them. Her lips quivered and panic shone in her eyes. So

33

much honesty, even without words. He felt certain, in that moment, that her body was the greatest lie he had ever known.

"You will have to guess," she said even as her voice shook.

He pulled her against him and crushed her lips, parting her mouth with force until their teeth clashed. He breathed deep, closing his eyes and tasting her tongue. How could she feel new? No one had felt new to him in decades. She shuddered and it made him push at her until they met with the opposition of a wall. She gave without resistance but there was a timidness about her fingers against his jacket, about her tongue touching his, about the way her breath shook in her chest.

"Give me a hint," Vaun huffed against her swollen mouth, his forehead rubbing hers to keep the back of her skull pinned to the stone wall.

She smiled shakily. "I have no hints to give." It sounded sad, even from a lust laden voice.

The prince grinned. "If we have met before, then you have hints to give." He delved his face into the curve of her neck. Again that smell, the one that screamed at memories. How could he remember the scent of her but not the name? His hands stroked the dip of her waist, then the curve of her hips. Eager fingers coiled, pulling the length of her dress upward. Simple gowns gave little resistance; it was one of their few charms, but it repented well.

For a moment her breath hitched and he wondered if she would actually decline. Some lovers liked to play at modesty, few as they were, and others simply liked to tease. His teeth grazed her throat before his tongue tasted her skin, giving her the moment to pick the game, but only small gasps came from her widely parted lips.

With his boot he slid her heel along the rough ground until her legs parted, his hip pinning hers into the wall. Cold air wafted over her exposed thighs and when his hand cupped her sex she actually jumped. He wanted to laugh against her neck. She was either better than he thought or it had been quite a while for her. She made the most beautiful sounds when he touched her. As expert as his fingers were, he had never heard anyone sound that pleased, not without the cheap pitch of over exaggeration. Her breath quickened and her head rolled farther back as she gasped for swallows of air.

He grinned against her cheek. "Tell your prince your name."

She swallowed hard, her hips still rubbing blindly into his touch. Her eyes pressed shut and he wondered if she was trying to gain enough focus to remember it herself. "You are not my prince—" the lady finally breathed "—you are my king."

The words struck him and his entire body jerked back. Her skirt fell back into place but her arms were still up, her back still pressed against the wall, not entirely unlike the last time he had seen her. Those words had poured from her lips that night as well, just as low and honest as they were now. With shaking fingers he snatched the mask from her face, practically slapping it from its perch.

Vaun hissed and staggered another step back. "AviSariel." He breathed her name like a curse.

Her arms sank slowly back to her sides as the weight of his hate returned. "Husband."

The prince bared his teeth at the title, taking another long stride back. "I told you never to stand in front of me again."

"It has been twelve years. I have stayed in the Tower, as you said."

"And today?" he snapped, voice rising. "You saw the party lights and thought you would come down?"

Her head dipped lower still. "The Queen sent me. I thought you knew—"

He let out a harsh laugh. "Knew what? That my mother released my wife from the Tower and sent her down to... what? Seduce me in the garden?"

Her head lifted a little. It took her a second to choose her words, her voice holding that unwavering calm that his mother desired in all people of value. "I was not the one seducing."

Vaun reeled, his lips pulling into a snarl. "The rules of our marriage have not changed. Do not slip up again or you will regret it." He walked away, abandoning her to the labyrinth. It occurred to him that she might become lost without him, and his steps quickened. Let his mother retrieve her.

He still didn't understand why his mother had been so bent on forcing his marriage to a woman no one knew. The Queen had seemingly produced AviSariel from thin air just to announce their engagement. It had been a delightful scandal all those years ago—the prince marrying the only noble the Realm had not yet corrupted.

She had worn white. He remembered because it had been the first time he had seen her in person and the last time he had seen her until now. He hated her completely; the sweet way she smiled. Her sickeningly polite words. She had refused to cry or shout, no matter what awful things he whispered while they danced. Even Vaun knew he was being unreasonable. He did not know her, so how could he hate her?

Sometimes reason had nothing to do with a matter, and it certainly had nothing to do with the prince's heart.

CHAPTER THREE

Vaun woke in less comfort than usual. He tried to find a better position on the bed, one that might afford him a few more hours of blissful sleep. Though his arms spread out, they found no blankets or pillows. With a curse on his lips he finally gave in and opened his eyes.

Laughter filled his ears. It was a deep, wholehearted amusement that he had heard on many occasions. Propping himself up on his elbows, he squinted against the lamplight filling the narrow parlor. He recognized at once the thick rug beneath his bare legs and the broad, overstuffed furniture lining the walls. His head throbbed, making his eyes squint tighter when he looked up at the only other person in the room.

A lean man reclined on one of the couches and grinned down at him: Udaro, a bastard son of the Belholn family. Had Vaun come to the Belholn province then, last night? He couldn't remember anything after swirling on the dance floor with one of the Vym twins at his party. It seemed likely, since Belholn bastards weren't welcome far beyond their own borders. Udaro moved more freely than most, despite having a Low born mother, but only because he alone masterminded the Realm's most sought after event, The Circus, a party that occurred only when and where Udaro chose.

"You didn't come to my party," Vaun accused.

"I wasn't invited." Udaro grinned wider.

Currently half dressed, which was half more than Vaun, Udaro cocked his head and the short, inky strands of his hair formed spear tips stretching for his stone green eyes. "Did you black out again, prince?"

Vaun pushed himself into a full sit, rubbing his neck to get at the ache in his spine. "Are you such a bad host that you would have me sleeping on the floor?"

Udaro laughed again. Long fingers with black painted nails brought a cigarette to his lips. "Not my house," the Belholn corrected. "But I did suggest we leave you on the floor."

Before the prince could ask, a sweet vanilla scent wafted into the room. He glanced up to see her enter from a side door, dressed in lace panties and a short, silk robe caught eternally between opening and closing, giving the eye dominion over navel and throat, as well as that taunting valley between, but little more.

Of all the things Meresin possessed to enamor and enchant others, it had always been her hair that caught Vaun's eye. How could such a shade of vivid red not? It wasn't a fashionable hair color before she showed up with it, and now that it was hers, no one else could have it. Women and men had tried and failed, because everyone that saw that hair expected her face and even the most beautiful creatures of the Realm held no illusions of competing with Meresin. It was not just her face or the oddly large, yellow eyes set in it. It was not even the shape of her body, the long legs or thick curves. Meresin had a way about her that invited others, that made thoughts turn sensual, that made voices turn deep and hearts lonely.

Meresin leaned onto the couch, planting one knee beside Udaro's thigh. She plucked the cigarette from his lips and turned her face away in what might have appeared to be politeness but was actually crafted to give both of her companions her profile. They watched in reverent silence as she inhaled, drew the cigarette away from her lips, savored, and finally tipped her head back to blow out a stream of gold smoke.

She smiled when she returned the red stick to Udaro's mouth and rolled over him to nestle herself comfortably into the other side of the couch, leaving a leg across his lap. "Coffee's being brought up." She turned her head to look at Vaun, warmth and friendship brightening her features and making her all the more enchanting. "Are you feeling well?"

"Your rug did not exactly offer the best sleep I have ever had."

Meresin giggled, the sound cut short as her fingers pressed at her lips in apology. "You seemed happy enough when you fell asleep there." A small warning knock sounded at the door before a maid entered, carrying a silver tray and setting it on one of the side tables. The woman stayed long enough to pour and hand out the white cups of black liquid. "Anyway, sweetheart, you weren't exactly expected," Meresin continued.

Udaro made a somewhat inelegant sound of agreement between a huff of smoke and a sip of coffee. "You barged in here, insisting that you had an appointment."

"You didn't," Meresin clarified. Her lips pursed, always glossy, and blew at the steam of her cup. Even that small act made parts of Vaun that had moments ago been forgotten and flaccid suddenly aware of just how naked he was.

"But, like an ass, you stumbled in and started stripping down." Udaro waved his cigarette about in Vaun's direction. "You really should lay off the tea. It's too much if you're forgetting your own nights."

Vaun sighed and crawled into an armchair without spilling or setting down his cup. Sitting on the floor was only allowed when one was half asleep, in the midst of something devious, or dusted, and he was, to some disappointment, not currently classifiable as any of those things. "My apologies." He sipped the coffee. It tasted awful, but the test of class was not to cringe.

Udaro shrugged, the gesture drawing attention to the dark lines of tattoos that scrolled over his naked shoulders and fanned the sides of his neck. Vaun knew a lattice work of ink covered the man's back, though his chest bore only a thin x slashed over his heart. Vaun had inquired about it before, since Udaro didn't strike him as the poetic sort, but his friend only laughed.

Not many among the High, or even the Main, would wear permanent tattoos. Vaun still thought it cringeworthy. Why would someone with the means to print and maintain a mark with vanity crafts stoop to putting needle to flesh instead? It was a level of slumming that the prince had yet to reach, his own bouts limited to searching out delightfully wretched teahouses in the Main.

He suddenly remembered the riot in the Low that claimed the life of Ferrin Gray. Proof, if ever he needed it, that there was no pleasure to be found below the Main.

"I will pay for the evening, of course," Vaun offered, if only to stall before having to take another sip of coffee.

"Don't worry. I made you work for it." Udaro grinned wickedly, one of the few gestures that showed his Belholn side.

Meresin put the edge of her cup to her lip in an unsuccessful attempt at hiding a giggle. All three provinces had the pleasure of Meresin's business and she kept a residence in each, but only Belholn allowed her to live at the top of the Main, just a block from the High. In Vym, she resided in the middle of the Main. Maggrin went so far as to banish her to the slums of the Low. Nothing kept the High born from making appointments, though. Whether she resided next door or near the Ash, she was still worth their money.

"How was the party?" she asked curiously over her porcelain. "The pictures in the paper looked lovely."

Meresin sounded excited even though she hadn't been on the guest list. Disreputable individuals were not allowed on the grounds of the Queen's Tower, which unfortunately included the Realm's favorite prostitute and Belholn's bastards. A shame. It would be a more exciting party if they had been there.

Udaro snorted smoke. "It couldn't have been that great if he came stumbling in here at midnight."

Vaun shrugged, sucking down the last of his bitter drink and trying not to shudder with revulsion. He succeeded and set the porcelain aside before stretching, utterly unabashed.

Meresin stood as though this was some sort of queue, fingers entwining with Udaro's to tug him up beside her. Udaro must have paid for the morning, as well, otherwise his casual lingering would have been rude. Meresin would likely have played the kind hostess anyway, but Vaun doubted Udaro would be so presumptuous.

"Care to join us for a shower?" the bastard joked with a broad smile, cigarette precariously clinging to his lip.

Vaun managed not to sneer at the disgusting thought of sharing tile. "I would rather spend the morning in my funk, thank you."

Meresin giggled and tugged Udaro toward one of the side doors that led further into her network of private rooms. Before they could leave, Vaun raised a hand in their direction. "Udaro, I'm having a dinner tonight. Will you be joining?"

The Belholn made a sound of uncertainty that could have easily been taken with offense. "Who's attending?"

"No one I am related to will be there," the prince promised but followed it with a sly smirk. "Though probably a few that you share blood with, and I also took the liberty of inviting Addom Vym."

That brought Udaro leaning back into the room. He laughed and smoke rolled out of his lungs, like clouds born from a dragon. "A Vym is not going to walk into the Belholn province, prince. Not even for you."

They both remembered Angelica Vym, the last of her house to trespass into enemy territory. She hadn't started the grudge between families, but it took her life all the same. Vaun didn't think all the pieces of her had ever been found. Belholns sometimes kept trophies.

"He has an official invitation," Vaun said, no grudge weighing on his shoulders.

Udaro straddled the threshold with Meresin leaning discreetly on his arm. "From Xavian Ren?"

Udaro might not have been a full sibling of the Belholns, but that shared blood allowed him to speak the name of the household's Lord with a casual ease that few others could muster.

"From the prince," Vaun countered.

"It won't go over well."

"I know."

"I'll be there."

Vaun eyed Meresin. "Do you have plans tonight?"

She smiled brilliantly. "Of course." She booked weeks in advance, a fact that discouraged Vaun only once or twice before he set up a few regular appointments. "But I'm sure it won't take long."

Grinning, Vaun waved and walked out of the parlor and into the lobby. A maid waited there, holding his cleaned and pressed clothing. He took the slacks and pulled them on. Through his lashes he checked to see if the girl blushed. She had not. Why would she? Suddenly feeling irritated, he snatched his jacket and abandoned the rest of his things, including his shoes. While Vaun was of the opinion that most possessions were made to be tossed away on a whim, he never willingly left a good jacket behind. It was not likely that he would wear the same one again, but he would rather see them stuffed away in a closet or burned than see them worn by someone else.

The sidewalk chilled his bare feet as he walked down the steps of the house to the street. Faces pressed to windows to peer out at him. The high sound of voices squealing gossip assaulted his ears. His car was waiting, just as it always was, and the driver opened the door when Vaun approached.

He slid in and threw his jacket onto the floor.

Grayc Illan did not even look at the garment or inquire about his general lack of clothing. "To the teahouse?" she asked instead, her tone only mildly judgmental today.

That pulled him from his intended sulking to look up at her sitting across from him in the spacious cab. She was in a suit today, wearing high slacks that hugged her waist and hips before falling wide around her legs to swallow her heels. He imagined how nice it would look when she stood. Her short sleeved blouse was mostly hidden beneath a matching vest.

"How do you stay so well pressed when you sit so long in my car?"

She glanced up from her planner, dark green nails hovering over the page with a white pen. "Magic."

Laughing, he nodded and reclined into his seat. "Take me home."

She hesitated. It was only a fraction of a second, entirely unnoticeable to anyone that hadn't sat across from her every day for seven decades. She rapped the window partition and the car pulled out into the street.

Vaun studied her more carefully. She appeared just as tense as always and just as disinterested in him. But he saw her waver. "Who's at my house?"

She focused on her lap, the newspaper tucked behind her leather bound planner. "Are you still having that dinner tonight?"

"It's Fay, isn't it?" He groaned and dropped his head back against the cushion. "I wish marrying a Vym kept her out of the other provinces."

"She's a princess," Grayc Illan said simply. A stretch of silence followed that nearly lulled Vaun into a nice car nap when, contrary to past experience, his valet started another conversation. "I saw your wife."

His eyes opened slowly but he did not sit upright just yet. She said it just the same way she said everything else, mildly annoyed but thoroughly unamused. "Did you know my mother was going to send her to my party?"

"No."

He lifted his head to study her. "Would you have told me if you had?"

43

Something changed in her features, something shadowed her eyes, and he could have sworn her already firm lips tightened. Was that regret? "If I could."

He watched her for a moment longer. Was this her way of reminding him that she was, in the end, under the employ of his mother and not him? He was well aware of her loyalties. No one crossed the Queen, not even her children. So, why did a part of him expect different from Grayc Illan?

The car pulled to a smooth stop in front of his townhouse in the Belholn High. He was halfway out of the car when Grayc Illan emerged from the other side. Vaun frowned. Grayc Illan was a creature of habit. She always stayed in the car until it parked in the underground garage, then came up to the residence on her own.

"What happened?" he asked grimly.

She rounded the car casually and started up the stairs, expectant that he would follow. "There have been riots in the Low of Belholn."

He raised an eyebrow and followed her up the steps. "You're worried about my safety?" Vaun scoffed as she opened the door, though inwardly loved how she held it for him. He stopped in front of her, to keep her standing there longer. He was right, those pants did look perfect on her when she was upright.

Vaun could not resist stepping closer. It was so rare that she stood with him, especially outside with no one around to grab his attention away. Ever more unlike her to not be in the midst of a task or focused on something else. She simply stood there, waiting, staring back at him. How long had her eyes been that shade of green?

"I feel like you are keeping something from me today," the prince said as he touched the waist of her fitted slacks, thumbing the stitching. Had she been using his tailor?

Grayc Illan smiled, a tart little twist of lips that gleamed beneath some cruel mirth. "I always keep things from you." Her free hand swatted his arm away like the nuisance that it was. "Today is no different."

He tried not to smirk, really he did, but some part of him loved her rejection. She was the only woman in the Realm, not related to him, that gave absolutely no thought to his flirtation before turning him away. Not once. Not in the seventy plus years that she had been his valet. How could she not even be curious? He brushed past her as he walked into the quaint receiving room of his home. A man sat at a desk there, much like in the lobby of an apartment building, and stood when Vaun entered. The lobby attendant looked surprised to see Grayc Illan entering with him, making Vaun wonder for the first time in those seventy years if she had ever used the front door.

"Attend my party tonight." He glanced at her from the corner of his eye as she reached his side.

"I'll be in the house if you need anything. I prepared a guest room in case you need to house Addom Vym for the night," she said, slowing to make sure she did not walk past him on the stairs up to his private floors. He tested this by lingering on the landing before taking the last stretch of steps upward. She would not pass him; it would put her higher than him. He wondered if etiquette prompted her, or if she did not trust him behind her. He hoped it was the latter because that meant she thought about him more than proper.

"Are you worried about him?" Vaun inquired.

Grayc Illan cracked a smile, a little one full of spite, and moved ahead of him at last to open the double doors at the top of the stairs. She stepped aside to let him enter first. How had he managed to open his own doors all these years? Surely, she would have to walk him in every day from now on. "Try not to get a Vym killed tonight," she said. "It would be hard to explain to his brother."

They parted ways in the foyer and he stood for a while longer to watch her retreat, slacks swishing like the whisper of pixie wings.

He sighed and headed for the bedroom wing.

"I'll be up with some tea shortly," Grayc Illan called over her shoulder.

His fingers stilled on the banister, gaze jerking back to her just as she disappeared behind swinging doors. Grayc never suggested tea; in fact, she barely managed to restrain a judgmental sneer whenever he requested it.

Suddenly, the stairs took on a sinister shadow and Vaun found himself creeping up them like a cowardly child in the dark. His gaze honed in on the corridor as it came into view. Nothing was out of place, although its sheer length and abundance of doors along the path to his own bedroom felt far more excessive than he remembered. Was he to check each room? Did he dare?

Vaun skulked along the plush carpet, grateful for the silence of his bare feet. He made it nearly the entire length, only an arm's reach from his bedroom door, when sound broke his silence.

He twisted to the side, pulling away from the hum of an escaping voice. He stared at the door of a guest room for a long while, studying the dark shadows against its carved and painted surface. Was that laughter? Vaun reminded himself that this was his door, in his residence, and stepped up to push the panel open.

He considered more than a dozen potential unwanted guests in the split second that followed, but she had not been one of them.

She curled into an overstuffed chair, legs tucked beneath her. One hand shielded a smile on her lips while the other held a book. It only took her a moment to look up, see him, and all happiness drain from her features.

AviSariel stood, dropping the book onto the chair behind her. She opened her mouth to speak but the weight of the silence between them pressed her lips together again.

"What do you think—" Vaun started, voice low, jaw set.

"Do you remember giving this to me?" AviSariel held out her hand.

The prince blinked at her shaking digits, and the tacky ring gleaming on her finger. "I wouldn't—"

"You did. Not at the ceremony. That was just words and signing the papers for your mother." She withdrew her hand and rubbed the tiny gold band. "After the party, before you left, you put this on my finger. You looked at me and said, 'If you need wealth, you will have it. If you wanted status—'"

"'—you've got it,'" Vaun continued in a low murmur. He remembered these words. He remembered that moment at the end of his wedding before the rest of his life. And he remembered that little ring that had weighed down his pocket all night. "'I do not know what you traded for this. I do not care. Keep the ring. Remember what you got yourself tonight but do not expect to be loved by me. I have never hated anyone more.'"

AviSariel exhaled with a funny little smile, tears in her eyes. She looked relieved that he remembered and, childishly, he wished that he had pretended that he had forgotten.

"I meant what I said," the prince persisted. "I do not want you in my house or in my life."

"And I do not want to be here," the princess admitted, looking up finally to stare back at him. "But the Queen ordered it."

His gaze hardened. Did his mother think she could spy on him with this woman? Did he have anything to hide? Of course he did. His teeth clicked. "Don't touch my things." He yanked open the door and stalked to his own quarters, hating her, hating his need to retreat, hating that he couldn't breathe again until he slammed his own door behind him.

He always knew she would be thrown back at him one day. It had been a blessing that his mother said nothing in objection when he left his bride behind at the Tower and returned to his life as though the wedding had never occurred. The entire Realm knew, of course, but marriages were easily forgotten when the couple was never seen together.

He had never asked anything about her. He had not wanted to know; he still didn't. His mother's will brought AviSariel to him and that alone was reason not to trust her. But the truth that chafed was his absolute lack of choice. AviSariel was his wife; he'd never asked her, never courted her, but still she claimed him. Now, by the Queen's order, she claimed part of his home, as well.

At times like these he almost understood his sister, but then he recalled the length of her anger, her dark clothing and unsmiling lips, her resolve to remain in her shackles, though Vaun felt certain that she could cast herself away from Quentan easily enough. Fay Dray Fen Vym was one of the very few "good spouses" in the Realm. She kept no lovers and said nothing in public that might scorn her husband. It was possibly the only matter in which she was incredibly unfashionable.

Just thinking of his bitter sibling exhausted him, much less coping with an unwanted houseguest. Though, as he retreated to the last safe space in his home, he wondered if a wife could really be considered a guest. He knew very few couples that lived together but they did seem to come and go from one another's homes comfortably enough.

He showered longer than usual, his body finding comfort leaning naked into the cold tiles while almost scalding water poured over the rest of him. It made his skin feel raw, hot and cold at the same time. It was the most comfortable discomfort he had ever felt, cradling him between complaint and sleep. Since he was a boy he had insisted on having complete privacy in the bathroom, taking longer showers when he needed more time to think. Normally, he emerged with a newfound calm or, at the very least, a scheme to make himself feel better. Today, he had no scheme or plot in hand when he left his bathroom for his bedroom.

He pulled on a pair of black lounge pants while his hair dripped. He could all but feel the letter propped on his desk glaring at him, like a malevolent eye. He'd seen it upon first entering but hadn't dared open it without a fortifying shower. Trying not to hold his breath, Vaun picked it up, wincing at the all-seeing royal emblem in vivid blue wax. The handwriting made his skin tight. The Queen had written the letter herself, as though her signature did not carry enough command on its own. As he read he could hear her pen scratching at the paper, see her hand rubbing against the lower edge of the page, feel her eyes going over the text.

He shuddered away from where it fell on his desk.

By the Queen's word, AviSariel was to live with him, wherever he moved, in any province and in any district. There was no escape.

A tap sounded at the door a moment before Grayc Illan entered with a tray of tea. He stood silently as she set it prettily on the coffee table in the sitting area and poured the singular cup full.

"No tarts?" The prince tried to sound disappointed. He lowered himself onto the couch not unlike a skeptical mouse sitting down to a plate of spring-loaded cheese.

"You hate tarts," she said.

It was true. He was sick of food but it was fashionable to eat.

As though he needed more surprises today, Grayc Illan sat beside him, leaving just enough space so as not to actually touch him.

Frowning suspiciously, he picked up the cup and breathed in the steam, smelling the bittersweet dust that swirled in its waters. "Nothing different about today," he repeated her words from earlier that morning sullenly. He did not need to ask why she had not warned him.

Her sigh sounded regretful.

He drained the cup quietly before setting it back down. "Is there any way to get rid of her?"

"Your mother, or your wife?"

Vaun laughed bitterly and fell to the side, his shoulder landing in her lap and his cheek on the couch arm. It was a risky move but, with his skin warming to the tea, he felt bold. He expected her to dump him on the floor, but she laid her palm on his shoulder, instead. She rarely touched him, and never tenderly, yet her other hand stroked his hair.

He exhaled and it almost felt like his problems had gone with his breath. "It must be truly awful."

"I drugged your tea. You'll be sleeping soon," she said and

continued to pet his hair. "You'll need your rest before dinner." Her fingers curled around the shell of his ear and he felt his entire body shiver. "It's time to face the music, prince."

Her voice was soft but no more forgiving than usual. Her nails stroked his scalp and he shuddered again. "Face music?"

His eyes closed, the nails of her other hand stroking his shoulder gently. "I think you will have to wake up soon," Grayc Illan whispered.

"I'm not even asleep yet," he complained absently and felt her smile.

"You have always been asleep."

He wanted to open his eyes and ask her what she meant. It was the longest and strangest conversation he had ever had with her, but he could not seem to form the words. His mind focused on the feeling of her fingers and the way they made his skin ripple with warmth. It occurred to him, though he fell asleep too quickly to remember it, that Grayc Illan knew things, things she might have told him if only he had asked.

AviSariel refused to pace in the hall like a child, though she couldn't help lingering in her doorway. Finally, after far too long to be proper, Vaun's valet emerged from his bedroom. The woman paused after closing the door behind her, then turned.

The servants here were silly things with covetous eyes and whispers of gossip in the corners of their mouths, completely unlike the servants in the Tower, a handful of severe maids ghosting through the rooms, always with a purpose and never with a whisper. Vaun's valet was not like either sort of servant that AviSariel knew. The eyes of Grayc Illan Sanaro did not covet, they saw, and, to the princess's discomfort, they judged.

With that gaze on her, in those spare seconds before the valet looked away, AviSariel felt lacking. She felt like the intruder in what should have been her own home. She had already heard the whispers and read enough copies of the paper to know about her husband's valet. Grayc Illan was a rat from the Low. She didn't have any right to judge anyone, and yet AviSariel felt her chin dipping and her gaze averting as the shorter woman walked by.

"Is he unwell?" AviSariel pried, some corner of her heart hoping to explain away the other woman's time spent in his room.

Grayc Illan paused but didn't look back. "Always, your grace."

AviSariel waited until she had gone before retreating into her suite. She'd decorated it to her taste, but still it differed little from the one in the Tower: a pretty cage with a window to watch the Realm from and a stack of books for company.

Dread swelled in her heart at the prospect of attending the party without a friend. Fay had sent a card promising to come for brunch tomorrow, but that only implied AviSariel would face the Realm alone tonight.

The door opened and the three maids Fay had sent to serve her entered, all but invisible behind racks of dresses and boxes of accessories. Their bright chatter filled the room, and they commenced fussing over her in such a cheerful, intimate way that it was easy to imagine they were friends and not merely staff.

She hardly recognized herself by the time they finished, and a whisper of almost-confidence fluttered in her breast; even if her skin felt a touch too warm from the vanity crafts they'd used to improve features and colors she had not realized she lacked.

Too many strangers filled the long dinner table for her to keep track of their names. Vaun sat at the head of the table, so far away that she could only hear his conversation when he raised his voice above the chatter of the guests in the middle. AviSariel found herself relegated to the end of the table; not the very end, directly across Vaun, but the last seat down the left side, next to a woman she soon learned came from an obscure family in the Main and the date she accompanied, a dust peddling Belholn cousin named Jacobi. Both seemed unsure whether to make conversation or ignore her, as her husband did.

Her earlier flutter of confidence died away as the evening wore on, smothered by a rising sense of doom. The prince's guests hung on his every word. If he hated her, so would they. She'd told herself that she could survive the Realm as long as she had either Vaun's love, or the love of their people; she hadn't counted on being denied both. She looked down on her plate while they talked about clubs she had never been to and people she had never met. She wanted to despise him for despising her, but couldn't resist sneaking long, sideways glances up the table.

Vaun was the most beautiful man she'd ever seen and she knew, *just knew*, that he could love her the way she loved him. They were meant to be. The Queen had called it fate—his fate. Turning the ring on her finger, AviSariel reminded herself that she was his wife. He was already hers. He could fight all he wanted, but the battle was long lost. And now that she was living in his home, she was determined to show him that she was the princess he needed. She could be an asset, a good wife to him and a good princess to his people, if only they would let her.

Vaun spent the bulk of the first course wondering if he had dreamed his conversation with Grayc Illan. No evidence of the tea remained by the time he woke on the sofa and his valet gave no indication that anything out of the ordinary had occurred.

Unfortunately, he had not dreamed discovering his wife in his house. He'd seated her at the farthest end of the table, beside Jacobi Belholn's mistress for the evening. It was a sad sight to see a princess of the Realm sipping her perfumed soup in silence as even the most nameless of women ignored her, but it gave Vaun some joy. He smirked while Ollan continued regaling the table with a wild, ranting story. Jounas laughed hysterically by the woman's side, both paying more attention to their tea than their soup. Charlie had not arrived and, though the man was often late, both Ollan and Jounas admitted they hadn't seen their friend since the day before. No one else seemed to have heard about Larc being sighted in the Low. In fact, all gossip on the matter had gone suspiciously unheard by the general public.

Vaun eyed Addom, but the Vym shrugged it off innocently, which in itself was an admission of some guilt. Unfortunately for Charlie, no one at the table cared much about what had become of him and conversation went on without a stall. To Vaun's pleasure, Addom and Udaro appeared willing to provide entertainment by chatting amiably with each other, leaving the other Belholns to scowl at their bastard relative for speaking to a Vym at all. The snarl of a gaunt face near the middle of the table caught his attention. Wendry, the youngest child and only daughter of the Belholn family, eyed her dinner companions like a dog deciding where to attack first. Vaun enjoyed inviting her strictly for the gossip that invariably followed. The paper frequently noted her penchant for mischief, preference for violence, and tendency toward sadism.

Throughout the first course of perfumed soup and the following cups of tea, Wendry remained suspiciously silent. Her dark eyes darted curiously up and down the length of the table, from the prince at the head, the Vym at his left, and down the row of others to the princess sitting quietly near the shadows. Not until after the metal cloches were lifted from the second course of flawless, red apples, and the guests took up their forks and knives to cut through the thin flesh and into the perfect, white innards, did she speak. "You have such curious taste in company, your highness: Vym trash at your side, my bastard cousin beside him, and a tacky bride in the corner."

Vaun caught AviSariel's gaze briefly, long enough to see a flicker of hurt there before she looked to Addom and Udaro for their reply to Wendry's cruel words.

Udaro smiled with dark, painted lips. "Sweet Wendry." He spoke her given name with acidic familiarity but never bothered to lift his attention from his plate. "Are you upset to find yourself lost in the middle of the table?"

Vaun grinned at the flash in Wendry's eyes. Everyone knew it was most offensive to be seated at the middle, judged too dull to be a favorite at the head of the table nor dangerous or unwanted enough to be banished to the foot.

Vaun washed down a small mouthful of apple with a large gulp of tea. He cast his eye to the midsection of his table. Wendry was the sort of woman that might have been called ugly had she not been so terrifying. She was bone wrapped in flesh draped in scant amounts of fabric. She smoked even at the dinner table, trails of cherry red slipping into the air above her. Her youth, coupled with her dress and expression, made her look like an abused adolescent.

She was one of the few High born ladies in the Realm that Vaun had never crossed the threshold into a bedroom with. It was not her appearance that kept him from her—he had been with less attractive and even more frightening individuals—but her love of bloodshed. It was said that her bedmates never left without a scar and Vaun loved his own body far more than he had ever desired anyone else's.

"My apologies, dear Wendry," the prince said, pitching his voice louder than was needed in the sudden silence. "But I like you too much to seat you with my wife, and I fear you will mar me with the cutlery too much to bring you closer."

She smiled at what she perceived to be a compliment and returned her scrutiny to her plate. Vaun glanced at AviSariel, too quick for anyone to catch. She looked stricken, flushed, and embarrassed. Good. Perhaps she would not impose herself on his dinners again.

"Vym," Wendry spoke again before someone else could divert the conversation. "I hear you've been screwing that twin of yours."

Vaun saw Addom's fingers shift on the cold silver of his knife, caressing it, turning it against the flesh of his apple, though he suspected no one else did.

"I have heard nothing of it—" Addom sliced into his fruit "—

54

though you would be the expert on incest. However do you manage, having so many brothers and being only one, tiny cunt?"

Stillness struck the table and breaths drew in. The Belholns stared at their cousin, waiting to take her lead. Suddenly, the small woman broke out into laughter, setting the table back into an awkward sort of ease. Jounas quickly started up a new conversation, offering tidbits he had heard about the riots in the Low, spinning tales of madness. One of the Belholn cousins speculated that the chaos sounded like dust madness, but another pointed out that the Low born could not afford dust.

"Bad dust would be cheap enough, wouldn't it?" Jounas argued.

"Sure, if it weren't a myth." A Belholn lady rolled her eyes. To Vaun's knowledge, she had never left the High. "Imagine mixing perfectly good dust with trash, just to make it stretch? Who would risk the Queen's wolves for such a thing?"

"I heard a whisper," Addom Vym offered to the table between bites of apple, "that someone tried to make their own dust from scratch." His voice dropped and, coupled with the sudden silence of the table, took on the tone of a horror story. "They couldn't get it right, though, and cut their losses. Now the bad dust is scattered throughout the Realm. Dust so bad that it drives a person to kill with their bare hands. I heard a man ate his own family because of it."

AviSariel dropped her fork.

Another man scoffed loudly. "A child's story, made up to keep the High born from slumming."

"It should be easy enough to make dust," Udaro said skeptically, eyeing Addom. "Find some pixies, fatten them up, and give them a good roasting. How could anyone fail?"

"Do tell me you've tried." Wendry smiled toothily at her bastard sibling.

"Undercut the Queen's monopoly?" Udaro's gaze swept the table, as if noting that dust infused virtually everything on it. "I am not yet so tired of life."

"I think we would know if someone had made their own dust." Vaun laughed and sipped his tea without hesitation.

"And how is that, your highness?" Jacobi asked from his banished end of the table.

The prince shrugged one shoulder. "We would have read about it in the paper. The wolves do not come down from the Tower without howls and the Queen's Wrath does not move without drawing a great deal of attention." Nervous laughter fluttered around the table. "No soul is dragged to the Tower without a report in the paper for our enjoyment and, as of yet, I have read of no dust inventor." Justice was swift in the Realm, but it did not go without notice.

After the apples were eaten and the trays taken away, the chefs carried in the main course: a three-tiered strawberry cake with gold frosting, accompanied by trays of jam-filled tarts. It met with enough praise—which Vaun accepted as though he had baked it himself—that he didn't bother scowling at the tarts. Meresin arrived shortly thereafter, making herself comfortable at the corner of the table between Vaun and Addom. She cheerfully picked at their plates while insisting that she needed none of her own.

The cake was halfway into its bottom tier and the party had started on their fourth round of tea when Ollan began to regale them with some strange story of her squandered youth, of which she had many. From what Vaun had gathered over their decades of friendship, Ollan had at least three centuries of youth behind her. The duster was nearly upon the punch line when she suddenly squinted, gaze cast down the length of the table. Fingers squeezed her empty cup as she leaned forward to get a better look. "Alison?" she said, sounding completely astonished.

Everyone blinked at one another, a few trying to understand how this fit with her story.

Ollan smiled so widely that her gums showed. "Alison, dear, is that you?"

AviSariel's brow pinched. She stared back at the strange and rumpled woman.

"Olly, that is the princess," Jounas looked up and down the table between the two.

Ollan laughed, starting to wheeze. "Alison's no princess! Why, she's the carpenter's girl. She played with my Kortney when they were in school."

Jounas looked to Vaun, helpless. The prince touched his friend's shoulder, waiting until Ollan tore her eyes from the woman at the end of the table and settled on him. "That is AviSariel. I do not know an Alison," Vaun said clearly, staring back at the old duster. "Who is Kortney?"

"Kortney?" Ollan inhaled to answer, but the breath came out again with a sudden loss. She blinked, and for a moment Vaun thought he saw tears gathering, but then Ollan smiled, face wrinkling with dumb cheer. "Why, I haven't a clue."

Jounas laughed, always ready to enjoy a joke even if he did not understand it, and the table followed if only to be rid of the strangeness.

Near four in the morning, Grayc Illan sent the last of the kitchen staff to bed. The trays and plates had been taken away, washed, and stored. From the kitchen she could hear bursts of laughter from the dining room, and their hysterical nature indicated that Vaun's guests had plenty of refreshments. She was pouring herself a glass of wine when the kitchen door swung open, her gaze lifting momentarily to address the stray guest.

Jacobi stood in the doorway. "I suspected you would be in here," he said, leaning his cheek to the wood. His almost white hair fell around his cheeks in a well cut sort of disorder, nearly obscuring his hazy black eyes. His body, like his words, was sharp, easily ignored but subtly threatening. "You are a good dog, Grayc. Always close by."

She set the wine bottle down and lifted her glass. "On your way out?"

He smiled cheerfully. "Yes, dear, but I wanted to thank you for your efforts. If only the company had been different, the party might have been a delight."

She shrugged. "You always complain about his highness's events, but you never fail to appear." She swirled the wine in her glass. How close were her suspicions? How much did he know about her? Anything? "I could wonder why."

"Because I was invited." Jacobi Belholn slouched deeper into the doorway. "And because you are here. Your talents are wasted on Vaun."

Grayc Illan smiled and drank deeply before responding. "You think I would rather waste them on you?"

The twist of his lips never faltered. "No, darling. I think it is a waste to leave you sitting in the kitchen, or in the car. I could consider a partnership if you had interest."

Grayc's eyebrows rose. He'd started offering her a job in his staff decades ago, and tried to sweeten the offer every few years since. Someday he might even offer her his house and his title. Anything, if it meant he could take the prince's valet from him. Why he thought it would scorn Vaun so much, she didn't know. "I am happy in my position, thank you."

A high and whimpering voice came from his side, beyond the door and out of sight. "Consider it," he said before leaving with his date.

Sitting on her stool in the kitchen, drinking her glass of wine, Grayc Illan thought about many things, but not about his offer. Not from a Belholn. Never from a Belholn.

Her thoughts wandered, gaze lost in the deep cradle of her glass and the swaying liquid there. The color reminded her of a red coat she had as a child. It had been the loveliest thing she had ever owned. Her mother had been a seamstress and made it using the scraps of another woman's dress after it turned from being a full length gown to a knee length dress on the Lady's whim. Her mother had curbed her excitement with a warning: wear it freely in the Low, but never in the High.

She had been obedient, for a time, as many children were, but then, also like most children, she forgot. It had been pure misfortune that they saw her, of all the people in the High district. The Lady that had ordered the red gown had been the wife of Dorian Belholn, the Lord of the Belholn province. It turned out that his Lady, Vinnia Belholn, did not like to share. Red had been her color then, and hers alone. The Lord and Lady had smiled at the child and inquired about her lovely coat, and foolish young Grayc had boasted of her mother's talents.

She cried the day she came home to her mother's little shop, everything tossed about and broken, and there, among the fabrics, lay her mother's body. Her death made all the other fabrics red. Dorian and Vinnia had been waiting there, waiting for the girl to return, waiting to see her life crumble.

The sound of a gunshot and a scream brought Grayc Illan back to the present so violently she nearly dropped her glass. She set it down hard, already off her stool, and ran from the kitchen.

The dining room was wild with laughter. Jounas had fallen back, still in his chair, but making no effort to right himself.

AviSariel had been the one to scream, standing with her hands to her mouth. Meresin hurried to the princess's side to calm her.

Wendry and Vaun each held a small pistol, positioned at opposite ends of the table.

"What are you doing?" Grayc Illan asked in the calmest voice she could muster.

"What does it look like?" Vaun laughed.

"He's defending my honor," Addom Vym explained with a wolfish smile.

"Six, five, four—" Wendry leveled her pistol at Vaun again. The prince followed suit.

Grayc Illan frowned at Addom, ready to note that he had no

honor, when she noticed three Belholn cousins asleep at the table. Jounas' chortles silenced with a sudden sigh.

"Oh, dear." Meresin exhaled when Ollan and Charlie passed out, Charlie's cheek landing in a plate of icing.

"—two, one—" Wendry slurred the numbers, arm wobbling.

Grayc walked right into the firing zone. Meresin shouted. The dueling pair fainted and fired at the same time. A bullet tore into a painting on the wall behind Grayc as she crouched, arms out, to catch the prince as he fell. She sank with him to lay him safely on the carpet.

AviSariel wailed, voice high and hands aflutter against her neck.

Meresin curled an arm around the princess's shoulders. "Calm down, dear. It's all right."

Grayc Illan sighed and patted Vaun down, making sure he wasn't shot before going over to begrudgingly check Wendry, too. "It's a dust sleep, your grace," she told AviSariel. "It happens when the dust is too strong in the tea and they drink too much. They'll wake in a few hours."

AviSariel looked at the teacups with new horror before her nose scrunched with confusion, looking at the red-headed woman beside her. "Weren't you drinking the tea?"

"I never drink tea." Meresin giggled and led AviSariel away from the table of sleeping guests. She settled the woman in one of the plush sitting areas nestled beneath wide windows. "It's best in my profession to keep one's wits, so I only pretend to sip. Plus, it's best to have a clear recollection of the night when it comes time for payment."

Grayc Illan rang for one of the maids, directing her to remove the guns, clean up the spilled tea and replace it with coffee for when the guests woke. She brought a bottle of wine to the women on the sofa and two clean glasses. Meresin did most of the talking but the princess looked relieved to finally have some conversation. Grayc suspected they would become allies of sorts, if for nothing else than because AviSariel was desperate and Meresin was kind.

Grayc lingered, waiting to make sure Wendry didn't wake before Vaun and decide their duel was still in play.

Meresin insisted she join them for wine and reluctantly the valet did, using a glass to hide her amusement at their chatter. Soon, Meresin embarked on detailing veritable biographies of every important person in the Realm, calling on Grayc to fill in the blanks when she found herself forgetting something.

It wasn't until they got to Fay Dray Fen in the list of important people that the conversation got truly interesting. As it turned out, AviSariel was not completely without friends in the Realm.

CHAPTER FOUR

Vaun rolled onto his belly and buried his face in a pillow. Breathing deeply, he could still smell the vanilla of Meresin in his sheets. It was not until he heard the soft draw of a porcelain cup from its saucer that he realized someone was in bed beside him.

He turned his head, forcing his tired eyes to bear the light and glide up the body that stretched beside him. Addom's naked torso leaned against the pillowed headboard as he drank from his coffee cup. He looked overly thoughtful. His eyes, still a dark shade of red from the night before, were fixed on the door. From the perfectly askew nature of his hair and the fact that he seemed to be wearing a pair of Vaun's lounge pants, the prince surmised he had been awake for a while.

Groaning, Vaun wondered what was outside his door that even Addom Vym had retreated.

"Would you like coffee?" Addom asked politely but absently.

Vaun made a juvenile sound and rolled onto his back. "If I must."

"I am not so petty as to gossip about whether you take your morning drink or not." A small smirk curled at the corner of Addom's lips, though his gaze remained on the door. "I know worse things about you."

The prince stared up at the ceiling, wondering if they could continue this conversation and simply pretend something unpleasant didn't wait outside his room. "What happened to Charlie, by the way?"

Addom sipped his coffee.

Vaun narrowed his eyes at the ceiling. "You didn't kill him, did you? You should have at least dueled. It's bad form to hide it from the public."

"You do not remember last night, do you?"

Vaun's face scrunched in reply. He remembered dinner, and maybe gunfire, and waking to see AviSariel and Meresin drinking wine together and giggling. He didn't like that memory at all. The prospect of his favorite mistress befriending his unwanted bride was not a bright one.

The Vym took another drink. "Charlie would not have stood a chance in a duel, anyway." After a moment of silence, he sighed. "I will let him go in a month or so."

"All that trouble just because Larc has a beau in the Low?" He grinned at the rhyme. "It's hardly the worst thing you Vyms have ever covered up."

Addom drank his coffee.

When another stretch of silence went too long, Vaun finally sighed. "Why are you in my bed?"

"It seemed the place to go after the party. Meresin was here."

"I'm glad the trip out of your own province has been worth the effort." Vaun sat up, running fingers over his scalp. His bed was stripped down to the sheet now pooled around his waist. "But why are you *still* in my bed?"

"Your sister is here."

Vaun winced. "So? You like my sister."

"She is having brunch."

"You do not like brunch?"

Addom's red gaze swung to him at last. "She is having brunch with your wife and Meresin."

Vaun jerked as if doused with a cold bucket of water, all but tangling himself in the sheet as he twisted. "No." He laughed, but it came out more like a nervous squeak. "Not possible." Fay was a snob to her core. No matter how much she liked someone, without the right lineage, they may as well be invisible. Meresin might be a favorite of the Realm and enjoyed privileges that made it easy to forget her Low birth, but she was still a whore. Fay had never set foot in the same room with her before.

Addom's attention returned to the door. "I was getting coffee when I saw them. Your sister looked angry, as usual, but she was sitting at the table with Meresin."

"No," Vaun said again, this time a little stubbornly.

"I would have taken a photo but... Well, I imagine my kidnapping Charlie is nothing compared to what Fay would do to me if I had."

They tensed at a knock, only to sigh with equal relief when Grayc Illan pushed through the door with a tray.

"Is it true?" Vaun asked uneasily.

His valet sighed. "Yes." She set the tray down on the small dining table. "You have other concerns, however. Xavian Ren Belholn has requested your audience." She waved a card at him, sealed with the Lord of Belholn's crest.

Vaun scrubbed his face. A Lord's request was a Lord's summons, even for a prince. He couldn't refuse without a good reason.

Addom hummed with interest around another sip of coffee. "Can I come?"

"You don't have a choice." Grayc lifted a second calling card, bringing it and a cup of fresh coffee to Addom, taking his nearly empty one in exchange.

She did not bring him a cup, Vaun noted. Fine. He stood and stretched, watching her lips thin in irritation at his leisure.

"I told you it wasn't a good idea to bring a Vym here," she said.

He flicked a hand at her. "What's done is done."

"Apparently not done enough." She turned away as if she didn't care how many people he got killed. "Get showered and dressed, your highness."

He smiled at her command and strolled into the bathroom.

Grayc arranged the intimate table with Vaun's coffee, breakfast cakes and newspaper.

The shower started and Addom made no move to follow the prince. He had spent enough time with Vaun to know that he wasn't welcome in his shower.

"You should go home," Grayc Illan said quietly. It wasn't in the nature of the High born to listen to their staff, so shouting wouldn't help. "Even the Lord of Belholn would not follow you there."

She felt his eyes even before she turned. She had never made conversation with Addom Vym before, so his amazement didn't surprise her. He recovered quickly, though, smiling wide.

"You're from this province, aren't you?" The Vym cocked his head. "From Belholn?"

Grayc waited for the jab; High borns always thought words were meant for fighting, for cutting or tricking. "I suppose." If he wanted to call what was below the High a part of any province, she wasn't going to correct him.

He brought his cup to his mouth, blowing at the steam. "You're from the Low. A little rat."

"Everyone knows it." Born in the Low. Raised in the Main. The daughter of a gifted seamstress that managed to make the great leap from one to the other. Now valet to Prince Vaun himself. The newspaper ran the story every few years when other gossip ran dry.

"I suppose that is why you are afraid of men like Xavian Ren," Addom remarked. "I am the son of Casion Vym. My brother is Quentan Vym, Lord of our province. I have won hundreds of duels and govern several streets in the Vym province." Addom managed to sound bored and prideful at the same time. "Keep your fears to yourself, or one day you might find you've been cast back to the Low, little rat."

Addom smirked and sipped his coffee, undoubtedly expecting her to slink off.

When he finished his cup, he looked up. She could see the verbal lashing in his eyes, ready to spring from his lips, but it all caught in his throat when he looked back at her. He hadn't expected her to be smiling, had he? "I am surprised you lived so long being so stupid," Grayc Illan said. "The Belholns will not be impressed by your lineage. You can go home to Vym now and say that you stayed the night, had your fun, and lived to leave, or you can go to the Belholn House and try your luck again."

She picked up the empty tray and headed for the door, but Addom got there first, slamming his palm against it. Tension pulled at the back of her shoulders, her chin rising when she turned around in the small space his body allowed.

"Careful with your words." The son of Vym spoke in a whisper that ground out as harsh as a howl. "I think no one would miss you if you were gone. And no one would think I had anything to do with your misfortune."

Her heart pounded against her chest but her hands remained steady. Her eyes narrowed and her nose wrinkled in a glare that could easily be a snarl. "Would anyone miss you?" Grayc Illan whispered back. It wasn't the first time a house lord threatened her; it wouldn't even be the first time one tried to kill her. Addom Vym thought he was frightening because he was powerful; he had no idea what the desperate could do.

The sound of the shower in the other room ended abruptly. "The High has grown comfortable with you at the prince's side. They speak of you as though you are important," Addom uttered low, leaning closer. "But no one forgets what you are." His hand found her hip and her throat tightened, clogged with old fury. Long fingers slid under the silk of her blouse and the embrace of her vest. He waited, expectation in his eyes. He wanted her to be afraid. He wanted her to back into the door, to cry, to scream. He must have felt the skin under his fingers jump but she wouldn't give him what he wanted.

His teeth ground together and he leaned in closer, his hip pushing hers. "I think you are a very good pretender, little rat, but you are still just a frightened Low girl."

Grayc Illan's shoulders relaxed and her mouth parted in the slightest smile. She waited, watching to see the moment when he felt that cold metal of her knife touching his bare abdomen. She could have given commands, or hissed threats, but she didn't need to. She could just open him up right there and leave him bleeding on the rug.

His hand left her skin and he took a lazy step back, never breaking eye contact. He colored his eyes red to inspire fear, but she had looked deep into them and found them lacking. He had no idea how frightening red could be.

Grayc Illan looked over Addom's shoulder to the bathroom door to see the prince standing there. "Be ready in twenty minutes." She tucked the short dagger up into her sleeve, hugged the tray, and left the room.

Vaun left the door of his walk-in closet open behind him. He dumped his towel on the floor and picked out a pair of slacks. "You pissed her off," he said, trusting Addom to hear him. "I am going to have to deal with that all day."

The Vym came to stand in the doorway, leaning his shoulder into it. "There is something about her... She is..."

The prince nodded and pulled on a shirt. "I know. It is practically impossible to get a rise out of her." He moved to a dresser and drew out a long drawer of ties. "Get yourself together if you are coming to the Belholn house." He pulled out a cord of pale silk and turned just as Addom backed away. "Oh, and friend—" Vaun waited for the full attention of those red eyes. He hadn't heard everything that was said, but he'd heard enough. Vaun met Addom's red gaze with no welcome or hint of humor. "Do not talk to my Grayc like that again."

The Vym lord blinked, then tipped his chin. "I see," he said. "I will meet you in the hall." Addom closed the door softly behind himself, leaving Vaun to his mirror.

The prince took his time dressing, fixing the collar of his jacket and the fall of his hair.

He found Addom waiting in the hall, dressed in a jacket that could almost rival his own. Their steps slowed with mutual curiosity as they passed the dining room. Vaun wouldn't say he actually craned his neck for a better look—he had his dignity, after all—but he should at least be able to confirm or deny gossip originating from his own house.

Fay skulked beside Meresin, dark and morbid as always, drinking joylessly from her cup. AviSariel smiled, somehow oblivious to the social abnormality she'd created.

Vaun didn't exactly hold his breath, but his shoulders loosened when they reached the front step. "Please say I can move in with you," he said as his car drew up to the curb.

The Vym smiled. "Of course, my prince, but I only agree because I suspect they will follow."

Grayc Illan waited for them in the car, saying nothing through the ride to the Belholn house. It was not a far drive from Vaun's residence, streets giving way to a small statue park and then iron gates already standing open; even a Belholn knew better than to make a prince wait. It was easy to lose Vaun's attention.

They pulled up to a vast, brick-faced residence. Vaun found it elegant enough, but so much red reminded him uncomfortably of dried blood, though such suited the Belholns. He'd heard once that the builders left spaces in the foundation to hide bodies of those who fell afoul of the family, but Vaun doubted they'd bother to hide their tracks. Inside, Grayc Illan stayed close, trailing behind them down the halls. Belholn cousins and staff lingered about without purpose; a show of their numbers for Addom's sake, Vaun guessed. It certainly wasn't to impress a prince. Vaun ignored most of them but kept his steps slow enough to see that each and every one tipped their head in a bow.

Xavian Ren, Lord of the Belholns, met them at the door to the dining room. He would have been lanky, were it not for the tight muscles that wrapped his bones and the powerful spread of his shoulders. It was a look most fashionable men sought after these days, but came naturally to the Belholn boys. Ren grinned, smile toothy. The Belholn siblings were called jackals for many reasons, and their mouths were not the least of them. Most of the siblings used magic to give themselves a longer set of canines. Ren gave himself two.

"Your highness." Xavian Ren tipped his head graciously. His predatory eyes weighed Addom briefly before returning to the prince. "Be welcome in my house. Come, we were just sitting down to an early lunch."

Vaun allowed the man to lead the way. The table was set with platters of treats and tight bundles of flowers. Only three more Belholns waited at the table, Wendry among them. She grinned.

Wendry stood out from her brothers, and not just as the only daughter of the house. She wore her hair dark, while the others kept theirs in varying shades of blond, like their parents. The brothers followed Xavian Ren's trend of letting his strands grow longer than usual, waves of pale hair loosely drawn back and knotted messily. It reminded Vaun of the pictures of their mother, Vinnia Belholn. She had been known for her long, blonde waves almost as well as she had been known for her love of all fabrics red.

She'd been found in a wet, reeking pool of red one day, many decades ago, only hours before her husband was shot in the Low. Vaun couldn't imagine who might have had the audacity to kill the couple, save his mother, who surely would have made even more of a spectacle of it.

The Belholn children had never solved the murder of their parents and, from the way they eyed Addom, Vaun suspected they had their own theories.

Vaun accepted a place to Xavian Ren's left while Addom stayed at the prince's side. Servants filled plates for them and poured wine but did not, to Vaun's surprise, offer any tea.

Addom leaned back and pretended to sip at his wine. He accepted the food set before him graciously, but not even he would be fool enough to eat in the house of his enemy. Belholns were not known for using poisons—they preferred the way of the brute—but nothing should be put past them.

For the most part, Xavian Ren and his siblings pretended that the Vym was not at their table. Addom, in turn, pretended not to notice going unnoticed. Vaun found it entertaining for all of two minutes before losing interest.

Killian, one of the Belholn brothers known for his tea addiction, appeared surprisingly lucid this morning, if not entirely well. He blinked, swallowed, then narrowed his eyes in sudden recognition. Leaning forward, he peered around the prince and toward the entrance. "I thought we got rid of that girl?"

Xavian Ren did not bother to follow his sibling's gaze to the woman standing silently by the door. "That is Grayc Illan. She works for the prince now."

Killian blinked again, looking skeptical. "Are you certain? She looks different."

"It has been almost a century, Killy," Ren reminded patiently before hiding a wicked smirk under the lip of his glass. "And he dresses her better."

The younger brother took on a silly, sloppy smile. "Does she mend his clothes and bring him tea, the way she used to for mother?"

"No, she..." Xavian Ren stopped, his fork paused in cutting a piece of cake. "What is it she does for you?" He smiled—almost friendly—at Vaun. "I would not usually inquire but, you see, Killian is terribly inquisitive when he's sober. Just won't stop until he gets an answer."

Vaun took a long drink and nodded obligingly. "Just about everything, I suppose. I am sure I would never have gotten out of bed today, and most certainly would not have arrived here, if it weren't for her nagging." He thought for a moment, then nodded. "Yes, that is what she does. She nags. Sometimes, she looks at me with disappointment. It is dauntingly similar to my sister's treatment of me, really."

Ren barked a laugh. "That makes sense."

His attention snapped up from the table to the Lord of Belholn. So much familiarity in those few words about his sister. Was there a reason his valet should behave like her? Was there a connection? Or did Xavian Ren simply believe Fay's character to be infectious? "Why do you say that?"

Chewing, Ren flicked a dismissive hand at the subject and then, after swallowing, turned his attention back to his lethargic brother. "Killian, what was that other question of yours? The one that has been on your tongue for the past two days?" His younger brother's eyes drooped with exhaustion, not seeming to have heard the question at all, which did not stop Xavian Ren from continuing. "That's right, you have been dogging me about why you can't drink tea anymore." That got the man's attention, his head turning from side to side as he looked over the table, his face creasing with sorrow at the lack of teacups.

Xavian Ren picked up his wine glass and took a quick drink. "I am sure you have heard about the riots in our Low district. This morning we even had a few outbursts in the Main. It seems to be an issue of bad tea." He spat the last two words and Vaun realized abruptly that the man was no longer smiling. "Well, bad dust to be more precise. I am personally quite curious as to what the Low district people were doing with dust in the first place. Queen knows they don't have the money for it. I looked into the matter, but the men that went dust mad did not survive the night. The Queen sends out wolves to clean up the mess, you see. I did manage to come across rumors of someone giving away packets of dust, saying it was a new product." Ren's gaze fell fully on Addom Vym for the first time. "I don't suppose you know anything about that?"

Wendry smirked where she sat, watching the scene and not even bothering to pretend with her meal.

Addom blinked innocently, a look that was far from convincing. "Not at all, Lord Belholn." His voice sounded too sweet and it made even Vaun suspicious. "But I would not talk of it too much. I can only imagine how upset the Queen would be if she thought you were trying to make your own dust."

It was true. Too much trouble with bad dust in Belholn could draw the Queen's eye to the province household.

He found it hard to believe that Xavian Ren would test dust on his own people, even in the Low. The Lord liked his comfort and life too much. Brutal the Belholns may be, but not stupid. They had never shown signs of higher aspiration or work ethic. There was no reason to take such a risk. One of the other households would be a more likely culprit, using Belholn as a testing ground. Which one? Subterfuge indicated Vym. Recklessness and greed suggested Maggrin.

"No Vym has set foot in my province for decades. Yet my sister finds one at a dinner party last night." Xavian Ren leaned back in his chair, gaze fixed on Addom. "And wasn't your cousin recently taken by the Queen for treason? What was her name? Merriam?" Wendry and the others at the table had fallen so silent that it was almost easy to forget that they were there.

"That is quite a coincidence," Vaun agreed. "I would be ready to agree with you if I wasn't the one that invited him." The prince let out a short laugh, helping himself to another tart. "Not to mention, I happen to know that Addom saves all his efforts for the bedroom. He doesn't even sign his own name to documents." He shot his friend a stern glare. "Honestly, I can't see him doing any sort of work, let alone creating and peddling dust."

Addom made a show of offense and pretended to drink from his possibly poisoned cup. "I will have you know that I am very capable in a duel."

Vaun rolled his eyes. "Who isn't?"

"If I remember correctly, you were shot twice at a duel only a few months ago."

"It was four in the morning and I had had quite a bit to drink," the prince defended. "What is important is that I won."

Addom snorted. "Barely."

Xavian Ren stood. "You two can jabber on all you like, but I have not overlooked this happenstance and I will know what hand you had in this game, Vym!"

Vaun drained his glass, then picked up his napkin from his lap and dropped it beside his plate. "Lord Belholn," he said in a chillingly altered voice, no longer the playful and slightly absent tone he usually used, but one quite similar to the voice Addom had heard earlier that morning. "A prince never jabbers. Every word, senseless or profound, dropped from my lips is a treasure to your ears." He stood, the legs of his chair making an awful sound as they scraped along the polished floor. His gaze met Xavian Ren's. "And no one, not even the Lord or Lady of a province, stands without courtesy from a table where I sit."

A silence swelled in the room, so thick that it could choke. Xavian Ren stared back for a small, defiant eternity before his knees finally bent and he sank back into his seat. The Lord of Belholn turned his head to glare viciously at the wall.

"You will overlook whatever you think has transpired—" Vaun straightened his jacket. "—or you will find Belholn without the love of a prince."

It was not often in his hundred plus years that Vaun found himself having to remind his company of his birth, but it was not something he shied away from, either. He could handle a great deal of disrespect, especially if humorous or well-said, but would not tolerate his authority being forgotten entirely. Lectures or threats from a House Lord would not do.

"My apologies, your highness." Xavian Ren's mutinous gaze found Addom. "You entered my province under the grace of the prince, and you will leave the same way."

They left Belholn without incident. Vaun lounged in his seat, but even he breathed a touch easier once they entered Vym. The streets and buildings looked virtually identical, but Vym fashion imitated the province's Lady, making the wealthy women into a mass of oddly cheerful mourners, whereas the fashionable of Belholn forever strived for scandal.

Vaun preferred Belholn, but in light of their tea problems, it seemed wiser to take his afternoon drink in another province. With Addom for company, he thought it best not to bring the Vym into Maggrin and make yet another household testy.

When the car stopped, Addom jumped out first, stretching his long body and drawing a deep breath of home.

Vaun scooted toward the open door. With one leg out, he paused. Grayc Illan sat silently in the dark leather comfort of the cab. He waited for her to look at him, staring at the set of her lips and the dark curls resting against her cheek, but she didn't.

"Come in with us," he said. It was a request, even if it didn't sound like one.

Finally, those eyes looked at him, unreadable as always. There was a mystery there, if only he cared enough to find out what it was. "There is plenty of staff in there already, prince. I am sure they will pour your tea just fine."

He stared at her for another heartbeat. The words were cold, but something in her eyes waited. For what? For another reason, perhaps? Why should she expect anything besides what he gave: an annoyed scoff and a slammed door?

Walking up to the dark blue painted entrance of The Gentlemen's Club, Vaun resigned himself to a bad day. They knocked and waited half a second before the doorman slid back the peephole, looked them over, then unbarred the door.

The Gentlemen's Club was one of the old favorites of the Vym province, a knock-off of an even older bar in Maggrin. The key difference was that The Gentlemen's Club in Maggrin followed strict gender rules, barring women from entering, whereas The Gentlemen's Club in Vym barred anyone wearing a skirt. Vaun preferred the Vym take on the establishment, as it resulted in a delightful mash-up of the female, male, and androgynous, all donned in a variety of coat tails, top hats, suspenders, and slacks. The club was full of voices and bodies, laughter rising high with the tendrils of smoke. In most clubs, the smoke of cigarettes created a multicolored cloud, but in The Gentlemen's Club, thin cigars reigned, as their pale smoke did not clash with the severe motif of rough wallpaper in dark colors and stiff wingback furniture.

Addom veered toward the bar, working his way through friends that rejoiced loudly upon his return. He began regaling them with the story of his foray into Belholn territory before he even reached the altar of drinks.

Vaun stopped near the middle of the room to let a pretty creature set a cigar between his lips and strike a match. Inhaling, he stared at the soft face and high cheekbones of the man in front of him. It was not a forgettable face, and Vaun was sure he had seen it before, but the lack of familiarity probably meant that it belonged to a Main resident and not a High. Vaun inhaled deeply and plucked the cigar from his lips before grabbing the man's well-tied cravat and pulling him onto his toes, into a savage kiss. It was long enough to draw attention, small wisps escaping between lips before the prince finally let go, leaving the man to wildly cough up all the smoke he'd forced down his throat.

Continuing on, cigar in hand, Vaun met the dreamy eyes of those he passed, each hoping for the same mistreatment. He remembered a time when those looks had been exhilarating.

His gaze met something that was not hope, but rather a mild dismissal. Her eyes went through him, brushing over him along with the rest of the crowd as she rounded the billiards table. The height of her stilettos nearly set her on tiptoe. Sheer, black stockings clothed her shapely legs until giving way to the smooth flesh of her thighs and the straps of her garters. She wore a tailored coat with tails, unbuttoned to show off the matching corset beneath. One hand raised, ruffling the back of her hair as she looked over the green felt and its scattering of colored balls. She bent, taking aim. For another set of heartbeats she was even more enticing than he was, drawing attention from every direction.

The cue slammed against the ball, making a cracking sound that made every man in the vicinity wince.

Vaun took the last few steps to bring himself through the crowd and snatch away the worshiping eyes that had been hers. Evelet Vym straightened with an irritation that led him to believe that she felt their loss. She turned, her hip rolling along the side of the table until her back was to it.

She frowned at him, but it was a bored sort of expression that he felt certain could be righted easily enough. Hands to her hips, Vaun lifted the Vym lady and set her down on the edge of the table.

"Should I be welcoming you back, or are you still residing in Belholn, your highness?" Evelet took the thin cigar from his lips and turned her head to take a long drag. The movement of his official residence through the provinces was posted in the paper, not something easily missed or forgotten, but pretending not to know things was almost as popular as knowing everything.

He watched her exhale. Today, her eyes were red, like Addom's. "Belholn, for now." He took the cigar back, smiling deviously. "But I would take any welcome you offered."

She laughed and it was sweet, the way it had been when they were younger. Her thighs spread so that she could hold the cue between them with both hands, one end pressed into the floor beneath her dangling heels. Evelet idly rolled the polished stick against the crotch of her satin panties.

Vaun shuddered pleasantly. It had been a while since he spent time with Vym's most dangerous daughter.

He reached out to wrap his fingers around hers on the high end of the cue, stepping closer to stand between her knees, pushing the stick up against her sex. He watched her lips as they parted and waited for her gasp. He leaned in, brushing his cheek against hers. "If you are done playing billiards—"

A flash of green caught his eye. Despite the press of bodies filling the club, a familiar figure stood out: the curves, the fingers peeking out from the sleeves of her jacket, the slope of her collar. In the same moment that he was certain it was Meresin, he was just as certain that it could not be. The color and cut of the suit was all wrong for her and the woman's hair was a pale yellow. Not to mention the impossibility of Meresin getting this far into The Gentlemen's Club without the uproar of attention that always met with her entry. Why would she sneak into such a crowded place? Why would Meresin sneak at all?

Before he could get a better look, the woman in question slipped into the back room.

"Vaun?" Evelet hissed his name, probably not for the first time. With one hand, she shoved him back. He took the steps, barely able to tear his eyes from that back door to glance at the now angry Vym for more than a few seconds. She looked incredibly similar to her brother in that moment, just before she lifted the pool cue and punched him in the stomach with the thicker end, driving the air from his lungs and knocking him into a chair.

"Useless dusters." Evelet hopped off the table and stormed away.

His hand stroked his belly, wondering what the bruise would look like, but already his gaze had found that door again. It could not have been Meresin.

Vaun got up and crossed the room, pushing a few shoulders out of his way to reach that narrow door. He pulled it open only to find a storage closet stacked with wine crates. He stepped in, tapping the wood paneling, before eventually retreating to his chair again.

People swelled in his line of sight, but he kept a careful eye on the door. Meresin or not, he was certain he'd seen someone go into that closet. Perhaps he'd gone mad.

Jounas jumped into the chair next to him, giving a long whistle as he settled in. "What did you do to upset Evelet?"

Ollan sank into the seat on Vaun's other side.

In place of an answer, the prince offered a shrug and another puff of smoke.

It was enough of a reply for Jounas. He took Vaun's silence as an opportunity to deliver every bit of gossip he had. If Vaun did not know him well, he might have thought that the man was trying to impress him, but Jounas was just as quick to tell his stories to his tailor as his monarch.

"Hart said that the people in the Low district of Belholn have turned into cannibals! Udaro said it wasn't true, but what does he know? I heard his mother was one of those Low district women." Jounas scrunched his face around the words. He inhaled sharply when an idea struck him, forcing delight into his voice. "Maybe Udaro is a cannibal like the rest of the rats! It makes sense that he would try to hide the truth if he is one of them."

And so a new rumor was born. The Low born were cannibals and Udaro was among their numbers. Vaun rolled his eyes.

"You know he spends his time in the Low, right? He's got himself a pass to live in the High, like he's not one of those rats, and yet he chooses the slums. I heard he tried to buy a street at the bottom of the Low, right on the Ash."

"Why?" Vaun found himself prompting on reflex alone.

"Who knows?" Jounas drained a cup of tea. "Another, my prince?"

Vaun started to decline when he realized he held a cup in his hand. Apparently, he'd been sitting longer than he realized. The closet door had not opened. No sign of the blonde in the green suit. "Might as well."

"Jacobi would not sell it," Jounas said.

"What?"

"The land at the bottom of the Low."

Vaun scrunched his cheek in a confused sort of annoyance. Jounas reached for the pot of tea. Finding it empty, he sighed and lurched into the crowd to find another.

A hand grabbed his wrist and Vaun spared a sideways glance to see Ollan leaning forward, looking quite grave. Her features were sunken, as usual, but her eyes were a bland brown and the bags beneath them were a much deeper gray than ever before. "There is something wrong," the woman whispered, all the creases in her face shifting with every word. Her stringy hair straggled over the collar of her stained suit. Ollan's appearance alone didn't alarm Vaun; his friend often spent too many nights in the same jacket, sometimes in the same club. It was her voice that raised the hair on the back of Vaun's neck: not warm and wistful from tea, but deep and shaking.

"What are you on about, Olly?" He touched the hand that still clasped his wrist.

Ollan made a sound that had Vaun feeling as though whispering was vital. Was someone eavesdropping? "Nothing is the way it was. She has done something horrible." Her eyes squinted and her fingers pressed against her temple. "She has... I just... It is so hard to remember."

"Remember what?"

Ollan's hand fell away from her face and her large, sad eyes locked on Vaun. "The Queen." Her gaze flickered past him and saw something that spurred her to hasty words. "Cages. We are in cages. Our skin. Our hearts. Locked in boxes on her shelf."

Jounas sank into the seat beside Vaun, wasting no time in pouring the fresh tea. "Whose shelf?"

Ollan shrank into her corner against the wall, pulling her cold hand from the prince. Her thin lips pressed tightly together when she shook her head, looking down and swallowing hard.

Vaun shifted. "Olly—"

A wolf howled.

It was hard to hear, at first, but the ripples of silence it caused made the second cry as clear as glass on hardwood. The music stopped. Voices stilled. There was a unified swallow of air, a mass hesitation, and all eyes turned toward the exit, even those too far behind other bodies to see it.

Another howl. This one louder. Closer.

The door burst open. There was a gathered gasp and a few shrill cries before they were reminded that wolves did not open doors. Grayc Illan's sharp voice commanded people from her path even as she shoved them aside. "Prince!" she called loudly, careless of the fear stricken crowd. His valet was unstoppable, as always. Voices broke out, hushed but quick with panic. Bodies shuffled about in the room, some daring to press near the stained glass windows and peer out into the streets. The wolf cried again, nearly upon them. It would be only seconds, now, if this was the destination. Who would it be? Who had betrayed the Queen so grievously as to warrant execution by wolf?

Grayc Illan shove her way to him. "Prince!"

The pack burst through the walls, leaving stone and plaster untouched. A scream pierced the room, followed by a string of others and the sounds of tumbling limbs and falling furniture as the people tried to leap from the path of the wolves. They prowled the room, their massive, transparent bodies passing through couches as well as flesh without resistance. The furniture remained unharmed, but the people who failed to pull their legs from the path of beasts doubled over, heaving up whatever contents their stomachs had to offer. They dropped to their knees, palms to the floor, bodies shuddering with cold as they wept.

In darker social circles, this was called the Queen's Mercy. They knelt, they retched, they wept, but they were grateful to be spared.

The crowd split, climbing on top of one another to press against the walls on either side. The wolves stalked closer to the prince. Jounas clambered over the back of his seat to escape, teacup ever in hand. Vaun stared back at the beast leading the pack. Transparent lips curled to bare transparent fangs.

"Your highness," Grayc Illan exhaled as little more than an urgent whisper. "Get up."

He could not, or maybe, he would not.

The wolf crouched and he could do nothing but stare back. Had his mother sent for his soul? What had he done today that was different from any other?

It leaped, springing into the air, and the entire room inhaled to scream.

Small hands fisted in his jacket, ripping it as Grayc hauled him to his feet. She pivoted, trading places with him a split second before the wolf swallowed her, ghostly body soaring through hers and beyond. It leaped through her as if she were no more than a wall or lamp and dove, snapping, into the corner.

Ollan's hands spasmed on her over-turned chair, then went limp as the beast emerged, the wispy shape of her soul clutched in its teeth. It dragged Ollan's spectral form like a heavy corpse, her trailing limbs passed through objects without effect as the monster stalked from the room. The pack followed and vanished through the walls.

Grayc crumpled with a quiet sigh, fingers slipped from his jacket. Her shoulder thumped loudly against the hardwood, though not half as loudly as her skull. Her legs bent under her thighs and her dark curls formed a halo around her head, eyes staring blankly at the ceiling.

"Grayc?" The prince knelt beside her. His voice did not sound like his own, yet it came from his lips. The rest of the club had fallen into chaos, but not her. Never her. "Grayc?"

Addom loomed over them. "Is she dead?"

Vaun swallowed hard and tore his eyes from her unblinking ones to lean forward. He laid his head against her chest, soft skin beneath his ear and silk against his lips. He closed his eyes and listened.

Silence had never hurt him the way the silence of her heart did just then. He could not move; he did not dare. His arm curled around her side as though someone might pull her away. He listened and listened.

"Vaun," Addom spoke in a hushed voice, the room watching the strange scene of the prince bent over his dead servant.

He held her tighter. He thought he heard something. He could have sworn that he heard something.

"Vaun," Addom said again.

Her heart beat.

He sat up slowly just to look at her, to see if her eyes had closed, if her lips had moved, but she had not stirred.

"Vaun!" The Vym shook his shoulder, squeezing hard.

Her body jolted on the floor. The heels of her boots smacked the polished wood and scraped when her legs kicked out from under her. Her eyes squeezed shut and she gasped, sucking in an agonizing breath before twisting to the side and vomiting on the floor. Vaun held tight to her shoulder, waiting until she was sobbing to scoop her up, legs wobbling beneath them both when he stood. He did not stop to look at his friend's body in the corner chair or meet Addom's astonished stare. The prince cut a line for the door and the crowd hurried from his path like they had for the wolves.

He was not sure why, but he needed to get home. He needed to think about what had happened. He needed to get out from under the press of their attention. Perhaps he just needed more tea.

When Vaun laid her barely conscious body into the car, he could not help but marvel at his own vanity because, just now, he was certain her heart had beat for him.

Forests. Trees all around her, with branches so high she could never reach them. The leaves had turned colors and grown crisp. A breeze spun around her and she lifted her arms high. The leaves fell, twirling and tumbling toward the wet grass. The branches swayed and sunlight spilled between them. The sky was blue. Blue. Not the blue of a dress, a drink, or a cake, but a blue that reminded of summer lakes.

Grayc Illan drew a shuddered breath and blinked away the images that danced so readily before her mind's eye. It felt like a memory, lodged beside the real ones so firmly that she had to remind herself again and again that it was not hers. Vaun told her in the car that she had been struck by a wolf. *Struck* did not seem to be an accurate word but she could find no better. There was a moment, just before her heart stopped, when she could have sworn that she stood in that forest. She could smell autumn in the air. She could feel her skin tighten against the chill of the breeze. And she could almost reach one of those falling leaves.

Vaun also told her in the car on the way back to the house that she had died. She did not believe him at first, certain he was just trying to get a rise out of her, but there was a foreign thread of importance in his eyes that made her stomach knot. When they got home, Vaun went directly to his room with a demand for tea tossed back over his shoulder. Grayc Illan went to her room and cried.

The last time she had wept had been so long before she started working for the prince that she could not remember the reason, but today she crouched in the corner of her room and sobbed like the child she wasn't anymore.

It wasn't that she had nearly died, or that it had been for someone as petty as Vaun. Grayc Illan cried until her chest ached and her throat burned, until her eyelids swelled and her face creased with tears, because the memory was not hers. She wept because she had never known that forest. She had never heard the sound of real leaves. She had never seen the sky. Until that stolen memory struck her, she had not even known the color behind the clouds.

Even when they headed out the next day, she found it difficult to shake those images. Her gaze was drawn skyward to the tops of buildings against the ever-clouds. When she felt Vaun watching her, she forced her attention down to the bulbous lamp on the sidewalk below, nearly identical to the thousands of others throughout the High and Main districts of all three provinces. They were always lit, even during the brightest of afternoons, a soft glow that did little to illuminate but everything to press back shadows.

Shadows were an enemy that the residents of the High had long since forgotten. The lights kept back the pixies, hungry little bugs that would gladly feast on the magic residue that coated the walls and streets, not to mention the residents themselves. Grayc Illan had seen many pixies in the Low, where people had so little contact with processed magic that the pests ignored them and instead pressed themselves against the walls at the bottom of the Main to lick what magic they could from the bricks.

Warmth enveloped her hand and Grayc Illan looked down to see Vaun's digits wrapped around hers. When she looked up, she found the prince staring back at her. He had not said anything since they came home last night; this morning, she found him dressed and ready before she came to stir him. Another jacket, another party. She would give him the details of the event on the way.

Some part of her, probably the part with a mind to keep her head, knew that she should pull her hand back and look away, but he was warm and today she felt so inescapably cold. He looked at her the way she had always wished he would, with thought and clarity, and when his other hand traced fingertips along the side of her face, she closed her eyes.

"Why did you do it?" the prince whispered.

She opened her eyes to look up at him, forgetting that they were standing on the sidewalk where anyone could see. His hair was dark today, black as black could be, with a few strands intentionally askew, as though he did not control every detail of his appearance. His jaw was smooth and angled, more beautiful than handsome. She knew every detail of him, and yet she had never looked this closely before. He hid the lean muscles of his body beneath jackets, preferring to look small in the company of broader men. Vaun liked to be underestimated because he loved the taste of surprise, something that became more elusive with every passing decade.

"It's my job," she said.

He stared back at her and she thought he would laugh; his eyes shined just as they always did before his lips curled. He leaned in, so close she could see nothing but the flecks of silver forever drifting in his irises, despite the color of the week. His full lips pressed soft but firm against her own. His fingers slid from her cheek to curl around the back of her head, threading through her hair to send a tingle down her spine just as his mouth opened hers. At first, he tasted sweet and false, like dust and cakes, but the deeper the kiss grew the more the flavor became his own.

She kissed him back, her hands pressed against his waist between jacket and vest. She retained the awareness not to wrinkle his clothing, and it was that same awareness that had her breaking their kiss. She pushed against his chest, stepping back. His arms fell away. "It was just my job, prince, that's all."

His eyes sharpened, never leaving her face. He studied her, the prominent rise and fall of her chest, the flush of her cheeks, and her swollen and still saliva wet lips. She set her features to that unreadable mask again but her gaze would not meet his and for the first time he thought he knew why.

"You're lying," the prince hissed, alarmed to hear the volume of betrayal in his own voice. Was this what rejection felt like? He'd been turned down before, but he had never wanted the attention of anyone the way he found himself wanting hers. "I saw you, Grayc."

She laughed and it was an unpleasant sound. "You can't even see yourself." She turned away but he caught her arm. Through her wrist, he felt her heart leaping.

"Tell me why." He spoke softly, but those fresh bits of resentment were still there, caught between his clenched teeth.

She met his gaze then, but it was hollow and practiced. "You are the prince. The Queen wants you out of danger. That is all." She pulled her arm free and marched down to the car. She opened the door and waited, forever the patient servant.

Vaun remained at the top of the stairs for a while longer. To make her wait. To watch her stand uncomfortably beside the car. She would have to wait forever if he didn't follow. It was tempting to lock his knees. Bitterness settled in his heart as he descended the steps. Well, as long as she was going to play the servant, he was going to continue to play the spoiled prince. They would see who broke first.

CHAPTER FIVE

Vaun wondered how long it would take Grayc to find him. He didn't think Addom would betray him, not after so gleefully pointing out a hidden exit from The Library, but one could never tell with Vyms. His friend seemed delighted at the unspoken battle between Vaun and his valet, and the prince didn't doubt Addom might play both sides simply for entertainment's sake.

Well, let her find him. Vaun slouched deeper into the battered couch. A derelict teahouse this deep into the Main was a new low, even for him. He chose Belholn Province simply because she hated it. He certainly hoped she hated the time it took to track him as much as he loathed the effort it took to vanish. The Queen wanted him safe? Very well. Let Grayc earn her wage, if that's all he was to her.

He was enjoying the new teahouse, a gem of a find in the unspectacular stretch of houses, workshops, and factories of Belholn's Main. It differed little from the ones in the High, save that the establishment's mismatched and worn nature was genuine rather than cultivated. He was on his second cup of tea, the fine craftsmanship of his suit offended by the stains of the sofa on which he sat.

Vaun took another deep drag off the cigarette one of his new friends, Gabby, had offered him. She and the man sitting beside her pretended quite comically to be from the High. The prince did not ruin the show by telling them that he knew everyone in the High, to some degree. The quality of their vanity charms indicated they were not, not to mention the state of their clothing. Being rude was only fashionable if one's victim was up to the challenge and could strike back. Besides, Vaun never discouraged people who tried so hard to amuse him.

The prince exhaled black smoke. It was thick and dramatic, but his skin didn't hum the way it usually did after a deep breath of dust. In fact, the tingle was more of an agitation, making him shift in his seat and flick his cigarette more angrily than usual. Ash fluttered through the air. How much tea did he have to drink for a decent buzz? He all but dropped his cup back on its chipped saucer in disgust. "I shouldn't have come," he muttered.

"You're leaving?" Gabby's smile faltered. Her fingers clenched around her teacup. She wore fingerless, black lace gloves like his sister did on occasion and Vaun noticed that her skirts and bodice were also in dark colors with hints of lace sewn in wherever possible, some obviously added as an afterthought and not even matching the lace elsewhere. It would have been easier to try to imitate the High fashion of Belholn but Gabby had aimed even higher, for the princess herself.

"Yes. I'm sure I have a date somewhere." Some part of him enjoyed the distress of the people around him at the possibility of his departure. It made him want to leave even more.

"Wait!" Gabby grabbed at the man beside her, whose name Vaun had forgotten a while ago, and tugged at the sleeve of his obviously repaired jacket. "Show him," she whispered urgently.

Vaun took another drag of his disappointing cigarette. The best part about going to a teahouse or club in the thick of the Main was how the people tried so desperately to impress him. The people in the High knew him too well to try so hard. They feared his mockery even more than they desired his attention. But this group had spent the better part of the last hour trying to wow him with their trinkets and knowledge of the High. It was all nonsense read from the paper and mostly outdated. "I truly doubt you have anything to show me that I have not seen."

The man reached into his jacket a little uncomfortably and took out a small mason jar. Others giggled, recognizing it, but Vaun only blinked at first. Its glass belly was full but not with anything liquid or solid. Light, captured and pulsing, swirled inside the jar. Vaun felt it as much as he saw it. He heard it like a whisper against his senses and found himself leaning forward to see it more clearly: a soul. Vaun had seen them before, but they weren't common. So uncommon, in fact, that he was surprised they hadn't led with this in their attempt to impress him. He supposed they might have been afraid he'd take it. Soul capturing was an old craft that most considered barbaric now.

His gaze turned up from the jar to the man holding it. "Who is it?" The soul was a beautiful captive, but the person walking around without it was the real prize—the puppet, someone that could be made to do anything.

"I couldn't say." The man smiled. "He wouldn't be much of a spy if I did."

Vaun resisted the impulse to sneer, doubting this man had any use of a spy. "Then how do we know it is a soul at all? It could be a bit of magic in a jar," he argued, even though he could feel the truth of it from where he sat.

The man turned a shade of red in offense, sputtering in search of an argument appropriate enough to take up with the Realm's prince.

Vaun heard the door of the teahouse open and shut and somehow knew it was Grayc even before she stomped up to his side and glared down at him. He let out an annoyed sigh and leaned back into his seat. He couldn't decide what irritated him most: Grayc's dutiful presence, the soul-jar on the table beside his drained teacup, or the cigarette between his fingers that never seemed to get any better. Deciding not to be a quitter just yet, he raised it to his lips once more.

Grayc Illan clicked her teeth and smacked the cigarette from his hand. It hit the floor with a burst of embers, but before he could snarl in protest she opened up a metal case and offered him another.

"Did you get that here?" she snapped. "How many cups of tea have you had?"

He took one of the dark green cigarettes from the gleaming gold case and held it between two fingers, waiting for her to light it. "Why? Did you want to join me?"

His valet made a series of irritated sounds, putting the cigarette case away inside her jacket and taking out a matching lighter. His cigarette blazed to life and he breathed deep, finally feeling that pleasant haze rush over his tense nerves.

"How can you be this stupid?" she demanded. "You read the paper every morning."

"Maybe I just pretend." He exhaled green smoke and ignored the way his new friends leaned in to try to breathe in some of that high quality dust. He resisted taking another drag just to leave them without another cloud to suck on.

Of course. She wanted him safe, because the Queen commanded it. Perhaps bad dust would make him a cannibal, like the rats. Like Grayc, however high she climbed. He showed his teeth and reached for his cup of tea. She kicked the table away, tossing the whole thing over, sending cups, saucers, teapot and even the little mason jar flying. Porcelain smashed as the heavy plank crashed down, legs upturned.

"Even the High born of Belholn fear to drink tea, but you come down to their Main for yours?" Grayc snarled.

Vaun surged to his feet. "What of it? I have a servant to save me, don't I?"

"Perhaps it wouldn't rankle so much if you didn't need quite so much saving." Her green eyes flashed. "Would it?"

He stormed past her, pretending not to hear the distress of the man behind him, cradling the shattered remains of his jar, just as

Vaun pretended not to feel the freed soul drift past, rushing toward its owner somewhere in the Realm.

Grayc followed on his heels, opening the door and hurrying him toward the car. She wanted to get him back to the High before he could do something else foolish, he supposed. Her furious silence usually soothed him, but today it grated.

The prince smiled when he got into the car, refusing to slide over to make room for her. "Enjoying your job today? I thought it would take you longer to find me, but I forgot. This is your home."

Grayc's lips thinned and she slammed the door shut before walking around to the other side.

Vaun continued to smile to himself while they drove back to the High but the gesture felt hollow within only a few blocks. He wanted to be amused with himself. He wanted to rejoice in driving her to some emotion, even anger, but he could not shake the irritation creeping under his skin. No matter how many cigarettes he breathed into his lungs or cups of tea he sucked down, he could not quite smother that little flame of frustration in his heart.

A gunshot jolted Grayc from her thoughts. She blinked fast to take in the street before her, bathed in the pale gray of morning light. A heavy, wooden box weighed down her arms. A crowd lined both sides of the street, clad in coats and gloves. Some hid their faces from the drama behind lace fans, as if their hungry little eyes were not riveted on the scene.

AviSariel used her hands rather than a fan, covering her mouth when the guns fired. Grayc Illan stared at the princess on the sidelines, her eyes brimming with tears, wide and focused with a mix of horror and awe on the prince in the middle of the street. The valet turned her head to follow that reverent gaze. Vaun stood with his body turned toward his audience but his arm outstretched to follow the length of cobblestone. His gaze was locked on the aim of the gleaming weapon in his hand, his eyes sharp, his lips pressed, and his jaw set.

Someone screamed near the opposite end of the street. The other man in the duel, a son of the Maggrin household named Axel Grand, crumpled to the ground. Red blossomed on the middle of his vest. Vaun's lips twisted into a cold smile before he turned to his audience and bowed. His gaze met Grayc's for a moment, his eyes cruel and hungry, before he smiled and waved at the crowd. His fans erupted into cheers and Vaun dumped his gun into the velvet-lined box she held.

Grayc Illan watched him walk toward his waiting friends, enjoying their praise as they suggested forms of celebration.

Residents of the High took up dueling when bored or offended. In the Low, dueling took on the role of law, used only for offenses so grievous they called for death, because that was often the result in the Low, where no one could afford the magic charms to reknit flesh or restart hearts.

Vaun always enjoyed viewing a duel and never shied away from one when challenged. On one occasion, he had been so bored as to challenge his sister. Fay had chosen guns, Vaun had boasted his prowess, and she had shot him squarely in the chest, missing his heart by a hair. He had laughed with blood coloring his teeth and tried to rise for another round, but the princess walked away before he even lost consciousness.

This was different. Vaun instigated arguments with anyone who dared to speak to him, and those capable of holding their ground found themselves challenged to a duel. He'd fought three in less than a week.

In previous duels, Vaun wasted time and played with the audience, making a great show of it, and then only winning by the skin of his teeth. Grayc Illan had even known him to lose, on occasion, if he thought the retelling would be better for it.

Showmanship and boredom did not drive him anymore. He

relished violence and shot with deadly precision. She had never known him to seek out the pain of others but pain was all that made him smile now.

Grayc Illan closed the box, the latch swinging shut.

After his successful morning, Vaun's fans swept him off to enjoy a cup of tea and a book at The Library. AviSariel trailed behind him, tethered to her husband by the will of the Queen, and no doubt hoping Fay would be among the guests at The Library.

Grayc Illan spent the better part of an hour sitting in the car outside the entrance. She lowered the window when knuckles rapped against the tinted glass and a footman passed her an envelope. She flipped it over in her hands.

After a moment of consideration, Grayc Illan stepped out of the car. Her heels sang across the smooth stone floor, growing louder as she paced down the hallway toward the large doors of The Library's main room. Guards eyed her but did not interfere, given Vaun's orders after his brother's appearance. The prince wanted his warnings and his messages delivered promptly. She pushed the door open and stopped at the flurry of sounds inside, far too loud and panicked to be proper library behavior.

"No!" Vaun roared and the room flinched. Broken porcelain littered the floor around his table. AviSariel cowered in her seat, trying to stifle sobs.

Addom Vym and several members of Vaun's party rose to their feet, talking quickly in an overlap of soothing voices.

"Didn't you hear her?" Vaun snarled, his eyes darkening to a dangerous black that ate up the last of the silver flecks floating there. "My wife says I have had enough tea." He kicked her chair. "Isn't that right? I've had enough, or so you see fit to tell me, a prince, as if I'm a child."

"I didn't mean to upset you," AviSariel whispered. "I only meant—"

"You said what you meant!" Vaun picked up his cup. "But it's still full, princess. What would you have me do with the rest of it? Leave it to grow cold?"

"My prince, I am sorry if—"

He flung the steaming contents at her, splashing the hot tea into her face. AviSariel screamed, throwing up her hands as her skin reddened under the scald. She stumbled back, chair slapping against the marble floor as onlookers gasped. The prince smiled.

Addom Vym stepped between them. "Your highness—"

"This is not your affair." Vaun showed his teeth. "I have had enough of—"

Grayc snatched a book from a table as she passed and swung it against the back of Vaun's skull. The impact echoed in the room a moment before the scrape of chairs and chorus of alarmed voices drowned it out. She waited as Vaun's head turned toward her, clutching the novel like a weapon or a shield, bracing herself as the full weight of his rage settled on her. Black consumed his eyes like ink spilling from a bottle, blooming in his whites before saturating them completely. "Grayc," he growled.

"Madness is no excuse for bad manners or wasted tea."

His lip curled. "Mad? Me? Only the Low—"

"Drink bad dust? In Belholn Main district teahouses, perhaps?" She arched an eyebrow. "No, a fine prince of the Realm would never be so foolish. A prince would never overconsume without giving his body a chance to rest between highs. Surely a prince would know better."

The veins in his neck jumped when his jaw clenched. "You think you can speak to me like this? You think you can get away with striking me, in front of all of these people? I own you!"

"If you think that is true, then perhaps I did not hit you hard enough." Her voice rose with a spike of anger.

The prince's hand drew back but before it could sail she spoke again.

"Swords or guns, your highness?"

Vaun blinked. "What?"

"For our duel," Grayc Illan said. "Would you rather I shoot you, or stab you?"

His lips curled back into a snarl that twisted at the corners of his mouth. "You cannot challenge me, Grayc. I am a prince of the Realm. You are just a rat."

She felt the entire room watching her but his blackened eyes weighed on her nerves the most, urging her to abandon her pretense of confidence and beg for mercy. It was not an option. His madness would only worsen the longer they allowed him to continue sucking down cups of tea. With a lazy shrug she tossed the book onto the table, ignoring the way the porcelain suffered and more tea spilled. "Vaun—" She used his given name and heard the intake of shock-stricken breaths. "—if you are frightened, you only need say so."

His fists clenched. "Swords. Where?"

"Queen's Courtyard," Grayc Illan said. It would sound like a mistake born out of nerves and haste.

"Your spilled blood would offend the roses," he reminded with no lack of enjoyment. "No rats on Tower grounds, not even to die."

Grayc flexed her fingers discreetly against her thighs. "The Ash Yard at the end of the Low, then. In Belholn Province."

A murmur rose from the guests in The Library but Vaun's attention could not be stolen from her. His smile grew when he took a step closer, swallowing the space between them. "Agreed." His fingers touched her cheek, watching to see if she flinched. She didn't. "It seems right that you should die in that filth." His hand fell away and he headed for the exit with a timid trickle of followers quietly moving after him. "Find your replacement before morning tomorrow."

"Noon today, prince."

He stopped near the doors and looked back, smile smeared with cruelty. "So eager to die? Very well. Enjoy your last hours."

When the door closed behind him the room erupted with voices.

A few bystanders rushed out, ready to spread the news: Vaun Dray Fen was dust mad and today his valet would die.

One of AviSariel's personal maids and a cluster of staff from The Library hurried to the princess, easing her down into a chair and offering a magic balm to sooth and heal her scalded skin. The maid dabbed tenderly at AviSariel's cheeks and neck with the opalescent cream while the others fanned her with their gloved hands.

"He's mad, Grayc," Addom said grimly. "No one would think less of you for hiding until he gets well again."

She looked at him curiously, though the lord would not return her gaze in public. "And who will take his tea away so that he might get well? You, Vym?"

His jaw flexed, the idea rolling around in his thoughts before he shrugged and took to buttoning his jacket. "He will kill you. I won't weep for you, but I imagine when Vaun is himself again..." Addom's fingers hesitated on the last button. He turned toward AviSariel, seated across from him. The violent red of her face had already subsided and the maid was smoothing balm down her neck with long, careful fingers. "Would you like a ride home, princess?"

She sniffled delicately but managed to smile. "Thank you, but I'll stay with the prince's valet."

He looked just as surprised as Grayc Illan felt. He bowed before leaving.

No matter how AviSariel wiped at her dress it would not come clean. The splotches of tea had found a home in the print and would not be moved.

Grayc Illan sank into Vaun's chair, leaning back into its stiff design and allowing herself a moment to soak in what she had done along with the last of his warmth. She had never sat down in The Library before. She did not imagine she ever would again.

"What is your plan?" AviSariel whispered, brushing off her worried maid now that her skin was cooled and healing fast.

Grayc Illan touched the prince's cup briefly, rotating it on the saucer. "What do you mean, your grace?"

The princess shifted a little on her skirts. "Your plan for the duel. Do you have some sort of trap prepared?" She paled. "He won't be hurt, will he?"

Grayc Illan smiled but it was a small gesture. "No trap, princess. I suppose my plan is not to die." It was meant to sound like a joke but it stuck in her throat. How many decades had she spent shadowing the prince? Most of his life. Most of hers. She knew him better than anyone. He pretended to fumble with a blade the way he pretended to fumble with all devices that reminded of manual labor under the public eye. He pretended to forget names and news. He pretended a great deal.

AviSariel's hand stilled, handkerchief pressed to her dress. She stared at the valet for a long while before finally dragging in a shuddered breath and leaning off the edge of her seat. "What?" Her voice was so frail that it grated nerves.

Grayc Illan sighed and stood. "I must prepare. The car will be waiting outside for you when you're ready to go home."

AviSariel's jaw trembled, her already tear swollen eyes filling again. "Grayc, you can't duel with him. There's no point in it."

The valet nodded in agreement and straightened her vest. "Princess, have you not noticed? There is not much we do that has a point. Not one I think you might see, anyway."

AviSariel stood before she could turn away and grabbed her wrist. "Grayc, he could kill you!"

He will kill me, she thought with such certainty that it made her skin cold. "What would you have me do?" The princess parted her lips, but Grayc Illan continued. "It's poison, your grace. The more he drinks it, the worse he will get until it consumes him. Bad dust does not leave the system until all dust does. Eventually the madness and the anger will be all that is left."

AviSariel clung to her hand. "Someone will help him. His family. The Queen." She swallowed hard and a few of her tears overflowed.

"Fay!"

Grayc sighed. "No, your grace. They won't." With care, she took the princess's hand from her wrist. "I am the one that takes care of him."

"But why?"

Grayc Illan stepped away from the table. "The Queen wants him alive and well," she recited and left. She wouldn't have to watch the other woman continue to clutch the handkerchief she had already ruined. She wouldn't have to see the princess mulling over her answer, tasting it for a lie before being consumed by a wave of sorrow when she began to guess at the truth. Grayc Illan had other things to worry about because, today, she was going to die.

Grayc Illan returned to the prince's residence in Belholn and used the staff entrance, just in case Vaun had returned. She found he had not, but locked her bedroom door anyway. For a handful of minutes that felt like hours, she sat in the stuffed chair she used for evening reading and let her thoughts race.

She was a fool. She knew it with such certainty that even she pitied herself. Her hand clutched at the arm of the seat when she remembered the way her bones had reverberated when she struck him with that book. It had to be done. His madness had to be cured. She knew that, but why did it have to be her? He was the prince of the Realm, beloved by his people. Surely one of them could save him. One of his friends? One of his lovers? One of his relatives?

Her fingers relaxed slowly against the chair as resolution quieted her nerves. His people were useless, his friendships as hollow as his romances, and she had never once witnessed any love between the Dray Fen siblings. Grayc had done it herself because she could entrust no one else.

Pushing herself up from her seat, she made her way to the bathroom and took a long shower. She wanted to cry. It was childish, but she always told herself that it didn't count as crying if her face was already wet. Despite wanting to, despite knowing all the reasons why she should be crumbling, Grayc Illan could not work up the terror she knew was buried someplace inside her.

She left the cage of tile feeling hollowed. The steam of the room drew the tension from her body and left a quiet resolve in its place. Even so, she braced her palms against the cool marble of the sink and dropped her head forward.

"Do the right thing," she whispered. It was the creed of her mother. She had said it so simply in the past, as though the right thing was always clear and the wrong thing never tempting. *Do the right thing.* It was a cause and a reason all its own.

Grayc Illan took her time dressing and gave what might be her last outfit thought. She decided not to die in a suit. She chose tight pants with good movement, since she had to give him a quality fight if she had any hope of wearing down his madness. She added a loose top and vest to pretend she hadn't already given up. Stretching upward on her toes inside her closet, she coaxed a box down from the top shelf. She knelt when she placed the large rectangle on the floor, sliding back its lid to reveal a red coat inside. A child's coat, tattered from mistreatment and stained in blood that, no matter how it tried to fade, she could always see at first glance. Grayc ran her fingers along the frayed material.

After another moment, she returned the box to its place among her things. It would be thrown out with them tomorrow.

She found a pair of leather gauntlets and pulled them on, drawing the strings snug as she left her closet for her bedroom. Grayc Illan stopped, fingers still entwined with laces, at the sight of her unexpected visitor. A quick glance showed her door was still locked, so he had been polite enough to return it to its original state after picking it and slipping inside. She pulled the strings of the arm guard tight and dropped her hands to her sides, the long ties dangling.

"Why are you doing this?" Udaro demanded, his brow creased

with anger but his eyes grim with heartbreak.

"It's my job," she recited. It was true enough.

He hissed and stepped closer, chin lowering to keep his gaze locked with hers. "Let me break your shackle, Illi."

She stepped back. "Shackle or no, I would still do this."

"How can you know that?" His hands fisted at his sides. "He's going to kill you."

"I don't care."

"You hate him! You hate all of them!"

Grayc hissed at him to lower his voice before anyone outside her room heard.

"You've grown soft for him over the decades," he snarled in a whisper. "You think you see things in him that are not there."

"They are not all the same, Udaro! They need to be saved like the rest of us."

He clenched his teeth. "And you're going to save them? The High born?"

The weight of that improbability, its very absurdity, settled over her, stealing her anger. "I'm going to save him."

"And if you can't?" Udaro's shoulders sagged. "You know what he is."

"I know."

He sighed, then gestured toward a long wooden box on her bed. "My sword. You don't have one nearly as good."

"Thank you."

Udaro hesitated, then finally touched her cheek. He leaned in and pressed a kiss to her forehead. "He will regret it when he wakes." The breath of his promise rolled against her skin and she closed her eyes.

She waited until he'd left, until the feel of his lips against her skin had faded, and then she went to the box on her bed and finished preparing. Shackle or no, she was going to save Vaun. Some part of her had decided that long ago, though she had hoped that it would be from more than just himself.

Grayc knew the Ash, where ridges and mounds of blackened rock stretched from the outskirts of the Low to the horizon. This was the edge of Belholn, where the Realm fell into charred ruin. When she was a child, Grayc Illan had wandered this wasteland with small friends and played in the rubble, telling stories of monsters until fear drove them giggling home.

Glimpses of dirty children scampering into partially demolished buildings told her that this was still the same place to a new generation.

A handful of the High born had come down to these ruins with hoods drawn and scarves wrapped around their faces to shield their lungs from the air. Servants surrounded the visitors, holding up lanterns like the ones in the High and Main to stave off the pixies. The High born looked at the children pressing their small faces against dirty windows as though they were goblins, tearing their false bodies from puddles of magic and stretching awful arms to snatch a vessel.

Grayc wondered how many of the High born had even met a child, as they hadn't birthed any in nearly a century. Wendry Belholn had been the last child born among the High, and she was almost eighty now. The magic that fueled them, fed them, kept them young, also blocked whatever nature needed to create new life. The High born didn't seem to notice, or care. They considered babies a forgotten nuisance, now a burden of the Low. Those who even knew the cost of their luxury undoubtedly considered it a reasonable exchange for all the pleasures magic could give.

Xavian Ren and the whole of the Belholn family clustered near a fleet of gleaming cars. She felt their eyes on her, pressing her down, reminding her that her death had always been meant for their enjoyment.

As soon as she looked away from them, she found Udaro. He leaned against a wall of bricks, looking as at home in the Ash as he did in the High. At his stare, she touched the sword hilt at her waist and nodded her thanks.

The sound of tires rolling down the empty street tightened her muscles. She kept her gaze on the stretch of land between the last buildings of the Realm and the valley at the end of the world. She did not watch Vaun exit his car or turn to see him speak to his spectators. She did hear him draw his sword and the crunch of charred land beneath his boots. Finally, he entered her line of vision, framed in the gap bordered by rubble and city. He had handed his jacket away and rolled up his sleeves.

His eyes, a wash of darkness, fixed on her. More than two body lengths of dirt stretched between them and, even so, her fingers coiled around the hilt of her sword anxiously. She pulled it free and let the weight become a part of her arm.

Vaun looked at the weapon she held, eyes narrowing at the extravagant hilt, a beautiful cage of polished steel curving over her hand to shield her fingers. His teeth clenched. With a turn of his head, his dark eyes swept over their audience to find Udaro standing in the shadow of a building. The bastard of Belholn stared back at the prince. "I hadn't realized you were so close," Vaun said.

She drew a breath to answer but he rushed forward, swallowing the space between them in a single heartbeat. His blade hissed toward her unprotected side. Blood rushed through her veins as her body burst into motion, spinning away just in time. Her sword caught his and he pushed in tight, forcing their arms up over her head. She kicked to throw him back, desperate to return the distance between them but he only used that space to slash at her anew. He lunged closer, aiming to stab at her, and she was forced to pull fast to one side. The shuffle of their boots kicked up clouds of soot. Metal clanked in quick repetition and the steel reverberated through her bones.

"Do you think he will miss you when you are dead?" the prince sneered.

His blade slammed into hers, grinding the edges together until the hilts locked. He twisted, unrelenting, and drove both tips into the ground. Glee twisted his lips when he rammed his elbow into her jaw. Grayc recoiled in a twirling stagger, yanking her sword free. She swallowed hard at the metallic saliva flooding her mouth but lifted her chin to face him. Blood dribbled thickly down her chin and she spat the rest of it into the ash between them.

"No," she admitted, tears stinging her eyes, "but you will."

He bared his teeth. The black of his eyes crept out to stretch spiders' legs under his flesh. "Did you find your replacement? Will she be just as *dutiful* as you?" He ground the words out as he stalked after her.

"More." She took large, backward steps. Looking over his shoulder, Grayc Illan gauged their distance from the spectators. The prince had followed her deeper into the Ash, but their audience had not. "He'll be loyal to you, and only you."

"I'm glad you're at peace with this, rat." He surged forward, raining down a series of blows that drove her farther into the Ash. She retreated, keeping up a guard that barely kept his blade from her skin. Grayc dodged and spun. She swung around to strike but he kicked her back. She scrambled and drew her arm back to parry when her elbow collided with the flat belly of a boulder. Triumph sparked in his eyes and his arm jutted out to wrap his gloved fingers around her throat, slamming her skull back against the rock with a hard thud. She stabbed forward, but his blade knocked hers aside and pinned it to the stone bracing her back.

"If I didn't know better, I would think that you wanted this." His fingers tightened around her neck, making her lungs burn and a reply impossible, yet he stared down at her as if waiting to hear one. "I will make it slow," he breathed, voice low, as though they lay tangled in sheets. "I promise. You will be the headline for months, every time they find a new piece of you." His lips brushed hers, tongue stealing out to taste the blood he had already spilled. "No one will forget you."

He crushed his lips to hers, mashing their teeth and forcing her mouth open so his tongue could search for the source of that blood. When he found it nestled behind her bottom lip, he sucked it into his mouth, digging his teeth into the tear to draw more pain from it. The cut spread under his force.

Grayc fumbled for the dagger in her vest and jabbed blindly. The blade scraped bone as it shoved between Vaun's ribs. She ripped it free and stabbed in again, leaving it lodged tight in the side of his chest. The prince gasped and stumbled, giving her the room to drive her knee into his thigh. He dropped like a stone. Grayc scrambled up the side of the boulder. A hateful rumble from his chest spurred her to move even faster.

Rubble shifted under her boots, threatening her climb, but the sound of Vaun's roar below made her fingers dig deeper and her arms strain to drag her up. At the top, she turned to look down.

"You cheated!" Vaun clutched his side, red running between his fingers. She watched, panting, as he bled. The black veins around his eyes faded. A small swarm of pixies buzzed around him. Most focused on lapping up the magic in the thick drops of his blood, but a few were so hungry that they went straight for the source. Tiny, naked bodies clung to the fabric of his vest. Their hands pulled at the tears to get teeth against his wounds. The prince smacked them away without looking.

"What did you expect?" Grayc finally did the thing she'd wanted to do all day. She ran hard and fast, leaping rubble and darting toward the horizon of black upheaval and gray sky.

He roared again behind her and her steps almost faltered; the sound was not human. She told herself again and again that she *knew* what he was, that it wasn't a surprise, but it didn't change the way her stomach sank and her throat tightened. He shouted after her but the strum of her own pulse in her ears made her deaf to his words.

She leaped down from one ledge of black and landed on her knees in a valley of silt. The ground gave a little beneath her weight, her hand touching down to keep her from toppling over. The fine, black dirt shifted and fell between boards into an unknown abyss. She rose and darted across the small valley, a flat stretch circled by boulders and small cliffs. Grayc Illan had not been entirely honest with AviSariel. She had a plan, of sorts; it just wasn't a very good one.

The prince's valet turned when she reached the middle of the little valley, her boots scraping at dirt. She had found this place as a child. She used to push pebbles between the planks of filth and try to hear them strike the end. She had never been able to hear them land. Today, she would.

Vaun leaped from the ledge and landed in a cloud of silt. The air rippled with heat around him as he straightened, sword in one hand and Grayc's bloody dagger in the other. His valet faced him, readying her sword. He rushed forward, focused on the sound of her pulse. She spun as he reached her and he realized her fight in the beginning had been a lie. He had underestimated her training. His blade tore across her thigh, buying him a sharp cry before she backhanded him with the hilt of her sword. The flesh along his cheekbone broke open.

They lurched and spun across the landscape, stirring up a cloud of ash. Somewhere in the back of his mind, Vaun began to notice the oddity of the ground. It was too even for this landscape, and too soft. Confusion slowed him for a moment as thought clawed forward. Grayc's blade struck out and opened another wound across his ribs. His vision swayed and for the first time he realized just how much blood she had cost him. Rage boiled up in his chest once more and his sword caught hers, dragging her blade to the side long enough to yank her close and jab the dagger into her chest. She gasped beautifully. Her body stretched, her red painted mouth opened as shock drew the color from her cheeks. He pulled the knife out and jerked his body back to watch her fall. Her knees hit the ground hard.

Pride kept him where he stood. He didn't care if he had to stand on a nest of pixies so long as he could watch her die on her knees in front of him. Her hand crawled up her chest, fingers touching the soggy cloth torn by steel on their way to the clasp of her vest. Trembling fingers tugged the garment open. He grinned, expecting her to clutch at the bleeding wound, but her hand reached around her side.

Her body doubled over, the tips of her curls sweeping the ground and red saliva dripping thickly from her mouth. With a pained groan she forced herself to sit upright again. Her hand drew out of her vest, circles of iron glinting on her thumb and ring finger. She stretched her arm out, revealing a device nestled against her palm, the core containing a small glass circle of blue smoke.

Vaun's eyes widened as he took a step back. There was no time to escape or negotiate, so he did the only thing he could think of: he lunged for her arm and watched fatefully as it came down. Her palm slapped against the ground and the bobble of smoke burst.

Time shivered and the floor of the Ash trembled. Black dust rose into the air just before the ground gave way and the darkness of the Ash swallowed them whole, dropping them down until even the gray sky above vanished.

CHAPTER SIX

Vaun forced his eyes open to darkness, shivering as liquid lapped at his waist. A line of fire burned across his cheekbone and smoldered against his ribs. He rolled over and moaned, but no servants appeared with light or comfort. He clawed at the ground and dragged himself upright. Wet gravel shifted under his fingers.

He stared into the unrelenting blackness. After a few moments, faint drips echoed to him, the sound hollow, as if traveling across a vast, empty space. The air smelled clean in a way he had never known, wet like the rocks and cold like a grave. He lifted his hands and felt liquid trickle across his skin, back into the pool he sat in. Thoughtlessly, he brought his hand to his mouth and sucked two digits. The liquid was thin, like cold tea, but offered no discernible flavor, and yet, when it reached his belly, he felt overcome by the desire for more. For the first time that Vaun could recall, he was thirsty.

Cupping his hands, he dipped them into the unseen pool and drank blindly. The more he swallowed, the greedier he became. The taste was nothing and yet, at the same time, it was a subtle sort of sweetness that he had never known.

His arms stilled when a different flavor hit his tongue, a metallic zest he knew all too well. The taste brought memories and awareness with it. He remembered this taste; he remembered sucking it from her lips.

Vaun shuddered, remembering the mindless, insatiable rage that had built up inside him. It ate through his veins until all he could see, all he could hear, was insult and injury. It felt as if his very body was a cage of fury, and he must purge it or split his skin.

Black smoke. Duels. Scalds. Memories flashed through his mind. *Madness.*

And then… swinging the blade, sinking the knife into her flesh… Her gaze meeting his as her hand struck the ground, light bursting from her palm. Falling…

Vaun scrambled to his feet, staggering in the pool as pebbles shifted beneath his boots and his side screamed. "Grayc!"

His voice echoed back to him, followed by painful silence.

He coughed and ran his fingers tentatively along the tears in his shirt to find raw skin. Even with no light to see, he knew the magic of his body had begun to work the wounds closed. Desperation told him the same would be true for Grayc, but sense told him otherwise. Her blood wasn't saturated with magic the way his was, and, as far as he knew, she had none of her own, though most everyone who did kept it to themselves. Even he and his sister did not dare use their crafts in the open, not where their mother might see from her Tower and grow jealous.

Old stories claimed all people once possessed natural magic, before it became a commodity to be bought, refined, and sold. Some legends even said the greatest households in the Realm—the Vyms, the Belholns, the Maggrins, even the Dray Fens—rose to power on the strength of their inherent blood magic, but Vaun did not believe in fairy tales. He could not count on children's tales to save Grayc's life.

Could he? In this dark, hidden place, would the Queen see if he used his magic? Fay had always been fierce in her warnings not to tempt their mother. She said the Queen's greed knew no bounds; no one could have power in front of her, and her eyes were everywhere.

"Grayc!" he called again, the echo of his own voice mocking him. His stomach sank deep into his gut at the thought of her corpse floating in that pool of liquid while he had been sucking it down.

Vaun drew a deep breath and let it out shakily, the magic stirring in his veins. His arm slashed at the air, as though cutting a horizon into the cave, and a dull light swelled around him without any discernible source. Using his own magic made his skin warm and his spine tingle. It was like scratching an itch he'd spent decades convincing himself wasn't there. It came naturally, easily, if only he'd let it loose. If anyone was nearby they would feel it, too.

He turned in a fast circle, but saw nothing except a vast, calm lake stretching off into more darkness and winding around large, curving walls of stone.

He chose a direction at random and walked the rocky shore. The light followed, spreading farther along the beach until it spilled over her body. Vaun ran when he saw her and sank to his knees beside her. Her wet hair clung to her face and neck. A smear of blood, black in the dim light, stretched thickly from the corner of her lips to paint the side of her chin and cheek. She was breathing, her chest rising and falling in shallow, uneven gasps.

Cupping her cheek, Vaun spoke her name. She cringed, lips parting to push up more blood. She coughed wetly, black spraying the rocks and dribbling from her mouth.

Gritting his teeth, he ripped the front of her shirt open. For a moment it wasn't the stab wound that drew his eye, but the mark above her heart. There, nestled above the silk holding her breast, a delicate little X glared up at him. His breath shuddered at the thin, black lines, so imperfect they must have been inked freehand. He'd seen that mark once before, and his gut twisted to see its twin over her heart. The heart that had beat for him.

Her breath hitched and her body jerked. Fresh blood gushed from the gaping wound below her collar.

"Grayc!" He grabbed her shoulders. "Wake up! Grayc, can you

hear me? Open your eyes."

How could he have stabbed her? *Her.* His Grayc.

"Wake up!" He wanted to shake her. "Damn you, Grayc Illan! Why didn't you run? Why didn't you leave me be? Did you think I would thank a hero?"

Her breath thinned. He sat back on his heels, scanning the darkness pressing against his false light.

"Help!" he cried, unable to temper his voice. "Can anyone hear me?" Only his own echo answered. Vaun scrubbed at his face, hands trembling. "Anyone? Please! I am Prince Vaun Dray Fen, and I demand—"

He all but choked. Who was he to demand anything? He was a dusted fool and a prince of nothing.

Vaun settled beside her, letting the near silence swallow him. After a time, it struck him, miserably, to realize that he was waiting. He was sitting in the dark, beside her dying body, waiting for someone to come. Waiting for someone to save them. What shamed him most of all was knowing that the one he was waiting for, the one who would swoop in and direct him toward the exit, the one who would put him back into his car, his bed, his life, was the one lying on the ground in front of him.

The prince scooped her up, careful, though awkward, as he stood. The uneven ground shifted beneath his boots as he walked. He left the beach to trudge into the endless darkness. The ground grew more solid until it became firm soil beneath his steps.

He came to a wall and followed its curve. The ground rose slowly, leading him up an incline until his light splashed against another wall of packed dirt. Vaun's quickening steps faltered as shadows receded, revealing intricate lines carved deep into the hard surface. Long, sinuous curves and thick mounds bulged, creating a strange image. It looked to be a face, monstrous, protruding from the wall of dirt. The creature's head was wider than it was high, and something about the flatness of its wickedly wide mouth made Vaun think of serpents. It must be some kind of animal, one of the fabled creatures that populated legends, like jackals and birds and rats. The only real animals were the wolves sent down by the Queen to end lives. Curiosity made Vaun want to step closer, but the quickening of his pulse kept him where he was, frozen as if the mighty beast might wake.

Grayc's body, growing heavy in his arms, offered him an excuse to turn away. He left the strange carving, trying to ignore the spike of panic when he could no longer see the terrible face behind him. His steps picked up again, ushering him down the wall and around a bend. The silhouette of a door formed from the shadows, cut into the earth and framed in thick beams. He choked on relief, almost staggering in his rush to reach it. Through it, the prince found the first of countless steps, winding upward and creaking fiercely beneath his boots.

Grayc mumbled something in his arms and he held her tighter, thinking of how bold she looked before they fell from the Ash. Blood on her lips, life gushing from her chest, and still he could swear that she had smiled at him. Not snickered, or laughed madly at how she would take him with her, but a soft, plain smile. He wondered if he would ever get the chance to ask her about it. Wondered if he would ever know the truth behind that little knowing gesture of her lips. A shiver clawed up his spine when he recalled the cracking of the ground beneath him and the tumble into black. Strange as it was, he didn't feel that she had punished his madness by casting him down, so much as she had gone with him.

At the top of the stairs, his stomach dropped; a short stretch of floor ended in a sealed door, a metal patch in a wall of stone with no knob. He set Grayc Illan down carefully, propping her against the wall to let her breathe easier while he inspected the door. He tried to pull it open, his fingers searching the seam of metal and rock for hinges or any sort of handle. Finding none, he clawed at the edges until he could only curse at his bleeding digits.

"Someone!" Tears pricked his eyes. "Hello!" His bloodied fists beat wildly against the door.

No one answered.

He called until his throat ached but silence was the only reply. With another reverberating pound of his fists he commanded the door open, screaming until his throat was raw.

"Be quiet," his valet murmured, her face scrunched with annoyance. Her arms coiled around herself.

Vaun obeyed, more than ready for someone else to be in charge, and left the door to kneel beside her. "Grayc? Are you okay?" He reached out to peel back her shirt and check her wound but she swatted away his hand with a disgruntled huff.

"No, I am not okay." Her voice labored, as though she were far away and straining so that he might hear. "You stabbed me."

"You stabbed *me*." He settled beside her, wishing he could offer her anything, any sort of comfort. "Twice."

"Deserved it." Her eyelids cracked open, body cringing under the pain of even that small effort. "Where—?"

"I'm not sure. I carried you as far as I could. Is there another way out?"

A tiny, pained sigh escaped her. "I don't know."

"You don't know? You threw us into a pit without knowing a way out?" He scowled openly at her and hated that she couldn't even muster a trace of dismissal. "This was a poor plan."

To his surprise, her lips turned up. "It was." Her eyes fluttered closed. "It seemed better than staying where we were. I had hoped we would end up in the water."

"Water?" The stuff he showered in? He felt queasy thinking that he drank of it.

"The pool. We landed there, didn't we?"

He nodded, though she couldn't see. After a moment, he carefully wrapped his arms around her and drew her into his lap, wedging his back into the corner near the stairs so that he could watch the door.

She tensed and Vaun thought for certain she would tell him to let her go, but finally she laid her cheek against his shoulder.

He didn't know how long they sat like that, sharing warmth. Slowly, she stopped coughing and her breathing steadied. Eventually, he drew open her shirt again to find her chest still smeared with blood, but none welling from the wound. He draped the material over her chest again and laid his cheek to her hair. "Maybe you have a little magic in you, after all."

She laughed, the sound tired and raw, though he wasn't sure what had been funny.

"You keep things from me," the prince whispered.

"Yes."

"Why?"

Silence stretched between them so long that Vaun wondered why he'd bothered asking. Just when he thought she'd dropped off to sleep again, she said, "There are times when I wish I could tell you everything... and other times I hope you will never find out."

He sighed quietly and closed his eyes. It was the sort of reply that he expected. "I don't understand."

Another silence followed. The warmth of their bodies lulled Vaun toward sleep and he curled his arms tighter around her. "Thank you," he whispered into her hair. "For hitting me with a book."

A soft sound made him think she smiled, but he couldn't see. He didn't think she'd ever tell.

Vaun woke, whether by the sound of the door or the weight of the other man's stare, he couldn't be sure. Cold had seeped down deep into his bones and exhaustion made his limbs impossibly heavy. Though he willed himself to rise and rush past the bastard of Belholn, the prince could only sit there, propped against the corner with her body cradled in his lap. In the time that Udaro's gaze lay upon him, Vaun was certain that they had held a conversation even if their lips had not moved.

Udaro appeared different, standing in the doorway with gray light spilling in behind him. His build was the same as it had been that morning and his clothes were their usual folds of black but his features had lost their characteristically lighthearted form. His lips were caught in the moment before a frown and his eyes were narrowed, sharp and spiteful, on the prince.

For the first time in nearly a century of carefree friendship, Vaun realized that he'd never really known this man. He had enjoyed Udaro's company as well as his humor. They had shared tea, beds, and sharp wit, and Vaun had mistaken that for depth. He had mistaken that for friendship. Now, staring up at him, the prince realized just how little he knew the man. A penchant for slumming it in the Low, a blood tie to the Belholns, and a splattering of tattoos: that was all he knew, and for the first time, that was too little.

A rustle of sound came from behind Udaro, beyond the doorway, and in the blink of an eye the judgment in the man's expression vanished. He knelt before the prince and curled his arms under Grayc Illan. The warmth of his skin pressed in through the front of Vaun's shirt. For a moment, he refused to let go, but then his own strength failed and Udaro lifted her away. The prince sat, half conscious, and watched as Udaro left with Grayc Illan in his arms.

Vaun only vaguely noticed the men that entered after Udaro, kneeling at his side and asking him questions. He didn't realize someone managed to get him to his feet and down a long hallway until the full force of the gray light of day blinded him, making his head swim.

A haze of images, like waking dreams, followed. He found himself waking repeatedly but could never recall falling asleep. Meaningless, nonsensical conversations occupied his thoughts for stretches of time he could not count before he realized he was alone. Everything hurt: sound, light, his hair against his cheek. He was either burning hot or bone-shaking cold; either way he was in agony, coated in sweat and struggling to breathe. And when it all finally faded into a complete, consuming, darkness, he was more grateful than he had ever imagined himself capable.

He woke slowly in his own bed, in his own home, as though all else had been a nightmare. He sat up, cringing at the pull of muscles and the emptiness in the pit of his stomach.

The bedroom door opened and a man entered. He had a good face, youthful and pretty, with a wide mouth and large eyes. Given his slight build, he would probably be mistaken for a boy from behind. He appeared just as surprised to see the prince sitting upright as the prince was to see him at all.

"Good afternoon, your highness," the pretty stranger said with a quick bow of his head, sending strands of blond hair into his eyes. Vaun wondered if he'd been born in Belholn. With hair and features like that, he could even pass for one of the Belholn bastards. The stranger opened the door again and leaned out, calling to a maid before returning. "Lunch will be brought up, along with the papers you've missed."

Vaun stared at him. It was obvious the man worked for him, but he had no memory of him. "Where is Grayc?" the prince demanded and found his voice hoarse.

The stranger flushed uncomfortably. "Your wife will be in shortly, your highness. She will be glad to see you're feeling well, at last."

Vaun's eyes narrowed as he watched the man move confidently around his room, altogether too familiar with the layout as he prepared the small table to be laid out with a meal. He disappeared into the wardrobe through the bathroom and emerged with a plush towel. He draped it across the back of a chair just the way Grayc Illan always did.

"Who are you?" the prince asked in a low voice.

The man's cheeks colored with embarrassment. "My apologies, your highness. You were ill. My name is Samuel Sinol. I am your new valet."

Vaun stared at him long enough to see the man shift uncomfortably from one foot to the other. "Grayc!"

Samuel Sinol cringed. "She was dismissed, your highness."

"By whom?" he demanded, grinding his teeth after the words escaped.

"The princess Fay, your highness. She was here by your side most of the time, as was the princess AviSariel."

The door opened and, as though summoned by her name, AviSariel entered. Her blue eyes lit up when she saw Vaun. Her mouth pulled into a wide, honest smile and she hurried around Samuel Sinol.

"Thank the Queen," AviSariel exclaimed. "How do you feel? Do you remember the duel?" The speed of her words made his head swim. She reached for his hand. "We were so worried."

The sluggishness of his limbs almost let her touch him but he jerked away just in time. When embarrassment and hurt had sufficiently colored his wife's cheeks, Vaun turned his malice on Samuel Sinol. "Where is she?"

The young man hesitated only a second before straightening stoically. "I believe Miss Sanaro will be in attendance at this evening's festivities, to which both you and the princess have been invited, your highness."

The door opened again and a maid entered, pushing a cart of cakes, coffee, and an impressively large stack of newspapers.

Vaun rubbed his head and resisted the urge to lie back down on his pillow. "What festivities?"

"The birthday of Lord Xavian Ren Belholn, your highness."

He massaged his temples. Xavian Ren's birthday wasn't until next month. Just how long had he been asleep? Since when was Grayc Illan invited to High district functions? Had she returned to working for the Belholns? No, impossible. She loathed them, save for Udaro.

"Should I bring up the new suits, your highness?" Samuel Sinol inquired.

With a nod, Vaun pushed himself to his feet and stretched. He hadn't realized he was naked until AviSariel blushed and pivoted away, averting her eyes. He rolled his. How long had it been since the night of his birthday and her return? Why did she keep up this charade of innocence when it obviously wasn't working? She had neither seduced him nor succeeded in gaining the favor of anyone else. If he had been feeling sharper, he might have dedicated some time to wondering what other scheme she could be working up under that blush.

"I suppose you'll have to join me," Vaun said while watching her profile. Did her eyes light up at his words? Did she interpret his defeat as his will? "Try not to be too embarrassing," he added, and watched the hint of hope drain from her features. Her head ducked when she curtsied before leaving, and Vaun found, in her wake, that hurting her gave him no joy.

In his bathroom, finally alone, he faced his reflection only to find it slightly askew. It took him several minutes to put his finger on what had changed. The magic had worn off. Not his own natural blood magic, but the purchased ones that had saturated his body for a century. He touched his hair and was pleasantly surprised to learn it was naturally black, though without its usual luster. His skin was still smooth, though not quite so coated in the flawless sheen that made the High district residents stand apart from those who could not afford the finest vanity crafts.

He leaned closer to the mirror, the cold marble countertop pressing a chilly line along his naked hips. Somehow, he had forgotten his real colors. His eyes were dark, almost black, but the closer he looked, the more flakes of silver he saw in them: a thin ring of it hugged his pupils. Disappointment colored his cheeks, and his fingers tentatively touched the blushed skin. He frowned; it was so much more livid than usual, bold rather than graceful. It reminded him of AviSariel and the awkwardness of her expressions.

He continued to stare at himself while he brushed his teeth, gawking at all the small differences. The tiles of his shower were cold beneath his feet but warmed quickly once the water sprayed hot. He suddenly remembered the pool beneath the Ash. Grayc Illan had called it water, but it had neither the intense sweetness nor the slight fragrance of lemon that the water pouring from the showerhead did. His stomach growled and he nearly jumped at the unexpected sound, fingers spreading over his abdomen as though to squash the inelegant rumbling. The longer he stood beneath the spray, though, the more relaxed he felt, the less worried, and by the time he emerged his skin tingled pleasantly and all thoughts of lustless hunger were forgotten.

He opened a drawer and fingered the little bottles with their potion filled bellies. He drank one to restore the ethereal cast to his skin, one to make his hair vivid in its darkness, and another to color his eyes a stark and icy blue.

He stood there, naked, in front of the mirror. He had thought that he would feel better, once his vicious smirk could play at the corner of his red lips the way he liked. He was beautiful again, so why did even the most expensive magic suddenly feel tacky against his skin? Had he always been this discontent? He had everything he needed. Everything he wanted. And yet, as the seconds ticked by, his heart grew heavier. Without the haze of his usual dust stupor, nothing softened the reality of his life—an existence spent in excess, with nothing to show for it. The old weight of his life pressed down on him, along with a truth almost too horrible to bear: he could have anything and everything he wanted, so long as he played his role—a foolish jester to amuse the masses while the Queen watched from her Tower. He could have anything, so long as it was nothing she wanted for herself. He could do anything, so long as it was nothing that would offend her. He was Vaun Dray Fen, prince of the Realm, and he was a prisoner like any other citizen of his city.

When he left his bathroom, the new valet greeted him with a rack of suits. The stranger selected one. Vaun frowned pointedly, and the young man quickly put it back and stepped aside. He offered the prince his tea and Vaun almost accepted on impulse before thinking better of it. He wanted to think a little longer. He wanted to discover an answer or two, even if just for himself.

"Did I miss anything?" the prince asked, waving at the stack of newspapers on the trolley with his ignored treats.

Samuel Sinol jumped, moving toward the papers as though to retrieve them but they were simply too large a stack to bother. "'Anything,' your highness?" There was an almost pleading tone to his voice and Vaun nodded, pulling on a pair of slacks.

"Anything important," he amended. Samuel Sinol's delicate features pinched with some uncertainty but he began reciting events—duels, parties, and scandals. The prince made an irritated sound that involved clicking his tongue to the top of his mouth. It was alarming, even to himself, because it sounded like something Fay might do. "Did anyone die?" Vaun asked pointedly, deciding to pick just one topic.

"Yes, your highness," Samuel Sinol said. "But no one in the High."

Vaun chose a shirt and pulled it on. He glanced over his reflection's shoulder to eye his new valet, waiting for more information.

Samuel Sinol tipped his chin higher but didn't met Vaun's gaze. Most servants never did. "There was a string of executions in the Main and Low districts while you were ill," he explained, voice tempered as he tried to gauge when to stop talking. Vaun knotted his tie. "Traitors, it seems, your highness."

"Treason? I thought they gave that revolution nonsense up years ago," Vaun said idly, practicing his tone for the party. It wasn't as easy to sound like an unfeeling bastard as he made it seem.

"Decades, actually, your highness."

Vaun pretended not to hear. He recalled the occasional group of activists here and there in the past. They rarely developed beyond the secret meetings portion of rebellion before a pack of wolves brought their souls to rest in the Tower, or worse, Evan Kadem came down himself to put an end to any thoughts of disloyalty. "So, what did these traitors do?" the prince inquired, still working on his tone and expression.

"They were peddling dust, your highness."

Vaun stopped in the midst of taking out a jacket and turned, eyebrow raised skeptically. He caught a glimpse of himself in the mirror and raised his eyebrow just a tad higher. Dust was just about everywhere in the Realm. Had he slept so long that that had changed?

"It was not the Queen's dust," Samuel Sinol said quietly.

Vaun stood there for another moment before nodding and drawing on his jacket. Someone had actually made their own dust? Vaun remembered the cigarette in the teahouse in the Main of Belholn, before his madness. The one that had felt wrong. "Get me a list."

"A list, your highness?"

"Of the dead, of course. I can't be caught not knowing their names, can I?" Vaun practiced a careless shrug, as if the man might need a reminder that a prince did not need a valet to advise him, especially not a stand-in valet while his own was missing.

Samuel Sinol bowed deeply and left. Vaun scowled after him, quite certain Grayc Illan had never bowed like that. He couldn't imagine her bowing to anyone without at least a hint of sarcasm. How did she ever managed to become his valet? He tried to remember how she had been appointed the position, sorting through memories long since blurred by a wash of tea and smoke. He made such a terrible habit of forgetting things, too. And yet...

There had been some sort of scandal involving a string of lost pearls, and her. The details of it were lost to him but among them he found her. The first time he saw her. She stood over his bed, looking down at him, and through the haze of the dust in his veins pulling him back toward blissful sleep, he sensed that she would be the end of him. What a beautiful end it would be, at her hand. He had slipped back to sleep with her watching over him like death itself, a stranger in the dark, and never slept more soundly in all his years before or since.

But he hadn't appointed her, he remembered now. Grayc Illan appeared in his life as suddenly as Samuel Sinol.

Because of his sister. Fay brought him Grayc Illan, without request or explanation. Vaun adjusted the collar of his jacket and looked himself coldly in the eye. How had he forgotten all of these things?

The prince stood a moment longer, considering the trays of cakes and cup of tea that had long since cooled.

By the time he left his room, dressed for the evening, Samuel Sinol returned with a narrow slip of paper. Vaun took it, eyes skimming the list of names before looking at the valet with just the right amount of mild confusion and disinterest.

"What is this?" he asked.

Samuel Sinol did not miss a beat. "Nothing of importance, your highness."

Vaun shrugged as though he had forgotten asking for anything and dropped the paper. It fluttered to the floor, not yet settled when he had gone from the hallway. It had taken him only a second to scan the names and find the one he suspected would be there: Gabriella Foslin. He had known her briefly as Gabby. So, she'd put the bad dust in his hand. Who had put it in hers?

More importantly, where was his valet?

To her credit, AviSariel paid careful attention to her appearance. Vaun didn't know if she'd done it to impress or to avoid embarrassing him, but he couldn't fault her for either. She wore a dress that made her look incredibly uncomfortable, exactly what was high in fashion at the moment, as Fay herself frequently wore remarkably restraining and lavish gowns. AviSariel was corseted in so tightly that her flesh heaved over the top a little. The length of the bodice wrapped her curves all the way down to her hips, and Vaun wondered how she had managed to get herself into the car. He would be sure to watch her attempt at exiting once they reached the Belholn estate.

She took little breaths and he faced the window to hide his smile; not one of cruelty, but of honest humor. She had tried so hard. She looked beautiful, though he would never tell her, but it had come at such an obvious and ridiculous cost. He wondered how other ladies wore such extravagant dresses and made it look so easy. His smile faded when he wondered if AviSariel would become just as elegant as the rest of them over time. Would she get used to the dresses? Would she learn how to play their games? Learn to flirt, to tease, to mock?

He pretended not to wait after exiting the car while she tried to manage the bulk of her skirts.

Some sort of pearlescent magic smeared her skin and made it shimmer when the light hit her. Her hair was longer today but still a deep brown and swept up into a mess of pearls and pins. She followed him up the stairs and into the welcoming doors of the large house. Vaun barely acknowledged his wife's presence but as they entered the banquet hall, no one else could ignore her.

He realized, for the first time, that everyone was a shade of beautiful in the High. Some of them more than others, but all gems decorating the crown of the Realm. He had seen withered bodies, homely faces, and tattered clothing in the city, but never in the High and never at their parties.

Vaun felt the eyes of the guests move from him to her, voices whispering beneath the sound of violins and cellos. He knew it then, that no matter how he hated her, the Realm would not be able to resist a new princess for much longer. What surprised him was the relief he felt knowing that others might give her the affection he would not. He let her have his arm and led the way to the head table, where Xavian Ren held court with his siblings and their lovers fanned out at his sides.

Killian Belholn whistled when he saw the prince approaching, though his glassy gaze slithered past Vaun's shoulder to admire the princess. He'd either found a new supply of dust or his family had given up trying to keep him from his tea. Killian stood, his long legs wobbling when his chair did not slide back as easily as he had expected. "You're alive after all!" He raised his teacup toward the prince.

Philip Belholn smiled beside his younger brother and pulled Killian easily, though not so gently, back into his seat. "We did not think you would make it," the second oldest brother of the Belholns said more politely, though there was always a jagged edge to Philip's mouth that prevented anything he said from sounding entirely honest or kind. "We invited your sister, but she declined. I suppose it can't be helped, being tied to those Vyms." A snicker pulled at his lips, infecting the people sitting nearest to him. "Your mother should have married her to one of us. We would not have forced her to play the prude."

The table laughed. The guests without Belholn blood in their veins shielded their smiles because though they must join in the humor of the jackals, they hesitated to offend the prince.

Vaun smiled back at Philip. "I assure you, no one forces my sister to do anything without serious repercussion."

"I remember Fay Dray Fen well, before her marriage." Philip's voice softened, as though a tragedy had befallen her and, in a way, Vaun knew that one had. "She was colorful, before."

Killian clapped his brother on the shoulder. "Do you remember that year she spent in our house?" His glassy eyes swept from his brother to Vaun. "Fay was always sneaking off from her governesses. She said her own home was boring. We never minded having her. Well, Mother did, but she couldn't exactly tell a princess to get out of her son's bed." The duster chuckled hard at his own words, nearly choking.

"Killian." Philip sighed and handed his brother another cup of tea.

"What?" Killian glanced at the others, but everyone casually averted their attention. Hammish Tar, the youngest of the brothers, pressed his lips uncomfortably and turned to whisper explanations in his lover's ear. Vaun wished very much to have been that lover at that moment and hear those secrets told so easily. "Don't you remember? She was here constantly, before her marriage. And then she was gone. And then Mother and Father were gone, too." Killian sighed heavily, lost in memories. "She was so different, then." He smiled to himself as he drank from his new cup. "She had a lovely laugh, didn't she? Remember how she used to play tricks on us? I do wish she would come back."

"Killy," Xavian Ren said, and the table hushed. He leveled a long, sobering stare on his brother before turning his gaze to Vaun. The Lord smiled warmly and held out his hand. "I am honored that you came, your highness."

Vaun took his hand. "Congratulations on yet another fine year," he recited, but was considering the words Killian had let slip. He'd known Fay had fancied the Belholns before her marriage but he hadn't realized just how differently they remembered her. Nor had he remembered just how soon after her marriage tragedy had struck the Belholns, with the mysterious and brutal deaths of their parents.

"We are all relieved to see that you are feeling well again." The Lord of Belholn released Vaun's hand to take AviSariel's. He gave her a tactful once over before smiling politely and kissing her knuckles. "I hope you enjoy the party," Xavian Ren said sweetly while his lips were still close to her skin. Vaun watched the interaction just long enough to see her blush before leading her to their seats.

He drew out her chair, blaming guilt over his dust-mad mistreatment of her for the spontaneous act of kindness. She made it so easy to forget that she was a pawn of the Queen's sent down with mysterious purpose.

No sooner had he taken his place beside AviSariel than his attention was stolen away. Even in a crowd as large as the one that had filled the banquet hall, even over the music, the clatter of dishes, and the rise and fall of laughter, he could hear Grayc Illan's voice.

He looked beyond the man across from him and to another table. So many people, and yet it only took a second to find her among them. Grayc Illan was smiling; not a true grin, but a careful curve of lips that suited the High. He watched as she lifted a wine glass to her mouth and drank. The deep red of the liquid matched the color of her lips. Her perfect, dark curls fell around her face, framing those eyes he knew so well. Her skin shimmered, as if the shine of her dark silver dress had somehow rubbed off on her. Around her neck, she wore a thin ribbon, black and glossy, but no jewels. She didn't need any.

She wasn't serving dishes or filling glasses. She reclined at a table of High district residents, even nobles, sipping wine and dismissing the grandeur of the event with fashionable disinterest. The man beside her touched her hand, drawing her attention, and she leaned in to hear him speak. Her smile tightened and Vaun could see that she was trying not to laugh before nodding shortly. Vaun almost didn't bother to look at the man sitting beside her, so mesmerized by the oddity of seeing her so comfortable at a table of jackals. She hated Belholns. He was certain of it. Wasn't he?

Vaun's eyes narrowed when he did tear his gaze from her to look at her companion. He set down his glass with a hard thud that nearly broke the stem, wine sloshing inside and dribbling over the edge.

"Vaun?" AviSariel whispered worriedly.

He didn't answer, staring at the man beside his former valet. Jacobi Belholn caressed her hand as he whispered in her ear. His white hair mingled with her black curls, and for a moment, his lips almost brushed her cheek. From the outside, they appeared a strangely fitting match, but Jacobi had a well-documented preference for the dim witted. His date for the evening sat on the other side of him. Her blonde hair almost matched his own for paleness and her dress was little more than a sheer slip. The amount of flesh she showed indicated her district of birth, probably the Main nearest the Low. In the High, showing too much skin became boring decades ago. Jacobi liked his lovers to be from the Main so that their families would not fret over his mistreatment of them.

Was Jacobi mistreating Grayc? Panic rose in his chest almost as quickly as it faded. No. Not Grayc Illan. He couldn't imagine anyone harming her and walking away unscathed.

Had he really only slept for a month? How could the Realm change so much, that nobles would dine with a servant as their equal, leaning in to hear her gossip?

Why hadn't he dined with her when he had the chance?

The first course came, and then the second, third, fourth, and fifth. The trail of pastries, flowers, soups, and fruit went on for what seemed an eternity and he could only stumble through conversation with the guests around him while watching Grayc Illan. She was suddenly a stranger. The way she moved, the way she held herself, the way she ate. Had he ever seen her eat before? At one point in the evening, Jacobi turned his attention away from his date to stretch an arm over the back of Grayc Illan's chair. He leaned into her and picked at her cake with his fork. He whispered and Vaun would have given anything to know what he said that made her laugh like that before she parted her lips and ate the bite he offered her.

Jacobi caught his gaze across the room, held it, and smiled at Vaun's misery.

"Vaun," AviSariel spoke softly at his side. "You've eaten nothing tonight."

He looked down at his plate and then up at his wife. "Am I dreaming still?" he asked so frankly that she could only blink in confusion. He turned his eyes away from her again. "I must have slept years rather than weeks."

Her hand laid over his. "Are you feeling unwell?"

He pulled away and picked up his fork, eating the sickly sweet cake until it was nothing but blueberry flavored crumbs and smears of rosewater frosting. The flavor left in his mouth reminded him of his shower water: sweet and chemical.

His gaze sought Grayc Illan again just in time to see her stand from her seat. Jacobi rose as well, exchanging a few more words with her before Grayc said goodbye to the rest of the table and left. Vaun couldn't help but stand. Before anyone else could ask if he was unwell, he left the table and wove through the busy room. He kept his gaze fixed on Grayc Illan's curls and when she slipped from the banquet hall into the foyer, his steps quickened.

"Grayc!" Her name leaped from his mouth as he burst into the nearly empty lobby after her.

She stopped, and from the moment of hesitation before she turned, he realized she had known he would follow and had hoped to escape. She stared at him before scanning the lobby again, probably seeking a maid to fetch her coat.

"What is going on?" His footfalls echoed as he advanced.

She stared at him so blankly he wondered if he'd somehow mistaken another woman for his valet, or simply gone mad.

"You will have to be more specific, your highness," she said.

No, there was no mistaking her voice or the cut of her words. This was his Grayc. "Enough of this. What are you doing here with Jacobi? Why is there a stranger in my house calling himself your replacement?"

Her gaze softened momentarily. "Samuel Sinol is your valet now. I picked him myself. He will serve you well." Her head dipped after a moment. "If you'll excuse me, your highness."

She turned on her heel.

"You are not excused!" Vaun snapped.

"Go back to your dinner," she called over her shoulder.

"You are my valet. I did not agree to a replacement." He followed her through a door and into a crowded room of hangers and fabric. "I heard Fay fired you. I want you to come back. She can't fire my employees. She—"

Grayc Illan laughed and turned away from him, her fingers hovering over the pages of a book on a desk among coats to find her name and the number to her garment. "I was never your employee, your highness." Her smile dwindled as she looked up at him. "But Samuel Sinol is. I hired him to be loyal to you, and only you."

The musky, narrow room warmed his skin and he resisted the urge to tug at the buttons of his jacket. "Who are you loyal to?"

She stared at him for a long moment before returning her attention to the book. "Go back to the party. I don't take care of you anymore."

Dread tightened his skin and weighed in the pit of his stomach. "Is it because of the duel? Did Fay say something to—"

"The princess didn't fire me. I left." Grayc Illan moved along the racks of coats until she found her own. "I am not Jacobi's valet. I'm his partner. I'm helping him run his businesses."

Vaun stared at her, stricken for a moment. She had left him for a better position?

She tugged her coat from the hanger and folded it over her arm. "It is time to let me go, prince."

"This is a lie." He blocked her escape. "This... It isn't true."

"What isn't?"

"I wasn't just a job. I—"

"I cleaned up after you, Vaun!" Her voice cracked with emotion. "I spent more than seventy years following you around. The same teahouses, the same parties, the same scandals and lovers. Did you think I would spend my whole life handing you towels and bringing you the paper? I hated it."

"You didn't." He yanked her back when she tried to shove past him. She tried again, mouth set, and he pushed harder, tumbling her into a wall of coats. Terror made it hard to breathe, though he couldn't understand why. Yes, of course, he thought she would be there forever to take care of him. For nearly as long as he could remember she had been there, the only one that cared for him. She could leave him for a new job, a better job, but this couldn't be why. She couldn't hate working for him. She couldn't hate him. She couldn't, because he couldn't bear that.

"Liar," the prince whispered angrily, tears in his eyes. "You lie all the time but I won't be tricked by you. You don't want to be at that table. You hate this house. You hate Jacobi." His lips curled into a snarl as he came toward her, pushing her back against the lumpy wall of clothing and hangers just as she straightened. He rubbed his hand over her arm, looking at the fine magic that colored her skin in silver dust. "This isn't you. This magic. This dress."

Her hands shoved at his chest but he wouldn't back away enough to let her stand upright fully. "What do you know of it? What do you know about me?" Her voice broke around the last words.

He grabbed the side of her neck so that he could force her jaw up and rub his thumb along those red painted lips, the ones he hadn't been able to take his eyes off of all night. They smeared, not magic but real color, rubbing off on his thumb against the corner of her mouth. "This. I know that this was you." He watched her eyes for some hint of confirmation, but true to her nature they gave nothing away. He nodded as though she had agreed. "You picked this color. The rest is a lie."

Her mouth trembled against his thumb and he knew she was about to speak again, to lie again, so he smothered her words. He sealed her lips with his, delving his tongue in before she could close them. She tasted like the wine she'd been drinking. He took everything he could from that kiss, certain that she would push him away at any moment, but the moment never came.

Her tongue moved boldly to shove back at his and her hands curled in the front of his jacket. Vaun pushed her harder into the coats with a desire more forceful than any he had ever known. How had he spent decades so close to her without touching her? He couldn't imagine letting go. His hips ground into hers until one of her legs curled up against his side.

His fingers dug into the flesh of her thigh beneath her skirt, clawing at the top of her stocking and pulling her leg higher until she teetered on the toe of her other shoe for balance. His hand caressed the underside of her thigh before sliding down to meet the warm mound of her panties. She moaned and the sound rolled through him like a wave of heat.

Grabbing her other thigh, he lifted the only leg she had left to stand on and toppled them both down the wall and onto a pile of rumpled coats. She dragged in short breaths, her lips swollen and stained in that vivid red. Her hair mashed against the still hanging garments behind her, her skirt pooled around her hips and her eyes hazy with passion. Her fingers pulled the buttons of his slacks open while he kissed her. The flavor of wine was gone and all that remained was the taste of her.

He pulled her panties to one side before pushing her up against the wall with the force of his hips. She cried out and arched in what little space she had. He held her thighs as he moved, his knees digging into the floor. Mesmerized, he watched her arms stretch up, trying to find something to hold onto but only dragging more coats down around them.

It was the most honest he had ever seen her and the most certain he had ever been about her. She clung to his shoulders when the wall offered nothing stable. Her fingers flexed against his muscles when she neared her end. Her hips rocked up into his and her ragged breath quickened into sharp gasps before she finally shuddered beneath him.

He held her tighter when he followed and then stayed there, hips joined and bodies leaned against the base of the wall until their breath evened again. He stayed another few minutes just to keep her there, her heartbeat loud beneath him and her face leaned comfortably into the curve of his neck.

"Vaun..." she murmured regretfully against his skin. He nodded and pulled away from her, standing and taking one more look at her before she pushed her clothing back into place and crawled to her feet.

"No more lies," the prince said as he began putting himself back together. She sighed and was about to protest when he continued. "No. Do what you have to do. Keep your secrets. Play your game. Say nothing at all, if you must, but stop lying to me."

Grayc blinked, stunned, before finally nodding her agreement.

He kissed her again and tugged the little ribbon from around her neck. "I liked this," he said, casually tucking it into his pocket. "I wouldn't be surprised if it became the latest fashion." He walked away before she could say or do anything that might ruin the strange sense of peace between them.

He was still rubbing the red of her lips from his own when he walked back out into the lobby, his collar askew, his tie a disaster and his shirt untucked and wrinkled under his open jacket. A little gasp brought him to a stop, his shoes scuffing the polished floor. His eyes moved from the color on his thumb to the woman standing on the other side of the hall. Her blue eyes swam with tears and her features were stricken by an emotion he did not recognize. He watched AviSariel's bottom lip quiver and wondered if she planned to cry. No, it wasn't a plan. All at once, Vaun realized that those tears were not a plot or an aesthetic choice. The tremble of her lips were true, like the blush he had seen color her cheeks and the embarrassment that he had enjoyed putting in her eyes.

That perplexing expression that coiled in her smooth features now was the reflection of some pain he had caused her. She was trying not to cry. He could see it by the way her shoulders tensed and her mouth scrunched. It hurt to look at, and though he knew there should have been a better choice of action, Vaun walked past her and back to the banquet hall. He heard her breath hitch behind him and a small, smothered cry. He didn't understand her pain but, for the first time, he wished that it would go away.

CHAPTER SEVEN

Vaun watched Grayc slip from his sheets when she thought he was asleep. If possible, she appeared even more comfortable in her bare skin than she had in her clothes. Strange, because that skin seemed so much more intimate than any other he'd seen. She was riddled in scars, some tiny and thin, invisible to the touch and only seen under great scrutiny, while others were the puffy, glaring remains of cigarette burns and gashes.

The arch of the bathroom outlined her where she stopped, pressing her palms into the cold edge of the marble countertop. She leaned in, staring into her own green eyes. Her ringlets, messy from his mattress, pushed forward against her smoothly rounded cheeks. No matter how much tea Vaun drank, he would never forget that mouth, parting just slightly, drawing a breath as though to speak.

A conversation was taking place in her eyes and he heard none of it. She stared at a stranger in that mirror. His secretive valet. His liar. His Grayc.

Tension gathered between her shoulders the moment she realized he watched her. She didn't turn her head, gaze locked on her own reflection.

"You have never met me," Grayc Illan whispered, words biting with bitterness. "But someday you will."

It was a strange sort of promise and he had said nothing after it, watching her dress and leave in silence.

Sitting in the car now, slipping from Belholn into Vym, Vaun realized just how long it had been since he had lived without her.

"Vaun?" AviSariel said timidly.

He stared out the window rather than at her directly and found himself wishing he did not hate her as much as he did. He would not admit it, but AviSariel's awkward honesty, her very inability to lie, intrigued him. He could ask her a hundred questions, if only his pride would let him show interest in a wife he'd never wanted. As odd and sad as she might be, she was still a shackle put on him by the Queen.

"What?"

She hesitated and he closed his eyes to the streets moving outside his window to stifle his annoyance. How had such weakness survived so long in the Realm? How had *she* survived so long in the Realm?

"How long will we be gone from Belholn?"

If she had been anyone else, the question would have been a jab at his raw heart. "A year. Six months in each province." That was the rotation of his residences. He had never minded before but Grayc had always gone with him then. Now she was business partners with a Belholn and trapped in that province like the rest.

"Will you still be seeing Grayc Illan?"

His eyes opened at that name on AviSariel's tongue, slanting toward her from the corner of silver lined lids. "Why?"

Her cheeks flushed and she glanced away.

"Whoever I see, princess, it will not be you," he said, keeping his tone soft to make the words honest but not cruel. He didn't understand why it hurt her so much that he spent time with Grayc. Was it because she was from the Low? Or would his wife dislike all of his lovers the same?

Silence hung between them until, to his own surprise, Vaun broke it. "What do you want, AviSariel?"

She blinked and looked down at her lap until he realized that not even she knew.

"You should find a lover," he said.

AviSariel frowned at her hands. "So I have been told."

"We're staying at the Vym family house tonight." He turned his attention out the window again. He rarely offered her much in the way of explanations; such implied too much care and skated too close to help. But he didn't want to see her flounder anymore. He didn't want her to watch him as she did, hopeful and sad. He wanted... He wasn't sure. But surely there was something better for her, for him, than this. Surely there was something better for the Realm.

The gap between High and Low was vast and yet filled only by the Main, home to their staff and merchants. Every day he read about riots and deaths in the Low, wedged into the back pages of the paper to fill up space and offer the High born something to preoccupy their eyes with while sipping morning coffee. Had it always been so grim? Had he ever bothered to read those pages before, or had he simply forgotten?

At least half of his friends regularly forgot the bulk of their days, memories swallowed up by too much dust. A sparse few of them developed those little tattoos on their skin, like the ones Ollan displayed before she died. Vaun considered a connection between the bad dust plaguing the Low and Main districts and the appearance of the tattoos, but after careful observation of marked friends, found none. The weight of his city pressed back his shoulders. No connection implied there was more wrong with the Realm than bad dust, and he was tripping over more and more of it every day. He had no time to spare for an awkward wife. He could not bear her weight along with the rest.

"At Fay's home?" AviSariel brightened. "She didn't say. Is that custom? We... I mean, you do have a residence in Vym."

"It's tradition." Vaun watched a happy smile hover around his wife's lips. How much of it stemmed from his conversation, and how much from relief at entering a friend's home? His wife and sister enjoyed brunch regularly, but rarely away from his residence. "Since Quentan married my sister, I stay my first night in Vym Province at their home."

"It is a gracious gesture." Her chin tipped. "Thank you. For telling me."

A chill tickled his spine. He'd never considered staying at a Lord's residence any kind of gesture, but that AviSariel saw the politics behind it so easily, if innocently, raised the hair on the back of his neck.

Vaun chanced a glance at his wife. He didn't know her. Not really. Not at all. He'd worked hard not to. In the beginning, he thought her a part of a grand scheme hatched by the Queen. He was still quite certain that she was, because there was no other reason but scheming to explain why his mother would have him marry a woman no one knew. But he was almost as equally certain now that AviSariel didn't know what that scheme was. She would have to be the most cunning, deceptive, wicked creature Vaun had ever encountered, and it seemed more likely that she was the most innocent, simple, unprepared citizen of the Realm. Not knowing which, he found himself unsure how to handle her. If the latter, he could help. If the former, he didn't dare.

When they reached the estate nestled at the top of the High, they stepped out of the car.

Vaun walked his wife up the stairs, questions and conversation starters on the tip of his tongue, but uncertainty made him bite them back.

He had always felt that the Vym house was much like his sister: quiet, relatively dignified, and packed to the brim with unspoken hostility. With vaulted ceilings, dauntingly large chandeliers, and tall, cut glass windows letting in only the colors of light from outside, every room was an architectural masterpiece.

Fay waited in the dining room, seated at a table of small pastries and wine, speaking to a petite girl with pale blonde hair that looked strikingly like a doll. She welcomed Vaun and AviSariel with a nod, while the girl grinned brilliantly. Something about the spread of her lips and the gleam of her teeth reminded of Addom, and Vaun realized she must be little Larc, the youngest of the Vym siblings. He only saw her once a year at these dinners, and though she had a prettiness about her, she wasn't particularly memorable.

"AviSariel," Fay said as the maid filled glasses for the new guests, "this is Larc. I don't believe you have met."

The girl continued smiling, though the longer Vaun looked at her, the less childish she seemed. Despite being dressed and painted like a doll, the fine structure of her cheeks beneath the pink dusting of rouge and the fullness of her lips said otherwise. Vaun reminded himself that little Larc could not be younger than eighty, since Wendry held the title of the last High born child.

"It's a pleasure to meet you," AviSariel said as she sat. "How have we not met before?"

"Larc is practically a captive," Vaun answered casually. He grabbed the maid's wrist before she could slip away and quietly requested a pot of tea. Even if he had been restricting his dust intake of late to keep his wits about him, he liked to play his part all the same. So far, no one seemed to notice that he only pretended to sip.

Larc giggled and shook her head. "Not at all. I simply appreciate the comfort of my home." She leaned toward AviSariel. "Wasn't it dreadful in Belholn? I read such awful things in the paper. Just yesterday there was another riot. This one in the Main."

"More dust problems, it seems." Fay sipped her wine, the glow of the chandelier above making the glass sparkle in her hand.

Larc bobbed her blonde head in agreement. "Handfuls dead. The wolves were sent out to snatch their souls." She shuddered visibly at the drama of it all, holding her wineglass in both hands. "I suppose it was the only way to stop the killings." Her head tipped toward Vaun, eyes bright. "Did you not hear the wolves?"

The prince smiled back. "Little Larc, I fear not even the howling of wolves can compete with the sounds of my bedroom at night."

She flushed prettily and for a moment he was certain her eyes shone with want rather than embarrassment. Vaun could not decide whether to be enticed or alarmed. Childlike dress-up did not excite him and she boasted a true excess of frills, an empire waist, and if he peeked under the table he was sure to see her feet kicking back and forth in flats and white socks.

"Really, Vaun," Addom said as he entered the dining hall behind Quentan. "You should mind your tongue around our sisters. They have such fragile sensibilities."

Vaun laughed and stood to greet Quentan before the Lord took his seat across from Fay. Vaun applauded the man's forethought: he found it best to keep his sister within eyesight, too. One did not want to lose track of Fay Dray Fen. "Perhaps yours, Addom, but surely not mine."

Quentan shared his brother's smile but none of his mirth. Despite their similar height, build, and coloring, no one would ever mistake one man for the other, not even from behind, not even if they used the same impeccable tailor. Addom possessed a carefree, dangerous wonder about him, while Quentan exhibited nothing but polished calculation. Vaun considered him the worst sort of thoughtful: the greedy kind, with no aim for pleasure. Addom often said his brother was his own worst enemy, and Vaun couldn't help but agree. Not for the first time, he wondered what his mother had hoped to achieve in matching Fay with Quentan. Or was all that meddling just to ensure Fay's misery?

"And where is your twin?" Vaun grinned at Addom. "Surely Evelet would not be considered fragile, either."

Quentan huffed in agreement, a less than approving sound.

"Running late." Fay signaled the staff to bring out the first course. No one had bothered with the pretty tiers of pastel madeleines half-dipped in white chocolate that occupied the middle of the table because Fay had made no move for them herself. It was impossible to know if foods already served were for consumption or decoration unless the host gave direction.

Larc leaned over to AviSariel, seated conveniently at the small woman's side. "My sister has grown terribly scandalous as of late. She's even talked about opening a *business*." She whispered the last word with a pointed gasp.

The princess blinked back politely, setting her glass down. "What sort of business?"

Little Larc giggled and almost looked the age she was dressed to play. "Does it matter? Can you imagine, behaving like a merchant?"

AviSariel's smile strained, though Vaun couldn't be sure why. "I suppose not," she said quietly.

The serving staff emerged in one long procession, the last of which carried a small pot of tea, a cup and a saucer, that he placed beside Vaun's shallow bowl of spray roses. The pink, orange, and teal buds clipped from their stems and then delicately reattached to the nest of green vines gave it a lively look. Vaun did not miss the large thorns on those stems, sinister black tips warning him not to touch his own food. He took up the glass chopsticks above his plate while AviSariel complimented Fay on the beautiful food. Fay managed to tilt her head to the side and accept the flattery, though he knew for a fact that she hated pretending to have had a hand in any form of labor that didn't draw blood. He had seen her throw out close friends for the offense. Why did she care about AviSariel's feelings? Was it misplaced sympathy? Did she see them as being kindred, both forced to marry? Where was his sympathy? He popped a teal rosebud in his mouth. It was sweet.

"I've been wanting to ask, princess—" Quentan leaned into the high back of his chair and turned his chin down the table. "—which province does your family come from?"

Addom laughed darkly over the brim of his glass. "Trying to find us another connection to the Queen, brother? Isn't marrying one princess enough? Now you wish the other to be our cousin?"

Vaun poured his tea. He had given his valet, Samuel Sinol, the task of finding out where AviSariel had come from and who her relations were more than a week ago. He had not found anything.

"Are you our cousin?" Larc chirped.

"Don't be dim, dear," Fay said coldly before decidedly changing the topic—it was her table, after all. "Vaun, I found a new valet for you."

He plucked another rosebud, an orange one, from the nest in front of him. This one tasted sweet as well, but with a hint of acidity and a tart afternote. "Is that so?" The table went quiet.

"She worked for the Danors before she came to work for us. A delightful girl. Very professional," Fay continued and he looked up just in time to see that the red rosebuds from her salad were the exact same shade as her lips. A quick survey of the table turned up no other red buds but for the few on her plate. He wondered if she even noticed. It was terribly common for her staff to fall in love with her. Fay had been enjoying special treatment even among the most important residents of the Realm for so long that "special" had become nothing special at all.

"Funny. Didn't Grayc work for you, as well, before she came to me?" the prince replied, though nothing about his tone led the others at the table to believe that it was the least bit humorous. "After she worked for the Belholns, that is, and before she spontaneously appeared in my employ." Careful digging the past few weeks had led him to interesting tidbits of knowledge. "To think, all this time I thought she belonged to the Queen."

Fay's cheek twitched, ever so faintly but with endless fury. "You will like this one."

"I liked the last one."

"She is better qualified."

"Was Grayc underqualified? She's practically a lady of Belholn now."

Fay's chopsticks clattered against her bowl. "She is the whore of a Low bred, dust peddling, Belholn bastard. That is all."

Larc gave a prompt little gasp, though Vaun suspected she sounded more elated than offended.

"I did not know you had such contempt for the Belholns, sister. On my last visit to the family, I heard you used to frequent their home. They paint quite an interesting picture of you."

Something struck that porcelain mask he'd always known as her face. Was that shock or pain? More importantly, from the corner of his eye, Vaun saw Quentan's fingers flex against his glass.

Vaun couldn't help but smile. He was going to sit down with Killian for tea someday soon.

A strange sort of quiet settled over the table.

Silent servants looked on, lining the wall in Vaun's view over the brim of his teacup. He almost took a real gulp when he noticed the oil painting of Fay hung behind them. A thick, gold painted frame tried and failed to contain the princess. For such a slight woman, she was daunting in all her depictions. He imagined the artist struggling with her eyes, repainting them again and again in a desperate attempt to get them right. No one ever did. A thousand paintings, sketches and sculptures of Fay Dray Fen adorned the homes of the High but her eyes were always wrong. In the end, they often painted her looking away, because none could capture even a fraction of the true weight of her gaze.

Just when the silence almost felt normal again Fay said, "I'll send your new valet to your house."

Addom took a quick drink of his wine to stifle a laugh.

"I have a valet," Vaun replied simply. "I think his name is Samson. Stanton. Something."

"Samuel Sinol," AviSariel said softly.

"Yes, of course." He grinned at his wife. "Samuel Sinol. Lovely fellow."

Fay stared at him with the full, unnerving force of her gaze. "He has no qualifications for the position."

"What qualifications does the man need to pick up my bath towels and retrieve me in the mornings?"

"You will like this one more," she persisted and Vaun found that she reminded him of one of his childhood governesses, dismissing his will on account of her own. The valet was likely a spy, though why she wanted to spy on him he did not know. Surely she could read the paper like the rest of the Realm.

"I like my own valet well enough." He smirked across the table at Larc; her eyes were impossibly large. Was that some sort of illusion or a trick of her makeup? "He has a good mouth." He watched her eyes widen before she tore them away to stare at her plate. He would have loved to see whatever imagery was playing across her thoughts, pulling her lips into that strange little smile.

Fay inhaled, lips thin; Evelet entered the dining hall before his sister could speak. The doors swept open and the Vym daughter pranced in, giggling with the woman on her arm and stealing the attention of the room.

Larc gasped again; it seemed to be her signature sound.

Evelet wore a suit, with her hair black, short, and slicked back. Vaun noted the suit only because it was cut for a man and not at all properly fitted to her waist or bust. As she neared the table, Vaun could see the cuffs of her slacks had been rolled up several times and a pair of polished leather dress shoes peeked out from beneath, scuffing the floor with every step. The outfit was a curious choice that had several brows at the table scrunching. The tailors of the Realm had perfected women's suits decades ago and, aside from that, Vaun was almost certain that he had never seen Evelet wear pants before.

The thought struck him that the suit might not be hers, but possibly taken from a lover's closet, and with that the overall look became captivating.

Reluctantly, his gaze slid to the woman clutching at Evelet's arm.

It was a shock that he hadn't noticed her first; it was a rare event in which someone stole attention from Meresin. The redhead whispered in the Vym woman's ear, calm as ever, even when waltzing deeper into a house that had never permitted her entrance before.

Quentan Vym's glass settled on the table with a heavy sound that inadvertently drew the prince's eye. He rarely saw the Lord of Vym angry, though he rarely saw Quentan at all. He considered himself far too serious, with far more important things to do than attend parties, lounge into the wee hours of the morning, and wake in strangers' beds. What those better things were, Vaun did not want to know.

Larc pressed fingers to her lips in a failed attempt to contain her bubbling excitement. Evelet pretended not to notice as she drew a chair out for her date before taking her own as gracelessly as possible. "My apologies for our tardiness," she chimed, perfectly managing never to catch her eldest brother's glare, turning her attention instead to the prince across the table. "Good evening, your highness. How does it feel to return once again to the *great* province of Vym?"

"Evelet…" Quentan warned.

Vaun smiled at the two newcomers. "Increasingly interesting, I must say." The prince eyed Evelet's oversized coat. "That is lovely tailoring. I could swear that I've seen it before."

She shrugged a somewhat drowning shoulder. "You don't wear corsets and stockings, so why should I?"

Vaun smiled wider. "You never asked me to wear a corset and stockings."

"I suppose I haven't," Evelet conceded with a dangerous grin. "Another time, perhaps? You can borrow some of mine."

"I have never been invited to play dress up before, but I promise, you may dress me in anything you like," Vaun offered whole-heartedly. A miserable little huff from his wife surprised him. He raised an eyebrow at her and supposed she would, indeed, dislike all of his lovers. Perhaps she understood even less about the Realm than he realized. When she learned more, she would find herself disliking all of his friends, too.

"You may toy with the prince at your leisure, sister." Quentan rose to his feet. "But not at my table and not—" his gaze flickered to Meresin "—with that. Do not try me further."

Larc's humor drained as discomfort settled over the table, her large eyes shifting anxiously from her plate to Quentan. Timidly, she touched her sister's hand. "Evy, perhaps the joke has gone far enough."

Evelet looked appropriately confused before laughing. "Darling, she's a prostitute, not a prop."

Addom coughed into his tea—Vaun's tea, really, since he'd managed to steal the prince's cup.

"The men of this family enjoy her company. Why shouldn't I?" Evelet knocked back her wine and cast her gaze upon Quentan, at last. "I must admit, I wasn't sure what all the fuss was about until she—"

"Enough," Fay snapped. "Just because you and Addom see fit to make shameful fools of yourselves does not mean you can do it at our table."

Evelet's brow pinched. "So, we can sleep with her, but we can't eat with her? If even the great Quentan Vym can climb off his high horse for an hour or two of crawling in her sheets, why shouldn't the rest of us?"

Addom stopped laughing. Fay's head snapped back. Meresin's fingers tightened around her glass, and her gaze moved up the table to the Lord of Vym as though trying to deliver a silent message. Vaun couldn't be sure whether it was a plea or a threat.

Larc tried to laugh and the sound made the table even colder. "You must be mistaken, Evy. You know how our brother feels about the Low, as well as the Main."

"And yet there he was last week, walking out of her townhouse." Evelet smirked as she picked up her glass, filling it from a pitcher of wine on the table. "I was personally quite relieved to see that you've finally dropped this whole pretense of propriety, brother. It's become a little stifling."

Quentan's shoulders pressed back until Vaun thought they would snap. He expected the Vym Lord to fly right over the table at Evelet, but before those tightly wound muscles could launch the man into action, Fay stood. She moved decisively closer to Evelet's end of the table. Was she putting herself between them?

"Evelet—" Quentan began, voice ground out between clenched teeth.

"No, no," Evelet interrupted with a sigh as she stood, hands raised in a show of defeat. "We'll leave." She turned to the redhead at her side, holding out a hand and waiting for Meresin to stand and take it. "Enjoy your dinner."

Evelet led her date away from the table. The sound of their steps echoed, harsh little claps against hardwood that drifted further away, carrying the stress of the room with them. Someone sighed when they left the dining room, though Vaun couldn't be sure who. The sound jolted Quentan into motion.

His chair fell back completely as he stormed from the table. Fay called after him, then followed when he didn't stop. Tears spilled from Larc's eyes. After a moment, Vaun hurried after his sister. He couldn't be sure whether it was his own curiosity that drove him to the foyer, or actual worry. Either way, he skidded to a stop in the entry as the Lord of Vym shoved Meresin out the front door before snatching his own sister by the arm. He yanked her inside and slammed the entrance shut before spinning her into a wall.

"I warned you about shaming the family," he snarled.

"Quentan. We have company," Fay reminded, voice strange. For the first time that Vaun had ever heard, she sounded like no one was listening to her. He knew instantly that he didn't like it.

Evelet took a moment to absorb the sudden change before rolling her shoulder against the surface, leaning against it as she stared up at Quentan. She smirked. "Wouldn't want to cause a scene."

The back of his curled knuckles collided with her cheek, sending her to the floor.

Vaun heard Addom curse, but when he looked back at the dining room, his friend remained at the table, staring blindly at his plate. He shook, but didn't stand or turn his head to see what he surely knew was happening in the hallway. Larc fled through the kitchen to some safe place where no one would follow. AviSariel rose and crossed the dining room to join Vaun. He stared at her for a moment, at the tears gathered in her eyes as she looked past him, lips drawn in horror.

Another sound of violence and the expulsion of air from Evelet's lungs drew the prince's attention into the hallway again. Quentan drove his boot into his sister's gut while she huddled on the floor, rolling her hard into the wall. She wheezed and stared up at the ceiling.

"You brought a whore into my house? Into our mother's house?" The Lord of Vym seethed, taking a step back and dragging his fingers through his hair, giving her time to claw at the wall and sit herself upright.

Blood dribbled from her mouth and with one oversized sleeve she rubbed it away. "When will you accept it, Quen?" she rasped, her bold lips pulled into a wild grin with blood painting her teeth. "It is a scandalous Realm and we are scandalous people."

Quentan roared as though his anger was trying to crawl up out of his chest. His hand knotted in Evelet's finger-length hair and yanked her up, ramming the knuckles of his free hand into her face.

AviSariel began to cry. Vaun could hear it in the shudder of her breath at his side. She clutched at his sleeve. "Do something," she begged in a whisper.

Her tone unsettled him. What did she have to fear? Not even the Lord of Vym would dare strike a princess of the Realm. Whatever her awkwardness, AviSariel outranked nearly everyone in the Realm, even Quentan. Evelet, on the other hand, was the Lord's family and therefore his subject.

"Vaun, please." AviSariel strained forward, and then he understood. She didn't fear for herself. She feared for another.

Why should this be acceptable, simply because Quentan had been born to a title that made him head of his household, his district, and his province? Why should Quentan's will be the will of Vym, just as the Queen's will was the will of the Realm? Why should he rule over others?

Fay stepped back, turning her sharp chin away from the scene and setting an exasperated hand at her waist. Vaun's shoulders knotted at her silence. Was this so normal in their house that she had stopped getting in the way of it?

Behind him, Addom's tension coiled, misery and helplessness raging in his silence. No words of his could save his sister because he was a son of Vym, and not the Lord of it.

Vaun was not the Lord of anything. He was a prince, and, for the first time, that meant more than getting the best tables and finest suits. "Enough," Vaun said, stern, but not loud enough to be heard over the sounds of knuckles pummeling flesh. His lips twisted with a snarl and he left the doorway, crossing the stretch of open hallway.

"Enough," the prince said again, no louder than before, but this time Quentan Vym sucked in a sharp breath of surprise and jerked away from the sound in his ear. His breath rasped, staggered by the exertion of his own brutality. His nostrils flared and his fingers remained coiled into bloody fists. Vaun watched him struggle to contain some part of himself, pressing those fists into the sides of his slacks to keep from swinging them.

"Vaun," Fay said, voice still tired but the command of it never fully lost. "Return to the table and I'll send for some fresh tea."

He tried not to sneer at her dismissal. Once, an offer of tea had been more than enough to turn his attention away. "I think I have had enough tea."

Something clicked inside the moment he said it; never, in all his life, had he ever had *enough*. Today, he'd had his fill.

Samuel Sinol materialized from wherever it was that valets went when not being of assistance and handed AviSariel his handkerchief.

"Help lady Vym up, would you, Samson?" Vaun said in his coldest of polite tones. Not even AviSariel corrected him on his valet's name.

Quentan struggled not to curl his lip in a snarl. "My apologies for the display, your highness, but this is a family matter and—"

"Are we not family?" Vaun stepped closer, more out of curiosity to see if the Lord would back up than to give his valet room to help a vaguely conscious Evelet to her feet. "You married my sister, didn't you?" The prince grinned as an idea struck him. "That is what we'll do. We'll trade. You took my sister, and now I will take yours."

Vaun watched Quentan's fist flex, twisting tighter. Would the man hit him? Had the ruling Lord of a province ever struck a prince? Vaun racked his memories. Though a great number of knuckles had acquainted themselves with the fine bone structure of his royal cheek, never had they been the knuckles of a Lord. He leaned in, daring Quentan to be the first.

"Vaun, that's enough." Fay tried to wave him away, using the low, irritated tone he hated. "Why don't you take AviSariel upstairs to your rooms while we get things settled here?" She hissed at his valet when Samuel Sinol began dragging a semi-conscious Evelet toward the front door while trying valiantly not to get blood on his jacket. "Take her upstairs, man."

Vaun opened his mouth to counter her command but, to his surprise as well as his sister's, Samuel Sinol's steps did not falter. He dipped his head respectfully to Fay while audaciously ignoring her directions.

"*He will serve you, and only you,*" Grayc had said. Until this moment, Vaun hadn't understood the difference.

"Are you going to deny a prince, Quen?" Vaun's lips twisted around the familial nickname. When the man said nothing, the prince pushed past, strolling toward the door, though not so quickly as to help with Evelet. She really had made a mess of his valet's suit and he couldn't bear to see his own suffer a similar fate.

He stopped when he remembered his wife and turned to see her still standing in the doorway of the dining hall. Her hands hovered somewhere between her chin and her chest, frozen in shock. He extended an arm and gestured her to follow him. She stared at him with some emotion he couldn't place before she hurried to him, taking his hand, though he'd never really meant to offer it.

"Vaun!" Fay snapped.

"Another time, Lady Vym," the prince said over his shoulder before walking his wife out of the house, careful not to step on the globs of blood speckling the ground on their way to the car.

The weight of what he had done didn't strike him until they were more than a handful of blocks away. Fay wasn't going to let him hear the end of this for years, and the Queen only knew how long Quentan Vym would be sour. He seemed like the sort of man who would hold a grudge.

Vaun sighed and made to scrub his hand over his face when he realized AviSariel still clutched his palm, her fingers entwined with his. She stared at Evelet across from her but held onto his hand in her lap, clinging to it as though precious.

An old, childish part of him wanted to yank it away from her, wanted to despise her the way he had. But slow pride bloomed in his chest, and he found he didn't have the heart to be cruel to her tonight.

Vaun turned his attention out the window to the streets moving past and left his hand in the warmth of hers.

Vaun pretended to slouch downstairs to breakfast. The fact that all of his residences, regardless of province, shared a similar floorplan allowed him to keep his eyes half-lidded. Evelet and AviSariel glanced up as he slumped into a chair.

"Good morning," AviSariel chimed, fresh faced.

"Did Addom leave already?" Vaun smirked at Evelet. "Or shall I have coffee sent to your room?"

The Vym hesitated before picking up another pastry. By now, only the faintest shadow marked her cheek. Vaun could hardly remember the way her skin had puffed out around her eye, bulging and pressing the lids shut, or how her flesh had split along one of those finely ridged cheekbones.

"I wouldn't know." Evelet shrugged. "Did you have him over?"

How long had she taken up residence in his house? A few weeks? It may as well have been a year. In those first days when she was healing and heavily dusted, he had been able to get a few interesting bits of gossip out of Evelet. As it turned out, Quentan had always had quite the temper and was the sole driving force behind their family's obsession with looking appropriate for the public. She insisted that she really had seen him at Meresin's house but that Meresin, true to form, would not confirm any such meeting.

In those dusted days, Evelet had told him all sorts of rambling, useless stories about her family. But as soon as her skin healed and she went back to a more respectable amount of tea, she dodged all intimate questions and pretended expertly that she had only moved in with the prince because the invitation had been so tempting.

"I could swear I saw Addom here last night." Vaun tried not to scowl as a maid set his old foe, morning coffee, before him. All of his drinks were becoming enemies. Coffee for its bitterness and tea for its dust. In an attempt to avoid the stupor of dusting or the chance of another bout of madness, Vaun had taken to sipping slowly, sometimes only for pretend, and only taking tea in the High.

Since he could get no more gossip from Evelet about her family, and wasn't willing to send her home just yet, Vaun took to having the staff restrict her dust intake. He hadn't told her, of course, but he was having her tea served with almost no dust and her cigarettes replaced with a lighter, cheaper, version. He was almost certain she had noticed on the first day, giving him an odd look through the veil of smoke, but she said nothing about it.

It had only been a few days now and already she was sharper, less forgetful and more aware.

If she did remember anything interesting and long since forgotten, as he had, she wasn't sharing. Leave it to a prince to waste his experiments on tight lipped Vyms.

The raven haired woman laughed before taking a delicate spoonful of her custard and strawberry trifle, a flaky maple croissant in her other hand. "I do suspect your mind is beginning to slip. You had only the Dourdin sisters, Mr. LeTorn, and myself in your bed last night." She lifted her cup, eyes skimming over the lip toward AviSariel. "Unless your wife had him over. Avi, dear, have you finally found someone to be your bedmate?"

The princess choked on her coffee.

Evelet grinned, looking viciously similar to her twin. "No? Then what is it you do with all your time, dear?"

AviSariel dabbed her napkin to her lips, her cheeks warming with a mixture of anger and humiliation. "I... I..." She stumbled for a suitable retort but took too long for the Vym's tongue to wait.

"Does it bother you that I've slept with your husband and you still haven't?"

Vaun lifted his gaze from his half-conquered coffee to see tears welling up in his wife's eyes and the red of her cheeks spreading down to her neck. He sighed notably and turned his attention on Evelet. "You do realize that Avi can throw you out whenever she likes, don't you?"

AviSariel and Evelet blinked equally stunned eyes at him. He had hoped that exposure to a Vym would thicken AviSariel's skin and sharpen her tongue, but it only made him feel like a bully. "It's her house, Evelet. Tread carefully, or you might have to find new patronage."

Evelet's mouth gaped, half-eaten croissant forgotten on her plate.

AviSariel blinked away her tears, seemingly mute at the very possibility of her own power.

Before she could look at him with those doe eyes, Vaun stood. "I have an appointment." He left his coffee unfinished on the grounds of storming out, rather than because it was too disgusting to finish. Sometimes, he really did enjoy having bad company at his breakfast table, if only for the excuse to leave early.

Her house. The words resounded in AviSariel's mind as Vaun vanished into the hall. Not his. Not theirs. *Hers.* And she could put this woman, a favored daughter of Vym, out of it.

Did he mean it? Biting her lip, AviSariel's brief surge of hope faded. No. Likely not. Vaun might snipe at other nobles, but he still left her at the table with them.

Humiliation riddled every day of her life now, it seemed. She'd been so foolishly relieved when the Queen sent her from the Tower to live with Vaun. She thought a life with a man who did not love her could not be any more miserable or lonely than a life hidden away in a suite of rooms. She thought she could finally see the Realm, meet people, and live a real life. She had been naïve.

She stared down at her breakfast, a half-eaten serving of once lovely trifle and an empty coffee cup. How many months had it been? The Realm had looked so enticing from her Tower window and the people so beautiful. She frowned at her plate and the smears of pastel colored cream mixing with the yellow custard and the bittersweet strawberry filling. She didn't belong among these people. She could feel it. She didn't look like them and she couldn't act like them. Their skin was lush but their hearts were cruel.

"Well," Evelet exhaled, breaking the silence and drawing the princess's attention from her plate. "What should we do now?"

AviSariel scrunched her brow in confusion and just a little contempt.

"No point in staying here if there isn't a prince about." The Vym stood from the table and raised an eyebrow impatiently when the princess made no move to follow.

"Where will you go?" AviSariel asked, if only for politeness' sake. The Realm wouldn't take that from her, at least.

Evelet groaned. "*We* are going out."

She put down her spoon. "We?"

"Better to have a social leper of a princess for company than no royal at all," the Vym sang. Something in her grin made AviSariel feel as though it was intended as a compliment. Evelet's attention homed in on the soft floral print of AviSariel's dress. "You don't happen to own any pants, do you?"

AviSariel sniffed. "No."

The Vym grinned.

CHAPTER EIGHT

"Will you stop whining?" Evelet revved the engine as their car whipped around another and cut it off. "I didn't tear the dress from your back." Her teeth flashed. "Well, not entirely, anyway."

AviSariel tried not to cower in the passenger seat. She'd never even sat in the passenger seat, much less seen the road ahead swerving and skipping so quickly. "Have you ever driven before?"

Evelet scoffed.

"Take me home," the princess demanded.

"Don't be ridiculous. It took almost an hour just to get you into the car."

"Take me home!"

Evelet sighed and took a hard right. "How is it that I went from living with one princess to another?" She ignored the streetlights, cars veering from her path. "And how can you both be so dull?"

AviSariel hissed, clutching at her seatbelt and digging her heels into the flooring. She couldn't help but wish that Vaun had left Evelet at the Vym family house. At the time she thought he was so heroic in saving the poor girl, seeing her so brutalized in that hallway. Now AviSariel felt that perhaps Lord Quentan Vym had been onto something.

The car screeched to a halt and AviSariel shrieked. She blinked back a blur of terror to find them parked on a sidewalk, smack in the middle of a crowd of people making their way to a nearby entrance. Evelet hopped out as AviSariel read the sign hung over the dark blue doors: The Gentlemen's Club.

She jumped in her seat when Evelet opened her door and leaned in, dark hair falling around her shoulders and her breasts almost tumbling out of the impossibly tight constraint of her corset. AviSariel blushed and averted her eyes when the lady grabbed her wrist. Evelet tugged hard and she jerked back, pressing herself deeper into her seat. "I am not going out there!"

Evelet leaned back in, grinning. "You're making a scene. How lovely."

"You cannot expect me to go out there like this," AviSariel half hissed, half pleaded. People on the sidewalk stopped near the club entrance to watch the car, straining to see who could be of such interest to Evelet Vym.

"Princess," Evelet spoke softly, drawing AviSariel's eyes to hers, "haven't you had enough of being the ragdoll?" She reached out, fingertips stroking AviSariel's glitter-dusted cheek. "Everyone in the Realm wants to be you." She whispered it like the most wonderful secret. "Everyone but you."

The princess blinked. "Why?" she breathed back just as quietly.

Evelet smiled, wide and bitter. "Because you can do anything, and go anywhere." She stood and stepped back, holding the door open. "Now get out of the damned car."

A moment of heartbeats followed, full of nerves and hesitation, and then her yellow heels touched the pavement and her body left the safety of the car. The cold afternoon air chilled her naked legs. The black dress shirt Evelet had boldly borrowed from Vaun's wardrobe barely reached AviSariel's thighs; one of his vests cinched tight around her waist but couldn't button over her breasts. The widening of eyes that recognized her on the sidewalk caused her steps to falter, her ankles wobbling on her heels before Evelet's arm coiled around her middle, leaning their sides into one another before strutting toward the door.

Evelet wore the same ill-fitting slacks she had the night they brought her home. She refused to toss them out, refused to have them hemmed, and even refused to get the bloodstains removed. She wore them with heels now, the shoes almost completely lost beneath the length of the legs.

When they walked into the club, a wave of whispers rippled through the crowd. Heads swiveled their direction. They stared the way they always did when she walked into a room, but this time was different. This time, their lips did not curl at the corners with smirks and the whispers did not ring with mocking laughter. They looked surprised, confused, and envious. A shiver crawled up her spine as a strange new feeling coiled in her chest, wrapping around her heart. Maybe she wasn't so different from the people of the Realm, after all.

"Are you sure you should be here?" AviSariel craned her neck. "What if Quentan comes here?"

She didn't see where Evelet got the cigar, but when she looked at her companion, the woman released a long stream of smoke. "He doesn't care for the senselessness of clubs and teahouses." Evelet shrugged, taking another drag from the petit, black cigar. White smoke wafted from the glowing end, glittering as it curled into the air. Evelet held it out, but AviSariel shook her head. "He only ever comes here for his secret meetings," Evelet said, unimpressed. "Besides, he has a hidden entrance into the back room. He'd never see us."

Someone put a whiskey glass in AviSariel's hand and she took to sipping it while Evelet led the way in a slow circling of the club. There were people everywhere, voices crying out here and there to draw Evelet's attention with the offer of a little conversation. When AviSariel's glass emptied, it vanished and another replaced it.

Eventually, she found herself perched on a stiff, velvet sofa, surrounded by what she assumed to be Vym cousins and friends. By the way they praised Evelet for getting herself into the prince's household, they apparently had no idea how it had happened. A few tried to goad her into telling the tale, but most simply hung on her every word, desperate to hear any and every detail she could recall, invent, or exaggerate about his home life.

Evelet told stories that AviSariel was almost certain were not true, but she kept her eyes turned toward the door and sipped at her drink.

"You must know, then—" one of the gentlemen started, his voice low with eager scandal "—why Princess Fay is on the outs with the prince? Its been all the whisper this week. It seems she hasn't been seen except at her usual table at The Library, and she hasn't visited him once since he moved to Vym Province."

"Did you know that she usually visits him regularly?" the woman across from them asked, her voice a little too shrill for the comfort of her companions. "I read in the paper that she pays him a visit every day! How strange is that?"

"It's not every day," AviSariel muttered, watching the entrance with ever fading hope that her husband might walk in and see her new attire. "We used to have brunch, but that wasn't with Vaun. He was usually asleep or out."

The group around the low table of ashtrays, whiskey glasses, and teacups went silent.

"You have brunch with Fay?" Evelet asked, sounding as disbelieving as the rest of them looked.

AviSariel warmed, but for the first time in months, it wasn't because of embarrassment. She finished her drink and nodded. "Used to," she said, watching as a waiter appeared and took her empty glass. "She doesn't come over anymore. Not since—"

"Princess." Evelet laughed, reaching out to stop the waiter from putting another glass in her hand. "I think she's had plenty." The Vym looked around at the gossip hungry faces surrounding them and grinned. "What can I say? It's her first time out."

Their joined laughter prickled AviSariel's skin, stripping away the last of her confidence.

"I heard the prince isn't interested in his own wife." One of the women raked a glance over AviSariel that seemed to find her lacking. "Never even slept with her once."

Another woman giggled, eyes shining pink. "How can that be true? Everyone above the Main has been in the prince's bed."

The gentleman beside her smirked, gaze boring into AviSariel, judging her allure and her worth. When tears pricked her eyes, they all leaned closer, like wolves picking up the scent of prey.

Evelet clicked her tongue, stealing back their attention. "And how long has it been since you've been in his bed?" she jabbed at the pink-eyed woman. "Perhaps you left a bad taste?"

The woman flushed. Just as readily as their cruel tongues had turned on her, so did they turn on one another. AviSariel frowned, her hand empty and her lips pressed with bitterness. She stood and the group barely noticed, too busy tearing one another down. Evelet glanced up, but the princess walked away before she could speak. She was almost to the door when the Vym caught up, catching her hand and pulling her to a stop.

"Wait," Evelet said quietly, almost sounding apologetic. "Where are you going?"

AviSariel jerked away. "Why did you bring me here?"

Evelet smiled, her expression a little sloppy from the mild haze of her dust. "To have fun."

The princess laughed, short and bitter, a sound she'd never heard from herself. "This is not fun."

The Vym hesitated before nodding. "Fine. We'll try one of the other clubs."

AviSariel rolled her eyes and shoved open the door, welcoming the cool outside air on her burning face and prickling eyes. To her surprise, Evelet followed.

"Come on." Evelet hurried past her to the car, still parked carelessly on the sidewalk. "I know a better—"

"No." AviSariel pivoted and walked away. She couldn't be sure where she was going, or even where she was, but she wasn't getting back in that car. She was done following. Her solitary march down the sidewalk burned with power she'd never tasted before.

"Where are you going?" Evelet called, tone wobbling.

"I don't know," AviSariel tossed over her shoulder. "I don't think I care."

A moment of hesitation, a low curse, and then the clatter of heels down the sidewalk trailed her. "You're going toward the Main," Evelet said.

The princess shrugged as the Vym fell into line beside her.

"We could send for a car and—"

"No." She continued to walk, wishing for a pair of pants or a skirt.

Evelet huffed. "Do you have any idea how Low it is to walk?"

AviSariel laughed bitterly. "What do I care? You're just dragging me around so that I won't send you back to your horrible brother or tell anyone how he pummeled your face."

Evelet stopped, likely in shock, before hurrying to catch up again.

"You should drink more often." She smiled, a small, devious curl of lips. Her tone quieted. "It's not something Quentan would want known. He doesn't like people talking about him."

"You still care what he wants?"

The Vym shrugged lightly. "It was out of character for Vaun to play the hero, and few people hold his attention for long. Sooner or later, I won't be under his protection anymore."

AviSariel thought about this for another block before sighing her forgiveness. It was yet another block before she spoke. "Who does hold Vaun's attention?"

Evelet grinned, linking her arm with the princess's. "Well, Fay's always imposed herself on him, though I don't think he cares much for her. He and Addom have had a strange sort of friendship these past decades. On and off, as it is." She giggled. "Really, I think it's more of an infatuation. They've always run in the same circles and often occupied the same beds. For years they used to compete over everything. I swear, for a time they dueled every other week. Then, one day, they just stopped."

The princess nodded thoughtfully, not exactly sure how to compete with Addom Vym for Vaun's affections. He was intimidating, masculine, and cocky in a way that she could not imagine herself even pretending to be.

"And then there's Grayc Illan." Evelet clicked her tongue viciously against the roof of her mouth. "I don't know what Jacobi was thinking, making her his business partner. I heard he did it just to take her from the prince."

"Why?"

Evelet shrugged. "I don't know the inner workings of Belholn minds. But Grayc..." She smiled briefly, a strange pull of lips that suggested pleasant memories and beloved secrets. "Well, it's probably for the best that she's not working for Vaun anymore."

AviSariel nibbled her lip. He hadn't mentioned Grayc Illan since they moved to Vym Province but she knew he still thought of her; every so often she saw him coiling one of those ribbons around his fingers. Whenever she asked about them he would reflexively hold the bit of silk tighter, as though she might snatch it away. "Would it be bad if they were close?" she asked quietly, trying not to sound more than casually curious.

The Vym cackled, the sound fierce and unhindered. "Aside from the idea of a Low born servant sleeping with the prince of the Realm?" She sighed. "Grayc Illan is cunning, and that's dangerous in a rat. Did you know that she used to belong to the Belholns when she was a girl? She used to mend the Lady's dresses." Evelet leaned in to AviSariel's shoulder, too comfortable with the ways of telling secrets. "And after that, Fay bought her off the Belholns. She used to work in our kitchen. I don't know how she managed to get a job as the prince's valet, but now she's practically an honorary citizen of the High in Belholn. That's just too much cleverness to be trustworthy."

AviSariel thought it odd to hear a woman like Evelet, with the circles of friends she kept, talk about trust. "I liked her." It wasn't a lie, but it hadn't been that simple, either. She wanted to like Grayc Illan, but she found it difficult to like a woman who held her husband's attention so completely when she could not even catch his eye.

The Vym didn't reply, pursing her lips and looking about the streets as they walked. Without warning, she tugged the princess to the left and down a narrow road. "I think I remember a dirty little club around here…"

"I don't want to—"

"Oh, it won't be like the last one," Evelet promised. "It is too loud for conversation and not at all populated by the sort of people worth talking to." She all but pulled AviSariel into a run, fingers laced to keep them joined. The clatter of their heels changed abruptly as cobblestone gave way to pavement. A streetlamp bobbed by overhead, dreadfully plain without its customary ornamentation. Just how far from the High had they strayed?

Evelet pulled her around one of the dark, brick corners and a large lamp illuminated an open door and the clusters of people moving in and out. Music throbbed from inside, threatening to beat down the walls and escape into the streets.

"Why would we go if the people aren't worth talking to?" AviSariel demanded, her nerves wavering as they approached the entrance. The people in line showed far more skin than fashionable, revealing bodies in dull, uneven shades that cheap charms did little to conceal. Lackluster hair in varying tones of brown and blond brushed naked shoulders. Some of them wore makeup, but they had the sheen of paint, not magic.

Evelet squeezed her hand, pulling her toward the door as though it had its own gravity and they couldn't turn back now. "People in the Main are good for things other than conversation," she said, her smile turning lecherous and the mirror of her twin's. "Just give it a try. If you hate this place, we'll find another."

The music of the room swallowed any response from AviSariel. Bodies moved from their path, but only enough to suck them in. AviSariel's heels shuffled along a sticky floor.

She wanted to cover her ears against the blaring sounds. A few sets of dull eyes trailed her, but not with the piercing judgment she had known in the High. Did they not know who she was? She jumped when hands touched her, twisting to see where they had come from, but there were simply too many faces, too many arms, and too many blindly seeking fingers. Evelet stopped when they neared the center of the room where the crowd thinned into pairs of entwined, dancing bodies. She heard a piano beneath the stomp and drag of shoes against the hardwood floor that had become drums to the beat. An electric violin somewhere in the room shuddered out haunting melodies to spur on dancers, driving them all faster and faster.

Evelet stepped up to a tall man with black eyes and black hair, running her fingers down his chest with a wicked twist of her lips. AviSariel blushed and looked away, only for Evelet to tug on her hand. Her gaze flew back to the woman to find the man gone and Evelet tugging a cigarette case from her slacks. She took one out and snapped the case shut. There was no sound over the music.

She watched Evelet light the cigarette. It was white, almost opalescent, and she could see the dust glittering as it burned. The dark-haired Vym took a long drag, her eyes fluttering and her skin shimmering before she exhaled, red rolling from her mouth so starkly that for one horrible second AviSariel thought it was blood before it curled upward into the air. Everyone around them leaned closer and hands curled up around Evelet's waist to stroke lovingly at her abdomen, at her arms, and at her breasts. A woman whispered in the Vym's ear, pleading, by the way her lips trembled, and Evelet sneered.

Ignoring all of those wanting bodies, the Vym turned to her, large pupils swimming with glitter. For a moment the princess considered fleeing, but something in the way Evelet stared at her was so entrancing, so personal and deep, that she didn't dare look away. Evelet reached out, tucking strands of hair behind the princess's ear before offering the beautiful little cigarette now trailing white wisps of smoke.

AviSariel's first impulse was to decline, already beginning to shake her head, but Evelet only smiled, waiting. Waiting. AviSariel's hand shook. She licked her lips. She'd read the papers and heard about the madness of bad dust in the Low of Belholn and Maggrin. Even if the cigarette had come from the High with Evelet, caution warned her against it. Every sensible thought told her to say no, but the look in Evelet's eyes was so certain, so daring, so tempting.

She reached out and accepted the offering. She held it to her lips before she could lose her nerve and inhaled. She expected it to burn. She expected to cough and make a joke of herself yet again, but it felt like the sweetest air she had ever inhaled, cold in the back of her throat and hot in her chest, in her arms, in her legs. By the time her lips opened to shudder out the red smoke, her skin was tight and tingling. Her tongue searched her mouth for the taste, chasing it in want of more. It was familiar, so familiar, and yet she couldn't remember what it was.

When she brought her hand up for another drag she found the cigarette gone. Panic surged through her muscles. Had she dropped it? Evelet's laughter brought her eyes up again in time to see her handing the little white stick away to another greedy mouth before grabbing AviSariel by the waist and leading her onto the dance floor.

A distant thought told her that she couldn't dance, told her to fret and try to escape the embarrassment that was sure to come. The thought drowned under the wonderful feeling of the music beneath her heels and in her skin and the warm tingling sensation wherever Evelet's hands trailed. They spun and laughed, sometimes dancing slow and sometimes very quick. The room became a beautiful haze, and for a stretch of minutes or hours, AviSariel had no worries, no fear or shame, no thoughts beyond the feel of her own skin. When she stirred from that wonderful stupor it was to find herself leaning against a wall, watching the dancers on the floor. She rolled her head to one side to see Evelet at a booth, straddling the man from before while he attempted to devour her mouth. He was losing. She was devouring his.

The warm haze of cigarette smoke in her lungs had not worn off enough for the princess to feel scandalized by the sight. She smiled and shifted to watch the dancers once more. Less than half as many people packed the club as before. What time was it? Could it be morning already?

Her skin prickled as a steady gaze met hers. How long had he been watching her? He smiled, and the gesture looked too charming to be anything but dangerous. When he crossed the room, forcing dancers to swirl out of his path, she almost thought him a hallucination. She could not resist watching the way his hips moved, drawing him closer and closer. The cut of his thin, gray shirt showed off the smooth skin of his shoulders and collar.

He stopped in front of her, head tipped delicately to one side. His stare trapped her there, her heart beating so loud she feared he could see her pulse jumping.

His smile grew, and he held out a hand. She didn't hesitate, as she had with the cigarette, but slid her fingers into his. A shiver slipped down her spine when he pulled her away from the wall.

They were spinning, she was certain, but she couldn't tear her eyes from his to look at the spiraling room; one was green and the other a dark blue. "Are they real?" she asked.

He smiled wider. "Real?"

Her fingers, emboldened by the haze that coated her skin, touched his cheek beneath the green eye.

"Does it matter?"

Her legs stopped moving and it took the strength of his arms to keep her upright. She stared up at him for another second, her brows knitting together. "It does to me," AviSariel murmured and pushed herself away. Her legs dragged sluggishly and her fingers combed through her hair, pushing the damp locks away from her face. Fetid air—toxic with sweat, dust, and endless envy—clogged in her lungs. Nothing was real here. Not her marriage. Not her city. Not even a nameless man in a crowd. All illusions. All lies. Her plain little ring caught the light as she pushed the door open and she cringed.

"Wait!" a voice called after her. Her dance partner emerged from the club in her wake, pale hair damp with sweat. AviSariel scoffed and strode away, naked legs cold in the night air as she followed the bulbous lamps down the sidewalk. First Evelet, now the dancer. She'd never been so pursued in all her life.

"You're going the wrong way." The man hurried after her. "The High is back that way."

AviSariel eyed the cracked sidewalk and grimy buildings, both without any pretense of style, but kept going.

"It's not safe down here," the man said in a strangely casual tone. "Haven't you read the paper? We could get caught in a mob, go mad with the rats." He paused but only for a second. "Maybe even get eaten."

"If it's so dangerous, then you should turn back," she snapped. Reason told her she should listen, but stubbornness kept her moving. At this rate, she would walk herself right out into the Ash.

"Princess." He took her arm, halting them in a pool of streetlight.

"You know who I am?"

"You are not easily forgotten." His fingers flexed against her arm, suddenly far more intimate on a deserted street than in a crowded club. "Though I understand if you do not remember me. You were busy, and it was many years ago."

Where—? Oh. Shame curled in her belly. "You were at my wedding." Everyone from the three ruling households had been, along with their High born friends. "Are you a cousin of the Vyms?"

"Not exactly." He held out his hand, palm up and patient. "Havik

Lor, and the eyes are mine from birth, I promise."

"AviSariel." She placed her hand in his. He smiled, as if to remind her that he already knew, and brushed his lips against her knuckles.

A clatter behind them made her jump. She turned, hand still in his, and squinted into the shadows of the Low. A large, dirty man blocked the mouth of an alley across the street. He looked almost monstrous in contrast to his prey, a small woman backed into the wall beside a dumpster. Her powder blue dress wrinkled as she tried to wedge herself further into her corner. Matching hair ribbons twisted over her shoulder. She looked like a child before him. His large, grimy hand touched her cheek as if to demonstrate how easily his palm could encase her face and seal the whimpers from her painted mouth.

AviSariel stepped toward the edge of the sidewalk, straining her eyes to make out the scene just beyond the lamplight. The girl looked like a doll. "Larc," she breathed the name of the youngest Vym sibling. She had only met her the once but there was no mistaking her.

The grimy man's hand dropped to roughly fondle Larc's breast, crushing the delicate satin and lace. The Vym cried softly, nibbling her lower lip as he lifted the skirt of her dress with his other hand.

Sucking in a horrified breath, AviSariel stepped off the curb, ready to shout and scream if need be. But Havik Lor hooked an arm around her waist and dragged her back, lifting her until the toes of her shoes barely brushed the concrete. His hand sealed over her mouth.

"Forgive me." He spoke in a whisper that was difficult even for her to hear. "The Vyms have... interesting habits. It would be a shame for you to interrupt the young lady's evening."

She looked across the street to see Larc now lifted, her back to the brick wall and her legs held by the stranger, his dirty fingers pressing into the surprisingly lush shape of her thighs at the tops of her white stockings.

"She comes down here every few months," Havik Lor whispered against the shell of AviSariel's ear as she watched the stranger push himself against Larc. Her body strained with a shrill, breathy cry as he forced himself to fit. "She wanders around until some brute catches sight of her. Everyone down here knows about it. They know what she's looking for."

AviSariel shuddered in his arms, cringing at the intimate and awful scene in front of her. The stranger thrust wildly, greedily, into that slight woman. One of Larc's gloved hands came up to her mouth, fanning fingers over widely parted lips to stifle her own mewling sounds of dark pleasure.

Havik Lor stepped away from the scene, carrying the princess with him. "Everyone has their perversions," he said as though to reassure, as though they were words to soothe. He rounded a corner, onto a sleepy street where they could only faintly hear the distant moans. His arms loosened, returning her heels to the ground.

She blinked at the dark corners around the stretches of lamplight. Had she really seen that? Was it okay to walk away? She closed her eyes when she felt tears building up. "Everyone lies."

He stroked her arm soothingly. "Of course we do," Havik Lor said finally. "Don't you?"

She drew a shaky breath and let it out. "No. At least, I don't think I do." Weight settled on her shoulders. "Is nothing real here?"

Havik Lor laughed and the sound made her pull away.

He waved a pleading hand. "My apologies," he managed as he bit back his mirth. "But after so many decades, sometimes the truth just isn't very interesting. Everyone has secrets, because not having secrets would be dull."

"I hate it."

"I can give you something real, if you'd like." His fingers wrapped around hers again, pulling her toward him. She stumbled and his other arm curled around her back. Her chest hit his just before his mouth took hers. It was a soft kiss and when his tongue touched her lips she opened, eyes already shut, though she couldn't remember closing them. He drew back first and her body jolted with embarrassment. Her palms pushed at his chest before one hand came up to rub at her lips.

"I'm married," AviSariel said, as though it meant something.

"Yes, you are," he agreed before taking a breath and stepping back, running fingers over his short hair and down the back of his neck. "Shall we get on with it, then?"

She flushed. "On with what?"

"Come find out."

Before she could protest, he tugged her down the street and around another corner, toward a square closer to the middle of the Main. People bustled cheerfully in and out of shops and bars. Light and laughter echoed into the street.

"Where are we going?"

"You'll see."

Vaun stifled a yawn. He squinted out the window of the car at the gray morning glare bouncing off ugly buildings. "Simons, didn't you say I was supposed to be having lunch with my sister?"

His valet nodded from his seat beside him. "I did, your highness, and you are."

The length of his sister's frosty anger hadn't lasted nearly as long as he'd hoped. Given her talent for nursing a grudge, he'd anticipated at least another month of blissful distance. The car stopped, parking on a curb that looked particularly shabby. Frowning, the prince squinted out the window. "Has my sister started gracing the Main of Vym with her presence, Stevens?"

"No, your highness." Samuel Sinol smothered a smile. "We are picking up Princess AviSariel first."

That helped wake Vaun from his morning haze. He looked out the windows with new interest. "Here?"

Samuel Sinol nodded and got out of the car. His eyebrows winged up silently when Vaun followed. The prince straightened his night-rumpled shirt.

"Let me." Vaun pointed to the building in front of them. "This one?"

His valet nodded. "Second floor. Room 2B."

"Interesting." The prince grinned and took the stairs two at a time, not sure what he expected to find when he turned that dented knob and swung the door open. The small, one room apartment boasted no kitchen, though at least it claimed a bathroom behind a narrow door. Windows filled one wall, though he couldn't fathom why, since the view showed nothing but decaying buildings. No furniture save a stack of mattresses graced the well-scrubbed floor.

The subtle floral pattern of the new wallpaper invited him in. It was a hollow room, but a well-kept one, almost masking the flimsy construction of the building that let him hear the rustle of other tenants all around.

He closed the door loudly and watched her body jolt awake on those mattresses, her nudity tangled in a dark blue comforter.

"Good morning," he called with too much cheer as he practically glided over to the bed.

Her face tightened against the glow of morning, against the confusion at the intrusion, before rounding in horror. She bolted upright, covers pooling around her waist. She gaped at him with wide, shocked eyes before yanking the blanket up to her neck. "I... I..."

"You—" Vaun flopped down beside her, leaning back against the wall that served as a headboard. "—might have had an even more interesting night than I did."

"I'm sorry," she blurted out, tears trembling on her lashes. "I shouldn't have..." Her breath hitched, rasping while she hugged the covers to her chest with one hand and shoved back wildly tangled hair with the other.

"Why not?" He didn't know where she had come up with her monogamous notions, but perhaps they could both be free of them at last. Maybe now she would stop wobbling her lip at him every time he brought home a lover. "It wasn't with a Vym, was it? They're not bad company, and I've slept with most of them, but I wouldn't wish them on your first time. Terribly greedy lovers, the lot of them."

"No!" She rushed to answer and then flushed. "I went to a club with Evelet, but I left with—" AviSariel gasped and grabbed his wrist. "You will never believe what I saw!"

Vaun laughed. "Sweetheart, you haven't seen anything I haven't after just one night." He glanced again at the small but otherwise tidy loft. "And, I'm guessing, one lover."

Her cheeks colored slightly. "I saw Larc near the Low!"

He raised an eyebrow. "Were you dusting?"

"No! Well, yes, but it was her." She wiggled closer to him and lowered her voice. "She was there, having..." Her face turned a vibrant shade of red. "...having sex with a man in an alley."

He couldn't contain a peal of laughter, though he tried, given her serious expression. It burst from him, burning in his chest until he had to wipe tears from his eyes. "You must have had quite a time with Evelet."

"No. I was with Havik, then, and he said that she does it regularly. She goes down there and waits for... for someone to take advantage of her. But everyone knows. Everyone down there, anyway." The princess huffed, pulling away.

"Havik, is it?" Oh, she *had* found herself quite an evening.

AviSariel hesitated. "Havik Lor," she whispered, sounding uncertain about giving her lover's name to her husband.

The prince laughed softly this time and nodded. "Havik Lor Maggrin." Not a bad man, as far as Vaun knew. Unlike his particularly uptight relatives, he enjoyed a grittier and more liberated way of living.

"Maggrin?"

He nodded again and stood, stretching for the second time that morning. It seemed his princess was finally making friends. It came as a strange relief.

"I thought Maggrins weren't allowed in Vym territory."

Vaun shrugged. "No one cares much about the Main districts, as long as they don't cause trouble or get caught. Havik Lor doesn't cause trouble. The Main in Maggrin is just too dull for his taste." Too dull for anyone's taste. "Now, get—hold up. What's this?" He leaned over to peer at the ink on her ankle. Red, irritated skin puffed around delicate gold markings. A small, golden crown had been tattooed on her ankle. He grinned at her. "Definitely more interesting than my night."

He heard her gasp in surprise behind him when he started toward the door. She seemed to have forgotten getting the tattoo until he drew attention to it. "We have lunch with Fay. I'll send Sanborn for some clothes since you appear to have lost yours."

He all but whistled as the door closed behind him.

They arrived at The Library more than an hour late. To Vaun's surprise, Fay had waited, sitting rigidly in her seat at the long table of books, tarts, and tea. Larc sat to her left, chattering at a speed that made him wonder if the petite woman even breathed.

Larc paused as the attention of the room shifted, heads turning toward Vaun and AviSariel at the entrance. She beamed, standing from her chair to wave them over. The drama of their last visit must have been enough to tempt her into leaving her house, hungry for gossip.

"I apologize for our tardiness," AviSariel said, taking a chair. Her smile faltered when Fay neither spoke nor acknowledged them.

Vaun draped himself across the chair between them. "Is your husband not joining us today?"

Fay managed to frown deeper and lifted her teacup to her lips, perhaps to drown her bitterness in the sweet liquid. It had never been easy for her to let go of anything, especially when that something was one of her brother's offenses. "It's not like you to be so late, AviSariel. I hope my brother isn't rubbing off on you."

Vaun reached for the teapot and filled his cup. "I assure you, I was not the one rubbing her. Tea, my darling?"

AviSariel reddened but ducked her head politely at his offer. He filled her teacup.

"I thought you were sour with me, sister," Vaun continued. "Has your husband's foul temper cooled so quickly?"

"Careful with your words, Vaun," Fay warned. "This is his province."

"And our Realm."

"Not ours." Her voice sharpened until he was certain he could hear the points of her teeth dragging along her words. "This is *her* Realm. You may be allowed to prance around like an entitled fool but I have responsibilities."

He rolled his eyes. "I think you have invented these responsibilities for yourself." He forked a slice of perfectly yellow lemon and took a bite; sugared rind and gelatin flesh melted in his mouth. "You're angry. Being angry is easier if you can blame others."

"Pray tell, brother, when did you become such a thinker?"

Already in the process of lifting his cup, Vaun pretended to take a sip before setting it back down. "I don't rightly know. I suppose I took up the habit somewhere between Ollan's death and you dismissing my Grayc."

"Stop calling her that! She's a rat!" Fay shuddered in her chair, belatedly swallowing back some of her fury. Only in Vym Province could the High born resist staring at her outbursts with such practiced poise; no one so much as turned their head. Fay's pale eyes slithered to his wrist, where the gold silk ribbon tied around it peeked out from his sleeve. "You should stop seeing her. You're making a fool of yourself."

Vaun settled into the embrace of his chair. Fay had been wound tight for as long as he could recall but he had never noticed before just how unhappy she was. "Why does it bother you so much? I have always made a fool of myself."

Fay's teeth clicked. "You have a wife by your side now. How do you think your behavior makes her feel?"

He pretended to consider her side, though he knew she was only grabbing at ways to herd him to her goal, whatever that might be. "Your husband doesn't take lovers," Vaun observed softly. He had never given Fay's happiness, or lack of it, much thought before, but suddenly it was impossible to ignore. "Not publicly, anyway. Are you happy?" A unique quiet fell over The Library, different from its usual hush, as every pair of lungs held tight to listen. "Does his fidelity, loveless as it is, honor you?"

Fay pressed her lips and put her teacup down with excess attention, turning it just slightly to have the handle at the angle she liked.

"Maybe if you hadn't invented the responsibility of your fidelity to him, sister, you wouldn't be so invested in the question of mine." Vaun sighed and stood. For the first time in a very long while, their conflicts did not amuse him. He did not want to be her enemy, and not just because he had seen the fate of Fay's enemies, but because he suddenly wished she had an ally. "I have no intention of being like you, Fay. My marriage won't be bitter and loveless—" He held out his hand to AviSariel. She slipped her palm into his and rose from her seat. "—even if our love isn't for each other."

This time he walked his wife all the way to the car, rather than shaking off her hand as soon as they were out of sight.

"Do you think she will be angry for long?" AviSariel asked quietly.

"She is always angry," Vaun said before registering her dismay. AviSariel had few friends in the Realm and, selfishly, he had not thought about that. "Don't fret too much. She'll still have brunch with you. She enjoys gossip even more than she enjoys ignoring people." He let go of her hand, Samuel Sinol having opened the car door for her. The prince smiled. "She just won't make the mistake of inviting me next time."

CHAPTER NINE

Grayc Illan followed Larc through the shadows, wishing with every step that the little Vym would turn around. Instead, the woman wandered farther toward the Low, a tuft of pastel satin against the old bricks and filthy streets. She skipped through weak pools of infrequent lamplight, daring danger to find her. Grayc's fists clenched in her pockets, willing her prey to look back, to catch her closing in, to run.

But Larc never looked back. Even when she sensed someone drawing close, she didn't look. She thrilled to be caught in those dark streets, chasing danger in a world that had proven to be nothing but eternal comfort. Grayc Illan understood her reasons; understood the lengths one would take to break out of a prison, even a comfortable one. Once, on first discovering Larc's dirty secret, she'd taken offense. How dare the High born idiot sneak down to the Low to get her thrills out of the shadows that were a real, ever-present danger to those forced to live there? How dare she play at pain? Then, later, she began to understand. Larc knew little else. Had she ever known real fear? Real pain? Real excitement?

She took wider steps, closing the stretch of sidewalk between them and coming up behind the youngest Vym. She wasn't sure if she mourned her choice because of the end it might very well bring upon

Larc, or because of the end it might bring upon herself. The only comfort she could give herself when she grabbed Larc by the back of the neck and slammed her face first into a wall, was that it wasn't really her choice. And that was no comfort at all.

Larc let out a squeak of terror and then shuddered in excitement.

Grayc held her firmly to the wall, black gloved fingers sinister against those pale curls and the lace fringe of her stupid bonnet. No one wore bonnets. Not even the fools in the High.

The shapes of others approached. Grayc took the syringe from her coat pocket, twisted Larc's head to the side, and stuck the needle into that column of exposed flesh. Her prey's jugular jumped and her eyes widened, trying to look back now with a taste of real fright to see just what trouble she had found in the dark of the Realm.

Grayc held her to the wall until the woman's eyes rolled back and her knees gave out.

One of the paid brutes Jacobi had put in her command swooped in, catching Larc before she could hit the ground and dirty her dress. He hoisted her into his arms easily and looked to Grayc Illan. She hated him for making her say it. "Put her in the car."

Grayc strode down the private hallway, though even the large men trailing her hesitated. She tugged her leather gloves off as she entered the lounge. A breakfast table was already set up with a steaming pot of coffee and several gleaming cloches.

She held the gloves out and one of the men took them. It was easy to pretend to be important after watching the High born do it for so many decades.

Considering the empty room, she crossed it to rap against a tall panel of black wood.

"Come in," Jacobi's voice rang easily through the door. There was no lock. She pushed it open, spilling light into the otherwise dark, windowless room. She took four steps in as a show of boldness and managed not to cringe at the musky stink of sex, violence, and… was that vomit?

The men in suits did not follow. As it turned out, in the case of the slight and boyish Jacobi, not all men required height or bulk to strike fear.

He stood in front of an open wardrobe, pulling a jacket from a hanger. In that dim light, his youthful face held seemingly endless charm, but with the slightest turn against the shadows, that youth swelled with malice. "You have such a gift for punctuality, Grayc. I tell you to meet me at noon and damned if you don't walk through those doors at the stroke of twelve." His hands fussed with the collar of his jacket but his gaze met hers. Gray lined his white eyes and his lips twisted up at the corners, seeing her signature glower. "We can't all be so timely."

He still made an effort to be friendly with her. In the beginning, his offer to make her his business partner stemmed from a need to strike out at Vaun. Now he worried she would leave before he was ready to pin the whole mess of his crimes on her. He needn't have bothered. She couldn't leave no matter how desperately she wanted to.

He looked away first, fingers leaving his collar to rake back his hair. She turned her gaze to the other side of the room. Her frown deepened before she caught herself. Jacobi's latest lover didn't move, little more than a heap of tortured limbs and bruised flesh, arms bound to one of the bed posts. The woman must have put up a struggle, because the cuffs had cut deep into her wrists and the short chain had scratched the polished wood raw. Clumps of blonde hair stuck to the rug, ripped from the tangled nest atop her head. Her cheek lay in a patch of mattress soaked in blood, saliva, and vomit, and the visible side of her face had been rendered nothing more than lumps of swollen and bruised flesh.

"Forgive me for keeping you waiting. You must be famished." Jacobi crossed the room and escorted her out. "You," he beckoned to one of the guards. "Get the maids up here. My room needs cleaning out."

Grayc Illan followed him into the lounge and found a small smile for him when he pulled out her chair, seating her first.

While they put squares of black and white checkerboard cake and curls of gelatin lemon rind on their plates, a cluster of maids accompanied by a guard whisked past and into the bedroom. He was done with this lover. She would be returned to her family in the Main with a sum of money for their troubles. Jacobi filled his coffee cup as the guard returned a moment later with the body of his former lover tossed over one shoulder.

The Belholn cousin offered to fill Grayc Illan's cup, but she shook her head briskly and picked up the glass pitcher on the table instead.

Jacobi laughed. "Must you drink that?"

She filled her cup with the clear liquid. "I like it."

"You are so strange." He cut his fork into a corner of cake. "How much of my money did you waste buying that plot of Ash?"

Grayc Illan grinned and drank her water with pointed delight. "Our money, Jacobi. Our companies. Our land." If she was going to play his foolish lamb, she was at least going to get something out of it for the time being. She held the glass toward him in offering. "Our water."

He shuddered and picked up his coffee instead. "A waste."

"An investment."

"Why go through the trouble of digging up your own water when the Queen gives us all we need? No one is going to pay for something they already have. And no one is going to drink it straight like some rat."

Grayc Illan smiled, refilling her glass. "Why not? They drink coffee and it tastes like dirt."

"In that case, maybe we'll serve it in the teahouses in the Main. Let the High borns think they're slumming it when they buy water."

Jacobi laughed loudly, startling one of the maids carrying sheets out of the bedroom. She moved faster. "So, is it taken care of?"

Grayc Illan stiffened and nodded sharply. "She's in the basement." She took a breath. "It wasn't a smart idea, Jac."

He flicked a hand toward her. "It was a necessity. Little Larc saw our boys picking up the new shipment. She might be too stupid to know what she saw, but that doesn't mean she won't tell someone smart enough to figure it out. We can't take risks like that. There have already been enough mistakes." He sighed tiresomely. "Did anyone see you?"

"Not that I know of, but it's the Realm. There are eyes everywhere." She refused to drum her fingers, though she wanted to. How far could she push him? "Your partner could be setting us up. I assume you've thought of that? If we get caught with her—"

"We could kill her," Jacobi said thoughtfully. "Put the body in Maggrin and start a war."

"To what end?" Grayc sighed as though her interest was waning. "Let me return her."

Jacobi smiled now. "And then what? The Vyms would have you gutted."

"Even I can convince a silly thing like Larc to keep her mouth shut."

He shook his head around a bite of lemon rind. "No. We will keep her, for now."

Grayc Illan shrugged. "Very well. You should tell me who we are working with, Jacobi. I can't prepare us for betrayal if I don't know which House to watch."

"What makes you so certain he will betray us?"

"Do you share blood with him?"

Jacobi's pretty mouth pressed and Grayc cringed, biting back a bitter laugh. Jacobi was going to get himself killed, which would have been a delight if her head wasn't bound to roll alongside his.

"He'll betray you. Blood ties are the only ties High borns care about, when it comes down to it." She knew it well, having grown up in the Belholn family house. Oh, they did awful things to one another, but in the end, their blood was all they had. Vym had been the same. The only High born she'd ever seen without love for his siblings was Quentan Vym. Even Fay Dray Fen would move the Tower itself for her brother, though she was careful to keep Vaun from seeing it.

Grayc Illan eyed the far side of the room and the stack of clear, plastic wrapped packages of opalescent dust piled neatly on a low table. "A new batch?"

He nodded and drank from his coffee.

"Where should we test it?"

"The Low, in Maggrin this time." He hummed with satisfaction. "The last batch was better. This will be better yet."

"I thought it only took longer for dusters to feel the effects."

"As I said, better." Jacobi's smile turned wolfish. "By the time anyone notices what's wrong, it can't be traced back to anyone, much less us. If it goes poorly, perhaps we'll still get lucky, and the Vyms will eat each other alive."

Vaun trailed Addom into yet another shabby brick building. His friend shoved past the shattered door and swung burning, red eyes on the family huddled in the corner.

"The littlest Vym," Addom barked at them. "She comes here. This street. Where is she?"

"Not here, my lord," the woman managed. "Look for yourself."

Vaun sighed as his friend did just that, storming through the decrepit hovel, yanking open doors and kicking things out of his way. Finding no sign of his sister, Addom stomped out, undoubtedly on his way to the next filthy home.

"How long do you expect to keep this up?" Vaun said quietly as he fell in step with his friend outside. Other High borns flittered in and out of doorways up and down the street, but nowhere near as many as yesterday, or even that morning.

"Until I find her," Addom snarled. "You can go, if you want. Go back to your tea and your pastries. All the others will, soon enough."

"It is hard to keep the attention of High borns," Vaun admitted. "Especially when they do not understand why we are searching in the Low. If you suspected one of the other households, that would feed enough gossip that half the Realm would join the search. But the Low is... uninteresting, at best. What do they know of danger, anyway? Can you blame them for expecting Larc to reappear soon enough, as if by magic?"

Addom's sneer deepened in his haggard face, but his frantic pace slowed. "I will find her myself, if need be."

A sleek, black car pulled up at the curb. Addom growled low in his throat as the door opened and his brother stepped out.

"Enough, Addom," Quentan said, looking well rested, well dressed, and well polished. "Get in the car. You've embarrassed our family enough for one day."

Quentan had not come down to search.

Vaun had not realized that Addom was tired until that moment, until his head sagged to one side and the lamplight shone in the dark pits of his eyes. He glared at his brother, heavy bags under his lashes, like shadows the lamps of the Realm could never chase away. "Embarrassed, Quen? Do tell. How have I embarrassed your family by looking for our sister?"

"You draw attention to her disgraceful habit," the province Lord hissed, stepping closer and lowering his voice. He didn't seem to care that the prince was there; perhaps he assumed that Vaun already knew. "If her shame got her killed, then for the sake of the province, leave her. Let it be a blessing that she isn't found and her scandal brought to light. Since her birth it has been our family's burden to hide her. Let this be the end of it."

Anger rippled through Addom's stiff body. The veins of his forearms pulsed when his fists clenched.

"Get in the car," Quentan said, voice laden with exhaustion as well but relenting enough to open the door himself. "I've told the others to go back to the High. We will send out a more tactful search for her, Addom."

"You go back," he said, low, and the words sparked something furious in the Vym Lord's eyes.

"Addom—" Quentan warned.

"Don't keep your people waiting, *brother*. What will they think if you linger in the Low too long?"

Quentan's long stride swallowed the distance between them. He curled his fingers around his brother's throat, yanking him onto his toes. "I have been saddled with you for too long, Addom. Get in that car or forget about setting foot in the High again. You can live in the Low with the rats for all I care." He leaned in closer, his teeth mashing angrily. "And when you die here, I will leave you behind, just like Larc."

Addom shuddered but didn't move, didn't strike. "Enjoy the High, Quen. You have it all to yourself, now."

With a sneer, the Lord of Vym shoved his brother back. Addom scrambled to keep his balance, ruining the last of the finish on his once exquisite shoes. Quentan's gaze slid to the prince, looking him over as if wanting to speak and only barely managing to bite back his words. The Lord turned sharply and marched back to the car. Addom straightened his wrinkled shirt as the vehicle drove away.

"Was that the best idea?" Vaun asked quietly. "You've never spent more than a few nights in the Low."

Addom stared down the street, exhaustion under his eyes. Evelet stood on the next corner, leading another hunting party. She'd stopped long enough to watch the interaction, expression mirroring the desperate madness in her twin's. She nodded once in their direction before returning to the search.

"I'm not leaving until I find her," Addom said, like an oath to the night, or perhaps a threat to the Low.

Vaun marveled at his friend. In the thick of grim tragedy, he had shown himself to be a man of loyalty, passion, and resolve. Fay warned him once that truths of human nature were exposed in moments of hardship and Vaun understood now better than ever what she meant. He knew Addom now, after a day in the Low, better than he had ever known his friend before, but wondered uneasily if he would have shown such character if he had been the one facing loss.

Grayc Illan woke with a start. Her body rolled out from under the covers. The moment her bare feet hit the floor, she hurled herself toward the doorway of her bathroom.

Her body buckled, knees hitting pristine tiles and fingers combing through curls to hold them back as she vomited. It felt as if her stomach wanted to crawl up her throat.

Finally, after long minutes of misery, she sat back, curling into the cool tile at her back. The peace of her own home—the first house she'd ever bought—crept back to her. While modest compared to the homes in the High, it easily dwarfed anything she'd ever been able to call her own before. Jacobi had offered her a floor of his own residence in the High, so close to the Tower that one could almost smell the sugary fragrance of the Queen's roses. Grayc Illan declined politely, though she hid her joy at owning a place of her own, a refurbished townhouse at the bottom of the Main.

She shoved her hair back. Her first house, bought with money earned working as a partner with Jacobi Belholn. *Partners*, with a *Belholn*. She lurched forward, heaving again, but this time she could only cough and shake. When the clamminess of her skin receded and a handful of moments passed, Grayc Illan pushed herself to her feet and flushed the toilet. She stepped to the sink but didn't look at the mirror or turn on the faucet. With shaky hands, she opened a glass flask on the counter and picked up one of the cups from the tray. She rinsed her mouth out with her privately bottled water before watching it swirl down the drain.

Her maid, Harmony Pan, called out as she entered the bedroom beyond, pulling back curtains to let in streams of morning gray. After a moment, she appeared in the doorway with an unconvincing frown. "Are you unwell again, mistress?" She was terrible at faking concern, terrible at faking anything, really. It made her a subpar servant and left her working in the Main rather than the High, but Grayc Illan knew to appreciate a bad liar.

She focused on the woman's reflection in the mirror. The maid's blonde hair made Grayc's vision swim, and for a fraction of a second she saw the woman from Jacobi's bed standing there, body bruised, swollen, and bleeding, tufts of that yellow hair ripped out. With a sneer, she tore her eyes away from the reflection and poured the flask of water into a basin before dunking a wash cloth in it and proceeding to wipe the sweat from her face. "Change your hair color," she ordered, and the hoarseness of her voice startled even her.

Harmony Pan blinked, one cheek pulling in a flash of offense. "Excuse me?"

Grayc Illan sighed and shook her head, dropping the wet cloth in the sink before leaving the bathroom. "Never mind."

Harmony Pan had already set out a tray with breakfast and more water. "There was a massacre in the Low of Maggrin last night," the maid noted as she set the paper beside Grayc Illan's plate. "Some duster went mad and killed a hooker, which somehow turned into a brawl with a couple other people. The duster survived, until the wolves were sent out for him."

Grayc shivered. She had dreamed of running, of hunting, of narrow streets and the scent of blood.

The maid didn't appear to notice the way her mistress cringed. "It's not in the paper, but I've heard rumors that the lady Larc of Vym is missing." Her voice rose with excitement as she filled Grayc Illan's glass. "Some say she ran off with a lover, but most agree she's been taken. The Vym twins are going mad over it and vowed not to leave the Low until she's found." Harmony laughed, the bitterness she never quite managed to hide showing through. "You'd think they were starving, somewhere out in the Ash, the way they say it. Poor little Addom and Evelet Vym, in the Low."

The maid's features lit suddenly with excitement. "You must have met them, when you served the prince. Are they as they say? Beautiful demons?" Her smile almost split her face, and as much as she annoyed Grayc, she couldn't help but realize that it was the prettiest the girl had ever looked.

"Don't you have things to do?" Grayc Illan said.

Harmony Pan flushed, hesitating before staying where she stood beside the table. "Your house isn't much upkeep, miss. You don't exactly make much of a mess," she said quietly. She wanted to ask something, it was there in her simple features and it made Grayc tired to look at for too long.

"This isn't your first time as a housekeeper," she prompted, keeping this conversation going until her maid could muster the courage to get the words out.

"Not at all, miss." Harmony Pan shook her head. "I've been cleaning homes, making beds, and setting out meals since I was seven years old." She was staring at Grayc, fingers twitching against the front of her apron as she resisted the urge to fidget. "I always wanted to meet you."

Discomfort had her putting her glass of water down and looking away.

"I apologize," Harmony Pan rushed to add even as she took a step back. "My mother knew yours. She spoke of her often and fondly when I was a child. Everyone whispers about you now." She smiled but it was a thin gesture, on the verge of misery. "Everyone in the Low of Belholn knows who you are. The daughter of a seamstress. A slave to the Lady Belholn. A servant to Fay Dray Fen. The prince's valet. And now a mistress of Belholn and the prince's lover."

Grayc tipped her head back and watched the maid, studying the envy in her eyes and the bitter lines creasing her brow. "Are you going to ask or not?"

Harmony Pan sucked a breath and held it almost too long. Her fingers pressed against her apron, her eyes wide. "What do you have that the rest of us don't, Grayc Illan Sanaro?" she whispered, more vexed than accusing. "What made you good enough to serve Belholns, Vyms, and Dray Fens? What is it about you that they would let you become more?"

Harmony Pan waited a long minute in the silence that followed before humiliation brought a little sound of dismay from her chest. Shock at her own boldness colored her cheeks and had her ducking her head and shuffling two steps back, into the frame of the door. She parted her lips, probably to try at an apology, when Grayc finally spoke. She hadn't really planned to. She knew what the maid would want to ask—what they always wanted to ask. How had her fate changed so drastically? Why her?

"A little bit of fortune and a lot of misfortune. It was not as simple as you might think. First, it was misery, and then, it was vengeance. After that it was fear, terror, and finally, slavery." She studied the maid once more as though measuring her next words carefully. "I think, what you really wanted to ask, is why I am sitting here and you are standing there?"

Harmony Pan's fingers clutched at the doorframe. She was barely breathing now. "Yes."

"I was of use to them. More use than filling glasses and washing laundry."

The maid soured at first, perceiving the words as cruelty before considering them more carefully.

"Be careful who you are useful to, Harmony Pan. At some point, they might take your soul to keep you that way."

Harmony stood there a moment longer, then curtsied and left.

Grayc picked up her water and drank, alone, at a table of cakes and coffee she dared not touch.

Vaun leaned against the rough brick wall, no longer caring for the wellbeing of his shirt, and scrubbed a hand over his face. The air in the Low was bitter and the days had been long. A week of searching—even with most of the High houses of Vym sending their bravest to help scour the Low—produced no trace of the youngest Vym.

After a handful of days, Vaun realized that he was looking for a body rather than a woman, and that he was not alone in his pessimism. He watched Addom reign over the search and wondered if he still had hope, or if pure rage drove him to find the source of his pain.

Vaun had not realized that he had closed his eyes until he opened them and the grogginess in his head told him that he had fallen asleep against a wall. He smiled and it was purely a gesture of exhaustion. He wondered what that picture would have looked like; the prince, in rumpled clothing, asleep against a wall in the Low. It would have been a picture worthy of the paper if there had been someone beautiful on their knees in front of him.

Samuel Sinol stood nearby with a heavy scowl and one of Vaun's jackets over his arm. "Let me take you to the car, your highness," the valet almost pleaded. "You have not slept in days."

With a groan, the prince straightened and stretched. "Addom has not slept."

Samuel Sinol nodded carefully. "His sister has vanished, and he is overcome with emotion. Why are you here?" The delicacy of his words defied the youth of his face.

Vaun scratched at the back of his skull because the stimulation made it a little easier to keep his eyes open. That was the question, wasn't it? Why did he linger on this tragedy? Because Addom was his friend? Because he hadn't expected it to last so long?

"You missed an appointment with Meresin last night," Samuel

Sinol continued. "She sent a card to the house to express her disappointment."

Vaun eyed his valet; could the man be lying? It wasn't like Meresin to send cards, or to be disappointed, for that matter. "Take me home, Simons." The command felt nice on his lips, accompanied by a sense of relief. Going home would mean going back to the High, away from this tragedy and back into the warm sheets of his normal life.

The plush leather interior of his car was more comfortable than he remembered and before they had even driven a block, Vaun was asleep.

Vaun looked out the window, speeding across the High from Vym to Belholn.

"Do you think Larc will ever be found?" AviSariel twisted in her seat beside him to ask. The search had been going on for weeks and there had been no sign of her.

"No, but stranger things have happened."

"Well, I hope things go back to the way they were before," she admitted with a small huff. "Vym is terribly empty with so many of the families in the Low with the twins."

"They don't plan to return," Vaun found himself explaining. Why did he bother? She knew, she just liked pretending she didn't because Fay preferred her that way.

She made a sharp sound of tongue to teeth. "Some of the High born have started buying property in the Low," she whispered her bit of gossip. She'd become fond of gossip in those weeks, even more fond of it than tea, but she still wasn't so ahead of it that she could come up with things Vaun hadn't already heard or seen. The High born with more friendship or loyalty to the twins than Quentan Vym had begun making themselves comfortable in the Low.

To everyone's surprise, the bottom of Vym Province had plenty of room for the rise in population as a number of buildings had been abandoned long before anyone could recall, some with no records of ownership at all.

"The Dourdin sisters won't stop going on about renovations. They talk like they've been meaning to do it for years."

Vaun smiled a little. She was careful never to complain about his own frequent visits to the Low to help with the search. He guessed her silence on the subject was because she hoped he wouldn't move down there permanently and drag her with him.

Now and then she would slip up with her wording and he would hear his sister in his wife's prattle. 'There is no point in fussing over things you can't control.' 'Quentan will deal with matters.' 'Addom is simply grieving the loss of his sibling. He'll come to his senses soon.' It all seemed logical enough and a part of Vaun wanted desperately to pull those words over himself like a blanket and turn away from his friend's pain, turn away from the Low, and back to his own life.

He wanted to drown himself in cups of tea and rooms of smoke and forget the strange, heavy feeling in his chest, the one that had been growing for longer than he could remember. Had it started when Larc vanished? When he woke beneath the Ash in that lake of shadows? Or had it been when Grayc lay dead on the floor of The Gentlemen's Club? Whenever it was, it had built up inside of him until now, on some nights, Vaun found himself lying awake for no reason at all, no thoughts in his head, no wants in his limbs. He stared at the ceiling in a consumed state of unrest.

There was something wrong and, in a pile of things wrong, he could not know which it was that gnawed at him.

AviSariel's hand carefully captured his from his thigh to hold it in the fragile cage of her fingers, drawing him from his thoughts to his current place in the car. How much time did he spend on these leather seats? Was it always the same car, or did he have several of the same design?

"Do you think this dress will do?"

He didn't bother looking her over where she sat beside him; he'd seen her when he walked her from the house to the car not thirty minutes ago. Time spent in the teahouses and clubs of the Realm had made AviSariel more confident and more comfortable. She played more boldly with the vanity crafts in her bathroom, tonight coloring her eyes to match the lavender of her dress and giving her skin a faint silver shimmer.

"It's fine." It wasn't an adequate appraisal and yet she smiled at the scrap of a compliment.

Would Grayc be at the party? It had been all too easy to jump on an invitation out of Vym. Even more so with the hope of seeing her.

He'd thought about going to her, thought about the way she always set his world right in the past, but a strange sort of pride kept him from seeking her out. She couldn't exactly go traipsing into Vym Province herself now that she was business partners with a Belholn cousin. Vaun knew that, and yet he was disappointed every day that she didn't show up at his door.

He felt AviSariel watching him and without looking knew that she was frowning.

"Will Fay be there?" she asked.

He shook his head. Fay was always invited, as a princess, even if she had married a Vym, but she never attended parties in Belholn. She had a few friendships in Maggrin; their family flavor of bitterness and underhanded remarks suited her well. But as far as Vaun knew, she hadn't set foot in Belholn since her wedding.

"Meresin should be." It was the reason they were going. More than an escape from Vym or a hope of seeing Grayc, Vaun wanted to talk to Meresin. As of late, she'd become a recluse, but Samuel Sinol assured him that the Realm's favorite redhead was going to the Belholn party.

AviSariel perked up instantly. "Really? We were supposed to have lunch last week, but she had to cancel."

"I can't imagine her missing it."

189

AviSariel toyed with a bit of lace edging her bodice. "Do… do you think it's true? What people are saying about her?"

"That she's stopped taking appointments and canceled several already on the books? That seems true enough." Vaun stretched. "But the rest? That one of her clients knocked her around, and she's too vain to be seen with the bruises? That she's fallen in love? That she's pregnant, a common ailment of Low born women?"

AviSariel chewed her lip. "Could any of it be true?"

Vaun scoffed. "Not Meresin. No one in the Realm would be fool enough to strike a creature so beloved. Nor is she the type for monogamous romance. And if she were the sort to take up childbearing, it likely would have happened before now."

"Then why isn't she coming to parties? Why not come to see me?" AviSariel's frown deepened.

A good question. Vaun shrugged and kept his suspicions to himself. The last he'd seen the redhead, he'd lain in her arms and told her about the long days and nights searching for Larc. A quiver rippling through Meresin's body cut his words short, and he'd sat up to find the woman flushed and staring—not with sympathy, but with fear. No matter what assurances he made or bribes he offered, she refused to speak a word on the matter. Vaun couldn't know how, but he'd bet his best suit jacket Meresin knew something about Larc's disappearance. He'd nearly told Addom his suspicion, but if Meresin wouldn't bend to the wishes and offerings of a prince, the only thing more Addom could try was violence.

When they arrived at the Belholn estate, the prince allowed his wife to keep his hand and walked her up the steps and into the main hall. The clattering of glasses and dice greeted them as background music to laughter and voices. He led her into the crowded rooms of gambling tables and exquisitely well-dressed bodies.

Julia Amil, wife of Xavian Ren, found them quickly in the flurry of guests.

"Your highness." She grinned broadly in welcome. "Your grace.

You are most welcome to my house." She reached for AviSariel's hand and tucked it into the crook of her arm. "Won't you let me give you a tour, princess? You should see our renovations! It's all quite the rage, even if we're not in the dreadful Low."

Vaun smiled as Julia led his wife away, already chattering about colors and materials.

He snagged a wine glass from a passing server and eyed the tables as though trying to decide where to begin his revelry. He saw her at once: he always did, even in a crowded room. Some part of him knew she was there the moment he walked in, the very moment the weight in his chest eased a little.

She tried hard not to be extraordinary. She dressed in solid shades of gray, without flare or excess. Perfectly tailored, but nothing striking. He couldn't understand it. The more he knew about her, the less her fashion made sense. His familiarity with her skin made any clothing at all almost offensive, hiding her strange tattoo, that x over her heart, and the assortment of scars he had discovered ghosting her skin.

Grayc Illan looked unamazing in her plain dress, despite its scooped collar and the way the blue ribbon around her neck trailed long ends down her front from the tiny bow against her throat. Beautiful, but unamazing, when surrounded by the High of Belholn in all their glamour, color, and flesh. She sat at a crescent-shaped card table with a man wearing a fur-lined jacket in canary yellow to match the color of his hair and a woman who had squeezed her impressive bosom into a corset three sizes too small. With one solid laugh at least one of those breasts would burst free and the room would know whether her nipples matched the raspberry shade of her gown.

Vaun came to the table, smiling wider at the way his former valet pretended not to notice him. The raspberry and canary simpered at him, and a fourth player—a man Vaun had seen but not bothered to remember—jumped up to relinquish his chair for the prince.

Grayc Illan didn't so much as flicker an eyelash as he took his seat, but he thought her pulse jumped a little beneath that thin silk ribbon. She picked up her white backed cards, nails painted red, a color so deep it bordered on black. It made him think of the blood that seeped from her body in that hollow beneath the Ash.

He did drink from his glass then, not a pretend sip but an honest swallow. The memory made him thirsty but the cool poison of his drink gave no satisfaction.

"Prince," the raspberry said with a spread of painted lips. The shape of her mouth was familiar and it occurred to Vaun that he'd slept with this woman before. "I don't think I've seen you since Lord Xavian Ren's birthday." She said the man's name with a certain flourish that made it clear she desired his favor. She wasn't a Belholn, then; blood bought a fair amount of freedom from bootlicking.

Vaun had no memory of seeing her at Ren's birthday celebration, an astonishing feat on his part if she had been dressed anything like she was now. "I've been residing in Vym as of late," he said, as though the entire Realm didn't know his schedule. He picked up his cards.

Grayc Illan didn't sort her cards, he noticed; she simply looked at them once and set them face down on the table again.

"Is your bride accompanying you tonight?" the raspberry persisted.

Vaun nodded, though his gaze lingered on Grayc. "She's floundering about here somewhere, probably rejecting the amorous attentions of gentlemen."

The canary across from him smiled over his cards. "Rejection looks different than I remember." He jutted his chin over Vaun's shoulder and the prince turned his head to see. He managed not to grin. AviSariel, still linked in arms with Julia Amil, held court amid the attention of several charming Belholn men and women. Even from the back, Vaun identified one of her admirers to be Philip Belholn. AviSariel's cheeks were already colored in that blush that was fast becoming a badge on the prides of High born lovers.

She waved a cigarette at him when she caught him looking and

Vaun smiled back. He had yet to see her pick up or light her own cigarette, but somehow her fingers were often occupied and her lungs exhaling bright clouds.

Vaun returned his attention to his cards. "Vym has been good for her. Or rather, the Vym twins have."

The raspberry giggled, eager to make a sound, and even her false laughter made her cleavage jiggle dangerously. "Terrible news about that little Vym, though," she started to say, but whatever sympathy she was about to offer tapered off under the arrival of Belholn's own daughter.

Wendry Belholn ran her thin hand along the back of Vaun's shoulders. With one glance, the man in yellow stood and held out his seat for her. As Wendry sat, she exhaled pink smoke. She was dressed much the same as usual: no jewelry, adornments, or jacket. She showed too much skin for her class, though no one would say it. Her dark hair was wild and free, looking tangled in the way it fell down her back and over her gaunt shoulders.

"Do you think they will find her body?" Wendry inquired.

The raspberry put her eyes to her cards, trading out three and saying nothing more. Grayc Illan picked up the card on top of her neat little pile and exchanged it for a new one. The dealer remained silent, dispensing and picking up cards without lifting his gaze from the table.

The game stalled when it turned to Wendry and the cards in front of her, which she had not yet touched.

"What makes you think she is dead?" the prince asked. He had pressed a couple of the Belholn sons for information over the last few weeks, and while both had been enjoyable interrogations—saturated in dust to make answers fall easily from lush mouths—neither had been informative. As far as Vaun had been able to discern, the Belholns didn't have Larc. He had not approached Wendry, though. It was possible she had acted alone. She was just mad enough to start a war between the houses.

"She would have been found if she were alive. There aren't many Vyms in the Realm." Wendry smirked, because her own clan did not lack in numbers. "I hear her perversions killed her." Wendry lifted her cigarette.

"If only we could all be so lucky as to die in the throes of our secrets." He didn't mean to let his gaze linger on Grayc, but it had been so long since he'd been near her, looking was all he could do to keep from touching her.

Wendry snickered around her cigarette, pink smoke curling out the sides of her mouth. "I don't know that having a tendency for rats is so impressive a secret, prince. It's really just bad taste."

Grayc Illan didn't flinch. She looked bored, her face perfectly composed, but for the briefest of seconds Vaun saw something in her eyes, something true and contrary to the mask she wore.

Vaun rolled his shoulders and turned his head to eye the little monster across from him. "I suppose. Your fetishes, on the other hand—"

She grinned with those thin lips. "Are hardly secrets."

"No. But how lovely would it be, to die in the mess of your own lust? Painted in their blood, and yours? Your own vomit caked on your skin and their cum sticking in your lungs?" His voice lowered, leaning a little closer to hear her smoky breath hitch. Wendry Belholn shuddered, surprise shining in the black pits of her eyes. Everyone knew her habits, but Vaun had never spoken of them. She leaned in without realizing it. "Corpses of fallen playmates would still be warm beneath you, and he would be looming over, watching the life slip out of you. The one lover you couldn't get under you, couldn't slide a knife into. He'll wrap his fingers around your neck and you'll moan until his grip won't allow it. He'll squeeze until you struggle. He'll squeeze even when he fucks you and you'll try to stay alive just to make it to the end."

Her cigarette burned down to the cradle of her fingers but she didn't seem to notice, even when it met with her skin. Her other hand reached out across the table to touch his with her long, cold fingers. "Are you such a lover, prince?" she whispered, hopeful and skeptical all at once.

Vaun smiled and pulled his hand out from under hers, tapping his cards pointedly and eyeing the pile she hadn't touched in front of her. "Doubtful."

Her teeth clicked, and for a moment he thought she might snap. Instead, Wendry let out a little laugh of pink smoke and picked up her cards. "Such a tease." She tossed a card toward the dealer and he slid her another across the black surface. "I don't know why you bother, prince. There is no point in playing cards with Grayc. All those years in the gutter have taught her how to cheat."

Grayc Illan smiled at that, but it wasn't a smile Vaun was familiar with. "If by 'the gutter' you mean 'this house,' then yes, I learned to cheat in the slums of Belholn."

The raspberry gasped, making herself known again to the table but not drawing much attention.

Wendry glared at his former valet. "You think you can spit words like that just because Jacobi gave you a long leash?"

The prince snorted. "Neither her status nor her employment has ever curbed her tongue."

"I don't know about that. I heard she was quite different when she served my mother." Wendry dropped her cigarette on the floor and the dealer quickly produced a fresh one. "She was a quiet little rat, and skittish, too."

Vaun raised an eyebrow, leaning back into his chair. "Doesn't sound like the Grayc Illan we know today."

The Belholn daughter shrugged. "I guess time changes a girl. She has crawled a long way up from hemming my mother's skirts."

"An awful lot of speculation from a child who was still wetting the sheets last time I served in her house," Grayc Illan said.

Wendry's mouth twitched and she quickly returned the cigarette to it. "Weren't you the one washing those sheets?"

The curl at the corner of Grayc Illan's lips told Vaun that Wendry had walked into a trap. "No. That was probably your nursemaid, Sylvia Hal."

Wendry tensed, blood draining from her face, leaving her eyes dead and her lips parted, as though breathing were difficult. The name of the nursemaid meant nothing to Vaun but obviously it meant something to Wendry.

"You were a beautiful baby," Grayc Illan continued. "I was there when you were born."

There was a secret there, lingering over the table between them and Vaun would have given his wardrobe to know what it was. It felt old, and from the way Wendry seethed in her chair, he wondered if it would be important to anyone but her.

"I'll fold." Grayc Illan stood. "How could I possibly win at a table with the prince and Wendry Belholn?" She offered them a tip of her head, a curl falling over her cheek. For a moment, her gaze met Vaun's, as though she had tried not to but in the last second before she turned she just couldn't stop herself.

He watched her go, memorizing the direction before reaching across the table to take up her cards: four of a kind. Wendry made an angry little sound and stood, her chair scraping the floor. She mumbled polite words to the prince before storming off in the opposite direction. More guests quickly filled the empty seats and the prince played six hands before excusing himself to circle the room.

He pretended not to notice Jacobi at a table with his arm around a pretty blond man only because he knew how much the Belholn would want to meet his gaze. For a moment Vaun wondered if it was the same as Wendry not meeting Grayc Illan's gaze, as though looking at them would be an honor that they didn't deserve.

The thought didn't linger long. Vaun walked through rooms of gambling tables and sweet smoke but saw no Grayc among the tangles of limbs and fabric. He was about to ask one of the many familiar faces when a streak of red caught his eye. He turned just in time to see Meresin duck through a door with Xavian Ren at her heels.

He might not have bothered to snoop if it hadn't been for the stiff, defensive line of Meresin's shoulders, or the set of Xavian Ren's jaw. Vaun crossed the room and slipped through the door, stopping short upon finding himself in a cramped, colorless servant's hall. It was so ugly without wallpaper or hardwood that he almost turned back.

"Tell me what you know!" Xavian Ren's voice echoed somewhere near the other end of the hall, drawing Vaun closer to the thin door that stood between him and the developing scene.

"I said I don't know. I don't!" Meresin begged, her voice unusually high and thin. It cracked around the last word.

The sharp, shrill sounds of metal crashing to the floor struck out, stifling her screams.

"Who's poisoning my people, Merry?" Xavian Ren's deep voice demanded. "Who's making the bad dust?"

Vaun stood near the door and listened to her crying.

"Is it you?" Xavian Ren snarled. "You said you knew something. You know who's behind the bad dust. Don't pretend now that you don't."

She whimpered.

"What's your price, Merry? What do you want?" His voice lowered, but didn't soften, and her whimpering exploded into the start of a scream that only ended because Vaun shoved the servant's door open.

He staggered into the kitchen, blinking painfully against the bright lights. Pots and pans littered the floor. Xavian Ren pinned Meresin to the steel counter, hand knotted in her glorious hair and knife poised against her throat. Meresin's pale gaze flickered to him helplessly. The Lord of Belholn swallowed back a snarl at the sight of Vaun, but didn't move. His lips pressed tightly and for a stretch of time, no one was willing to speak first.

Vaun finally scrubbed a hand over his face as though struggling to sober up. "This isn't the men's room, I take it?" He peered at the gleaming counter tops and stacks of plates and teacups. His gaze lingered on the dishes littering the floor and then finally landed on the knife against Meresin's neck. His mouth spread in a sloppy smile.

"Since when do you play rough?" Vaun laughed and sauntered closer, leaning against the counter beside her. Her breath came in quick pants and tears tracked down her round cheeks. "I offered her my house in Maggrin to let me hold a pistol to her in bed—not even loaded—but she declined." He made a disgruntled sound and plucked the blade from Xavian Ren's hand. The Lord let him have it and released Meresin's hair as well. "This is much more dangerous than a pistol," the prince said too loudly and waved it about before looking up at the Lord of Belholn. "What did you have to pay her?"

Xavian Ren dragged himself back a step, allowing Meresin to scurry out of reach. He straightened his jacket. "Prince, I think you've strayed from the party."

"You're the host." Vaun laughed, ducking his head coyly and pressing a palm tenderly to Xavian Ren's chest. The Lord was a head taller than him. Long body, wide mouth, and blond hair—that was what made up a Belholn. Or, at least, most Belholns. "Isn't the party wherever you are?"

Meresin bolted for the door. It occurred to Vaun that he had never seen her run before; at least, not when she wasn't hoping to be chased. Xavian Ren sighed heavily and looked at the hand still against his chest. "You don't use the bathrooms in my house."

"Hm?" The prince blinked up at him innocently, still flicking the knife in the air beside them.

Xavian Ren wore a tight smile and looked the prince in the eye. Leaned back against the counter, Vaun was practically petite. If it wasn't for the knife in his hand and the confidence of blue blood in his veins, he might have looked like prey. "Even when you're completely dusted, you refuse to set foot in our bathrooms, your highness. Something about the size of the tiles."

Vaun smiled slowly and dropped his pretense. The knife stopped moving. "My mistake." He let his hand fall away from the Lord's chest and stood upright, leaving even less space between them.

"Are you involved in this?" Xavian Ren spoke quietly and Vaun could almost hear the storm in his voice. Belholns were dangerous when happy; only a fool would push one. Was Meresin a fool?

"I don't even know what 'this' is." He spun the knife in his hand and offered it, handle first, to the Lord. "Though I seem to have developed a habit of interfering."

The Lord took the knife tentatively and set it aside with a mild rush that implied he didn't want to look like he was threatening a prince. Vaun started for that dreary little door again.

"Has interfering worked well for you so far?" Ren asked.

Vaun laughed. "Not at all."

"Then might I suggest not interfering again."

The prince didn't bother to look back. "That's the trouble with being invincible. There's no incentive not to follow my impulses."

He took the shabby little hallway back to the party and wondered just what Meresin knew. He doubted she could be the mastermind behind the bad dust, but given the beds she tumbled into, she might well have heard what others preferred to keep hidden.

Vaun resisted the impulse to look for her upon rejoining the party because she'd surely have fled by now, tucked in her car and speeding toward another province. He'd wait until she went to ground and hope that in her distress, she'd confess what she knew. More importantly, he'd wait until Belholn eyes didn't shift oh-so-subtly his way.

The sight of Grayc Illan dancing wiped all thoughts of Meresin from his mind. Even with her back to him, he knew she was smiling, her expression reflected in Udaro's as they swayed. She laughed when he spun her and relaxed when he held her close. Udaro's smile vanished when his eyes, eternally lined in black, met Vaun's across the room.

A hand touched his, drawing his attention away from the crowd to look down at the fingers clutching his. "Do you want to dance?" AviSariel whispered, sounding hopeful and a little dusted.

He stared at their entwined hands. He had never taken hers, but she enjoyed taking his. "I do." The prince pulled his fingers from hers and walked across the floor. He didn't look back. Maybe later that night he would reflect on leaving AviSariel standing there, and wish he had been a better man, or even just cared enough to lie. Dancers spun out of his path. Udaro and Grayc Illan stopped moving. Vaun paused behind her to slide his fingertips up her spine, against the fine material of her dress.

"Thank you for the dance, Udaro," she said, and the other man stepped away. His relentless stare held another moment before he turned away, and once again the prince wondered what stood between them. They had not been friendly since Udaro appeared under the Ash to save them from the darkness, though Vaun had never asked why.

Finally alone, as alone as they could be in a ballroom, Vaun touched her naked arm, trailing his fingers up her shoulder to stroke the back of her neck at the bottom of her curls. "Aren't you done with this game yet?" he whispered near her ear and tugged the delicate blue ribbon. The bow gave, shrinking until it collapsed and he could slowly pull the silk from her throat.

"What game?" she whispered back, turning her head to the side so that his mouth hovered close to hers.

He smiled. She must have missed him as much as he missed her, to allow such a scene.

"The one that keeps you in Belholn." With the ribbon twisted in his fingers, he took her hand and pulled her into a dance. She didn't relax as she had with Udaro, but she matched every step and kept her eyes locked on his face, sometimes lingering on his mouth.

"Belholn is my home."

"You hate it," he replied, but offered a grin. "Leave it. Come home with me."

Grayc Illan laughed. "What would your wife think?"

"Whatever you're up to, it isn't worth it." Vaun's smile faded, thinking about Meresin cornered in the kitchen. He could not imagine his Grayc cornered so easily, but he could imagine the result being much worse.

She smiled and he wondered if his concern charmed her. "You do not know what I am up to, so how can you know what it is worth?"

He leaned in, brushing her lips with his. "If you are not with me, it is not worth it."

Her smile grew, and something altered about it, something almost honest, before it faded back into its normal, tempered shape. "She has a crush on you."

Vaun blinked. "Who?"

"Your wife." Grayc Illan stared up at him and all traces of humor faded. "Be careful with hearts." She touched his cheek, and his skin tingled from the contact of her fingertips in front of so many eyes. "They can be dangerous when they're broken."

"I have never broken a heart."

She looked at her fingers on his cheek and slowly drew them away. "Now who is the liar?"

They stopped dancing and she took a step back. His arms surrendered her reluctantly. "The song isn't over," Vaun remarked, hoping not to sound bitter.

Grayc smiled and brushed curls behind one ear. They didn't stay. "Someone wants your attention."

He glanced aside and was mildly surprised to see his valet standing along the sidelines of the ballroom, looking more than a little anxious. Of all the people he thought might seek his attention, Samuel Sinol had not come to mind.

Grayc Illan's hand tugged and nearly escaped his, bringing his gaze back to her. "I'm going home for the night." Was it an invitation?

His smile must have looked devious, because she laughed and pulled away from him. "Your valet knows the address."

He resisted the urge to follow, his head cocking to one side. "You think I'll come when you call?"

"Come or don't," she said as she backed away. "I'll always be waiting for you." Her lips curled around the promise and he shivered at the sincerity in her stare.

It hurt to watch her go, but he didn't follow, her ribbon still tangled around his fingers.

When he left the floor, AviSariel no longer stood on the sidelines. Hammish Belholn swirled her across the dance floor and laughter wiped away any sadness that might have tarnished her features. Vaun sauntered toward the main hall knowing that Samuel Sinol would follow. When the man caught up to him the concern that plagued his youthful features had not faded.

"Your highness," he said quietly, "we should leave."

"Leave?"

"I've found someone who says he knows who took lady Larc. He says he will only speak with you."

Vaun frowned, thumb stroking the ribbon in his palm. "Why me? Send him to Addom." For the first time in weeks, Vaun had something more interesting on his mind than Larc's disappearance and bad dust. Not quite as noble, but for the moment, more interesting.

Samuel Sinol's lips tightened. "He says you'll want to be the first to hear it." He took a step closer, almost invading the prince's personal space for the sake of discretion. "He says it concerns someone you care for and that you would regret not hearing it first."

Vaun hesitated before finally nodding and allowing his valet to lead the way. It wasn't terribly uncommon that someone tried to bait his attention with lies, but why use this particular ruse? Why bait him with news of a Vym, and not Addom?

Well, who was he to turn aside perfectly good gossip? Perhaps he wouldn't need to wheedle information out of Meresin, after all. If it concerned her—and he fervently hoped it didn't—perhaps he could save her pretty neck before the Vyms broke it.

At any rate, hunting up gossip was always an acceptable excuse to dash and an even more acceptable reason to be secretive.

Whether the man offered real information, or was just a liar looking for the prince's ear, perhaps he could thank him all the same for getting him out of the Belholn house early.

CHAPTER TEN

The prince followed Samuel Sinol up a dark, narrow stairway. Muted wallpaper peeled from the walls and an unimaginable stench drifted from somewhere above. "Why are we in the Main of Belholn, Sandy? If the rat saw something, shouldn't he be in the Low of Vym?"

"He lives here, your highness. He was in Vym to meet with friends, or so he says." Samuel Sinol's lips twisted on the words. "But he did speak of Vym as if he'd been there."

Vaun noted the stains on the walls and slid his hands into his pockets.

"He works for a craftsman that caters to the High." Samuel Sinol lowered his voice as they approached a dented door.

They stopped in front of an entrance with a brass number on it and the valet knocked soundly at the thin wood.

There was a rustle inside followed by the heavy release of locks. Vaun couldn't help but wonder what use good locks would be on a door that frail. It opened and he frowned at the creaking of its hinges. A disheveled man peered suspiciously out at them, barely visible from the dim interior. Vaun hesitated; he'd rather not have entered. He'd been in shabbier places, but this time he wasn't dusted. Samuel Sinol brushed past the man and some strained form of masculine pride forced Vaun across the threshold.

The furniture was surprisingly nice but upon further inspection Vaun realized that each hand carved piece was flawed or damaged in some way. The man himself was average, about Vaun's own size, but aged. Wrinkles gathered around his mouth and eyes, the sight of which made the prince inexplicably uncomfortable.

The man grinned and those folds of withered skin grew. "I knew you'd be interested," he said hurriedly before gesturing to one of those damaged chairs. "Sit, sit."

"No." Vaun had to draw the line somewhere. This whole evening had gotten out of hand in the least enjoyable way. He stood in a mediocre apartment in the Main with bad lighting, wearing a jacket he'd had designed specifically for this evening, and there was absolutely no sign of debauchery or humor taking place. He had a ribbon in his pocket and a woman waiting somewhere in this province, a fact he loved to savor and had no intention of wasting. "What do you have to tell me?"

The man's smile faltered but never quite faded. "Straight to business. Very well." He shifted on his feet. "I was in Vym that night the little lady got taken. I saw everything."

Vaun raised an eyebrow. "Really? And why haven't you said anything?"

The man huffed. "I ain't got much interest in meddling, you know?" He laughed nervously. "I don't want my throat cut over some rich girl."

"And that changed?"

"I saw her again," he said, seeming to panic upon hearing the disinterest in the prince's voice. "I saw her here, in Belholn! I didn't know who she was that night but when I saw her again…" He exhaled heavily and licked his lips.

Vaun frowned. He tried to remain skeptical but hope leaked into his thoughts. "You saw Larc in Belholn? In the Low, or—"

The man's laughter cut off the prince's question. "No! Not the

Vym girl. The woman that took her!"

"A woman?" Dread pitted in his stomach. Meresin?

The man nodded. "There were men there, too, but I recognized her. I can't believe I didn't realize who she was that night. Everyone knows her around here."

"Who?" He didn't want to hear it. He didn't. But he had to. He had to know so that he could get ahead of whatever was going on.

The man grinned and leaned in, closer than Vaun appreciated. "Grayc Illan Sanaro."

The prince swayed as if the man had punched him. He stared, chest heavy and fingers tight in his pocket. "Be careful who you name, sir."

"It was her," he insisted, standing taller. "I saw her, her curls and a little ribbon around her neck. I saw her!"

Vaun suddenly wished he had sat down when it had been offered. His fingers felt cold around the silk in his pocket. "Who else have you told?"

The man shifted on his feet again. "I don't want to cause no trouble and if the Vyms hear about it… well, that Grayc is gonna lose her head."

Vaun closed his eyes to keep from cursing. Why didn't he doubt that she'd done it? "Why did you tell me?"

"Everyone knows about you and her. I was thinking… I could keep my mouth shut about it, and maybe you could give me some sort of compensation?"

The prince opened his eyes and there must have been something frightening in them because the man took a step back. "You're blackmailing me?" His voice was smooth, curious rather than outraged.

"I… I saw her," the man stammered.

Vaun winced. "Yes, you did." He reached out and before the man could take another backward step those royal fingers clamped down on the sides of his face, dragging him close. Vaun saw the reflection of his now silver eyes in the dull ones of the other man before he pulled his face close, hissing through gritted teeth in the stranger's ear. "You saw nothing. You weren't even in Vym that night."

He threw the man back and black wisps of magic trailed from the stranger's eyes. He landed hard on the floor and blinked away the darkness. He breathed heavily and when he looked up at Vaun and Samuel Sinol, his face twisted with confusion. "What in Queen's name are you doin' in my place?" He exhaled uneasily and crawled to his feet. "Who are you?"

The prince turned away.

"Get out!" the stranger demanded behind him.

"Forgive us. Wrong room," Samuel Sinol said with a disgusted sniff.

Vaun headed down the stairs, hands fisted in his pockets against the impulse to do worse to the wretch. The door closed with a distant snap and clipped footsteps hurried after him.

"Your highness," Samuel Sinol said after a moment. "Was that...wise?"

Vaun heard what he meant easily enough. *Everyone knows some High born still have magic of their own, but no one dares use it for fear of offending the Queen.*

"Do I need to do the same to you?" Vaun snarled.

Samuel Sinol missed a step, but only one. "No, your highness. Do you have a plan of action?"

Vaun hissed. "Take me to her."

Grayc Illan had slipped out of her dress and returned it with care to the closet, along with her shoes. It was her bedroom, and her house, but it still felt borrowed. Her life felt borrowed and she couldn't remember the last time it had felt like her own.

When she returned to the large vanity, she wore only a thin silk slip and her garters. She stared at herself in the framed mirror. Her fingers touched her curls. Her hair had always been this way, she was certain she remembered that correctly. Her mother's hair had been the same, hadn't it? She remembered playing with her curls when she was a girl.

Her fingers trailed down and her eyes watched them in the mirror as they tugged at the low neck of her slip to touch the ink that crossed out her heart. She remembered the night she let a man with eyes that did not match put a needle to her skin and the way Udaro had laughed at her for cringing.

Her hand left the mark to glide down over silk and finally set her palm to her abdomen. Silence welled up around her and in the back of her mind she remembered her mother's whisper, *"I loved you before your heart beat and I'll love you even after mine stops."*

The clatter of some heavy piece of furniture toppling over in the house startled her from her thoughts. She turned toward her door and heard Harmony Pan's voice from the front hallway. "Prince Vaun! You can't barge in like this!" She sounded out of sorts and breathy. "Wait!" Two pairs of footsteps rushed down the corridor.

Grayc Illan opened her door just as he pushed in, sending her back a few startled steps. Heat rushed to her face. "What are you—"

"Is she dead?" He stopped just inside her room, Harmony Pan red faced and completely at a loss behind him.

Grayc felt the rage drain from her features. Of all the things for him to learn, did it have to be that? She managed to take her eyes from him long enough to look at her maid. "You're excused for the night."

Harmony Pan hesitated.

"Go," Grayc Illan ordered. The maid bit her lip and curtsied before stomping away.

"Is she dead?" Vaun yelled this time.

"Who—"

"Don't lie!" He pushed past her to look inside her bathroom and rip open the doors of her closet. "Where is she?" He stalked back out into the hall. She followed on bare feet, flinching every time he threw open another door and searched a room. Did he really think she'd keep Larc here? Tied up in a closet or stuffed in a trunk?

"Vaun..."

"Where is she?" He shouted, taking the stairs up to the second floor. She hurried after him, her chest feeling tighter with every step.

"Vaun." She tried to sound firm. When he found a door that was locked, he broke it open. Even strong doors caved. He pulled open the closets of her office and cursed violently.

"Where?" he roared.

"She isn't here!" She watched his body jerk to a stop at her words.

He turned enough to offer his profile, to see her without having to look at her. His silver eyes shone bright in the dark. "Is she dead?" the prince whispered. His voice was just as foreign to her as it had been when he shouted.

Her hands knotted together against her belly and though she wanted to drop them to her sides and stand straight, she couldn't. "No," she whispered back and hoped it was still true. Jacobi wouldn't kill a Vym himself; he wouldn't risk the retribution.

Vaun was quiet for so long it became nearly unbearable. He stared at her, his thoughts racing behind those bright eyes. Slowly, he said, "Give her to me. Give her to me, and I will find a way to fix this. I will return her, and—"

"I have it under control," she said stiffly. "She's safe."

Fury rippled across his face and the whole room felt hot with the waves of his anger. "Why did you take her? Is it Jacobi? Why does he want her?"

She swallowed and set her jaw firmly. "I can't tell you." But she wanted to. All of her secrets were beginning to choke her.

The prince cursed and turned briefly before spinning toward her. "When Addom finds out..." He shuddered and dragged his fingers through his dark hair. "Return Larc before this ruins you."

She shook her head. "I can't."

"There seem to be a lot of things you can't do!" He stepped closer to her. "It's a shame lying and kidnapping aren't among them."

Her hands finally unclenched and her neck strained up to glare back at him. "I'll handle this."

"Shut up!" The prince shook his head. "Addom is going to have you strung up if you don't give her back. I can't keep this from him. I won't!"

"Then don't!" Grayc shouted back.

"You think I will lie for you!" Vaun accused, his voice low and his hands shaking.

She laughed and it was miserable. "No, you don't lie for anyone but yourself."

"You're going to judge me? You?" His teeth mashed angrily and he came close to her again, looming over her. "You've lied and connived your way up from the Low and now you snatch people from the streets! Is this better than picking up after me? Will it get you another house, Grayc? Maybe one in the High this time?"

She shoved at his chest but she wound up staggering backward herself. "You don't know!" Tears that would never fall gathered in her eyes. She panted and took another step back, jarred by the pitch of her voice. She blinked and stared at him as though she had just now seen the scope of their conversation. "We've never even met."

Vaun groaned and rubbed a hand over his face, sighing heavily. "Give her back, Grayc."

She took a step to the side, offering him the door. "I can't."

He closed his eyes and stood still for a string of heartbeats. She watched his jaw twitch, his cheek cringing against his thoughts and her refusal. She half expected him to explode, to burst with the rage she had always suspected lingered beneath his amiable façade, but he didn't. He walked away. Without words of anger or plea, without a curse on his lips, he simply went and she was left standing there, replaying every word, moment, and action that had led her to where she was now, alone.

Vaun went home because there was nowhere else to go that would not tempt his tongue. The bitter parts of him wanted to go straight to Addom and see the world fall on her head. Surely his Grayc had a plan, but maybe in the midst of the mayhem and violence Vaun could catch some bit of her true agenda. Would her choices make sense if he knew her reason? Would there really be a reason good enough?

Vaun's shoulders slumped when he entered his house. The answers didn't matter. He wasn't going to tell Addom, or anyone else. Even the bitter parts of him knew that, had known the moment he wiped away the memories of the stranger who had seen her. He couldn't even approach Jacobi without risk of spoiling whatever she was up to and endangering her. Why did her safety matter so much? Why did it matter more than Larc? Grayc Illan Sanaro was a rat. She should be expendable.

He groaned and rubbed a hand roughly over his face because not even he believed that nonsense. Not anymore. Not without the haze of dust and the carelessness it had always brought.

A large gift basket perched on the entryway table drew his eye, tempting him from dark thoughts. Wings of fuchsia cellophane gleamed at him invitingly, offering long necked bottles of a much darker color. Grabbing up one cold, glass body in his hand, he absently plucked up the stiff card and flipped it open.

I want to talk. Brunch tomorrow.

The brief words appeared shorter than her name scrawled along the bottom. With a defeated groan, he dropped the card and opened the bottle. Where did his sister's obsession with brunch come from? It wasn't even a real meal. He drank deep from the first bottle while picking up the second and starting toward the stairs. It occurred to him somewhere between the eighth and twelfth step that the women in his life were going to drive him mad. He wanted to scorn them, he often did, but right now hating them only reminded him of how much he loved them and what little choice he had in the matter.

He was so busy swallowing that he almost missed the last step. The dark red wine sloshed inside the bottles. His skin tingled. The wine was good. It wouldn't have been like Fay to send anything but the best.

The hallway was quiet. He half expected AviSariel to come barging out of her room to smother him in her hopes and wishful stares. He saw. How could anyone not see?

He didn't wonder why his bedroom door was open but was vaguely grateful because it meant that he didn't need to tackle the logistics of two bottles and a doorknob. He kicked the door shut with his heel and noted over another deep swallow that he wasn't alone in his room.

He paused to lick his lips and look at his guest.

Meresin stood from where she'd been sitting on his bed. She didn't look herself, but rather frightened and helpless, exactly like she had earlier that night.

"Did we have an appointment?" Vaun asked, not feeling friendly at all. He had been building a list of questions for her in his head only an hour ago but it was lost now. Now, he wished it had been her name the stranger gave. He wished Meresin had been the one to snatch up little Larc and not his Grayc.

Her face scrunched as though she wasn't sure if they had an appointment or not. Her fingers crawled shakily up her side, clawing at the fabric. "No. No." She said it the second time with some certainty. "I need to talk to you." Her big, yellow eyes looked up at him. Had she always looked this young?

The prince laughed. "Talk? Not your specialty." He held out the bottle he wasn't already working on and she took it automatically. "What do you want?" He assumed it had to do with Xavian Ren Belholn and bad dust and yet more scandal that would lead to Grayc Illan. He walked deeper into the room and drank again before setting his bottle on the bedside table and shrugging out of his jacket. He dropped it on the floor.

She turned to watch him work the buttons of his shirt free. "There's something wrong." She held the bottle against her chest with both hands.

Vaun laughed at that and nodded, dropping his shirt to rest with his jacket. He took the few steps to stand in front of her, tugging the bottle from her hands. "Sweet Meresin," the prince cooed, opening the bottle with a sharp pop that made her jump. "I am beginning to suspect that everything is some sort of wrong." He held the bottle out to her again. He could see his silhouette in her glassy eyes. He looked dark and frightening but she wasn't afraid. Not of him, anyway.

She clutched the bottle again and shook her head. "No. There's something. There's something and I know it. I knew it." She laughed and he almost took a step back. She squeezed the bottle tighter, her fingers long and fragile against the dark glass. "I can't remember." There were tears in her eyes even though she smiled.

Meresin leaned toward him as though to reveal the punch line of a joke. "I think I've gone mad." A pair of tears spilled over but her forever red lips remained in a grin that trembled at its corners. She turned away from him and he was relieved for the moment of distance. She drank and sighed heavily, shoulders slumping a little and one hand dragging fingers through her scarlet hair. "There's something important. I know it." She sounded a little more certain now and somewhat less insane. "Xavian Ren said that I came to him last week and said that I knew who was behind the bad dust. He said that I told him someone was trying to make their own dust and testing it in his province." Tears spilled over her lashes again. "I don't remember that." She exhaled shakily and brought the bottle to her lips.

Vaun watched her drink. His skin hummed greedily and almost had him stepping closer. There was a pain in his temple but it was dull enough to ignore. "Maybe you've been poisoned," the prince suggested.

Meresin laughed bleakly. "The marks won't wash off. I've tried. They won't wash off."

He raised an eyebrow skeptically and looked her over again. Her dress had no sleeves, leaving arms, shoulders, neck, and face to the soft glow of the lights. Her skin looked perfect from where he stood. "I don't see any marks, Merry."

She made a 'tsk'ing sound and took a step toward him, holding out the bottle so he would take it from her. He did and managed not to look too happy about it, though he wasn't slow to drink. His temple throbbed.

Meresin had more trouble slipping out of her lace accented gown than usual, but when it finally fell into a pool around her ankles, he forgot the battle completely. He almost dropped the wine. Almost.

She stood there, naked but for a pair of black panties that clung to the thick flesh of her hips. He swallowed the space between them in two steps and his free hand came up to touch fingertips to the skin between her breasts. She inhaled pleasantly, a sound she'd learned to make so well that it came naturally now. Vaun ran his fingers down to her navel, following the line of black symbols, little scribbles that looked like no language he knew. They ran down her chest in four lines. The one in the middle was longest, the other three were shorter and started lower and lower down her chest to the right, printed over the ample curve of her breast.

She swallowed hard and he saw her chest move beneath his fingers. "What do you think it is?" she whispered fearfully.

He could say that he didn't know. It wouldn't be a lie. He had seen it only once before, but it didn't seem kind to mention since the woman was now dead. "It's pretty," he offered absently and took half a step back, though his hand was reluctant to leave her skin. What if it was an illness? Ollan had been addled before she died, but Ollan had always been some sort of mad.

She took the bottle from his hand and sighed, one of her arms curling up between them to rest her fingers on his shoulder, reminding him of his own exposed skin. "How does one become sane again?" Meresin asked, her eyes serious, though her back arched to rub her hips into his.

Vaun smiled lazily. The ache in his temple spread to form an uncomfortable ring around his skull, but other aches took precedence. "I don't know," the prince answered honestly, his arms coiling around her waist to pull her against him. "I've never tried to be sane before."

Her fingers crawled along the back of his shoulders until her arm hooked around the back of his neck. "Do you think people will still like me, even though I've gone mad?" There was a little giggle in her voice, frantic, as though she was frightened and excited at the same time.

He nodded and lifted her higher, until he was sure she'd risen onto her toes. "It's not as off-putting as you might think."

Her skin smelled sickly sweet and he couldn't resist licking it. She didn't taste like the magic she smelled of but he wondered if her sweat would. He turned them, not caring if her ankles twisted in her dress before they tumbled into his bed. Her body was warm and soft under his and she giggled when the wine sloshed out of the bottle to splash her skin and stain the sheets.

He smiled against her and drank up the red where it collected in her collar.

It really was her color.

And that was the last solid thought Vaun would remember of that night.

Red was her color.

Vaun stirred from a heavy sleep to discomfort. His skin felt cold and sticky and for a moment he wondered if more people had been in his bed last night than just Meresin. He moved, only a little at first, to test his limbs as well as his surroundings. She was still asleep beside him and the mattress felt wet. Had they spilled the entire bottle?

The air burned his lungs when he breathed. The stench made him cringe and turn but his movement failed when he realized that his right arm was pinned beneath her back. His fingers were numb and the whole limb tingled violently when he tugged. Her skin stuck to his. "Wake up," Vaun croaked, his throat painfully dry. His eyes opened but it took several determined blinks to work through the fog of his vision. The curtains were drawn and the room dim, but he could still see his arm where it disappeared beneath her bright hair.

He blinked again and cringed at the pain the effort sent rippling through his aching skull. She didn't stir, so, with a disgruntled groan, the prince pulled himself free.

Her hair was everywhere. It stuck to his arm and his side, plastered to the sheets around them. When he sat upright, his vision swam with a moment of nausea. He managed to stave it off and swallow hard before speaking again. "Merry," he murmured irritably, rubbing his face and opening his eyes again. Dark stains splotched the once white sheets beneath their legs. Too dark to be wine. His breath quickened in his chest. The stains coated their skin, smeared thick across legs and crusting from the wear of the night. Suddenly, whatever exhaustion that had clung to him was gone. That awful stink and its sweet undertone hit him anew. He knew that smell. Anyone that had ever been in a duel knew that smell.

His gaze worked its way up her naked body. His breath hitched in his chest at the first thick gash in her belly, the first of dozens that worked together to rip open her chest in a mesh of gaping black holes. Her yellow eyes were open but dull, her jaw locked in a soundless scream.

Vaun jerked away, scrambling off the bed without tearing his gaze from her. He staggered back, stomach heaving. He curled over and retched, clutching at the nightstand to keep his balance. Wiping his mouth with a shaking hand, he glanced back at his bed. A small, foolish part of him hoped she might be gone.

She was still there, red and savaged and staring at nothing.

He stood, shaking. Tears dripped onto his chest before he realized he was crying. His legs trembled, his whole body hurt, but he couldn't sit down. He couldn't move. He couldn't even think with his gaze glued to her gore and his brain throbbing against his skull.

He never heard the knock at his door or Samuel Sinol enter, but he felt the pause, the moment when someone else saw her body and the possibility of this being a nightmare vanished.

The valet stood in the doorway, caught in the stillness of horror until AviSariel's cheerful voice called from behind, somewhere in the hall that still didn't know what had happened—a place untouched by Meresin's death. Would it leak out the open door? Would the Realm feel it before the paper told them?

"Go to your room and wait there," Samuel Sinol said over his shoulder, alarmingly commanding, before shutting the door. He strode across the room. "Are you hurt? My prince? My prince, are you hurt?"

Vaun blinked dumbly at his valet, at the meaningless words he hurled at him. Hurt? Him? He looked down at himself and his stomach heaved again. He was painted in her blood.

Samuel Sinol touched him, pressing fingers over the bloodier patches of flesh to probe for wounds. Vaun watched it all distantly. Samuel Sinol found no wounds, but that brought no relief. His valet started talking again, but the words make little sense. Finally, his brain caught up, and his own questions poured in: When had she died? Had he been asleep beside her? How could he not have noticed? Had he just forgotten? Had she cried out for help?

Samuel Sinol cupped his face with warm hands, still speaking, shouting even. Vaun stared at his valet's face. It was scrunched with confusion and panic but he looked so young. Meresin had looked young. Tears burned Vaun's cheeks on new paths around his valet's fingers. "I'm going to send for your sister," Samuel Sinol said slowly.

Vaun wanted to protest but couldn't form words, let alone think of anyone else to send for. He wasn't sure if his valet said anything else or if he'd just pushed him along to the bathroom, but when the door shut Vaun finally found himself alone. The bright lights glared down on him, standing naked and smeared with red amid the pristine tiles. He retched again when he saw her crusted handprint on his bloody chest.

The prince huddled in the corner of his shower for what felt like hours, knees drawn to his chest. The spray of water that rained down on him had long since washed away any evidence of his accompaniment to her death. He watched the red turn to pink and finally vanish completely from the endless swirl circling the drain. With his head to the corner of tile he listened to the indistinguishable trail of voices in the other room. Some shouted. Some whispered. Then there came a stretch of silence before the door to his sanctuary opened and closed quietly. He watched her stand there, just inside his bathroom.

In as much of his life as he could remember, Vaun had never known Fay to hesitate. Not when they were children, not after she became a Vym, not with all the eyes of the Realm watching her, or even in the face of Evan Kadem. But that morning, in his bathroom, she hesitated.

She stepped out of her heels. Her dress rumpled around her feet when she crossed the room to his shower. One arm reached in and he watched her delicate fingers stretch from lace clad palms to turn off the spray of water. The silence that followed made him wince. She didn't bother to lift her skirt when she stepped into the shower. The intricate beadwork of her dress sounded beautiful against the wet tiles and the black material was breathlessly daunting where it piled on the white floor.

She crouched down and he remembered how small she was. Standing, Fay had a presence about her that fooled the mind into thinking that she was larger, taller, and generally more imposing than her petite frame would suggest.

His eyes fell on her arms, curled against her chest and hugging a pair of cotton pants. They were his; he recognized them as the kind he liked to wear in the mornings. They wouldn't make this morning better.

"Vaun." She exhaled his name and he remembered the way she used to speak to him when he was a boy. She hadn't been much older than he was and they had been raised in different houses with different staffs, but Fay had always come over to check on him or scold him. He realized that had never changed, only her tone. She wasn't as motherly or patient anymore because he wasn't a boy who listened to her every word.

He lifted his gaze to hers. She looked uneasy. Of course she did; she'd seen Meresin, too. Why did he let that happen? Why did he allow her to see that horrible room? He knew the answer as soon as he thought the question. He needed her to make it better, to take it away like any other bad dream.

"Is she gone?" he whispered, hating the words.

She nodded. "Tell me what happened."

Vaun closed his eyes. "I don't remember."

"You were drinking," she prompted, voice still soft, like it had been so long ago.

He nodded once, his throat dry. "Just the bottles you sent."

She was quiet for a long while, so long that he opened his eyes to look at her. "The knife was on the bedside table. Do you remember it?"

His heart hammered in his chest. "No." How could he not have seen it?

"Vaun," she whispered, and for the first time in his life, he wondered if his sister was frightened. "Did you kill her?"

The question jolted through his body, electric, burning his skin. "No."

She stared back at him with hard silver eyes. "Do you have any idea who might have? Was anyone else with you?"

His stomach twisted. "No. No one else. At least, I don't think so."

She nodded once and touched his arm, the one curled around his knees. "I can try to keep it out of the paper but it won't stop the people from talking. They probably already know." She stood and her affection vanished. His pants were held out in place of her touch. "Put something on and stop hiding in the shower. If you did not kill her, you have nothing to worry about."

He stared up at her. "And if I did kill her?"

The princess didn't think long on it, lifting her skirt on her way out of the shower as though the water would know to drain off her fabrics before she reached her shoes. "You are the prince. No one can judge you but the Queen, and she won't care about this."

He watched her leave and for the first time since he was a boy, wished that she would stay. In her wake, in the sweep of cold that fell over his damp body, the prince realized that as surrounded as he might be by lovers, servants, and subjects, he was alone.

CHAPTER ELEVEN

The Realm mourned the death of the red-haired lover. Addom would have mourned her as well if he had room in his heart for any more sorrow. The Realm may have forgotten Larc as the weeks passed, but he didn't. His gloved fingers tugged his hood further over his face as he turned a corner onto a busy street in the Main of Belholn. It was nothing extraordinary for a citizen of the Main or Low to slip between provinces, but it was something for Addom Vym to walk into Belholn. No one took notice of him. People in the Main looked much the same in this province as they did in any other.

He turned into a shabby building and made his way up the stairs, eyes searching until they locked onto the correct apartment number. With one leather boot he kicked open the flimsy door. The lock ripped off the frame and the barrier slammed into the wall with a sound worth more than its build. A thin man fell off the sofa, frightened from his sleep, eyes large and dull.

Addom Vym waited a heartbeat for the other man to stand or gather his wits, but when neither happened, the lord spoke. "Who took her?"

The man blinked those dumb eyes. "W-what?"

Addom strode into the room. His leather-clad fingers coiled in the man's shirt and yanked him from the floor.

"Who?" Addom snarled, slamming the rat into the wall. The wretch's flimsy shirt twisted easily in his hold, revealing black etchings along his shoulders. Addom's gaze traced them up the man's neck, where they disappeared into his hairline. He'd seen more and more of such tattoos in his own province, though they seemed to mean nothing to anyone.

"I don't—who?" the rat squealed.

"You were in the Low of Vym the night Larc disappeared," Addom accused.

He shook his head frantically. "No! No, I wasn't. I've never been to Vym."

"You're *lying*? To *me*?" Addom's fingers tightened in the ruined material. "You dare, you miserable—"

"I'm not!" The man scratched at his hands, clawing his skin. "I didn't—"

"Where is she? What did you see?"

"Nothing!"

Addom slammed him harder into the wall, making the cheap plaster crack. "You were there. People heard you bragging about it, about how what you saw was going to make you a bundle. Now, what was it?"

The man shook his head, but his brow furrowed as though he were trying to understand something difficult. "No... No, I wasn't in Vym that night."

"Shall I jog your memory?" Addom hissed. "I could peel you like an apple."

Something moved near the corner of his eye, crawling over the man's sweat-damp skin. Addom blinked, then peered at the tattoo as a line of the inked text uncoiled like smoke beneath the skin. It drifted upward to form a new symbol closer to the man's ear. The wretch continued to plead, repeating that he didn't know, while Addom watched two more strange letters form below the first.

"Okay," the lord said as gently as he could, uncurling his fingers from the cursed man's shirt.

He sagged back against the wall. "I don't know anything. I don't."

"You don't think you do." Addom pointed at the man's tattoo. "When did you get that?"

His hand groped at his shoulder. "I… um… A couple weeks ago, maybe?"

"Did you see anyone strange? Anyone you wouldn't have normally met with?"

"The prince. The prince was in my living room." His gaze darted toward the door, then to the floor at his feet. "Right here. I don't know how he got in, but he was here, with another man." His gaze shot back to Addom's with fresh panic. "I didn't mean to be rude. I'm sorry. I didn't realize it was him until he left."

The Vym stepped back, as though the man had swung at him. Addom wanted to call him a liar, but how could he? He didn't even know what he was saying and he didn't look clever enough for such a ruse. Vaun wouldn't have taken Larc and, if he had, he wouldn't have risked using blood magic to cover it up. He was the prince and, as far as this last month had shown, he could get away with anything, even murder.

If he didn't take Larc, then, he must be shielding someone. Someone he'd risk the Queen's jealousy for. Who? The question came with the answer trailing in his thoughts, her name a crystal bell that twisted his heart and aimed his fury.

Grayc Illan. It must be her. Addom could count the people in the Realm that Vaun would protect at the risk of their friendship. The number of people Addom would shield from the prince if the situation had been turned was equally brief.

Well, a shame for Grayc Illan that her royal protector had been in a dust stupor since gossip of his crime hit the streets. Perhaps he'd wake from it when her body joined Meresin's in the Ash.

Addom backed out of the apartment and hurried down the hall.

He took the stairs two at a time and pushed his way out onto the street, making his way down the Main. His boot scuffed the pavement when it came to an unplanned stop only blocks from the Low. Two men stood in his path with wide smiles. From the corner of his eye he saw another stepping off the sidewalk on the other side of the street to creep closer.

"I knew you would come back." Her voice was hoarse, as though pushed through a malformed throat. He turned around slowly to face the smallest Belholn. Even in the chill of the morning, she wore little, her thin legs exposed from ankle to thigh. The air swayed her dark hair against her gaunt cheeks. "No need for the hood, Vym." Wendry grinned and dropped her cigarette on the street, the three hulking men behind her making her look the size of a child.

He obliged her and pushed back his hood. "I mean no offense to your House, Belholn." At the moment, he meant it. If it was only Grayc Illan with a hand in his sister's misfortune, he would gladly take her and leave.

She grinned wider, baring her false fangs. "Your presence is offense enough, Vym. You were warned once before."

"I'm looking for Larc."

The men inched closer to him.

"And you think she's here?"

"I do."

Wendry stared back at him for a set of heartbeats. The curve of her lips never faltered. "Then I will look for her, and if I find her, she can die with you."

The men moved in, swinging hard. The ensuing struggle was a blur of limbs and a mess of voices. Addom blessed two men with his knuckles, sending them reeling into a brick wall one after the other. The other men were less lucky because when they expected knuckles, Addom had moved on to a knife. He sliced the short blade over two chests, sank it into one man's side, and then punched it into the back of the last man, scraping at ribs when he pulled it out.

Addom still held it when he turned and started running through the bottom of the Main. His cheek ached from a punch he couldn't entirely remember. There were more men up ahead but before he could think of what to do about them, he found his body falling, tumbling hard onto the concrete. Distantly, he heard the echo of a gunshot.

With a groan, he rolled onto his back, the sky glaringly gray above him and marred only by her silhouette.

Wendry frowned but there was no lack of amusement in it. She held a pistol in one hand. "I was trying to play nice." Her heel pressed down on his wrist while she leaned over to take the blade from his hand. "You played dirty first."

Her fingers had barely brushed the bloody knife when he twisted beneath her. He grabbed her ankle and jerked hard, knocking her to the pavement. Her back hit first, punching the air from her lungs and jarring the weapon from her hand. Addom scrambled to his feet and yanked her up.

"Tell them to back off," he hissed in her ear, dragging her backward. Panic sharpened the voices of her thugs, overlapping a flurry of clicks as pistols trained on them and hammers drew back. Addom's fingers became a collar around her slender neck. She weighed nothing, hardly more than a doll, and held just as still. His shoulders bumped safely against the wall and he hugged his human shield tighter. "Do it, or I'll snap your neck." Her body shuddered against him and he could have sworn she moaned.

With a curse and an extra squeeze, he shouted at the guards himself. "Back up or your lady dies right here in the Low!" He wasn't sure if they'd crossed from the bottom of the Main into the top of the Low—trash just looked like trash at some point—but the threat was enough to have the guards shortening their steps.

He took another sideways stride, almost to the mouth of an alley, almost ready to take another chance at running when the cold, metal barrel of a gun met his temple. He rolled his eyes to the side to find

Philip Belholn's arm stretched along the belly of bricks to hold a pistol firmly against Addom's skull.

Addom exhaled slowly. "I just want my sister." Wendry started to twitch in his grip, heels tapping his shins.

Philip's gaze sliced toward his suffocating sibling and then back to Addom's face. "That is not her."

Addom ground his teeth and lowered her until her bare feet touched the dirty sidewalk and she could finally wheeze in air, though he didn't quite let go. "Bring me Grayc Illan, and I will trade."

One side of Philip's mouth curled with a smile that didn't reach the other half or change the swirls of rage in his dark eyes. "Oh? And what makes Miss Sanaro worth trading for the only daughter of Belholn?"

Lie, Addom's instincts told him. Lying was always the first choice for a Vym. Make the story interesting. Dazzle your prey. But what lie could be more interesting than the truth? "She took my sister."

"A grave offense," Philip snapped.

"She's been manufacturing bad dust and selling it in the Low." The lie came so smoothly that it actually felt better in his throat than the truth had. "She's trying to ruin us, your house as well as mine, and Maggrin."

Philip Belholn didn't look overly interested. "I see. Then we'll handle that, and you can leave."

Addom exhaled slowly. Vyms knew lies when they heard them, but he had no options left. He could snap Wendry's little neck and it might give him some satisfaction before that bullet blew through the side of his head, but it wouldn't give him Grayc Illan. He let Wendry go and held out his hands.

She slumped to the pavement. When she rolled onto her back, he saw the red color of her face and the gape of her lips as she gasped. He had been closer to killing her than he realized. Her hand touched her chest, tugging a little at the material that held her small breasts and when her eyes fluttered open he couldn't help but look back. She smiled, a lazy gesture straining saliva slick lips, and he grinned back.

Philip spun him around, slamming him into the bricks. A savage twist of his arm expertly dislocated his shoulder.

Addom muffled a howl of pain, focusing on remaining still. Fighting back now would only get him killed. It was like running from a wolf: what choice did a Belholn have but to chase and bite?

Philip leaned in. "Don't worry, Vym. You'll probably survive this." He threaded his fingers through Addom's hair. "But you'll wish you hadn't."

Addom coughed a laugh through the agony in his shoulder and the bullet in his chest, trying to ignore the way his knees shook beneath his weight. "You've got nothing. I'm a Vym. You Belholns might run wild and play with knives, but we were raised under them. There's nothing you can do that hasn't already been done."

Philip hauled him around and smiled, signature blond hair shading his dark eyes. Addom realized that unlike his siblings, Philip didn't wear false fangs. Somehow, the flat of his teeth was more daunting than the glamour of his brothers and sister. "We'll see."

Grayc Illan dropped the paper in the wastebasket at the entrance before crossing the broad lobby of Jacobi's house. He'd designed the first floor to look like an office building. He said it seduced people into feeling safe and public. Grayc Illan didn't think there was anything safe about being in a public place.

The guards at her back muttered as she stepped onto the elevator. She turned to find them reluctantly parting to allow a lord of Belhon to slip past. Philip ignored their narrowed eyes and stepped onto the lift beside her. Grayc considered jumping off, or holding the door so at least one of her guards could join them. They stared at her anxiously, waiting for a command. She let the doors close. The air tightened now that she shared it with a Belholn.

"I didn't know Jacobi was getting a visit from one of his cousins today." She spoke first because waiting felt weak.

"He doesn't know, either," Philip said. He hovered close at her side, towering over her even with his head tipped down to watch her.

"I am sure he will be honored."

"Actually, I came to speak with you. Or warn you, I suppose."

She raised an eyebrow and looked up. Blood smeared his cheek and speckles of red stained the low neck of his shirt and splattered his collarbone. It reminded her of a time when she was a child working in his house. Philip and his brothers had liked to play hide and seek with her. The price for being found had always been bloodshed.

"We caught Addom Vym snooping around the Main today."

She shrugged and returned her eyes to the closed metal doors in front of her. "That explains the state of your clothing, I suppose."

He didn't laugh, but a twitch at the corner of her eye made her think he smiled. "He said something interesting. He said you were the one that took Larc." His arm crossed her back, his hand resting on her shoulder, thumb and two fingers curling toward her neck and past the shelter of her jacket. The feel of his skin against hers burned. He squeezed as he leaned down closer to her ear. "But more interesting than that, he said you were behind the bad dust."

She kept her gaze focused on the gleaming metal of her cage. "And?"

In the blurry reflection of the elevator doors, his lips twisted into a smile. In those distorted shapes, his mouth was wider than possible, eager to swallow her whole. It made him look like a shadow of his father.

"I thought you might just be able to come up with a lie if you had the time to think of one. It's possible Xavian Ren won't find out if Addom doesn't say it again." His fingers dug into her collar when he kissed her temple. "We wouldn't want you getting caught this close to the end," he whispered against her skin.

Her breath quickened. "What are you talking about?"

His fingers slid along the base of her neck in a slow, agonizing motion that twisted her guts in the hopes that he would withdraw his hand entirely. His fingertips lingered at her spine, one long digit stroking up and into her hair.

"You know?" It was the lowest of whispers and the loudest of disbeliefs.

Philip laughed and stepped back. "I know her." He leaned against the wall. "And I knew you, when you were a girl. You were never this strong or this cold, Grayc." He was still smiling when the elevator stopped. "You used to cry every time my mother scolded you. And when my brothers and I would chase you around the house, you always ran. We could find you because eventually the fear would build up and you would start making these little weeping sounds."

She looked up at him then as he moved to hold the impatient metal doors for her.

He answered the child's question in her eyes. "You didn't get better at hiding, Illan. You just weren't worth finding anymore."

She walked out of the elevator because she couldn't think of anything else to do.

"Good luck, whatever your plans." He remained in the elevator, stepping back to press another button.

She waited until the doors closed and then stood a while longer under the deafening beat of her own heart. There was a moment of almost fear, of almost something, before calm swept in again to remind her that she had no soul to fret over. Her shoulders squared and she brushed out the wrinkles his touch had caused her jacket on her way down the hall.

Jacobi was sitting at a large desk in his office of tall windows and gleaming surfaces. He lifted a cup of tea to blow the steam over the ridge of porcelain.

"Philip Belholn paid us a visit," she said over the echo of her heels on the dark hardwood. There was no point in hiding something he would find out about in minutes. "It seems Addom Vym suspects we've taken Larc."

That took his attention from his tea as well as his paperwork. The cup returned to the saucer without a sip being taken.

She pulled out a chair and sat down across from him. "Luckily, Philip doesn't seem to care about the loss of a Vym."

Jacobi cursed and leaned back in his chair. "And neither should we. It's high time we kill her and put her body out in Maggrin for the paper to find."

"If we kill her now, it would look like he was on to something and we panicked."

Jacobi's eyes narrowed. "You're awfully insistent on keeping her alive."

"You wanted her taken, so I took her, but I don't want to lose my head over this just because of Addom Vym." She spat his name and reached across the table, picking up Jacobi's teacup and pretending to take a sip. "Let's see how this plays out. They probably won't believe anything he says. If we have any luck left, your cousins may kill him by morning."

Jacobi considered this hope for a moment before nodding and returning his attention to the papers spread out on his desk. It was a bleak day the Realm over. "The new batch was even worse than the last." The news had been a sprinkling of disasters in the Low of Maggrin for weeks now. They had tested three batches in the past three weeks. Never large amounts, but the problems stemming from even a little bad dust were remarkable. For some the madness came suddenly, violently, turning them into more beast than man while for others the craze built slowly. Days, even weeks after consuming the bad dust, they could turn mad and another slaughter would be splashed across the pages of the Realm's paper.

Belholn had been on edge even though it had been some time since Jacobi had dumped any of the trial products in his home province. The High district's residents no longer visited clubs in the Main and there were rumors that Xavian Ren made his servants taste the dust before letting his brother Killian have any, an extreme that had spread to the houses in the High that still dusted.

"What your friend has promised is not worth the business we're losing," Grayc Illan said carefully, watching him through her lashes. "The clubs are empty and we can't sell the dust we bought from the Queen. Even if we get a cut of dust made by someone else for a tenth of the price, the risks of selling it won't be worth the punishment when she finds out."

Jacobi groaned and scrubbed a hand over his features. "We need to stimulate business."

"We need to cut our ties with this other party. He can't make a quality dust. We've had enough trials and failures. We're tempting fate."

The Belholn cousin laughed. "Oh, I think we are past temptation, Illan. No more talk of turning back. We're in deep and I won't leave with less than what I was promised."

She looked away, her sign of disagreement and her silent punishment.

"Do something useful. Get the people of Belholn dusting again."

She exhaled and stood. One hand straightened the front of her jacket while her heels started her for the door.

"Where are you going?" Jacobi demanded, more curiosity than anger in his voice.

One shoulder shrugged back at him. "As you asked."

AviSariel stepped out of the car and onto the sidewalk. It felt strange to go anywhere alone and the more she thought about it the more her fingers coiled nervously in the lace of her dress. She had bathed and changed but still felt wrinkled and out of sorts. It took all of her self-control to keep from tugging the woven strands of her hair loose from the braids and pins that held them back.

She'd tried everything she could think of. She'd tried to give Vaun space. She'd kept the house quiet, driven away attention seekers, disposed of the endless letters that poured in, offering condemnation or begging for gossip. She'd railed at him, too. Broken crockery. Taken away his tea. Begged. She'd do anything to break Vaun from his endless guilt, but nothing moved him. He merely sat, staring at his bed as if he saw Meresin still, or huddled in his bathroom. He barely so much as blinked. Sometimes, she wondered if he breathed.

If she couldn't reach him, perhaps someone else could. AviSariel lifted her chin and forced herself up the steps of The Library. She remembered it being a much livelier place. Most of the tables and couches were empty, leaving an echo where crowds of whispers had once been. She heard Fay even before she saw her, a spray of black lace and plumes against the backdrop of gleaming marble, polished wood, and colorful bindings.

"I said no." Fay's voice was stern, and though she was speaking to someone else, AviSariel nearly turned on her heels and fled.

"He's your brother, too!" Evelet snapped at the seated princess, her hands balled at her sides. The few guests in The Library struggled not to look up.

Fay snickered from where she sat and lifted her glass. "Do I strike you as sentimental?"

A snarl pulled at Evelet's brightly painted lips. "No. Of all the things I'd like to call you, sentimental would not be one of them."

Fay shot her a warning glare before taking a sip of her wine. The dark red liquid rolled captive against the curved glass in her palm. A stretch of silence followed and AviSariel herself felt almost faint. Somehow the daughter of Vym managed not to shrink under that glare.

"You are a princess," Evelet tried again, her voice softer and straining against her teeth. "If you ask for him, they will have to give him back."

The princess scoffed and the bodies of the room shifted nervously at the sound. "Why would I do such a thing for Addom Vym?"

"He's family!" Evelet shrieked.

Fay's glass returned soundly to the surface of the table. "Do not mistake yourself, *Vym*." Her voice lowered, as though every word dragged up from deep inside her chest, rushing forth like a curse from her lips. Her dark eyes glared up at the other woman with a glazed hint of madness—not the kind born of tea but of decades of bitterness rotting away some vital part of her. "I did not choose your family."

Evelet pressed her palm to the table and leaned closer, never one to shy away from insanity. "Only children and fools believe they choose their family. You did not choose Vaun, but he is your brother."

"That is blood."

"That is fate!" Evelet snapped. "Fate made you a princess. Fate gave you brothers. *Fate* made you a Vym. The Lady Vym." She shuddered angrily, her teeth pressing together to keep her already loud voice from rising higher. "Fate gave you power, more power than any other citizen below the Queen and her Wrath. So stop sulking and do something with it."

Fay stared back at her sister-in-law. "Something for you?"

"Your duty!" Evelet pushed herself away from the table, away from the princess, to circle the open marble floor. When she came back to the table she looked like she might say something else. Her finger pointed and her hand shook in the princess's direction. With her lips curling around whatever words she'd thought better of speaking, Evelet turned away and marched out of the room.

She didn't seem to notice AviSariel though she passed within arm's reach.

Silence followed. AviSariel couldn't convince herself to move. She simply stood near the doors and watched Fay's stiff profile sitting deep in the large room. Between breaths, she looked like a painting, unmoving and mesmerizing.

"Are you going to sit?" Fay asked without looking up, retrieving her wine glass once more.

AviSariel shook her head, though the other princess could not see it. She'd come to ask for help with Vaun but it occurred to her now that if Fay had wanted to help, she would have. AviSariel took a step back. It was difficult to tear her eyes from the princess. She watched Fay swallow, a perfect and practiced gesture, before setting her glass down again. Every movement was planned, fluid and beautiful.

AviSariel took another step back and was struck by the whispered thought that perhaps it wasn't that Fay would not help Vaun, but simply—sadly—that she could not.

The car ride back to the house was bleak. She sat in a stupor, trying to imagine what she could possibly do for her husband if not even Fay Dray Fen could resurrect him from despair. The thought to leave him in his current state occurred to her not for the first time. He deserved this misery, didn't he? A man should be overcome by guilt after what he had done.

It wasn't until the driver tapped at her window that she realized they had arrived at the house. She dabbed her eyes and smoothed her hair before he opened the door. When she stepped out she noticed another car parked in front of hers, a sharp black twin to her own. She thought little of it until she walked through the main doors of the townhouse and into the gleaming lobby that occupied the first floor.

A smudge stood there in tight curls and a tailored suit. The anger that swelled up in AviSariel's chest upon seeing Grayc Illan in her lobby was as surprising as it was bitter.

"You've seen him?" The princess spoke first—it was her house, after all—and tried to keep her voice hollow. She walked toward the stairs, never quite turning her body toward the rat. She tried to move the way Fay would have and felt the slightest bit stronger for the attempt.

"No." Something small in Grayc Illan's voice hinted at surprise and AviSariel could feel the Low woman watching her. "I just arrived."

"Then you should leave." She found herself saying stiffly. "I'm given to understand that business partners of Belholn are no more welcome in Vym than the Belholns themselves."

"I only came to see that he is well."

"Well, he is not," AviSariel snapped before she could compose herself. "He went dust mad and killed a woman, or did you not hear?" The words rushed out of her, leaving her weaker for having admitted them. "He did not send for you, so he does not want you. Nor do I." She flicked a hand at her doorman as she reached the landing, and he closed the tall doors behind her.

AviSariel exhaled a breath of exhilaration and misery. The silence of the stairs enveloped her and for a handful of seconds she was alone, between problems and worlds. Holding her skirts, she marched upward, chin tipped high. She told herself that when she walked into their home this time she would be stronger. She would march into Vaun's room and demand that he pull himself together. She would—

Her heart sank when she reached their private floor, beyond those last doors at the top of the stairs, and stepped into the residence that had become her prison. She wanted nothing more than to leave again. She only made it a few steps into the hall when she stopped, her heart gripped by uncertainty. She hated this place. She wanted to leave, to abandon him to his misery. He deserved it, didn't he? He had killed Meresin, hadn't he? She had begged him to tell her he hadn't. Just to say it so she could cling to it, but he would give her nothing. Not even his gaze.

Just as fresh tears welled in her swollen eyes, a door closed around the corner, following by advancing footsteps.

AviSariel's eyes widened as Grayc Illan stepped into the corridor. The woman paused on her path to look down the hall at the princess. The former valet answered her unspoken question. "Staff entrance." Grayc Illan glanced at the short set of stairs leading to the bedroom wing, then back at her. For a moment AviSariel was certain Grayc Illan would simply walk away, but the woman hesitated with something unreadable in her eyes. "I will not pretend that I do not know why you dislike me, princess, but I am no enemy of yours."

"Then—" the princess started, not even sure herself what she planned to say, but the rat cut her off before either of them could find out.

"But that does not mean I will tolerate your foolishness. I wish you happiness in this Realm, just not at the cost of his." She walked away with the same certainty that she had walked in with, disappearing up into the private hallway.

AviSariel stared blankly at the now empty corridor in front of her, her cheeks red and her face tight as tears finally spilled over. A sob broke free of her when she heard his bedroom door close and agony clutched her chest. She clasped her mouth but couldn't smother her childish cries.

The parlor of his private quarters was dark but Grayc could make out trays of untouched cakes on the table. A small light glowed from inside the bedroom and she pushed the door open to find him sitting in an armchair, staring blankly at the bed. Her heart ached with every step she took and a small breath she did not know she was holding escaped when she finally touched her fingertips to his hair. He didn't move or speak. She wanted to apologize, but found no words for it. For all the little wrongs she had done to him, she had nothing to do with what hurt him now.

Grayc let her hand slide from his hair to his cheek. It felt wrong how much comfort touching him gave her; she'd told herself she'd come for his good. She leaned forward to kiss his hair before laying her forehead to his. "How many times do I have to ask you to wake up, sweet prince, before you finally do?"

He sighed and the sound became a slow sob. "I killed her," he whispered, his voice hoarse.

Grayc Illan crouched low to look up at him, her hands on his knee. When she found his eyes she saw only sorrow and loss. "You did not."

He stared back at her. "I think I did."

"You didn't."

"Her blood was soaked into my bed. Everyone—"

"They don't know you," she persisted, shocked that he could believe that he had done this. She had come to his house in hopes of stirring him from his grief, never expecting to find him trapped in guilt. Since when did her prince know guilt? "They believe everything they read, every bit of gossip they hear." She cupped his cheek again, thumbing away stray tears. "You did not kill Meresin. She was your friend and you loved her."

"What if—"

"Vaun." She held his gaze and waited until she was sure he was looking back, not lost in the nightmares he had created for himself. "I promised that I would never lie to you. I might not always answer, but I will never lie to you. You did not kill her."

"But I—"

"No. You didn't." She shook her head but didn't lose his gaze. "And that means that someone else did."

"But why would anyone—"

"She had enemies." Grayc Illan sighed and dropped her hand. "So do you." She stood despite the urge to lay her head on his thigh and close her eyes. She had no time for comfort. Neither did he. "You've wasted weeks in this stupor."

He caught her wrist and her heart leaped into her throat.

He looked up. Bags bruised the skin beneath his eyes, but some of the insanity faded from the gleaming darkness of his irises. "Did you give Larc back yet?" He said it quietly, a secret he had just remembered.

She shook her head.

Disappointment darkened his features. "Is she dead?"

"No."

His fingers hesitated before letting go of her wrist and turning his attention away from her. He looked at the bed again but with new eyes. "I didn't kill her?"

"No."

"Did you?"

She cringed but he didn't see it. Her jaw tipped higher; funny how pride only grew when abused. "No, and I don't know who did." Grayc Illan waited for him to say something else but when his jaw flexed she knew that he wouldn't. He was waiting for her to leave, so she did.

AviSariel was still standing in the hallway when she passed but the princess didn't say anything. She just stared and Grayc Illan didn't look back. A small voice in the back of her head screamed out, as it often did, 'Too bold! Too bold,' but she ignored it because acting her station had never served her well.

She took the front stairs on her way out, right through the lobby and out the front doors. A car pulled up. It wasn't hers but when the passenger door opened, pushed from inside by an arm with a rolled-up sleeve, too many tattoos, and black painted nails, she got in.

Udaro lounged against the seat across from her, putting his heels up on the leather beside her thigh. She closed the door and he raised an eyebrow. He looked rumpled and she couldn't tell if he'd slept in his clothes or just decided he liked that particular look.

"You wanted to see me?" he said, the car pulling away from the curb.

"It's not safe for you in Vym."

"It's not safe anywhere." Udaro's lip curled. He hated her working for Jacobi, even if he knew she didn't have a choice. "Especially for you."

She shrugged. What else was there to do? "I need you to do something for me."

"What?"

"Throw a party." She smiled a little. Just a little.

He let out a barking laugh and rolled his head against the headrest. "Now? Why? No one would come with what's been going on with dust lately."

"They'll come if it's your party. You always have the best dust." She didn't bother to plea or negotiate. He was going to do it because she was asking. She didn't ask for much, and no matter what she asked for, no matter what he did, he could never repay the debt between them. She hadn't considered it a favor, long ago, when she avenged his mother. She hadn't even done it for his mother, but he felt the weight of it all the same and never forgot.

Udaro sat up and planted his feet on the floor of the cab. "I'm not using any of your shit dust, Grayc. I'm not poisoning people."

"I'm not asking you to," she said. The car crossed into Belholn and wove toward the Main. "I just need you to make them forget what they read about in the paper for a night."

He stared at her for a whole block and she studied his always impeccable black eyeliner. He had been wearing too much black since they were adolescents. "Why?" Udaro asked and she understood exactly what answer he was looking for.

Grayc Illan waited, in the silence, because that was the only answer she could offer. She had no choice. Jacobi said he wanted the people dusting again.

Udaro swore and leaned back, abusing the upholstery with his shoulder blades. He didn't look at her, but he nodded.

The chains rattled violently from the ceiling all the way down to the dark pool in the middle of the stone room. The icy water sloshed angrily where those thick links of metal broke the surface. Xavian Ren Belholn turned his head to the side to see those dark waves roll over the smooth floor, lapping at his sister's naked toes.

Wendry leaned forward with wide eyes, watching something wiggle in the darkness beneath the surface. Her wild hair stuck out in all directions, her pant legs rolled up and her sleeves bloody. It wasn't her blood, though, so it wasn't an offense to him to see it there.

"You're going to kill him," Philip said over the lip of his teacup. He lounged on a couch in the sitting area with Xavian Ren. It had been prudent when they first decided to move a lounge into the torture room that they keep the furniture as far from the water as possible. Of course, with time, they came to realize that it made little difference. Everything ended up stained in a room with intentions such as this one. Luckily, Belholns never shied away from a good stain. They often made for the best conversation starters.

"He's not going to die while he's still wiggling!" Wendry twisted her shoulders around to shoot a glare at her brothers.

Xavian Ren smiled when Philip gave her one of his 'are you so sure?' glances before pointing at the chains just as they stopped rattling.

"I don't know why you're so intent on keeping him alive," Ren said to his brother while their sister cursed and started jerking at the chain to haul her victim up from the depths.

"You know why," Philip replied tightly and drank from his cup.

"He wouldn't want to upset the princess," Hammish teased, putting his heel on the low table between them.

"Wendry will be so disappointed," Ren said. She'd been excited when they brought the Vym back to the house. It had been more than half a day and she hadn't left this room once.

She slipped on the slick stone floor in her struggle to pull Addom's still body from the pool and roll him onto his back. It was quite a struggle considering their difference in size. Hammish let out a laugh and a puff of black smoke when she managed it. Wendry crawled on top of Addom, her narrow knife scraping along his battered chest, poking at flesh already bruised, burned, or cut, but he didn't move. He wasn't breathing.

"I told you," Philip remarked before taking another sip of tea. "You've never been good at water torture."

Wendry made a dismissive sound and lifted her free hand. She brought it down in a fist once, then twice, against Addom's chest. Together Xavian Ren and his brothers watched her with scantly hidden humor as she aimed to beat the Vym's heart into starting.

Finally, Ren stood from the small sitting area and crossed the floor. With a huff, Wendry rolled off her victim. Ren drew one hand from his pocket and licked the tip of his index finger, a blue spark sizzling from his tongue to the digit. His blood heated, his ears popped, and his skin crawled with a tight, tingling sensation. Crouching without letting his knees touch the wet floor, he tapped that fingertip to the deeply bruised flesh of Addom Vym's left breast. Before the Belholn Lord stood upright again, the body on the floor seized, head and heels digging into the floor as torso bowed upward. Addom's broken lips parted wide in what would have been a gasp if his esophagus weren't so preoccupied with vomiting water.

Wendry squealed in delight and clapped her hands. "Oh! Teach me?" Her glee turned instantly to pleading when she twisted to grab at her brother's arm.

Xavian Ren laughed and shook out his hand, fingers tingling painfully as though they'd fallen asleep. "Never." It was a trick his father had taught him in this very room and one he dared not use anywhere else. Iron lined the walls to keep out the Queen's sight. It was built long before anyone living could recall and came only with superstitious warnings passed down through the years. Don't stay too long or dare use it to hide from the Queen. If she seeks you and cannot find you, it will only draw her scrutiny. Though surely every household has such a place, never speak of it in public.

With every lesson, his father had told him the warning tale of an ancestor that had used his magic in Queen's sight. A Queen's envy was nothing to be desired. Many said that the wolves came for him but Xavian Ren's father, Dorian Belholn, had told him clearly that it had been nothing as kind as wolves. The Queen had sent her Wrath, Evan Kadem. The fight had been brief and the Belholn that had dared to use his own magic had not even been granted death. Evan Kadem had taken him back to the Queen's Tower and his name had been stricken from the family registry.

A stern knock sounded at the doors, locked from the inside. Philip reached them first and opened one to allow a cousin of theirs to loiter in the opening, handing him a card.

He looked down at it briefly and from the press of his shoulders and the expanse of his chest, Xavian Ren knew exactly who the card was from even before his brother said, "She's here."

He slid his hand into his pocket again, crossing the room toward the door slowly.

Wendry whined loudly behind him. "No! I found him. I want to keep him!"

Ren grinned at Philip. "She has a point."

"Do you want to be the man that displeased a princess?" Philip smirked around the words.

The Lord Belholn rolled his eyes. "She is a Vym," he spat the name and looked at his brother hard. "She could have been a Belholn if you hadn't been so set against it."

With a tight smile Philip inclined his head. "Forgive me my childish past." He laughed to ease the tension, or maybe his own heart, Ren wasn't sure which. "Perhaps it would have been better to marry you rather than the Vym, but that time has long since passed and, whatever her union, she is still Fay Dray Fen."

Xavian Ren groaned but nodded. "Not one to be brushed aside or made an enemy of."

Wendry screamed furiously behind them but the Lord of Belholn had already pushed the door into a wide swing and gestured the handful of his kinsmen in the hallway into the room. It would only take one to drag Addom Vym upstairs; the rest were let in to keep Wendry from following. Xavian Ren loved his sister but he had not lived as long as he had at the head of a household by ignoring the weaknesses of his siblings. Wendry's weakness was insanity just as

Killian's was dust. Though obviously dangerous, Xavian Ren often wondered if their weaknesses were any more crippling than Philip's.

When he left the room and started up toward the main lobby, Philip followed while Hammish stayed behind to finish his cigarette. Hammish had the weakness of common sense. He had no desire to take part in foolishness that would result in future discomfort or trouble but he was too loyal a brother to escape it altogether.

Philip acted casual when he followed Xavian Ren out of the basement but he knew the difference between his brother's true disinterest and this pretend. He could have sent Philip alone to handle this situation if it were anyone other than Fay Dray Fen waiting upstairs.

The passage from the basement came up narrow stairs to a door in one of the dozens of private parlors on the first floor. "Should we make her trade for him?" Xavian Ren mused.

"What do you think he's worth?" Philip asked tightly from behind him.

Ren didn't answer. Fay was a daunting sight standing in the middle of his foyer, not at all like the girl he remembered in their youth. The last time she stood in his family home, his parents had still been alive and she still had a penchant for mischief and eccentricity. He supposed that she was still eccentric, even if it had lost its color and joy.

Would she have been like this if he had married her instead of Quentan Vym, back then? Would it have been enough to be in the same house as her lover? He doubted it. It still wouldn't have been her choice, but at least then it would have been the Belholns that had a princess and not the Vyms. Xavian Ren knew his own weakness just as well as he knew his siblings and spared a glance for the brother standing at his side.

"Is he still alive?" Fay spoke first. A princess didn't need to be acknowledged by a Lord.

Xavian Ren nodded and returned his gaze to hers. "It's been touch and go, but he's still breathing."

"Good. Put him in my car." She turned away and one of her many valets quickly opened the door.

"Is that all?" The Lord of Belholn grinned. "I knew you wouldn't ask in words… but not even a thank you?"

She paused to give him her profile before turning her head to look at him, her gaze stuck on Philip for a second too long before her hard stare found Xavian Ren. "Do you desire a favor of your princess, Ren?" Danger dripped from the question, daring him to make a demand, warning him what could happen if he did.

Xavian Ren bowed, deeper than he ever bowed to anyone, and it was easy because it was Fay. He looked up at her skirts through his lashes, his hair against his cheeks, and smiled the way only Belholns did. "I would only ever beg your blessing." He sang the words before lifting his head cheek first, looking up until he found her dark eyes looking back. "Put me out of my misery, your highness. Did he poison my people? Are the Vyms my enemies?"

Fay looked down on him for so long that he was sure she would not answer, but he did not dare break that moment of stillness. He could not imagine the thoughts that moved behind those dark eyes and flawless features. And then her lips parted, darker than lips should be, and he held his breath.

"Addom is not the fiend you hunt," she said before the hint of a smile pulled at the corners of her lips, a curious gesture born of too much amusement, "but he and his kin are most certainly your enemies, just as you are theirs."

She held his gaze for another heartbeat before turning away. Xavian Ren straightened. Both he and Philip watched her leave and in some way or another, he was certain that neither could help but wish that she had stayed.

CHAPTER TWELVE

It was both a relief and a disappointment to find that being believed a murderer had so little effect on his social standing. His sister was right; no one but the Queen could judge a prince, and the Queen didn't care.

Vaun abandoned the room of Meresin's death. Samuel Sinol moved his wardrobe to a spare room without being asked. Vaun didn't care about the room's size or sparseness, so long as the bathroom suited. He intended to make the sofa of his new parlor his new bed, but to his surprise, being suspected of killing his lover didn't stop others from inviting him to their mattresses.

The only occasion he saw his wife was when he returned home to bathe and redress, assuming she wasn't out herself. She had not said much to him since he emerged from his bedroom. Vaun had never been one to break a good silence but every time they inhabited the same room he felt her eyes on him. She had lost some of her naïvety during the time of his mental absence and he found something severe residing in her gaze now, studying him with a care that bordered on obsession.

At first he thought her intensity was simply a form of fright. She believed he had killed Meresin, after all. But he realized quickly that it wasn't fear he sensed in her; it was anger in the press of her lips and the gleam of her eyes. Anger and something else, something he either couldn't place or didn't care to think long enough on to recognize.

When he came home that particular late morning, she was sitting in the dining room taking her tea with sugared petals and cream puffs. The silence of the last week prevailed on his path to the hallway but her voice broke the tension like the snapping of the first bone in a long tumble.

"No ribbons lately." The sound of her cup nestling not so gently back onto its saucer followed her words. "Has she run out of them?"

Vaun paused, one hand to the corner of the wall and one foot on the first step. Her words surprised him more than her voice itself: bitterness. It rang so crisp and familiar; how could he not have noticed before? The prince almost laughed, dropping his head back to look up at the ceiling rather than turning to look at her. "Either you have been drinking too much tea, or you have been spending too much time with my sister. Both can be utterly depressing habits."

He didn't see her expression but he imagined it to be some beautifully honest mix of anger and embarrassment. He took another step up when her chair crashed against the floor.

"Wait!" Her voice lost the strength of bitterness quickly; not all women could soak their souls in fury as absolutely as his sister. AviSariel floundered for a moment in search of something to offer, some way to keep them from returning to the silence. "Your mail," she blurted out.

He turned to find her standing at her end of the table, pointing at the small pile of letters in the entry.

He nodded briefly. "I'll have Sanford bring them to my dressing room."

"One of them seemed important." She strode toward him, or at least toward the letters. "The man that delivered it was a servant of Udaro's." She brushed a few letters aside to find the long, thin, black envelope. "He said Udaro wanted to deliver it himself but... well, with us residing in Vym, at the moment, he simply couldn't." She held it out to him.

Vaun felt much like a duster being lured with a glittering cigarette. He descended the step and leaned close enough to snatch the letter from her fingers. He opened the black envelope only to find a single, long card smeared in bright neon colors inside.

AviSariel stared at it, taking a step to his side to read it. "It's just an address."

The prince smiled. "It's The Circus."

"The Circus?"

"The most exclusive party in the Realm, princess." He called for his valet and ascended the stairs. "You should get ready. We'll leave at dark."

A unified inhale and resulting hush met Grayc Illan Sanaro as she stepped into The Library. The only one who didn't look up was the one she had come to see. She had been thinking about it for days, weeks, months, maybe even years. How does a woman ask for freedom?

She crossed the large room to stand beside the chair of Fay Dray Fen Vym. The princess didn't acknowledge her in any way, so Grayc Illan placed the black envelope beside the woman's tray of tarts. "Udaro felt it important to invite the Princess Fay."

Fay put down her fork delicately and picked up her glass, pretending quite expertly that no one had spoken to her and no letter existed beside her pastries.

The silence of the room would have been unbearable if she hadn't known such gawking before. She touched the back of Fay's chair, wrapping her fingers around the high back and hearing the reverberating shock in the onlookers that filled the seats of this establishment. She bent over to speak softly near the princess's ear, though many others were close enough to hear even the slightest of whispers. "I want a word."

Fay drank from her cup before setting it back down.

"And I'll have that word, with or without an audience."

The princess was silent for another set of seconds before turning her eyes to one of the women at her table. "Clear the room."

The Vym cousin blinked at the Lady of the province before hurrying to stand. The rest of the table followed and started for the door, and soon enough so did every other guest of The Library. The doors closed and Grayc Illan stepped away.

"You—"

"Let me go," Grayc Illan whispered, the plea exhaled as though another voice spoke it deep inside her.

Fay turned her head, and with no one else to see, looked at Grayc Illan Sanaro.

"I have served decades, your highness. Have mercy and let me free of this shackle."

Fay's chair slid back but never fell and the princess stood, every bit of lace and layer of fabric in its place. "You think you have served long enough? Your debt is paid?"

"I never owed a debt," Grayc Illan bit out before checking herself and looking down at the floor. "Please. You offered me freedom for my slavery, and I have paid."

"Hardly. You've been playing around with my brother."

"Princess—"

"Are you begging, Grayc?" Fay's voice took on a curious tone and her skirts shifted as she stepped closer.

Grayc Illan stared hard at the floor. "Yes."

"Then kneel."

Her jaw clenched but her legs caved. "Please, Lady Vym, Princess Fay. Let it be enough."

Fay smiled and buried her long, dark nails in Grayc's black curls. "Enough?" She wrenched Grayc's head back. "All your life someone has been trying to put you on your knees and today, of all days, you drop willingly?" She shoved her away. "I don't think so."

Grayc Illan clenched her teeth. "I'll still work for you!"

"And what use would you be then? I gave you power, rat. Purpose. I took away your fear, your hesitation. You should be thanking me. You should be begging me not to give it back to you."

"Fay, if you leave it like this it's only a matter of time before Jacobi asks for Larc's life. I can't stall him much longer."

The princess paused and something close to guilt fluttered across her features, there for a moment and then lost to the hard resolve of her high cheekbones and darkly painted lips. "Then don't. If Jacobi Belholn tells you to kill Larc, do it."

Grayc Illan stared up at the woman, eyes wide and heart taking a heavy beat that blurred her vision. "Princess—"

The princess returned to her seat. "If he tells you to hang yourself, you tie a good knot and climb up on that chair, Grayc."

"Fay!"

"Be quiet," the princess snapped and Grayc's mouth closed though her jaw trembled. "Leave and never return to this establishment."

Grayc wished she could slap the cruelty from the woman's face. Wished she could rail, or fight. Instead, she silently rose to her feet and obeyed.

Even with the dust scare gripping Belholn, the residents of the High could not ignore the call of The Circus. Udaro always promised the best quality at his parties and it seemed that promise was enough for an entire province to gamble their lives.

The drums in Belholn reverberated throughout the Realm. Music thrummed from a converted warehouse in the Main, and by the time Vaun and AviSariel arrived, everyone that mattered in Belholn—and everyone not tied to Vym and Maggrin by blood—packed the floor. AviSariel looked her part, dressed in a full-length gown of vibrant fabrics and striking colors, with a corseted top and a skirt pushed outward by layers of blue tulle. Her hair had been piled high with a feathered fascinator seated among the gold tinted locks, and a veil curtained one blue eye. He wasn't sure who had dressed her and might have suspected one of his own tailors if their contracts didn't explicitly forbid such sedition.

Despite all of that fabric and color, it was not difficult to lose her in the mass of bodies that danced and shuffled through the warehouse. She stayed close until tempted by one of the naked beauties dipped in dust-laden sugar. The treat that coated their skin glittered by perfect design in the traveling, multicolored lights. She giggled nervously when invited to take a lick and Vaun lingered just long enough to see her lean in and run her tongue along the man's dust-caked collarbone.

The prince spun through the party, moving from teacups that he pretended to sip to cigarettes that he pretended to smoke. Eventually, Vaun found himself near the heart of the room. With an arm extended blindly into the crowd he gave his cup away, sure that some eager hand would relieve him of it. Fingers tugged at his belt and he looked down to see a pretty woman dressed in skimpy bits of sapphire crouching on her heels in front of him. She smiled up with lips as eager as he imagined the hand that took his cup to be. She pulled his pants open and if she'd been any rougher about it he would have slapped her for creasing his slacks. A low rumble vibrated through his chest but not even the woman with her lips around his sex would hear it over the music.

There was another rumble, this one heard by all, and he wasn't so prideful as to think it came from his body. His head tipped back with eyes already glazed and looked up at the piles of clouds that filled the high ceiling of the room. They swam with colors: peach, violet and yellow. They reminded him of AviSariel's dress. The clouds rumbled again and the crowd below called out, arms stretched high as though begging a deity. Oh, what a kind god it was that had made those clouds. A streak of blue lightning struck horizontally across the pillows of color, splitting them open to pour forth their shimmering bounty. Dust fell like rain, sticking to cheeks, soaking into skin, making already frantic pulses race.

Greedy as they were, they stuck out their tongues and tipped their faces high, breathing in and swallowing down their fill. There was a moment of near silence, an inhale, and then a mewling groan of delight that sent the room back into the engulfing sounds of music.

When the first rain of dust touched his face and soaked into his skin, he turned his head away. The rush of his blood in reply to the rich dust reminded him of red hair.

Keeping his head down rather than turned up to embrace the dust fall, he couldn't help but look at the sapphire woman. Not a friend or a lover, just eager and first to his belt. With the sort of bored sneer only a prince could muster, Vaun pushed her away and tugged his pants up. He didn't bother with the buckle, stepping over her on his way to familiar faces.

AviSariel had been standing near the wall when the false clouds erupted. It was amazing how easily she could find his face in a mass of others. She watched for another heartbeat and then turned away, giving unheard apologies to the people she couldn't help but bump into on her path to the exit. There were hands everywhere, eyes trying to meet hers, fingers reaching out to touch her. There was no space to shy away, for every direction only led her into contact with another stranger.

Holding her skirts up, she nearly fell through a pair of swinging doors and into a narrow hall. The doors closed and muffled the sounds of the party. She found herself drawing deep breaths of only slightly cleaner air. Everything tasted sweet now. Her skin tingled and when she closed her eyes she could still see Vaun standing there among his people, haunted by the feeling that he belonged with them in a way that she never could.

"Your grace."

The familiar voice came from her side. AviSariel turned sharply. Grayc Illan stood with her back to the wall, dressed in a strapless black dress that showed off shins and heels. A bright yellow ribbon circled her neck.

"Do you feel well?" the rat asked and the princess disliked her even more for her concern.

"I'm fine." AviSariel tried to snap but it felt foolish to be impolite in the face of manners. "Shouldn't you be out there?"

Grayc Illan shrugged, her naked shoulder moving her loose curls. "I thought I'd wait until after the storm." There was a stretch of quiet before she spoke again, voice raised over the pound of music through the wall. "I can send for a car to take you home, if you like."

AviSariel turned away to hide the roll of her eyes. Of course Grayc Illan wanted her to leave, to go home and hide. She hated how tempting that offer was.

"Your grace, if—"

"Illan!" The music muffled the shout, but it echoed down the narrow hall nonetheless.

AviSariel jerked her gaze to the man striding toward them. A drawn hood shielded his face, but something about the set of his shoulders and the narrow of his hips seemed familiar. As he passed under a hanging lamp, his eyes shone like rubies in the depths of his hood.

Grayc inhaled sharply and pushed herself away from the wall. She darted for the door but the man closed the distance in a heartbeat, snatching the rat up by her hair and lifting her onto her toes.

AviSariel screamed, but she may as well have been a shadow. Grayc Illan struggled, pulling a dagger from some hidden pocket. The man's hood fell back, revealing Addom Vym. He grabbed Grayc's wrist and twisted; the blade fell from her hand with a crack. AviSariel gasped as he slammed the woman face first into the wall, crushing her between the metal and his weight. Her toes beat a frantic cry against the wall, like an answer to the drums beyond. He palmed her skull and slammed her head again; her struggles quieted.

"S-stop," AviSariel whispered.

"Go back to the party, princess," Addom Vym huffed, ignoring the way Grayc Illan tried to tear his fingers from her hair. She didn't look afraid, not even now. Angry and flustered, but not quite afraid.

Her large, green eyes looked to AviSariel and the princess stared back. She couldn't tell what the woman was thinking, what that look was supposed to mean, but she found herself taking a step back from the brutal scene. Then another. Why would Addom attack Grayc Illan? Was he going to kill her? AviSariel spared the rat one last look and some wicked little part of her wished he would.

She slipped through the doors and back into the party.

"Wait," Grayc Illan ground out through her teeth just before he jerked her away from one wall to throw her into another. When she slumped to the ground she saw the knife she'd tried to pull on him. She reached for it only for his boot to stomp over her hand, grinding her fingers into the concrete.

"Where is she?"

She shivered at the calm of his voice and hissed back, "Who?"

He growled low and kicked the blade further down the hall before pulling her upright again by her curls. His knuckles smashed into her cheek, spinning her into the wall. She coughed red and sank to the floor, hands out and vision swimming.

"You think you can lie to me? I'm a Vym." He grabbed her arm and hauled her up. "What did you do?"

She leaned into the wall, ankles wobbling on her heels. Her chest heaved with every breath and hot blood dripped from her face. She smiled despite herself, agony lacing through her features. "What have I done?" she whispered, and thought of such a long list of answers.

He grabbed her jaw and yanked her face toward his. Red eyes

stared down at her. "I don't care why you took her. Just tell me where she is. Tell me she's still alive."

It was tempting to say Larc wasn't. He would kill her, wouldn't he? It would be over. "There's nothing to tell." Grayc Illan coughed.

He laughed and it was an awful sound. Vyms were not laughing creatures. They had smiles that could steal souls but their laughter was almost purely reserved for the dying. "You're playing a game you can't win, rat. They won't even find your parts when I'm done with you." He jerked Grayc off her feet with his fist curled in her hair. She scrambled beside him as he dragged her down the corridor, clawing at his wrist, trying to pry his fingers free of her hair and ripping up trails of flesh with her nails. Her knees scraped against the wall and ground as she staggered. A metal door banged and he hauled her out into the night.

"Tell me where she is!" Addom flung her into the street, pavement tearing her knees. Grayc crumpled into a ball, sucking in shallow breaths. "Where?" he roared.

Grayc tried to focus on his blurred form, shoving hair from her eyes. "Vym…" Light flickered beyond him, a strobe of safety that never—*never*—wavered. She blinked, and it swam into focus. A streetlamp. It blazed, then dimmed, then shuddered out.

"Grayc—" Addom snarled.

"The light," she exhaled in disbelief.

"Don't—"

Her head jerked, following the flickering as more lamps dimmed. Down the length of the street, the enormous hanging globes of safety wavered, rallied, and died. In the distance, toward the Low, entire buildings vanished into the night. "Vym, the *lights*."

Addom gazed into the nearing dark, eyes widening and mouth parting to suck in a gasp of disbelief. "That can't be."

"It's a blackout," she whispered in horror, crawling to her feet, heels long lost in the struggle.

"No," Addom said, staring in a morbid daze. "The lamps never go out. Not in the Main. Not in the High."

Because the lamps kept the swarms of pixies at bay. Kept the magic-soaked residents of the Main and High safe. Sometimes the lights flickered or failed in the Low, but the vicious bugs didn't bother the rats much, with so little magic on their skin to be worth the bother.

Grayc watched the Realm be swallowed up one block at a time, then bolted for the warehouse. Addom shouted her name, but she flew through the doors, down a corridor, and burst into the full blare of The Circus.

She pushed her way through bodies, grabbing at shoulders to catch glimpses of faces, searching for one she knew, one that could help. Her body jerked to a stop when she saw his top hat bobbing along behind a group of heavily dusted dancers. She didn't apologize when she shoved her way through them. She lunged forward to twist Udaro around. The man smiled down at her at first, still playing his role as ringmaster, but the grin gave way to shock and fury at the sight of her. He hurried her away from the center of the party and toward a vaguely quieter corner.

"Turn off the music!" she yelled at the top of her lungs so that he might hear. "The lights are going out. You have to evacuate. Get them back to the High."

Udaro scrunched his face in confusion. "What?" he shouted over the music.

"Blackout!" Grayc Illan screamed.

He stared at her. Blackout. Pixies. The Circus. The gravity of it drained the blood from his face. "Run!" He pushed her in the direction of the exit and shoved his way toward the stage. Precious minutes ticked away until he cut the music and raised his hands.

"Ladies and gentlemen, The Circus is hereby post-poned. Exit the warehouse immediately and proceed to the High…"

Grayc Illan sneered as Udaro advised them not to take any dust with them, not to risk attracting the swarms, as if they weren't all living beacons by now. She moved through the bodies, straining to see over those that were so much taller than herself and find him in the mess of others. The grim thought that most of these people were too dusted to understand the danger or find the exit struck her, but she couldn't spare them the time that kindness would take. She could only push them out of her way and call his name louder.

Of course, he didn't call back. He never did.

"Grayc?" AviSariel whimpered, probably more than a little surprised to see her alive. Grayc Illan wondered if the princess understood what was happening, what was about to happen.

"Where is he?" she shouted over the other voices that were finally starting to panic.

AviSariel hesitated before pointing toward one of the walls deeper in the room. The dim lights went out, plunging them into darkness. "What do I do?" the princess pleaded, her voice louder in the dark.

Screams started; not the shrill, excited screams of fright, but heart clenching cries of pain and terror. The crowd lurched, shoving in all directions, pushing toward the doors with new vigor, but it was too late. If they were screaming in that direction, then the pixies were already inside.

She grabbed AviSariel's hand and pulled her along the wall, making their way to the couches arranged near that far corner. The swarms poured in through the front doors, frail wings beating in the thousands. She saw the shapes of them in the shadows, clouds of ill intent moving up the walls to lick at the magic. Soon they were everywhere, crawling over the floors, the chairs, and the tables. It wasn't long before they found better meals in the guests, taking greedy bites from those magic-filled bodies slow to escape.

The crowd grew thicker around them as people fled toward the back, desperate to find another exit. They reached the couches but Vaun wasn't there. A man so dusted he merely smiled at the screaming crowd lounged there, instead. His female companion stretched her arm high and watched in addled awe as a pixie wrapped itself around one of her fingers, gnawing at the tip with its sharp, little teeth. She didn't flinch or panic even as blood began to drip down her wrist and the bone of her fingertip shone.

Cursing and slapping a pixie from her hair, Grayc Illan spun around. Her eyes strained in the dark. There were shapes of bodies everywhere and moving clusters of shadows in the air, dipping down to attack flailing limbs. She called out his name but the growing buzz of wings drowned out her voice.

AviSariel pulled at her arm, tugging her closer to the mass of bodies. "The door," the princess wailed. "We have to get out."

Grayc tried to let go of the other woman's hand. AviSariel could try the door if she wanted, but even from here she could make out the shape of a pile of bodies clogging the entrance. People were trampling each other and attracting the swarms with their blood. They were everywhere now, nipping at every bit of flesh they could find. With her free hand, Grayc swatted them away. A few of their small, naked bodies broke against the force of her palm but there were always more.

She cursed AviSariel when she pulled at her again, almost knocking her over. This time Grayc pulled back, jostling the princess on her heels. "Go, if you want!"

AviSariel sobbed in reply and clutched Grayc Illan's hand harder. She pushed on into the room along the wall, shouting his name over the sharpening screams. AviSariel screamed, too, when they stepped over a fleshless body on the floor. His skin had been eaten clean off his sinew with no clothing at all to get in the way. It took little time for Grayc Illan to realize that he had been one of the dust-dipped treats roaming the party.

The pixies crunched beneath their feet, so greedy for the mess of dust on the floor that they couldn't be bothered to avoid their footfalls.

People ran blind in the darkness that had only grown as those swarms filled the air around them. Grayc pulled AviSariel along, fingers digging into the back of the princess's hand when she staggered behind her.

"Where are we going?" AviSariel sobbed.

Grayc didn't answer, running her free hand along the wall. The sounds of wings and wet carnage grew louder than the cries. Her fingers found a crack in the wall and her body jerked to a stop, AviSariel running into her from behind.

"Grayc?" The princess pleaded, frantically swatting away the bugs that tore out chunks of her skin.

"It's here," Grayc Illan assured, only realizing when she spoke that her lips were bleeding. Finding the doorknob, she yanked open the door and dragged out the brooms and mops stored inside. The tiny space was smaller than she'd hoped; room for one. She hesitated, then shoved AviSariel inside. The princess stared back, face shining wet with tears and blood even in the darkness, eyes wide with blind terror just before Grayc Illan slammed the door.

Her body curled against the barrier. She couldn't run, even if she knew where to go. There was a chance someone might open the door if she left it. Her skin burned and she knew it was their teeth. She pressed her forehead to the door, trying to think while at the same time trying not to scream and run. Perhaps Vaun had already made it out. The door quivered and scratching filled her ears. At first she thought it was her own nails, only to realize the sound was getting louder and more frantic. Her arms skimmed the surface, prying pixies away where they clawed at the seams of the door. They could smell AviSariel inside, soaked in the finest vanity crafts the Realm had to offer. It was enough for the bulk of the bugs to ignore Grayc in their attempt to tunnel through the wood.

She cried out as she fought them off the door. Splinters of wood dug into her flesh, indistinguishable from the bites. As though the insects possessed a unified thought, most of the swarm abandoned their assault on the door and turned their fury on her. Grayc wrapped her arms around her head, trying to shield her face, and sank slowly to the floor.

AviSariel continued calling her name through the wood, voice trembling with sobs. She must be twice as frightened now that Grayc had stopped screaming. She should be. The world blurred and faded around her, and curiously, Grayc found herself thinking about trees. Tall trees, in a wood, with branches that blocked out all but thin slivers of daylight. Leaves shifted in a breeze. Grayc thought about running, her legs strong, her heart beating wild. Fury bubbled up inside her, because this wasn't a thought. It was a memory, and it wasn't even hers. Her last thought was being wasted on something gleaned from the mind of a wolf.

There came a stillness in which Grayc was certain she had lost consciousness, only it was that same certainty that told her it wasn't so. The buzzing of wings grew quieter, almost distant. Battered wood filled her vision, bathed in a soft, white glow. She pulled back, frowning at her hands. They looked too bright in that gentle light, slashed with vibrant blood and gouged with splinters. The stillness broke, and something breathed deeply behind her. Grayc turned slowly and stared into the eyes of a wolf.

Its ghostlike body gave off a pool of light as it stood within arm's reach, its large head swung toward her, eyes so icy a blue that they shimmered white. It tore its gaze from hers to tip its face high and howl. The cry was so loud that she covered her ears. Other wolves echoed the call of the first. One sounded as though it might be right outside the building while others were far away. The beast eyed her once more, almost as if it might speak, before it turned away with a snort. It prowled the perimeter of the room, snarling to keep the pixies crawling high up the walls. Some had fled out the doors, either full or ready to seek their meals elsewhere, while others lapped at the ceiling and watched the beast with cautious, beady eyes.

A group of people rushed into the warehouse, each wearing plastic suits with masks and carrying weapons she recognized as torches, the kind they used to fend off pixies around the Dust Factories out in the

Ash. Flames burst forth, so bright it made her eyes ache. The fire curled in the air, growling like the beast that stood nearby.

"Grayc!"

Her eyes had closed against the painful brightness of the flames, and for a heartbeat she thought his voice was a hallucination. When his fingers found her face she opened her eyes. Vaun breathed heavily. Her vision swayed and for a moment his pupils sharpened and his eyes looked a shade of silver like the eyes of Evan Kadem himself. Before she could recoil, the hallucination passed and Vaun wrapped his arms around her. He pulled her up, his cheek bleeding from tiny, crescent cuts that trailed down his neck, but otherwise he looked well. Samuel Sinol lingered nearby, looking more than a little rumpled himself.

Vaun pushed her hair back to study her face. His fingers hovered over her torn skin, making their way down to her arms. She held them out to her sides, blood dripping in thick globs from her fingertips to the floor.

"The closet." Grayc Illan swallowed and then coughed. Her voice was raw and foreign. "The princess is inside." She gestured to the ravaged door and Vaun's gaze followed.

Samuel Sinol crossed the space to examine the assaulted door before prying it open. The wood cracked and fell into two large pieces. AviSariel screamed and the light of the flames made her tears shine. It was absurd that a person could still look so lovely with her cheeks wet, her hair tousled, and blood smearing her skin.

It took more than a little effort for Samuel Sinol to coax the princess from her broom closet and when he finally did, she promptly fainted. It was probably for the best; the warehouse looked almost as bad as it had sounded. Somehow, the prince's valet managed to carry AviSariel and all of her skirts with no sign of trouble.

Grayc Illan hadn't realized that she, too, was being ushered out until she found herself looking back at the wolf. She could have sworn that it watched her go.

CHAPTER THIRTEEN

Vaun kept his arm around Grayc's waist until they got out of the warehouse, worried she might faint. Had someone punched her? Had she run into a wall during the uproar?

Cold air washed over them as they left the warehouse. Chaos reigned outside as much as in. Bodies bled in the street, victims shrieked, rescuers wielded flame-spouting contraptions, and fat pixies broke underfoot, weighed down by their swollen bellies. Flashes of light drew Vaun's gaze toward the higher streets of the Main, where more stark flames lapped out in the darkness and another wolf prowled in a pool of its own glow to ward off the pests. He'd never known the wolves could repel pixies, but was grateful all the same.

With as much grace as possible, Samuel Sinol placed the princess in the back of the car and held the door, waiting for them. Vaun nudged Grayc forward, but she blinked and pulled away. With a little shake, she scanned the busy street. "I need my car."

"I'll drop you off," Vaun said.

"No. I have to—" She swayed but brushed him off when he reached out. "I have things to do."

"Get in the damned car," he snapped, eyeing her arms for a spot least injured so he could haul her into the car if need be.

"I can't." She studied the crowd, as if noting particular faces, sorting them into columns or searching for someone. Her gaze drifted up the street, peering at the lamps blazing less than a handful of blocks up the road, beyond the wolf and the flames. The blackout hadn't gone farther than the Main.

"You need a physician," he snapped, but she turned away. "Grayc—"

Blood smeared down her back, trailing like a gory ribbon along her spine. Ridges of torn flesh peeked out from beneath her hair. Her shoulders and the rest of her back appeared relatively unharmed, but the pixies had torn into that tender flesh as if seeking the sweetest magic—

Shock rippled through Vaun, rooting him to the spot. Pixies cared only for magic, stalking those with the best quality and highest quantity first. It was why the pests preferred the flesh over the meat beneath; it was saturated in magic for beauty and sprinkled with dust for sensation. And Grayc, his Grayc, who recoiled from the excessive use of magic in almost all its forms, had enticed them from better meals.

He came up behind her, grabbing her hip while sweeping her hair aside. The pixies had torn their way along her spine from hairline to shoulder blades, tiny wounds coming together to open larger gashes aimed for her spine.

Grayc Illan tensed but he held her in place. He could hear her heart beat faster when he leaned his face into the curve of her neck beside that angry wound. He breathed in deeply and his eyes fluttered shut. There, inside her scent, beneath her skin, was the heavy smell of magic. Not a charm purchased or a power within but a curse folded tightly into her vertebrae.

"Vaun," Grayc exhaled his name. Was that a plea?

He drew back to look at the wound again and through the blood he could almost see it, the intricately woven threads of pale light running along her spine. He let go of her and stepped back, pulling away as though the shackle might reach out and ensnare him next. His mind spun and he took another step back when she turned to look at him. Again, that look in her eyes, the one that he could never quite read, like she wanted to say something but couldn't.

"We have never met," he whispered words he had heard her say and felt his heart crushing beneath the weight of what they meant. How many times had he heard people who knew her before him say that she had changed? How many times had he seen that look of conflict in her eyes despite the confidence of her body? "You're a puppet." He almost choked when he said it.

She didn't say anything. She probably couldn't.

"Who holds the strings?" His voice sounded cold but his skin felt hot, like it seethed against his muscles. How much of her was a lie?

She stared at him the way she had so many times before, her lips pressed firmly but her eyes begging him to guess the answer.

"How long?"

Grayc Illan swallowed and looked away. "We have never met," she repeated quietly and Vaun's heart nearly broke. Never. When had she come to work for him? Who had she worked for before?

Anger swept over the pain and he took another step back, toward his car. "I will fix this," the prince whispered, managing to drag his eyes over her one more time, though he wasn't sure who he was looking at anymore. She stood there, silently watching him back away. Never quite afraid. Never quite sad. Grayc Illan Sanaro. His Grayc.

"How will you fix it?" The corner of her mouth turned up, as if to smile. "Will you ask me to do it for you?" Even in her exhaustion, her words dragged with bitterness. "I have tried."

A sleek black car he recognized as hers glided to a halt beside them, one of her guards springing out to open the door.

She held his gaze a moment longer, then vanished into the vehicle.

Grayc Illan demanded her driver take her to the offices Jacobi kept in the bottom of the Main. One of the guards in the backseat tweezed bits of wood from her arms while the other filled her in on what little they knew: Jacobi had been among the first to escape the warehouse—he was likely locked safely away in his house in the High—and the blackout had struck only the Main and Low of Belholn.

She closed her eyes at that bit of information. So, this was an assassination attempt, by someone who didn't care how many died so long as their target perished. She'd once thought only the Queen could be so cruel. But the Queen wouldn't send her wolves to mitigate a slaughter she'd orchestrated.

If not the Queen, then who? Who had the power to darken a province? Who had a secret worth risking the Queen's fury to protect? And who hadn't been at the party? Whoever Jacobi's partner was must have decided to close up shop. The blackout in the Main during The Circus could have been a scheme to destroy them, hoping that they would be eaten with the rest of the guests and that the evidence of the treasonous dust would be gobbled up in the night.

Grayc spent fifty minutes in traffic, crawling along roads congested with cars fleeing to the safety of the High while others ferried more staff from the factories with flamethrowers through the Main.

By the time she arrived at the office, both of her arms had been cleaned and a thick bandage taped over the deepest wound at the back of her neck. Some of the lamps along the main roads began to flicker to life again, offering whispers of hope in a night that had only just begun.

Before opening the door, one of the guards pleaded with her again, insisting that it was best to head farther up the province since there could be more attacks and they would be safer in the High. Grayc Illan ignored him and opened the car door herself. She remembered she was barefoot when her soles touched the pavement.

Someone in a suit hurried to open the building door for her. "Get me a change of clothes," Grayc Illan demanded. The building manager fell in step beside her as she headed up the stairs. "Any problems here?"

The older gentleman looked flustered but not injured. "A broken window. They got into the dust stash in the second and fourth parlors. I'm afraid the little beasts ate just about all of it before we could board up the windows and exterminate them."

She nodded. The second parlor was the Queen's dust, a legitimate and costly loss, and the fourth was the experimental dust, nothing they could ever claim. "The basement?" Her voice remained steady, as though she inquired about wine and not an abducted Vym.

The man straightened beside her office door, pulling out his ring of keys and diligently unlocking the barrier for her. "Not a peep, miss."

She nodded again and dismissed him. Larc was alive and the building was standing; she'd ask no more tonight. She eyed the couch against the far wall and considered doing nothing more than collapsing on it for a few hours, but the sting and ache of her skin drove her into the bathroom. Blood crusted a split and bruised cheek, but it was nothing to the torn flesh down her arms and back. She stripped and stepped into the shower, carefully scrubbing away crusted blood and filth from her skin.

The adrenaline keeping her on her feet began to fade, leaving a faint tremor in her hands and growing pain in her body. After showering, she pulled a roll of gauze from the bottom drawer and quickly wrapped her forearms. She glanced in the mirror when she finished. Her bottom lip was scabbed and bruised, whether by the teeth of a pixie or the knuckles of a Vym. Addom wasn't her biggest problem tonight, but he would bury her if she survived to tomorrow.

She glanced at the door in the reflection, then turned and locked it. Her hands shook as she pulled her hair up and tied the damp locks back. Leaning against the sink, she carefully peeled the bandages back. Picking up a hand mirror, she turned to examine the back of her neck. The ugly wounds were still raw, but scabbing over and healing quickly. Magic, even curses, had some perks.

Vaun had called her a puppet. She put down the smaller mirror and stared into the larger. She tugged the tie from her hair to let heavy curls press against her cheeks. She *was* a puppet.

When she left the bathroom, she found fresh clothes folded on the arm of her chair and Jacobi Belholn sitting in it. His hair was out of place and the collar of his shirt splattered in blood, though not his own, if the pristine state of his face was any indication. He looked her over, but neither her nudity nor the abuse she had suffered relieved his features of their glower. She crossed the room to stand beside him, picking up the clean clothes to dress: a pair of slacks, a black blouse, and a pinstripe vest.

"Bad night?" he said.

She smiled a little and bent to roll up the bottoms of her slacks; they had been hemmed for her heels, without which they would be intolerable. "Worse than yours, it seems."

"I heard you saved the princess."

Grayc Illan thought on that for a moment before replying. "I suppose I did." She sighed. "Jacobi, that blackout..."

"I know." He groaned and stood. "I've destroyed the papers at my estate. I'm going to burn the rest here and make sure all of the dust is gone."

"Is that wise?" She leaned against the wall when he stood from the chair. "We won't have anything to use against him."

"If he was trying to kill us, then he will soon find out that he failed," Jacobi hissed. "He could try to frame us for the whole thing now."

"Just tell me who it is." Maybe she could find a way to save herself by saving Jacobi.

"No!" Jacobi barked and she realized that he was afraid. Of course he was afraid; he was running dirty dust in treason to not only his cousin, the Lord of Belholn, but to the Queen herself. "We're done. We had nothing to do with this." He pushed past her on his way to the door. "Make sure no one finds the body."

"You've killed her?"

"No," he hesitated at the door, "you will. Now. Get rid of her somewhere no one will look."

"Jac—"

"Enough," the white-haired lord snapped. "Put a bullet in her head and be done with it."

He left the door open in his wake. Grayc's body shuddered under the weight of his command before her legs carried her to her desk and her hand, so newly cleaned, reached out to take a pistol from the drawer.

She wanted to run. She wanted to come up with a plan that would keep Jacobi from getting suspicious and keep Larc alive. She wanted to do anything other than what she was about to do. The gun felt heavy, straining the joints of her arm as though it begged her to drop it. The hallway seemed shorter than ever before. Had the carpet on the stairs always been red?

She didn't want to do this. The bottom of the stairs was upon her and the hardwood was cold beneath her naked feet. The large doors of the entrance stood only a short sprint away, she could run for it, but she turned away and continued down the narrow hall to the storage room and the basement door tucked inside.

She was a puppet.

She couldn't even cry. Couldn't even feel the weight or guilt of what she was about to do. She knew it was wrong. She knew she didn't want to. She knew to be sorry. But she didn't feel it.

Three guards waited at the bottom of the steep cobblestone stairs. Jacobi must have sent them down to help her get rid of the body.

With a flick of the gun she gestured for one of them to open the door. "Wait here." Grayc Illan exhaled before walking inside. When she waited another moment, they obliged her unspoken order and closed the heavy door behind her.

The room was small. A mattress lay in one corner where the damsel sat with her back to the stones and her knees to her chest. She looked up with large eyes—brown, as it turned out, after the charms of her magic wore off weeks ago. Without the powder and the paint, she looked more like a young woman than a child, but there was no ignoring the naïvety of her eyes or the tears that stained her cheeks.

"Grayc?" Little Larc Vym cried softly and Grayc Illan knew her heart would have broken at the small sound of hope in the other woman's voice if only her heart could break.

Her arm shook when it lifted the gun; shook because she tried so hard to lower it. Her fingers felt numb and her mouth parted shakily because she could not stop her digit from sliding over the trigger.

Larc cried loudly in shrill sobs. She wailed and begged. She offered anything and everything. She called for her brother—not Quentan, but Addom. She pleaded and then, at last, when her tears blinded her, she cried out for her mother.

Vaun ignored the pleas of the servants on his path up the stairs just as he'd ignored the guards at the door. He called her name in the halls of the Vym family house because though he had once thought he knew her, he had never pretended to know the architecture of her home.

She appeared at the end of the hall, hurrying through doors flung wide.

"Vaun, thank the fates." Fay exhaled, and he couldn't help but think that it didn't sound natural for her to thank anyone, even fate. "We heard about the blackout." She reached up, bare hands seeking the small wounds of his face.

His fingers caught hers a breath from his cheek. Their dark eyes met and all softness slipped from her features, hardening right before his eyes into the woman he should never have underestimated. She jerked her hands free and stepped back.

"You don't understand." Fay sneered as though he had wronged her.

"You cursed her."

"I made her useful."

"To spy on me?" he snapped.

"To protect you," Fay countered. "You know nothing, Vaun. This Realm is not as simple as you think." She spun on her heel and sailed down the hall, as though this conversation could so easily be concluded.

"But she doesn't protect me anymore, does she?" He caught the door before it could slam in his face, slapping it against the wall hard enough to make picture frames shake. Fay jumped, a slight response of flesh that never reached her face. "You sent her to Jacobi."

"She has better uses now," Fay huffed, pacing the room. Her fingers pressed stiffly to her bodice. Was this what his sister looked like when flustered?

"What use?" he demanded. "What plan do you have for your slave now?"

Her lip curled at his tone. "Temper your mood! My plans are my own."

"What about her plans?" He swiveled to follow her as she paced, sweeping around what must have been her private parlor, for everything matched her severe taste and wardrobe. He had never seen it before. She had never invited him here. "Set her free."

Fay stiffened, chin rising. "I will not."

Vaun bit back a scream. "Let her go, Fay!"

She planted herself in the corner of the room, hands balled at her sides. "I cannot do that. You do not understand."

"So I keep hearing."

"She is only a good liar because she cannot tell the truth. She is only strong because she has no choice."

"You stole that choice!"

"This is her penance for her crimes!"

He upended a chair, sending it careening against the wall. "How convenient for you that your servant could be blackmailed into such use!"

"I made her better!" Her long nails dug into her bodice to rip at the delicate beadwork there.

"I know what you did! I know the curse! You stole her soul!"

She shook her head and he thought she looked almost afraid in the face of his disgust. Quick steps brought her closer. "It was for a cause, Vaun." Her voice softened, pleading for him to understand. "Sometimes spies are the only ones we can trust."

His heart hammered painfully in his throat as more pieces of the puzzle slid into place. "You know about Larc."

She touched his arm, gripping it tight. "There is nothing I can do to save her without exposing Grayc Illan, and my part in why she is there." Tears glassed her eyes. Was that real remorse, or just what she thought she should show? "I didn't do it to meddle in your love life, Vaun. I needed someone close to the situation. I needed to make sure he didn't go too far."

"Who? Jacobi?"

She shook her head, lips pressed tight over an answer.

With a groan, he bit his lip and looked away from her. "Fine. I don't care. Just let her go."

"I won't do that," she said softly, like an adult explaining facts to a child.

He jerked his arm free, not caring how she staggered in his sudden absence. "I am not asking." His voice chilled, eyes slanting down his nose to look at her as though she were any other subject in his Realm.

Her features shuddered with fury. "Jacobi will know instantly." The plea vanished from her voice, swallowed up by callous certainty. "He will kill her."

Vaun shoved his sister aside, forcing her into a sofa as he passed.

The moment she realized that he knew about her curse in the hallway she had moved toward this parlor, and when he followed her in, she managed to keep herself between him and the next set of doors. He pushed them open while she screamed at him to stop. The study inside was much like the room before it, lavish and gothic with furniture that had a tendency toward severity. The whole place reeked of her—not Vym, but Dray Fen. He studied the walls and shelves, books and trinkets, roving past a heavy desk and another cluster of chairs.

"You can't do this, Vaun!" She grabbed his arm and hissed when he shook her off.

"Be quiet," he warned.

"I will let her go when the task is done. I swear!" She trailed after him as he circled the room.

"Shut up!"

"Vaun, listen to reason! I—"

He spun, yanking her against him and clamping a hand over her mouth. "Shhhh," he breathed against her cheek, squeezing her tighter when her lips moved against his palm, a warning she reluctantly heeded.

Silence swelled in her study, the sound of her heartbeat hammering against his senses before he set it aside. There was... a humming. A quiet, miserable humming that drew him slowly toward the far wall. Her skirts dragged along the rug as he walked them toward it, her fingers clutching his arm in silent negation as though their pressure could slow his stride.

He stopped when they stood in the little sitting area, his eyes fixed on the blank wall. With a small shove he released her, tumbling her and all of her skirts into a chair.

"Vaun..." She started but seemed to have finally run out of threats and pleas, watching instead as he grabbed the side of the couch that rested there against the wall. In one swift motion, he shoved the furniture aside, legs scoring the hardwood. His hand touched the wallpaper and the humming grew beneath his fingertips.

With a curl of his lips he dug his fingers through the paper. The false wall caved easily, bits at a time peeling back and dropping to the floor. He used both hands, then, and when he finished he stared in silence at the rows of shelving housing more than twenty glass jars and bottles, each humming softly from within.

More than twenty. More than twenty puppets in the Realm. Each had to have agreed to her curse, whether she had blackmailed or tricked them into the agreement, for no one but the Queen with her wolves could take a soul that wasn't offered.

"Which one?"

Fay didn't answer. Whatever control he'd managed to maintain broke and he lashed out, sweeping fragile containers from shelves to smash against the floor. He tore every bottle, every jar, every capped flask from her hiding place and crushed them at her feet. Shards of glass skittered wildly across the hardwood in all directions. The humming turned to breathy screams as those captive lights flared, swelling into deafening cries before vanishing, drawn like magnets back to their bodies.

When silence returned and every prison lay smashed, he half expected her to scold him, or scorn him, but she only sat there, stubborn and unapologetic. He'd always known his sister to be strong, sometimes cruel, and sometimes kind, but he'd never thought her a thief.

He strode past, crushing fragments underfoot. Fay called after him, real fear in her voice. The puppets were just another game lost, but her brother was a price she'd never thought she would have to pay. He heard her question in the silence that followed, heard her worry, and though he knew he could never truly abandon her, he wanted her to be afraid just a little longer.

He paused at the door. "The last time I saw jars like these was in the Tower." He turned, giving her his cheek because she didn't deserve his eyes. "Mother was mistaken, sending you away and keeping Evan Kadem at her side. You would make a great heir."

Larc's cries cut off. The stench of gunpowder hung in the air.

Grayc's hand shook violently and every muscle screamed. Her legs buckled and the pistol slapped against the floor as she bent over, gasping for air. Her whole body ached. Her heart hammered in her chest and her lungs burned. After decades of drowning, she could finally breathe and it made everything hurt with a clarity that she had forgotten.

At last, she raised her head to meet Larc's gaze.

The girl didn't move, or speak. She huddled in the corner, consumed with terror. Or perhaps she'd bitten off her tongue in the height of her panic. Either way, she still breathed.

Grayc sat up, eyeing the gun in her palm. Jacobi's guards would have heard the shot, and be ready to remove a body. She could work with that. At least Jacobi himself wasn't outside. He would know the moment he saw her that something had changed, if he hadn't felt the curse break already. She shuddered and stood, legs wobbling.

"Grayc?" Larc whispered, her voice so soft that Grayc wasn't sure she'd even heard it. "A-Are you going to kill me?"

Grayc stared down at her. She couldn't hide or bolt for the door. She still had to get Larc out of the house. "No." She swallowed hard when she heard her voice, heard the softness she had forgotten and the way that it shook. "No. Get up." She held out the hand not holding the gun and the timid Vym reached up to take it, crawling to her feet. She couldn't pretend Larc was dead. One of the brutes in the hall would notice she was alive and unbloodied—even if Larc could manage not to squirm, shake or sob—when he went to lift her body. "Don't say anything. Just stay close. I will fix this," she whispered. Vaun had said it to her, so she said it to Larc. Vaun had meant it and so would she.

She swallowed hard and squared her shoulders before opening the door. The three men on the other side straightened, though none hid their surprise at seeing the Vym girl standing behind Grayc Illan. "Change of plans," she announced and again her voice threatened to wobble.

"Miss?" one of them asked cautiously.

"We'll take her to the Low. Slit her throat and leave her for the pixies. With tonight's mess they'll never be able to tell what happened, if they find her at all." Her voice sounded stronger this time and Larc started crying again behind her. Grayc Illan wasn't sure if it was for show or not.

"You two, go get the car and meet me around back." Grayc waved off the two who knew her best. They hesitated, but inclined their heads and lumbered up the stairs. She focused on the last. "Go tell Jacobi the plan. He's in his office. Let him know I'll be back for breakfast."

He nodded like the others and hurried up the stairs ahead of her. Her stomach almost turned with relief and it took more effort than she would have liked to admit just to get her legs to launch her up those steps. Larc followed, fingers clutching at the back of Grayc's vest. She pushed open the door at the top and stepped out into the large room, quiet and dark. Her skin tingled with nerves but she didn't dare stop.

The hall was empty but long. Her feet were cold but silent on the hardwood, bringing them closer and closer to the front of the house. She paused near the mouth of the corridor, where it opened into the lobby, more entrances on either side and a staircase to the left. The door was right there, on the other side of those checkered tiles. Larc whimpered, the sound bubbling up from nerves that couldn't take the suspense of silence. For the first time in a long time, Grayc Illan completely understood the feeling.

She stepped out of the shadows and into the open lobby. Her lips parted to shudder out a breath, but met no damning answer. The second and third steps grew faster and the door loomed before them.

Her hand touched the knob just as Larc's sobs pitched, gushing through her nose. She pressed hard into Grayc's side.

"Grayc." Steel laced Jacobi's tone, and she found herself thinking of the blonde woman in his bed with bits of scalp missing.

Her eyes closed. She straightened her spine, but couldn't bring herself to turn around just yet. She was going to die in this house. She was finally able to breathe again, and she wasn't even going to reach the sidewalk.

She heard his shoes on the steps as he came down the stairs. Larc started crying again. She had good reason.

"Oh, Grayc," Jacobi sang with a mocking sigh, but she heard the fury beneath his words. "I only have one question."

She didn't wait to hear it. She jerked the heavy door open, grabbing Larc to push her out first. Perhaps they wouldn't get far, but maybe they'd get far enough.

The door slammed shut, Jacobi's palm against it and his breath on her neck. He shoved Larc away and leaned his cheek into the back of Grayc's hair.

"Who do you work for, little spy?" he whispered into her ear. She couldn't keep her mouth from trembling when his fingers traveled down her arm to wrap around the gun. She couldn't make herself release the weapon, her last pretense of strength, but with another growl and a hard tug he took it.

"Jac—"

He spun her around and tossed her toward Larc. She scrambled to keep her balance. He followed, looking at her anew.

"I knew the change was too extreme. Frightened little Grayc doesn't grow up to be this." He stopped when he was close enough to tangle his fingers in her dark curls. "How about we change you to a nice blonde, and then we can have a long talk?"

Tears welled in her eyes, and he smiled. She pressed her lips together, as though that little gesture could possibly stop her tears from spilling over.

Decades. She had spent decades like a ghost, and now she would die for it. She would die afraid. Had it always been her fate?

Larc screamed when he grabbed her, shoving her to her knees. Her sobs pitched and her eyes shut. Jacobi cocked the pistol and aimed it at her face.

After everything, Larc was still going to die, for no reason other than she might have seen something she was too stupid to realize. Grayc's stomach churned, but she lurched away from the wall. Her fingers slid into the perfectly tailored pockets of her slack and came out with a thin, black dagger. Grayc Illan Sanaro always had a weapon; everyone knew that. She threw her body into his and they tumbled to the floor. The gun skittered across hardwood and into the hall.

Blood roared in her ears, drowning out Larc's sobs. Grayc scrambled free, kicking Jacobi in the face before stumbling backwards to get some distance. Her knuckles screamed from clenching the knife so hard. Jacobi hissed through his teeth to catch his breath, propping himself up against a wall. He noticed the blood on her knife before the growing stain on his shirt.

Surprise looked ugly even on his delicate features.

"Run!" Grayc Illan hissed at the little Vym. "Larc, go!"

With a deep, shaky breath and the slightest hint of courage, Larc crawled to her feet. Jacobi snarled and pushed himself away from the wall but Grayc staggered between, sticky blade in hand.

"You will regret that," Jacobi hissed, one hand pressing against his wound.

The door opened and closed and she was alone with him.

Grayc smiled softly even as a tear slid freely down her cheek. "I don't think I will." She might die in this house, but Larc wouldn't. She hadn't killed the only innocent Vym in the Realm.

He charged. She set herself, ready for the impact, ready to spin back and use his momentum to lurch them across the floor in a crazy dance. They crashed into the wall, and her knife sank beneath his ribs. He howled but didn't back away, using his height and weight to box her in.

His fingers wrapped around her hand and the blade to pull it out of himself. Her whole arm shook when she tried to push it back in but couldn't. The wounds on her arms from The Circus bled bright through the bandages. Slowly, he brought her arm and the knife between their chests and she watched in stunned horror as he turned the narrow dagger toward her. She tried to push back but he forced her arm across her body, setting the blade just under her collarbone.

His lips twisted into a smile again and his forehead pressed intimately against hers as he forced the knife slowly through her skin until it scraped against bone.

She screamed and it was a ragged, wild sound, filled with terror and rage, but no matter how loud she cried the blade didn't stop. He grunted at the resistance of cartilage and her sounds pitched into a near breathless wail when he shoved through.

Her vision blurred and for a moment she thought she'd lost consciousness. Jacobi pulled his head back from her to stare, lips parted and eyes confused. He let go of the knife and took a step back. His hand clutched at his chest while his mouth struggled to gather air. She could have sworn he was glowing, bright, as though embers ignited under his skin.

Confusion turned to agony. His eyes widened. Veins bulged in his face, and when he finally did manage to exhale, steam rolled off his tongue. The brightness grew and his skin began to bubble. He tried to scream, but more steam seared the inside of his mouth. His beautiful white hair curled and singed in the heat and Grayc Illan looked on as Jacobi Belholn burned from the inside out. He exhaled ash, and like a wooden toy tossed into the flames, he peeled and fell apart right before her eyes, husk collapsing to the floor of the lobby.

She stared down at what was left of him. Her vision swayed and she wasn't sure whether she would vomit or faint. Her gaze dragged up from the floor to see Vaun standing in the drifts of ash and she could have sworn a wisp of smoke slithered past his lips. As quickly as relief struck her, her knees buckled. She sighed when he caught her and leaned into him when he picked her up. She wanted to ask him to take her outside, because if she was going to die, she wanted to do it out there, but she wasn't sure she could speak.

His lips brushed her temple and she almost thought she heard him laugh and reply, *"You're not dying. We only just met."*

CHAPTER FOURTEEN

Fay picked up her coffee and leaned back into her chair, watching Quentan finish his cup at the other end of the long table. He was one of those men that liked coffee and was quick to get a refill. She cradled her cup to soak the warmth into her fingers.

Quentan shook his head at something he read in his copy of the paper and flipped it over. She waited until he drained his second cup before she set hers down without taking a sip.

"Why his bed, husband?"

The Lord of Vym raised an eyebrow. "Excuse me?"

"Meresin. Why kill her in Vaun's bed? Why not in her own house? Why not the street? You could have killed her anywhere you liked."

Blood drained from his face, taking any bemusement with it. "What? Your little spies couldn't tell you?"

"I want you to tell me."

He barked a laugh. "Didn't think I knew about your pets, did you? Do you really think I'd ever let you get enough dirt on me to force my soul into one of your jars?"

"I don't need your soul." She folded her hands. "I want an answer. Why kill her in Vaun's bed? Did you do it yourself, or send someone else into my brother's house?"

"It was *my* house." Quentan idly tossed his napkin beside his plate. "Before Vaun made it his playground, it belonged to my family. I know every corner and every passage, just as I know every corner of this province. Trespassers so often forget that."

"Did Meresin trespass?"

"She poked around, Fay. She suspected me of producing the bad dust. She wouldn't let it go, and wouldn't take a bribe." He laughed, short and bitter. "A whore, who wouldn't take a bribe. She demanded I stop making the dust. Stop selling it. She worried about the people. Worried about the Low." His face twisted. "She should have worried about us all."

"You are a fool to think you can change the Realm."

His gaze met hers, eyes full of the cold contempt and rage she'd seen day in and day out since she married him. "Someone has to do something, Fay. We're drowning in her dust. She makes us weaker to hide her own struggles. When was the last time she left that tower? When was the last time the Queen was seen in her Realm?"

"You would have seen her yourself, if you'd been caught." If it wouldn't have led to the death of the whole family, she might have made sure it happened that way. She'd suspected he hoped to use a new dust to steal wealth and power from the other families. She had not imagined he aimed higher. Not even Quentan would dare test the Queen.

"But I wasn't caught." He shrugged. "And now, I never will be."

"Because you stabbed a woman to death in my brother's bed? How does that protect you?"

"I was protecting us!" he hissed. "Can you imagine what would have happened if that whore told people what she knew?"

She watched him like a creature she had never seen before. He said 'us.' Said it like she was a part of it, but kept all his secrets to himself. That was the power of a Lord. He could do whatever he liked and in the end use all his people, his power, his name, to make himself feel safe again. She understood that power, because it was hers even more than it was his, but she also saw the danger of it.

"You never liked Vaun, but to put that mess—your mess—in his bed? I sent him an invitation, but not wine. Certainly not wine laced with so much dust that he wouldn't be able to remember the night." She shuddered remembering the lost, broken stare of her brother huddled in the shower. "It's too far, Quentan. Even for you."

"He needed to learn a lesson, Fay." He stood, straightening his jacket and heading for the door. "He was getting curious and too bold, even for a prince."

"*The* prince," Fay corrected. "And royalty doesn't learn lessons from lords."

"Well, at least Meresin did." He laughed. "I'd have used poison, but a blade is more honest, don't you think? We're better than that."

"No," the princess said firmly, "*we're* not."

He reached for the doorknob but his knees faltered, his fingertips only brushing the brass handle before he sagged to the floor.

Fay closed the space between them and kneeled in front of him, peering into his flushed face and wide eyes. "Perhaps you'd have preferred a knife, but I suppose this is just as cruel." His lips worked to form sounds he couldn't give breath. "We won't be testing on the Low, Main, or High anymore, husband. We won't be making a new dust. *We* won't be doing anything at all." She lay a gloved hand against his cheek, not even worth her skin. "I meant what I said on the day we married: I hate you. But I never wanted this for you, either."

She stood, watching saliva drip from the corner of his lips as they turned blue. "You should have shown mercy." She swallowed back the lump in her throat when he stopped breathing, his eyes wide in pain and panic as they looked up to her with a frantic, bloodshot plea. "But most of all, husband, you should never have put your mess on my brother. It was your choice to risk Larc, but Vaun?" She stared down at him, cold and unforgiving. "Never Vaun."

A strangled sob burbled in his throat, and his body collapsed, going from rigid to limp, from occupied to empty. She took a moment to steady her breath, lips pressed tight. Her gloved fingers dabbed at the corners of her eyes to steal away any liquid before it could be called tears. After another moment, she pulled open the door.

Addom Vym stepped past her to check the body and she waited for him in the hall. The stillness of his silence and the gravity of his eyes were unlike any she had seen in her brother-in-law before, but when he emerged again he seemed his old self.

"Well, widow, the High of Vym is all yours," the new Lord of Vym declared.

Her gaze narrowed at the edge of his strangely chosen words.

"I'll be keeping the Low," Addom added.

Fay's eyes narrowed. "Why? I told you, you and Evelet may return home."

"Don't take this the wrong way," he smiled, "but I don't want you near my food."

Her expression soured. "And if I'm not satisfied with part of a province?"

Addom Vym grinned, his red eyes gleaming at the prospect. "You're more than welcome to come down to the Low and take it back, Lady Vym."

"What about the Main?" she hissed when he turned away.

He laughed over his shoulder and shrugged. "We'll share. We're family, after all."

Fay watched him leave and let the word 'widow' sink in. She tugged off her black gloves and let them fall to the floor, followed by her jacket and shoes on her way to the stairs. She would go to her room and strip down. She would bathe, maybe cry, and then she would throw her black clothing out the window and dig up something with a little color. Maybe red. No battle was won without it.

ABOUT THE AUTHOR

Cheryl Low might be an Evil Queen, sipping tea and peeping on everyone from high up in her posh tower—a job she got only after being fired from her gig as Wicked Witch for eating half the gingerbread house.

...Or she might be a relatively mundane human with a love for all things sugary and soap opera slaps.

Find out by following her on social media @cherylwlow or check her webpage, CherylLow.com. The answer might surprise you! But it probably won't.

ᘓ

Watch for *Detox in Letters* by Cheryl Low, Crowns & Ash Book Two, coming soon!

ACKNOWLEDGEMENTS

Linn, you're the best reader any writer could ask for. Thank you for all the help, advice, support, and work you put into this project. Thank you for the amazing cover. And, most of all, thank you for being you. A big thank you to Laura for her ruthless red pen work and enthusiasm; no one's ever loved flesh eating pixies more. Thank you to April for supporting my daydreaming since childhood, Whitley for having that dark humor that always makes me laugh, and Diana for all the great advice. You are each a constant support and source of positivity and I would hate to face a day without you.

Thank you for reading!

We hope you'll leave an honest review at Amazon, Goodreads, or wherever you discuss books online.

Leaving a review means a lot for the author and editors who worked so hard to create this book.

Please sign up for our newsletter for news about upcoming titles, submission opportunities, special discounts, & more.

WorldWeaverPress.com/newsletter-signup

OPAL
Fae Of Fire And Stone, Book One
Kristina Wojtaszek

White as snow, stained with blood, her talons black as ebony…

In this retwisting of the classic Snow White tale, the daughter of an owl is forced into human shape by a wizard who's come to guide her from her wintry tundra home down to the colorful world of men and Fae, and the father she's never known. She struggles with her human shape and grieves for her dead mother—a mother whose past she must unravel if men and Fae are to live peacefully together.

Trapped in a Fae-made spell, Androw waits for the one who can free him. A boy raised to be king, he sought refuge from his abusive father in the Fae tales his mother spun. When it was too much to bear, he ran away, dragging his anger and guilt with him, pursuing shadowy trails deep within the Dark Woods of the Fae, seeking the truth in tales, and salvation in the eyes of a snowy hare. But many years have passed since the snowy hare turned to woman and the woman winged away on the winds of a winter storm leaving Androw prisoner behind walls of his own making—a prison that will hold him forever unless the daughter of an owl can save him.

"A fairy tale within a fairy tale within a fairy tale—the narratives fit together like interlocking pieces of a puzzle, beautifully told."
—Zachary Petit, Editor *Writer's Digest*

CHAR
Fae of Fire and Stone, Book Two
Kristina Wojtaszek

"*Char* was a beautiful book that'll have my mind reeling for a long time. It's a faery tale you can taste and smell. Give this book a try if you like faeries or are a lover of nature; I promise you won't be disappointed!"
—Mariella Hunt, author of *Dissonance*

THE FALLING OF THE MOON
Moonfall Mayhem, Book One
A.E. Decker

In the gloomy mountains of Shadowvale, Ascot Abberdorf is expected to marry a lugubrious Count and settle down to a quiet life terrorizing the villagers. Instead, armed with a book of fairy tales, her faithful bat-winged cat, and whatever silverware she can pinch, Ascot heads east, to the mysterious Daylands, where her book promises she can find True Love and Happily Ever After, if she only follows her heart.

Determined to win the hand of Prince Parvanel, Ascot storms the Kingdom of Albright. With the book's guidance, she's confident she'll overcome any obstacles the imperious Queen Bettina Anna throws in her way, be they witches, evil stepmothers, or Big Bad Wolves.

Unfortunately, the book doesn't cover reluctant princes, wolves who read Dostoyevsky instead of blowing down houses, or a guild of Godmothers whose motivations may not be as pure as three drops of blood on a sweep of snow. Most annoying of all is the captain of the guard who swears he'll see the moon fall before she weds Prince Parvanel.

There are stories … and then there are *stories*, and if this parade of shifty shenanigans continues, Ascot might have to rewrite her own tale lest she end most Unhappily Ever After!

THE MEDDLERS OF MOONSHINE
Moonfall Mayhem, Book Two
A.E. Decker

"The characters are truly amazingly amusing and frightening at the same time. They are magical and compelling with unbelievable talents. This book is fantastic for a night at the campfire, or a spooky Halloween night."
—*Girl Plus Book*

SHARDS OF HISTORY
Shards of History, Book One
Rebecca Roland

Feared and reviled, the fierce, winged creatures known as Jeguduns live in the cliffs surrounding the Taakwa valley. When Malia discovers an injured Jegudun in the pine forest of the valley, she risks everything—exile from the village, loss of her status as clan mother in training, even her life—to befriend and save the surprisingly intelligent creature. But all of that pales when she learns the truth: the threat to her people is bigger and more malicious than the Jeguduns. Lurking on the edge of the valley is an Outsider army seeking to plunder and destroy her people. It's only a matter of time before the Outsiders find a way through the magic that protects the valley—a magic that can only be created by Taakwa and Jeguduns working together.

"A must for any fantasy reader." —*Plasma Frequency Magazine*

"Fast-paced, high-stakes drama in a fresh fantasy world. Rebecca Roland is a newcomer to watch!"
—James Maxey, author of the *Dragon Age* trilogy

FRACTURED DAYS
Shards of History, Book Two
Malia returns home the hero of a war she can't remember.
Rebecca Roland

SHATTERED FATES
Shards of History, Book Three
Sometimes unlikely alliances are the only way to succeed.
Rebecca Roland

THE KING OF ASH AND BONES AND OTHER STORIES
Four story collection.
Rebecca Roland

BITE SOMEBODY
Immortality is just living longer with more embarrassment.
Sara Dobie Bauer

"Do you want to be perfect?"

That's what Danny asked Celia the night he turned her into a vampire. Three months have passed since, and immortality didn't transform her into the glamorous, sexy vamp she was expecting, but left her awkward, lonely, and working at a Florida gas station. On top of that, she's a giant screw-up of an immortal, because the only blood she consumes is from illegally obtained hospital blood bags.

What she needs to do—according to her moody vampire friend Imogene—is just … *bite somebody*. But Celia wants her first bite to be special, and she has yet to meet Mr. Right Bite. Then, Ian moves in next door. His scent creeps through her kitchen wall and makes her nose tingle, but insecure Celia can't bring herself to meet the guy face-to-face.

When she finally gets a look at Ian's cyclist physique, curly black hair, and sun-kissed skin, other parts of Celia tingle, as well. Could he be the first bite she's been waiting for to complete her vampire transformation? His kisses certainly have a way of making her fangs throb.

Just when Celia starts to believe Ian may be the fairy tale ending she always wanted, her jerk of a creator returns to town, which spells nothing but trouble for everyone involved.

BITE SOMEBODY ELSE
Immortality is being a horrible influence on your best friends.
Forever.
Sara Dobie Bauer

"*Bite Somebody* is the *Pretty in Pink* of vampire stories; fun, self-consciously retro, and not afraid to be goofy. Sara Dobie Bauer knows how to keep a reader smiling."

—Christopher Buehlman, author of *Those Across the River*